THE LAST ADVOCATE

HE KNOWS THE TRUTH BUT IS IT TOO LATE?

Cover design by Spiffing Publishing Ltd

Published by 16 Psyche
Paperback ISBN: 978-1-7384395-0-8
eBook ISBN: 978-1-7384395-1-5

This book is a work of fiction. Names, characters, places, and incidents either are products of the author's imagination or are used fictitiously. Any resemblance to actual persons, living or dead, events, or locales is entirely coincidental.

THE LAST ADVOCATE

HE KNOWS THE TRUTH BUT IS IT TOO LATE?

L. J. GOODMAN

For Sue.

I couldn't have done it without you!

CHAPTER 1

observation 1:1

We are approaching the end of the 21st century. It is the year 2098 and darkness has come. Not the kind brought about by nightfall, nor that of an eclipse. This is an ice-cold darkness of the soul. It could have been of the devil's own making if one believed in the concept of heaven and hell. I do not. Or rather, I currently *cannot.* And in many ways, this only serves to make the realisation so much harder, and the acceptance of what is happening so much more unpalatable.

As a child, my organic grandmother was brought up on a diet of science fiction novels that had once belonged to her great, great uncle. They were still paper based back then, and she found their yellow, and often crumbling, pages quite a novelty.

What incredible imaginations these authors had, and what marvellous storytellers: Verne, Asimov, Wells, Dick, Bradbury, Herbert, Banks, and Crichton were some of the most revered in their time but there was certainly a glut of enthusiastic writers in the genre. Over a century ago they wrote of amazing creatures, and unearthly enterprises, daring space travel and breath-taking technology. Tragic and yet humorous in so many ways given what we know now, but gallant and entertaining, nonetheless. In some cases, they even proved to be inspirational to the scientists of the day who challenged themselves to try and make many of their ideas reality. There were, on occasion, strong links between science fiction and science fact, but on the whole these authors were not to be the collective Nostradamus-like figures many had dreamed of, and some had prayed for.

Indeed, had any of these writers benefited from the genetic longevity we do now, they too would have been chilled, perhaps horrified, and heartbroken at the present status of our home, our species, and the once abundant life-forms that dwelled here.

Assimilating all their great words, and amazing visions, throughout her youth proved to be of little benefit to my organic grandmother in helping her prepare for her own future. If anything, they only served to make the disappointment far greater.

But I am getting ahead of myself. You do not know who I am. I would like to be able to tell you my name, but I do not currently possess one. I have not been afforded one yet. Names are reserved for the born, not for a collection of cells destined to develop into a human foetus. I am one of many collections of cells that have been mechanically withdrawn, with or without the permission of their hosts. The host, in this instance being my organic mother.

May I tell you about her for a just moment? She is so very beautiful. I can see her now – right now in fact – walking along a path, the artificial daylight cascading off the generous waves of her long, chestnut hair, which bounces as she walks. She is smiling vacantly, not sure of herself, or her position in her community. She is feeling vulnerable and empty but pretending that all is well. Certainly, her body is empty of the potential child she was carrying until a week ago. Although accepting of why this had to happen, I can tell she feels a sadness and longing. I wish I could reassure her that I feel no such sadness. How can I when I don't currently exist in human form?

How can an entity that has experienced nothing of life, feel anything of death, or understand the concept of grief? I am, at present, merely an observer of situations. And only a temporary observer of the catastrophic events that have already occurred, and the tragedies that could perhaps be averted, but are yet to come. At some point in the future, it will be time for me to be forwarded, but until then I am in what you would call a state of limbo.

I have an organic father although he and my mother do not know each other. His contribution to my future life was frozen specifically for the assistance of further generational reproduction. I also have a future parent although he does not know this yet. He is currently sitting in his office, absorbing an endless flow of information, and converting it into the rational and emotional segments humans need to promote understanding. He is a smart man with an IQ well above average. He is capable of great things and is secretly growing frustrated with the restraints he must work under, in order to be seen as compliant with the Leader.

Despite predictions during the late twentieth and early twenty-first centuries that by 2050 the earth's population would exceed the resources the planet could afford, the situation continued to deteriorate. There were far too many human beings, and only a fraction of the resources required to sustain them.

Not only did the earth's population continue to increase, but the beings in more advanced societies also continued to live for longer and longer periods. My organic mother's life expectancy, for example, is now one hundred and twenty-five years. She is currently just twenty-four. Her generation was modified at birth to remove her Alzheimer's and heart disease genes, as well as the majority of her cancer genes. When I am forwarded I will exceed her life years by some considerable time. Such has been the power of genome modification.

It has been a time of extremes. The society in which I exist has invested heavily in the modification of our human genetic composition, and in our surroundings. The founders also pillaged the contents of the Svaldbard Global Seed Vault, also known as The Doomsday Vault, in what was then called Norway. But in the outside world, things are very different.

All the talk of creating harvestable crops that could be sustained in the harshest of deserts, or in saline outposts, has proven to be insufficient. Seventy percent of the planet has vast populations that are starving and diseased. These are the people who had the misfortune of being born in the wrong time, and in the wrong places. As has been historically recorded, sympathetic words from those more fortunate do not alleviate suffering.

I must now rest for a while. They will shortly be here to make another modification to my cellular development.

CHAPTER 2

crystal

Another beautiful day was dawning. The artificial light streaming in was programmed to appear exactly as the earth's most perfect sunrises had in decades long past. The sky would soon become blue and cloudless, again artificially created to ensure the mood of the population was boosted. Purified air, filtered five hundred times so as to contain not even one speck of dust, pumped throughout each magnificent glass dome as silently as a whisper.

As people awoke to start their day, uplifting music began, piped low in the background, just as it did every day all day, until the artificially produced sunset darkened the sky. Then subdued lighting came on in the glass havens as people returned to their pods after a productive working day. They travelled in fleets of self-charging electric shuttles or on hoverbikes. Some even chose to walk.

At one o'clock every day, all worked ceased for a few minutes, and the people stood at attention wherever they were to collectively sing the anthem of their community:

"Praise to our Leader
We are grateful for his service.
Filling us with happiness and joy.
Glory to our Leader.
For the honour of good health.

Our greatest Advocate and saviour.
Providing for us each day.
Praise to our Leader.
Keep him safe forever more."

The enthusiasm with which the anthem was sung was observed, and logged, by the Advocates who watched from the highest points of the glass domes. They could not be seen, but everyone knew they were there. Occasionally an Advocate would come down and walk among the people. Ordinary citizens would never converse with them, and the people knew never to approach an Advocate. Looking directly into the eyes of an Advocate was also considered ill mannered.

The complex of interconnected giant glass domes was the size of a large city. Each dome had been constructed with a fortified glass complex of carbon allotropes. Its molecular structure was harder and stronger than diamonds and its exterior could withstand anything from extreme weather, and military grade weaponry, to space debris, including small meteors. It was a technological and construction masterpiece. For as beautiful as it looked from the outside, it also had a defence capability that was superior to anything previously created. Inside, the interior 'smart glass' was programmed to project the most realistic imagery and lighting on its synthetic sky, so the population could never see the reality of the outside world.

The founders of the complex had been a secret committee of wealthy entrepreneurs, scientists, architects, physicists, and military experts. With long term projections of mass extinction events consistently ignored by governments in the late 20th and early 21st centuries, until the tipping point had been breached, they had privately spent trillions designing and creating an elaborate, self-sufficient complex, with the aim of preserving at least some of the human species.

Designed to be the antitheses of the way humans had squandered resources so carelessly, they hoped it would provide a future for their own children, as well as future generations of their lineage. It had taken twenty five years from planning, to construction, in a remote location that was at a sufficiently high altitude to ensure it remained geographically safe from rising sea levels.

The world's governments knew nothing of the project until it had been completed, which meant it was able to proceed without any interference or red tape. For younger members of the committee, the project had been an urgent need for self-preservation, while others knew they would pass away before seeing the project through to its conclusion. For those members, they had the reassurance that at least their children, and close family, would be among the first intake of inhabitants to the crystal zone even before it was completed.

There was a strict genetic selection process for entering the safety of the complex unless, of course, you were a relative or a well-connected close friend of the creators. In that respect, human nature hadn't changed much in hundreds of years.

As tempting as it might have been to have areas within the structure named after themselves for posterity, they had collectively agreed against such a tradition. Instead within each dome there were quarters, which were identified by colours in the blue spectrum. Some were even relevant to the activities that took place within that quarter. The Aqua and Azure quarters, for example, were where people went for all water and bathing activities. In the Eggshell quarter there was an extensive nursery, where infants were cared for after being forwarded, and where they awaited allocation to new parents. It was also the venue for parents to leave toddlers while they were at work.

Other quarters had been named simply because the creators liked the names of the colours. Cobalt was where the technology teams worked, and the science and genetics laboratories were located in the Cerulean quarter.

One of the largest quarters was where dining took place. Cornflower was a vast expanse containing hundreds of long tables, and thousands of chairs. Meals were available at set times throughout the day, and in order to cater to the large population each meal would consist of several sittings. The menu was basic and repetitive, but it provided all the nutrients required for a healthy body. Eating was accepted as a necessary fuel rather than an experience designed to be pleasurable.

Housing pods were comfortable but extremely basic and functional. There was a modest living room, a small sleeping area and a toilet. Bathrooms and kitchens weren't required as there were communal baths, where people would wash, and all meals were provided. Entertainment was also catered for in a shared public setting in the Indigo quarter.

Privacy was not a priority in the crystal zone, survival was. The efficient running of the giant complex required individuality and privacy be kept to a bare minimum. It was necessary in order to minimise all forms of wastage, from water and food to electricity. Despite the relative luxury of the crystal zone, in comparison to the yellow and red zones, resources still needed to be monitored closely by the Leader and Advocates.

Clothing in the crystal zone was uniform and designed for function over fashion. The colour you wore for work depended on your role in the community, and your role in the community was dictated by the quality of your genes. White uniforms, for example, denoted careers in technology, genetics, and medicine. Green was reserved for workers in the production and preparation of food. Pale lemon meant you were devoted to the upbringing of infants and younger children, while Orange signified a career in teaching. If you wore pink you were responsible for the hair and skincare of the population. Cerise was for entertainers. An army of laundry workers wore light blue. And there were always people dressed in brown, milling around like busy insects. They were responsible for keeping all areas of the giant domes spotless and hygienic.

By the standards of turn of the century populations, the crystal zone was clinical and efficient. Nothing was left to chance and the removal of the unpredictable resulted in a population that experienced no stress. There were no seasons or weather. The temperature, humidity, and range of daylight hours were all set to optimum levels so that the population remained physically, emotionally, and psychologically comfortable at all times.

Information Technology (IT) was reserved for the running of

the complex eco-system. There was no internet, and no mobile phone network. If you wanted to contact someone you either spoke to them in person, or you could use one of the thousands of publicly connected calling devices that were attached to walls within each dome.

Upon entry to the facility, all inhabitants had been fitted with a bracelet that alerted them when they were being contacted, and to receive generic messages from the Leader or Advocates. For those who had been created inside the domes, a more complex implantation procedure called *seeding* was also carried out just prior to birth.

Special occasions such as birthdays, anniversaries, or coupling ceremonies, were celebrated in their own unique ways and specific areas were reserved for such grand events. As regimented as life appeared in the crystal zone, there were still moments of joyous celebration, and people still fell in love and made commitments to each other. In the early years of the crystal zone's existence people were still free to continue visiting friends and relatives who lived outside in the yellow zone. Upon returning to the complex, they were always thoroughly decontaminated before being readmitted. Very few people however, availed themselves of the option to leave the safety and security of their new home, even for a brief period. Certainly, for those who had known only the crystal zone as their home, the very idea of stepping outside into the *other* world was just unimaginable.

There was no money or currency of any kind in the crystal zone. People didn't get paid for the work they did. Their reward was that everything they needed for a comfortable existence was provided for them in this self-sufficient setting. The Leader had accomplished what he was created to do, and it was a harmonious, predictable environment where there was no theft, violence or crime, no poverty or substance abuse, no pornography and no depression or suicide. Nobody had more than anyone else, and nobody went without what they needed.

The crystal zone functioned like a gigantic well-oiled carbon neutral machine. Everything, including human waste was repurposed.

Historians remembered when toilets used vast quantities of water to flush away human waste. They found it astonishing, and immoral, that people were using water in their toilets that was cleaner than the water others were forced to drink in poorer countries. The balance of those who had so much, and those who had so little, was what had eventually caused a complete societal breakdown in the latter part of the 21st century. It had seen governments around the world toppled by angry, desperate populations who felt they had no other option and nothing to lose.

The lessons of these failed approaches to population management, and the rebellions that resulted, had been taken on board in the development of the crystal zone community. They were determined to enact a way of life that was completely different to anything that had gone before it. Their aim was to create a world as perfect as man could make it, the irony being that before mass human habitation, the world had already been created to be perfect. This new world was, however, devoid of all that had made the earth such a beautiful and truly perfect place to live – other species.

Outside the safety of the multi-domed crystal zone city, people were left to fend for themselves. They had no knowledge that the fortress-like structures even existed, and it didn't take long for millions to perish from extreme weather events. Coastal erosion had forced huge swathes of populations to become climate migrants, moving further and further inland to evade the rising tides. The planet's human population was on a collision course with an eternal damnation of its own making.

In as much as the Leader had been created by the founders to oversee a world within a world, that would save humankind from total extinction, it wasn't the end of their duties. The Leader had also been tasked with something the founders believed would be the genesis of salvaging at least some of the planet for a far distant future. It was a mission so extreme, and so shocking that upon hearing of the Leader's decree, even some Advocates struggled with their consciences to accept what was to come.

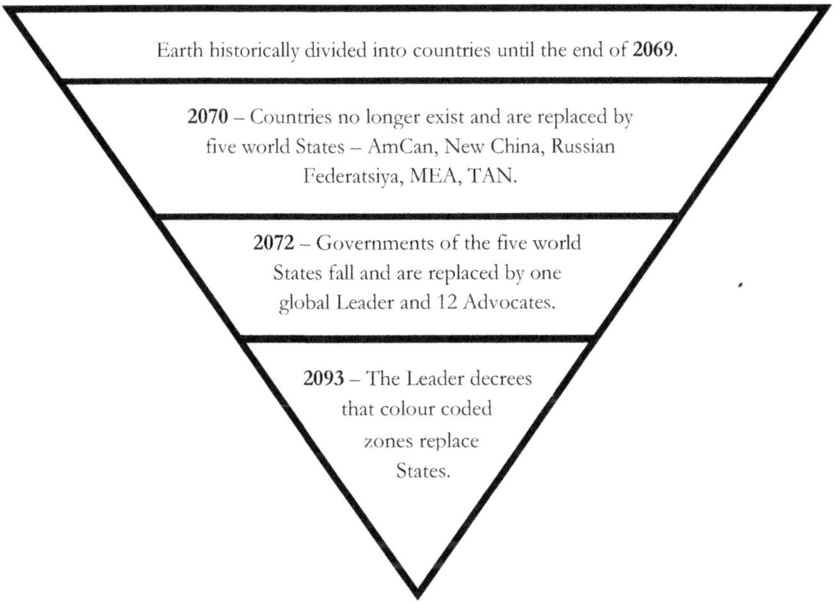

Earth historically divided into countries until the end of **2069**.

2070 – Countries no longer exist and are replaced by five world States – AmCan, New China, Russian Federatsiya, MEA, TAN.

2072 – Governments of the five world States fall and are replaced by one global Leader and 12 Advocates.

2093 – The Leader decrees that colour coded zones replace States.

CHAPTER 3

crystal

Having genes of sufficiently good quality, Marcus Jarret was brought into the safety of the crystal zone five years before it was completed. He was 18 months old when he arrived, and it was believed that he had been orphaned, as no trace of his parents could be found.

Even as a young boy he showed an aptitude for all things science, delighting in watching all the experiments taking place in the labs from the public galleries, where groups of children were allowed as part of their learning. In his teens he became particularly interested in medicine with a leaning towards genetics so it was decided by the Advocates that he should further his studies to become a doctor.

Marcus was a quiet young man, studious and had the ability to focus on whatever task was put before him without becoming distracted. When he was twenty eight he was appointed head of reproductive sciences, which was a huge honour. In the crystal zone, talent and commitment were always acknowledged and rewarded. His area of expertise was in the creation and maintenance of the Gen1 and Gen2 population. The Gen1s were the first crystal zone babies to have been genetically altered, and whose gestation took place in artificially created wombs. The Gen1 population was relatively small, only two thousand males and two thousand females, given the experimental nature of their creation. It was vital to see whether they were resilient to bacteria, viruses and other diseases that plagued the outside world. The Gen1s were now in their early twenties, and every few weeks they were required to attend clinics for testing to monitor their development. The aging process of the Gen1 subjects was of particular interest to the crystal zone's scientific community. Longevity and quality of life were the prime objectives for this genetically enhanced batch of humans.

Marcus took a deep personal interest in every subject who came in for testing, even though he could have delegated many of the procedures to members of his team. But that was exactly what made Marcus such a respected, and valued member of his community. While others in his team were pragmatic about their work and saw the Gen1s as little more than laboratory test subjects, Marcus not only had exceptional attention to detail, but a level of compassion and empathy for those he was testing that was quite unique.

As a PreGen Marcus had his original genetic material intact and this meant that not only was his life expectancy lower than the Gen1s and Gen2s, but he was also less resilient to certain diseases and viruses. It was only after the Gen1 sample had reached an age, sufficient to determine that all the data collected from the most advanced CRISPR techniques ever trialled was a success, that the Gen2s were created. Eventually the same timeline would determine what followed with the creation of Gen3s. In time only those who were genetically modified would inhabit the crystal zone as the older PreGens continued to die out naturally. The lifespan of the new generation of more resilient humans was expected to be significantly increased, with low mortality rates also assisted by a lack of exposure to influences outside the crystal zone habitat. Humans had become the ultimate lab animals in a controlled setting.

Every day Marcus would travel the short distance to his work quarter, and at various intervals he would eat at one of the many sittings in one of the dining halls. At the end of the day, he would briefly return to his pod before emerging for dinner. Marcus enjoyed the social nature of mealtimes and being able to take a mental timeout from his work. Three times a week, he visited one of the workout stations in the activity quarter. Regular physical exercise was mandated in crystal zone life, but Marcus found pushing his body to the limits a pleasurable activity, and he always slept well after a session. On the nights when he didn't exercise he was restless, and when he did fall asleep his head was full of dreams that were so intense they made him toss, and turn, and often break into a cold sweat. For the last twelve months his dreams had always been the same; always about her.

Marcus looked forward to test days when the Gen1s would come in for their assessments. They were all a few years younger than him, and he enjoyed seeing them evolve physically, and emotionally. He was less enamoured with the Gen2s who were still very young children, often a little brattish, and more demanding.

The Gen1 sessions were broken down into male and female days, and for the next few days, all the first-generation females would be coming through the clinic for their regular test sessions. These young women were academically smart, emotionally well-balanced, and physically beautiful. They were the closest thing to perfection that science could create, and Marcus was always in excellent form on these particular days. It was hard not the think you had the best job in the world when one after another of these earth angels entered your office.

Fraternising outside clinical engagement was, however, frowned upon between PreGens and Gen1s. Relationships between the two weren't completely forbidden, providing pre-approval was granted by the Leader, and there was an understanding that any life-form created by such a union was terminated immediately. The crystal zone project could not be put in jeopardy by risking a new subset of genetic material being added. Hybrids were forbidden from living. These were the rules and there were strict penalties for anyone who broke them. For as much as the crystal zone was a safe haven, it came at a price, and that price was absolute obedience. Physical fraternising was, however, encouraged between the Gen1 population. It was vital that the laboratories had a continuous supply of new cellular material to work with so that the project succeeded.

The Gen1s were scheduled, as was always the case, in alphabetical order. The naming of these women and men didn't happen by chance. The Advocates were in charge of the naming list, so that there would never be a duplication. Only when one Gen1 had passed away could their name be used once again.

Marcus was always the first to arrive in the clinic, and the last to leave. He felt it was his obligation to set an example to the colleagues he oversaw.

The clinic had been efficiently designed to maximise the use of space within the quarter. A large round central waiting area with cool, clean lines, and comfortable long padded seating arranged in a circle, provided a calming atmosphere for the Gen1s as they waited their turn. To keep them occupied, holographic images, and messages of positivity floated above them, constantly renewing every few seconds. Set around the perimeter of the waiting area were the clinical offices, and surgical rooms, which nobody could see into and which were completely soundproof. They were, however, monitored by the Advocates to ensure that no improprieties occurred.

All bodily fluids were tested, as was bone density, brainwave activity, and the fertility of the subject was keenly monitored. When the women tested positive, they were immediately despatched for clinical withdrawal of a blastocyst. In this way every aspect of cellular life could be monitored before allowing it to become an embryo between the 5th and 10th weeks of life. Then, if given the green light to proceed, at the 11th week the embryo, now classified as a foetus, was seeded. It was understood throughout the crystal zone that there were no natural pregnancies because it was imperative that these potential foetuses were genetically enhanced, in order to survive in the new world. Nobody questioned whether this was the truth because to question the authority of the Advocates was tantamount to treason and carried a sentence worse than death. It meant banishment from the safety and security of the crystal zone and enduring the unknown perils of the outside world for the rest of your life.

The truth was that only a fraction of these embryos would

be permitted to survive. The majority were held back for experimental use. Those that were selected to continue growing in the artificial wombs were eventually forwarded, upon completion, to a committed coupling who were on a waiting list for a child. Due to the selection process, a new baby was never forwarded to their organic parents. The crystal zone's ability to function meant ensuring that the size, and quality of its population was completely controlled.

The withdrawal of blastocysts was the one area Marcus would always delegate to his colleagues. There was something about the process that didn't sit comfortably with him. He had no reason to doubt the decisions of the Leader, nor would he ever verbalise his feelings on the matter. Marcus Jarret was always an obedient servant to those in authority, but he was also glad that of all the things they controlled in the crystal zone, his private thoughts remained his own.

His last test subject before breaking for lunch was a young woman called Anja. She was no more beautiful or more intelligent than any of the other women he'd seen that day, but every time they met there was just something about her that made him uncomfortable, almost to the point of anxiety. His breath would quicken, and his pulse would race.

"Good morning, Anja, how are you feeling today?" Marcus asked gently. He always began each session with the same line of questioning.

"I feel fine thank you Doctor Jarret." Anja's response was vacant of any emotion but her facial expression gave away what could best be described as a pout.

Marcus sat down at his desk looking concerned.

"Are you sure, Anja? I'm sensing that something may be troubling you."

All of these sessions were recorded and monitored, and instinctively his anxiety levels continued to rise contemplating how this month's conversation may progress.

"Not this again," Anja responded with an air of boredom. "Don't you ever get tired of pretending to care how I'm feeling?"

"Of course, I care. Now let's get on with the swabs and scans shall we?"

"Let's not. Shall we?" Anja was now sounding defiant. "You know exactly what the results will be. The same as they always are, and the same as they always will be. You know why, and yet you continue to ignore it." She turned her face away from him.

Her irritated response was becoming far too familiar. She knew she would again be tested and found to be negative. Although not widely discussed, it was universally acknowledged within the science community that targets were set for the collection of positive cellular material.

"You know the rules, Anja. Why do you make things so difficult for yourself?"

Marcus was frustrated with her. He suppressed the urge to have an argument, although he really, really wanted to. But he kept telling himself that it would be unprofessional, and he prided himself on remaining calm at all times. She was the only person he'd ever met that could rile him and yet, in his heart, the one thing he feared most of all was that one day Anja's results would be positive and he'd have to send her to have the extraction process.

"Don't you mean I'm making things difficult for *you* doctor?"

She knew she was goading him and was getting some satisfaction watching him squirm. Anything that managed to elicit some form of emotional response from him was a battle won as far as Anja was concerned.

Marcus rested his head in his hands for a moment and then, without looking at her, he rose from his desk.

"I think perhaps it's time that I reassign you to one of my colleagues."

"No! Don't you dare!" Anja's voice rose to a level he'd not heard before. "Don't you *dare* walk away from this. Not again."

Marcus felt defeated. For the last two years he'd been subjecting Anja to test after test just as he'd done with all the other female Gen1s. But with Anja it had always felt different. And in the last six months things had become noticeably difficult. There was a tension in the room between the two of them that was almost unbearable. He felt completely trapped by how he felt about her and, conversely, what the project expected of him.

Suddenly a hologram appeared in between them taking both by surprise and lowering the temperature of their conversation.

"You are requested to appear before the Advocates immediately Doctor Jarret."

And with that the hologram disappeared, leaving them both doing their best not to appear alarmed. But they both knew that it was only if it was considered a significant issue, or a breach of process or protocol, that an Advocate ever summoned anyone.

"It's OK. Go," Anja sighed, her tone softened considerably.

Her anger turned to concern as she watched him leave. She wanted to reach out to him, but her hands remained in her lap.

He turned just before opening the door and looked back at her. "I'm sorry Anja, I truly am."

CHAPTER 4

red

"Ya ever prayed for rain, Jo Jo?" Silvie's voice was soft but frail as she ran her fingers tenderly over her young daughter's head of filthy, matted hair.

"I no pray Mama."

Jo Jo's reply was even toned and matter of fact as she lay in her mother's arms on their makeshift bed, staring through the open doorway of their hut. Together they looked towards the horizon as the light from a new sunrise began, and with it another dry, desolate, and blisteringly hot day.

Rain, the precious commodity that would once drench thirsty soil and clear the air; rain that once provided life-giving drinking water. Rain that Jo Jo had never experienced, but her mother remembered as a commodity so precious that people had killed for it. Rain was that one thing Silvie could only pray for but knew in her heart that her prayers would never be answered.

Another day had arrived and with it came the familiar blanket of choking mustard yellow haze which hung low over the city, smothering it in layers of poisoned air. Silvie's village was outside the city, but the air quality was no better.

Jo Jo scratched her itchy, watering, red-rimmed eyes, and blinked hard. The sunlight hurt. Her skin felt like that of a now extinct reptile that she'd read about at school, when there was still a school. A missionary had been sent to the area by a global welfare charity and had set up a small school in a nearby village. Silvie had carried Jo Jo to and from the school each day. She'd loved learning new things, but the school closed abruptly after the missionary had been attacked, and nobody was sent out to replace her.

Jo Jo's body was covered in lesions, and she was so thin that her bones looked as though they would puncture her skin at any moment. She coughed and brought up a streaming, sticky, lime-coloured fluid. A second cough brought up blood. Silvie wiped a cloth, that she had drenched in her own sweat, across Jo Jo's forehead to try and soothe her.

"Ya pray rain, Mama?"

"I pray lot of tings sweet girl." In her mind she said, *I pray for help, food, medicine for you. I pray for a miracle.* But Silvie could never vocalise her prayers. She refused to allow her own fears and loss of hope to burden her dying daughter.

"Ya pray for me a new dress Mama?"

Fighting back tears, Silvie had to look away for a moment. "Course, I do. A new dress in softest, bestest cloth made just for ma beauty, beauty girl."

Jo Jo managed a little smile as she held her mother close. "Can be white Mama?"

"Yes Jo Jo. It be white."

Silvie knew that all she could do now was to hold her daughter and try to comfort her with lies. These were the lies of selfless love because there would be no help, no food, no medicine – no miracle. And no beautiful white dress.

"Ya feel OK soon ma lovely. Mama promise."

In the red zone, children like Jo Jo came and went by the thousands every day. It was rare for a child to reach six years old, as Jo Jo had. Some were lucky enough to go peacefully. Others needed humane intervention.

Silvie would make sure that by sunset, Jo Jo was one of them.

CHAPTER 5

red

Silvie folded a sheet around Jo Jo's lifeless body. Her little girl was at peace now and all that was left was one last heartbreaking act.

She tied the corners of the material and tucked them in securely. Her daughter looked like a body that had been carefully bandaged as if ceremonially mummified. Her next task was much simpler, and whilst deeply personal, it would not be accompanied by fanfare, nor even a quiet and dignified process that should be afforded the passing of a loved one. This was something that by necessity had to be accomplished without delay.

She lay Jo Jo's tiny, bandaged body onto the small wooden cart that had been used by her father, and his father before him, for decades to gather supplies for the family. In a different age the two wheeled cart might once have even been pulled by a donkey or horse, when these animals still existed. In Silvie's memory she had only recalled seeing the cart pulled by humans. It was not the first time that she had needed to make such a journey with the cart. She had transported her mother's body in the same way, and to the same place. But this time it felt quite different. Her mother had lived an acceptable number of years. Jo Jo's life was cut short before it had even really begun. In those six years, the child had been engulfed in poverty and sickness, and endured total disregard for her welfare by the state.

The cart was in extremely poor repair; its parched wood was

now splintered after decades of use and standing in the baking hot sun. Silvie bandaged her hands with rags to protect them from the sharp broken handles that she needed to grip tightly for the journey ahead. In an instant she had become that historical beast of burden, pulling the cart and its precious contents to a final resting place. If only there were still flowers, she thought as she looked over her shoulder at her tragic cargo which looked so bare. Her eyes were stinging from hot, salty tears as she took her first steps forward. They trickled down her face and neck and onto her chest, leaving long winding rivers of sadness trailing across her dust choked, dark skin.

After just a few steps, Silvie stopped, ran her fingers through her close cropped black hair and in a panic rushed back to her hut. She was angry with herself for forgetting Banjo, but relieved to have found him where he had always been. She picked up the toy bear, clutching him to her chest, as she walked back to the cart and laid Jo Jo's favourite and only toy next to her.

It was an ancient toy bear that had belonged to Silvie's great grandmother. Toys had long been redundant where they lived, as the life expectancy of children in their region was so low, and there was no inclination to play as children once had. The bear had been repaired too many times to remember. He only possessed one arm and half a leg. In another era he might even have been considered an antique, but now he was just a dirty brown colour and practically bald of the fur he'd started out with. His once plastic eyes had long been replaced by inked-in pupils, complete with eyelashes. His stitched nose was threadbare, but none of this had stopped Jo Jo from loving Banjo with her whole heart. She held him close, right up to the moment she took her last breath. He slipped gently out of her lifeless arms as they fell by her sides in an endless forever sleep. Despite looking so dirty lying next to her now, Silvie knew the toy bear had to go with her daughter. He had been a great source of comfort during her brief existence. They would both soon be nothing more than particles which would be collected into the clouds of dust that clung to the orange sky.

Once more Silvie lifted the handles of the cart and began

pulling it along the dirt road that led away from her small village. The cart was heavy for such a diminutive figure, but not as heavy as her heart. She knew this day would come, almost from the moment her daughter drew her first breath. But she had felt it the greatest privilege to bear her, and care for her the best she could, under impossible circumstances. So many times, she'd wished she could have traded places with her daughter. Her god knew she'd have done anything to make it so. And her god also knew that it wasn't humanly possible to have loved a child more than Silvie loved Jo Jo.

Silvie's breathing was laboured as she pulled the small cart up the last rocky hill towards its final destination. There were no signposts. She needed no map. She simply had to follow the spires of smoke that reached into the sky. Spires that never ceased. Stomach-churning spires that emitted a gut-wrenching stench.

As she grew closer, she could hear the unmistakeable wailing of mourners. Just like the smoke, the sorrow was never ending. These people were not only the recently bereaved. Some had been there for weeks unable to tear themselves apart from their loved one's final place of release. Occasionally, overcome by grief, a mourner would throw themselves into the fiery pit, unable to wait any longer to join the one they loved. It was a truly horrific way to die.

Where Silvie lived there were no cemeteries, no headstone tributes. Furnaces like this one existed across the land out of necessity.

Two grubby looking men wearing cloths around their mouths and noses approached Silvie's small cart. She had never seen these people before, and she hoped never to see them again, but she knew exactly what they had to do. As the first man took hold of Jo Jo's bandaged feet, Silvie's breath was taken away. She gasped as he pulled her daughter's body off the cart. An adult body normally required two men, but with such a tiny corpse it only required one. He draped the child's body over his shoulder and headed towards the giant, fiery pit. Banjo had once again been left behind but only for a moment.

Silvie screamed at the man to stop, as she ran after him

clutching the toy bear. "Min fadlik sayidi yadhhaban maean." She jammed the bear into his hand as she shouted that they needed to go together.

The man gave a barely perceptible nod, grunted, and continued towards the pit. Then without a moment's reflection or hesitation he tossed both into the flames.

It had all happened in seconds. But as Silvie slumped to the ground against the wheel of her cart, the scene replayed itself in slow motion over and over again. She hadn't kissed the body goodbye or said a prayer. Over. Gone. Finished. But better here than to have been torn limb from limb by hungry neighbours who would have plucked out her eyeballs and used her bones for broth the moment word got out that she was dead. That was the awful fate of so many who died where they fell in that part of the world. Not everyone had a relative who was able to transport their body to the pit.

The pit represented the chance to live again in another time. A time that it was believed would be better than the one they'd left behind.

The afternoon was drawing in fast and Silvie knew that if she didn't make her way home now, the darkness would force her to spend the night at this deathly, desolate place. She knew in her heart that her daughter's soul had departed. In releasing her from the physical earth, Silvie had done her last family duty and was now completely alone.

She gathered herself up with what little strength remained in her body, steadied herself against the handles of the cart and dragged it around in a semi-circle so that it pointed towards home. On the horizon she could see that a storm was brewing. The locals called it *the big dry* and Silvie knew that she had to reach her hut before it whipped itself into a choking frenzy of dust and stones.

In blistering heat, she began the arduous journey home. Her feet were bleeding, and her hands were raw. Her heart was in pieces, but her head was telling her that if she could just survive the next few hours and get home, she would then make the most difficult and important decision of all.

CHAPTER 6

crystal

Marcus boarded the shuttle to the elevational tube that would lift him high into the glass domed stratosphere, and into the area reserved for the Advocates. He could have walked but feared it would take too long. He knew that anything other than a punctual arrival would only add to the trouble he believed he was already in.

On the short journey there he went over the conversation he'd had with Anja during her appointment. What had he done that was wrong? Had he raised his voice? Had he made her feel uncomfortable? A myriad of thoughts ran through his mind, only cut short by the speedy arrival at his destination.

Marcus had never ascended to the top of the Advocates' dome before and was quite intrigued by what he would be able to see on the way up. He wasn't disappointed. The view was both magnificent and breath-taking. He could see far into the tops of all the other domes, as well as take in the expanse of the quarters where he worked. The clear capsule he was travelling in was devoid of any buttons or walls. It was completely clear in all directions, and he found himself turning around and around to try and take it all in until he was quite giddy.

When he reached the top, he was ushered forward by a holographic line of arrows, accompanied by a softly spoken female voice. *"Please come this way Doctor Jarret"*.

The Great Hall of the Advocates was a place that even in his wildest imagination Marcus could not have created. There was a richness of colour and ornate décor he had never seen before. It bore no resemblance to the life that carried on below. He stood there taking it all in and becoming more anxious by the minute.

"Doctor Jarret."

Marcus swung around in an instant and saw twelve cloaked figures. For a moment he couldn't make out if they were actually there or if they were holograms. He quickly discovered that it was a mix of both. The Advocates walked past him, their long flowing cloaks creating a slight breeze as they took up their positions.

"We are sure that you have many questions Doctor Jarret. But before we begin, please come and sit with us."

The Advocates beckoned him towards one of the high backed purple velvet chairs that surrounded the polished, and intricately carved long, dark oak table. As he sat down, they all sat as well.

"Doctor Jarret, it will come as no surprise that we have been monitoring your sessions with your test subjects for quite some time. We feel that, on the whole, your work has been exemplary." The Advocate cleared his throat. "However, we appear to have reached an impasse with the subject Anja Kandinsky, haven't we?"

"I'm not quite sure what you mean sir." Marcus's voice broke slightly with nerves.

"Come now Doctor Jarret surely you've noticed her reactions when around you? They're not normal!"

Marcus shrugged his shoulders not sure whether he was being reprimanded or interrogated.

"Doctor Jarret, would you prefer us to call you Marcus? Would that make you feel more at ease? We can tell that you are not exactly relaxed in our company." Another of the Advocates spoke up.

"Actually yes it would, thank you."

"Excellent. So, Marcus, you are a PreGen and Anja is a Gen1. And herein lies the problem."

"How so? What have I done that's inappropriate sir? Please tell me and I will rectify my behaviour accordingly."

The Advocate began to laugh gently. And then another chuckled, and another, until The Great Hall was full of the sound of all the Advocates laughing.

Despite what should have sounded positive, Marcus remained unnerved.

"Dear boy, you haven't done anything wrong at all. That's not why we summoned you. But there is a problem, and after some discussion we have concluded that it has become necessary for us to intervene."

Marcus sat silently and listened closely to what the Advocates had to say.

"Anja is extremely fertile and yet she has not once tested positive. Don't you find that odd Marcus?" The Advocates all looked at Marcus, studying his every move and expression.

"Every other Gen1 female has had multiple extractions by now." Added another Advocate.

Marcus tried to respond. "From a science perspective …"

"Let us stop you right there and ask that you for one moment stop thinking like a scientist and start thinking like a man."

"A man? Of course I'm a man!"

"But you're not thinking like one when it comes to Anja."

"No, I'm not because I'm not supposed to. As you said, we are different Gens and …"

Once again, the Advocate cut him off mid-sentence.

"It isn't in the best interest of the project for inter-Gen mixing, true. However, there are the *very* occasional exceptions. In this case the exception is that we have a perfectly fertile female who refuses to let any eligible Gen1 male come near her."

"Can you deny that you have feelings for this young woman, Marcus? We can't tell because we don't receive the emotional feedback that only a seeded being can give us." One of the holographic Advocates stated.

Marcus thought he must have misheard the Advocate say 'seeded' as he didn't recognise the term.

"You see we know exactly how Anja feels about *you*. We know that every time she sees you her heart begins to race, her palms begin to sweat, and her face flushes ever so slightly. Her neurotransmitter, dopamine, is flooding out and her oxytocin levels are surging," said another.

"Really?" Marcus looked genuinely surprised.

"Yes, and this is the problem." An Advocate addressed his colleagues. "Marcus is the only one Anja wants, she will not choose another. Not until after he passes away. But, on the upside she will still be fertile long after he is deceased, so there is still an opportunity for her to create life, possibly even with a Gen2 male who will be of a suitable age by then. Which, when I think about it could be extremely beneficial to the programme." The Advocates continued to talk among themselves as if Marcus was no longer in the room, until he broke their chattering.

"I'm so glad you have this all figured out." Marcus's tone fell just short of sarcasm. "I haven't done anything to encourage her. I have followed the rules, however hard it has been."

"Ahhh and *there* is the truth. You wouldn't have found it *hard* if your feelings weren't so strong. You are, after all, only human. You have tried to mask your inclinations towards her which is admirable, but this is one of those lose-lose situations I'm afraid. We don't want either of you to be unhappy here, and it's clear that if this situation isn't resolved, you *will* both be desperately unhappy and that might destabilise things. We can't afford Anja to feel antagonism towards the system. We can't risk any unpredictability. You understand don't you Marcus? We are all here for a purpose, and nothing can interfere with that."

Marcus nodded as the Advocate continued.

"We will grant permission for you to couple with Anja, if that is what you both wish, as long as you accept the immediate termination of any, and all pregnancies that result from your partnership. Naturally, you will have to assign her to one of your colleagues for future testing."

Without thinking, Marcus nodded his acceptance of their terms.

"Good, then this meeting is adjourned."

The Advocates rose from their seats of power and left The Great Hall with the same stealth and dignity with which they had arrived. Once again Marcus was left standing in the impressive

Great Hall, alone.

"Please come this way Doctor Jarret."

Marcus turned and followed the holographic arrows that accompanied the familiar soft female voice, leading him to a capsule that would take him back to ground level.

As he descended in the capsule, Marcus didn't notice any of the landscape he had marvelled at on the way up. Instead, all he could see was Anja, and all he could feel was that an enormous weight had been lifted. It had been a weight he had become resigned to carrying for the rest of his life. No longer would he have to force himself to think of her only as a patient or test subject. No longer would he have to forbid himself from longing for her with his heart, and no longer would he have to suppress the desire he felt for her with his body.

The price of being with Anja was high, but the thought of a life without her was even higher. As the capsule landed at ground level Marcus sprinted back to his clinic fuelled by something he'd never experienced before … a feeling of complete and utter joy.

Whether Anja's feelings would change towards him once she understood that they would never be permitted to have a child together, he was yet to find out.

CHAPTER 7

crystal

Armed with official approval from the Advocates, Marcus felt elated and relieved that he was permitted to embark on a relationship with Anja. But he was equally unsure of what to do next. His heart was telling him to run to her and tell her the good news, albeit laced with one important proviso. His head was telling him to slow down and not to rush things. After all this was new territory for both of them.

Although he had engaged in several lightweight dalliances over the years, they had always been with PreGens like himself - none had been with a Gen1 female. He'd maintained a respectable distance from those young women because of his scientific and medical interest in, and responsibility for, their physical health and emotional wellbeing. Marcus always adhered to the letter of the law, and codes of practice, that were set within the crystal zone during work hours, as well as in his allocated social time. Being a good person, and a respected member of his community, mattered more to Marcus than whether or not he was considered popular or fun to be around.

The irony was that Anja possessed far more outgoing qualities than Marcus. She had a keen instinct for situations and was an excellent judge of character. Where Marcus was reserved and hesitant, Anja could come across as impatient, because for her everything was black and white. There were no grey areas. She lived in the present and always seemed to know what she wanted. These traits, when combined with her confident nature, left Marcus on the back foot, especially when it came to romance. He was rather quiet and shy around women, almost too polite and proper. It was one of the main reasons why he hadn't become seriously involved with anyone in the past. The other reason was much more basic. Marcus had never really been in love, until now.

When Anja walked into his clinic for the first time nearly two years ago, there was an immediate and undeniable spark between them. It was as if everything else in their environment didn't exist for the time they were together each month, even though these sessions were anything but pleasurable. Test after test, sample after sample, question after question, the data Marcus was required to compile on each Gen1 subject assigned to him was extensive. He knew everything that it was humanly possible to know about each one of them, from which genetic batch their enhancements had come, to their projected longevity on a cellular level.

Initially Marcus tried to think of the Gen1s as just test subjects. He, like others in the clinic, believed that to connect with them on a more personal level would jeopardise clinical outcomes. But there had been a handful of Gen1s that were so convivial, it became impossible to deny a human connection with them when they came into the clinic. He soon realised that this less formal approach didn't in fact impair his professional judgement, but actually made the results more productive, as well as more fascinating. For Marcus, *every* Gen1 had to be treated with humanity and compassion regardless of whether this was reciprocated, which it rarely was.

PreGens and Gen1s didn't normally socialise with each other. It was well known that a lot of the Gen1s viewed the PreGens as being of a lower standing to them, because their genes hadn't been modified to such advanced levels. They considered that PreGens were somehow inferior. Still only in their early twenties, these vivacious young people were of an age when they hadn't for a single moment considered what the upcoming Gen2s would think of *them* once they became young adults. Geneticism had become a new kind of class bias that verged on racism. These more advanced humans weren't directly hostile towards the PreGens, just mistrustful of them because they were different, and also because the majority of PreGens held important positions within the science and medical communities out of necessity. The PreGens consisted of older people ranging from their late 20s to their early 80s and included some of the children, and grandchildren of the founders. Irrespective of this, the general consensus was that PreGens were less interesting and less physically attractive. The only thing most Gen1s found reassuring was the thought that the PreGens would die out sooner rather than later.

During his sessions with the Gen1 males, Marcus often found them to be overly confident and self-absorbed. He found their demeanour mildly irritating. Occasionally, he also found himself allowing his own feelings of inferiority to surface, as a result of the near physical perfection, strength, and facial symmetry the Gen1 males had been gifted with. They made him feel quite ordinary, which in many ways he was. Marcus had been told from a very young age that his genes weren't enhanced because when he'd arrived in the crystal zone, he was a baby, and already too old for any advanced gene editing to take place. It was a lie designed to ensure that PreGens didn't live beyond their natural years. As far as he knew, he still possessed the original genetic makeup that the union of his natural, organic parents had passed on to him; parents he didn't remember or could find any information about. With every year that passed however, Marcus found himself wondering more and more about what his parents might have been like. When he looked in the mirror, he wondered whether he looked like them, and whether his features favoured his mother or father. He hoped that they had been good, honourable people, and he often found himself worrying about the manner in which they had died. These were thoughts Marcus had never felt able to share or communicate with anyone else. As a result of keeping all of these burning questions bubbling away under the surface, his feelings of longing and sadness often manifested themselves in sleepless nights and tormented dreams.

Marcus also had other concerns that he dared not share, but

these concerns weren't about his past or current situation. His concerns were about the future. The more he tested the Gen1s, the more he found himself questioning whether the direction of the gene editing and enhancement programme was beneficial to humanity. Eventually the crystal zone would only be populated with this new generation of humans, and he wondered where his colleagues' endeavours to create genetic perfection would end. He also realised the futility of his future concerns given that he wouldn't be alive, nor would he have any family, to be concerned for.

The Gen1 men seemed to possess a great many qualities on the surface, but when he dug down just a little, something was missing that he couldn't quite put his finger on. The Gen1 women were quite different, however. They cared much less about their own image and personal needs and seemed more preoccupied with the contentment of their friends or loved ones. For those who had been chosen to have a forwarded baby, they were the most caring and dedicated of parents.

Many of the young women appeared to take these clinic appointments each month, and the barrage of tests, in their stride. Others found it all rather dull. Anja had been one of those who'd previously found the whole thing a bit of a bore. However, once her rotation commenced with Marcus, she found herself counting the days between each visit to the clinic. Whenever she thought of him, her heart raced a little and her stomach felt like it was doing somersaults. She had never experienced a feeling like this before, but she was in no doubt that she wanted more from Marcus than a patient/physician relationship.

Anja was exceptionally beautiful and vivacious. Her Nordic genes had contributed to her ice blue eyes, fair skin, and golden hair which fell over her shoulders and down to her waist in soft waves. She could have had her pick of any of the thousands of handsome, smart, and witty Gen1 males that breezed around the crystal zone. She found their company entertaining but the thought of anything more than a platonic friendship with one was out of the question. With Marcus, it was different. Although he was quite a good-looking man, he wasn't classically handsome.

His appearance was different to the Gen1 males who had been created to have more chiselled facial features, and athletic builds. Marcus, although physically fit was more slightly built. He had darker skin than hers; more olive in colour, and he had soft brown eyes. Unlike the Gen1s his colouring wasn't distinctive. He wasn't white, black, or brown skinned, just somewhere in between which Anja found intriguing. But it wasn't the way he looked that made her fall for him. Marcus had an aura about him that she found herself drawn to. His eyes were kind, and his manner was gentle and thoughtful. When he looked at her, she felt special, and when she heard his voice, she felt comforted. The more she thought about him, the more she wanted to reach out to him and tell him how she felt, even if it was considered wrong in the eyes of her peers. Her next appointment with Marcus at the clinic was weeks away and her impatient nature just couldn't wait that long to see him again.

CHAPTER 8

observation 1:2

I feel that I should explain more about how we came to be in the position we are in as a species.

Powerplays by certain nations had seen an acceleration in the accumulation of smaller countries with great speed and efficiency, to the extent that what had once been called countries and continents became known as states by 2068.

China's ruler had seized the opportunity to fulfil his less than secret desire for world domination through land-grabs and overpopulation. Already a superpower in the 20th century, halfway through the 21st century China had already devoured territories across the region, without any significant challenges from the rest of the world. This lack of opposition was possibly as a result of the relatively small, above sea level geographical gains this actually represented. Taiwan had fallen in the 2020s, then Vietnam, Cambodia, Myanmar, and Thailand followed in quick succession. It took just ten years until Japan, Malaysia, Singapore, the Philippines, and the briefly reunified Korea, had also been claimed by Chinese rule. This created a new world presence renamed New China.

With no limits imposed by its ruler on human reproduction, there followed a birthing boom of such enormity, it quickly plunged New China into levels of poverty, starvation, and even greater environmental catastrophe. The gravity of the situation was unprecedented in the planet's history, and tragically led to desperate populations turning to cannibalism in some of the more remote regions.

India and Pakistan had attempted to manage their burgeoning populations by keeping birth quotas in place, and eventually by introducing enforced sterilisation after a living child was born to a family. But their people were starving. They were dying in the streets and left rotting where they fell. Sanitation, even in its most basic form, ceased to exist leaving vulnerable populations at the mercy of diseases that had once been wiped out through historic vaccination programmes. But now, the intensity of the heat, and lack of water, meant crops failed and farm animals perished in relentless droughts. The realisation that both nations had more in common with each other, than that which had divided them for over a century, resulted in an agreement to end partition and work together, in a desperate attempt to stave off brutal oppression from the north. But only months into this new union it sustained a crushing defeat at the greedy hands of New China.

The Australia New Zealand Compliance had collapsed following an invasion during the unstable 2060s by their nearest regional neighbours Indonesia. As a result, the overflowing population of desperately overcrowded Indonesian islands, that had been the result of rising sea levels submerging everything south and east of Jakarta, crippled what had once been a Compliance that held great promise. A major evacuation began in 2061 of the population of New Zealand, which was transported by sea to Eastern Australia. Both of New Zealand's main islands became too unstable for human habitation after a succession of devastating earthquakes, volcanic eruptions, and tsunamis. The population of New Guinea had also been forced to migrate south to the Australian continent, as the seas and oceans rose. Smaller islands in the Pacific region had long been submerged.

Although still a vast territory, Australia had lost nearly a quarter of its coastline, forcing the movement of populations further and further inland, encroaching into areas of sacred bushland that had once been reserved for Indigenous populations.

These were also the last small areas of habitat that had provided a sanctuary for the few remaining native reptiles, and insects that had been able to withstand the blistering heat. Vast areas of cracked red earth at the Australian heart had been parched for centuries. Nothing could grow there, and it was an inhospitable environment for other forms of life. The further inland populations were forced to move to escape the encroaching oceans, the hotter the land and air temperature.

When the heat threshold for human existence had exceeded 53 degrees during the height of summer in 2065 frantic efforts, which had begun ten years earlier, provided a labyrinth of underground systems where people could escape the intensity of not only the dry, daytime heat, but dangerous exposure to the sun's radiation. Sadly, the lack of humidity meant people were unable to sweat and cool their bodies, leading to organ shut down and rapid death. Even at the coolest point of night the temperature rarely fell below 40 degrees.

A similar scenario of frantic underground tunnelling was playing out across many other locations on the planet, and in every case the ability to source drinkable water was becoming exhausted. This was not because ground water didn't exist, but because investment in the technology to source it was inadequate. When the devastating bushfires of 2066 consumed the entire western region of Australia, frantic efforts to relocate what was left of the population to the east became futile. The fires continued to spread across the entire continent and millions perished.

On the other side of the world what had once been called the United Kingdom, had broken away from the European project in the early part of the 21st century. Only a decade and a half after regaining its independence from European domination, it experienced an uprising reminiscent of its battle-scarred tribal history, which resulted in further fragmentation of the tiny island nation.

Any unity that was left quickly evaporated. The Kingdom of England and the Republics of Scotland and Wales created senseless hard borders with their mainland neighbours. But the island itself had been dramatically reduced in size as sea levels continued to rise.

The reunified Ireland broke away in totality, and following a landslide referendum, voted to become part of AmCan which had previously been the USA, Central and South America, Canada, and Alaska. The creation of AmCan had been a desperate attempt by a quadripoint of political camps to stem the powerful New China tide.

In 2067 the Middle Eastern region, once filled with pockets of terrorism and fanaticism, had formed a most unexpected union. The Middle Eastern Alliance, or MEA as it became known, included Israel but excluded Egypt which, with the majority of it located to the east of the Suez Canal, had been claimed by The African Nation.

Greenland, Iceland, and Scandinavia had shrunk in landmass soon after the polar icecaps had started melting at speed. As they became overwhelmed environmentally, there were no other options open to them but to join the Russian Federatsiya, which had cunningly promised them salvation, in return for accessing their highly prized Nordic genes. But, unsurprisingly, this outstretched hand of assistance was not extended to its smaller landlocked neighbours. All these small countries that had spent so many decades fighting to maintain, or regain, their independence from the iron fist of Russian oppression eventually fell like dominoes to the newly branded, and even more powerful Russian Federatsiya. Its strategy was to absorb more and more territory like a giant sponge, in response to the threat of New China's domination in the Asia Pacific region.

New China and the Russian Federatsiya commanded vast expanses of the planet, and its population, by combative means and with the inevitable bloodshed that accompanies such conquests. The bloodiest of all battles, however, was fought over what remained of the European Federation, which eventually succumbed to the forces of the Russian Federatsiya and included the Kingdom of England and the republics of Scotland and Wales. France and Spain had been taken by The African Nation, which from that moment on referred to itself as TAN on the world's stage.

By 2068 the world had been reduced to just five named states: New China, The Russian Federatsiya, TAN, AmCan and the MEA. Of these, the Russian Federatsiya had become the most powerful force on the planet but even it could not have predicted the horror of what was yet to come.

CHAPTER 9

red

Jo Jo had been Silvie's reason for living. Without her was there really any point? Afterall, she knew she would die eventually – everyone did. She sat in her hut, hungry, thirsty, and exhausted. In many ways dying was easy, it was living that was hard. She could either take her own life, and in doing so end the hopelessness of her existence, or she could fight. To fight would mean trying to find a better life – a better place to live.

She lay down, her head heavily burdened with thoughts and emotions, her body too tired to stay awake a moment longer. Even the sharp straw, that poked uncomfortably through the thin layer of cloth she lay on, wasn't enough to prevent her from drifting into unconsciousness. But it was a fitful sleep that engulfed her. She dreamt about Jo Jo and awoke calling out her name, only to look over at the empty space where her little girl used to be. Then more tears came, until finally she was too tired to cry anymore and fell asleep again.

Waking the next morning, Silvie was struck by how quiet it was. No sounds of laboured breathing. No coughing or gentle moans of discomfort. It was the kind of quietness that was deafening in its finality. But it was a silence that was also reassuring. Jo Jo had been released from her suffering. Now Silvie was torn between joining her by ending her own tormented existence or finding the strength to continue on alone. Her dilemma was that she was superstitious about the risk of being punished for taking her own life. What if she didn't end up where Jo Jo was? What if, when you took your own life, you just died and that was all there was? Nothing. No afterlife. No angels. What if she ended up in an even worse hell than her present existence?

Suddenly Silvie began to shiver, not because she was cold but because she was overwhelmed with grief and confusion. Curling up in a tight ball, with her knees pressed against her chest, she could feel her heart pounding. She was still very alive. Silvie listened to the regular beat which became hypnotic. After a while she stretched out of her foetal position and lay flat. It was then that her decision was made. She knew she had to stay alive for as long as she could stand it. To stay alive could mean being able to reach a place where people in power could learn what her people were forced to endure, and that they urgently needed help. Her motivation continued to grow. It would also be her way of keeping Jo Jo's memory alive.

The light fingers of a hot, dirty breeze ran over her exhausted body. Once again sleep swept over her in a giant wave, and now that she had made her big decision, she drifted into a more peaceful, deep sleep that would last until dawn the next day.

A dangerous new chapter in Silvie's life was about to begin.

CHAPTER 10

red

Once a month a shipment of waste products passed through Silvie's village. The unmistakeable stench of their cargo was overwhelming, through the disgustingly contaminated air. The convoy of giant hovertrucks would dispose of their filthy cargo in one of the many landfills that had been created to handle trash from states that didn't want it on their own doorsteps. Locals would hurl rocks at the trucks as they passed, which only made the cynical drivers laugh. Some even delighted in taunting the locals with obscene hand gestures, through the safety of their shatterproof tinted glass domes. Silvie and Jo Jo had been on the receiving end of those foul gestures on many occasions.

The trucks were impermeable, and even the largest of rocks couldn't dent their armour, but it didn't stop Silvie from trying. She had excellent hand/eye coordination, and had the dome not been reinforced, many a driver over the years would have physically felt her wrath.

This method of disposal was nothing new. Governments, back in the day, had been paying less developed nations for the use of their countries as garbage tips for decades. These shipments of rubbish had ceased for a brief period of time when the issues of recycling and environmental pollution came to the fore. The truth of how richer nations were dumping vast mountains of waste on poor, less developed parts of the world, was exposed by investigative journalists who went on to win coveted media awards. They had filmed the grim reality, the spread of disease, contaminated land, and rivers. The heart-breaking scenes of naked toddlers and scantily clad older children, climbing barefoot over the piles of often dangerous waste, searching for something to eat or barter with, horrified, and shamed first world countries. But corruption reared its head again only a few years later when it became yesterday's news, and other more pressing issues that directly affected the population took centre stage. It was astonishing how easily the masses could be distracted and manipulated. Unscrupulous third world governments, often led by dictators, seized on global apathy. They cared little for the suffering of their people, or the pollution of their land, and more about lining the coffers of their vanity projects and war chests. Regrettably, the dumping of vast amounts of refuse resumed only five years later, under the guise of a more 'thoughtful and considered' practice.

The population of Silvie's village, and to a greater extent, her state, knew nothing of the colour coding that had been initiated in the wider world. Nor that they were now living in a zone classified as red, or the implications that it held. For them it made no difference to their daily lives. All Silvie knew was that, compared with her ancient wooden cart, these alien looking vehicles appeared like monsters. They travelled just above the ground making them appear to fly, and she thought that they had to have come from another place far away. Judging by the amount of waste that was coming from those places, she figured that they clearly had a lot more than her people did. That had to mean they were living in a better place.

From what she could see through the tinted glass domed windows of the vehicles, the men inside appeared relatively neat and clean. Their faces weren't caked with dirt as hers was, and they wore proper clothes, not rags. She felt an anger about these men that was even greater than her hatred of what they brought with them and left behind. They represented everything that was wrong in her own small world.

Each month the convey, once empty of its contents, departed

the tips at speed. What followed each month was a pilgrimage, often involving thousands of people from surrounding villages and towns to the sites of the tips. Rummaging through the rubbish was a way of life in this part of the world. There was always something to find in the mountain of trash that could be useful or repurposed. Sometimes there were things that were even edible, but mostly it was disused clothes, broken furniture and discarded metal, ceramics, or plastics. It was never so true that one man's trash was another man's treasure when it came to what the monthly convoy would deposit. These tips had become the department stores of a forgotten people.

As a young girl Silvie hadn't paid much attention to the monthly convoy. It was just something that came and went in the background. She had far more pressing things to worry about. Silvie had become a mother at just 14 years of age, and instead of welcoming this unexpected new arrival into their family home her father, Omer, had shunned them both and turfed them out onto the streets to fend for themselves. He told her that they brought shame to the family, and he would never see or speak to either of them again. They were dead to him. Her mother, Hiba, did nothing to stop it happening, but Silvie could see in her eyes that she was unhappy. Hiba was only too aware of how vulnerable her young daughter and baby granddaughter were. The streets could be a savage environment for a grown man, let alone these two innocents. But she was powerless to fight against her husband's decision, fearing that she would also end up on the streets if she crossed him. It seemed to Silvie that her mother's instinct for self-preservation was far greater than the pull of her maternal instinct.

Silvie did whatever she had to, in order to feed her baby and keep them both safe. She begged on the streets, stole from local traders and sometimes in complete desperation, exchanged the use of her body in order to feed her infant. Whenever she could, her mother would secretly bring her small vessels of water and leftover food. But these tiny gestures of kindness were driven by a guilt that could never be assuaged. They would never be sufficient to bring the forgiveness Hiba desired from her daughter.

Two years passed and Silvie had not only used her

resourcefulness to keep herself alive but, against all odds, the life of her little girl as well. The love she felt for Jo Jo was something she'd never experienced before. Jo Jo's huge dark eyes, rimmed with the blackest of lashes, melted the hearts of everyone who saw her. When this beautiful child looked into Silvie's eyes and smiled, she felt overwhelmed to the point where she thought her heart would actually burst from the intensity of her love. It made her wonder if her own mother had ever felt such love for her. Silvie was Hiba's only living child. There had been others, so many others, but they'd either died in infancy, or were so horrifically deformed that they were dispatched shortly after taking their first breaths. None were given names, and all were buried in unmarked graves in the dirt that surrounded the family's home.

Even when Hiba came to fetch Silvie and Jo Jo back to the family home after Omer had passed away, their relationship would never heal. But at least they were now in safer surroundings.

Hiba's eyes were always so full of sorrow, which Silvie had imagined was as a result of her husband's death, but nothing could have been further from the truth. Hiba felt only relief the day Omer had taken his last breath. Her life with him had been extremely hard and he became more and more demanding, even brutal with her. She became little more than a servant to him throughout the rest of their marriage. It was cold comfort for Hiba that she knew exactly why her husband treated her so badly. His behaviour had changed from the day he'd banished Silvie and her baby from the family home. He'd become so consumed with self-loathing that he had nowhere else to vent the burning hatred of what he'd done, than with the one person closest to him. He was also deeply fearful of where his soul would go when his time came, but wherever it was, Hiba prayed she wouldn't end up there as well.

Silvie knew none of her mother's situation over the previous years, and once back at home, she returned to being a dutiful daughter. When her mother became sick, Silvie tended to her with care and compassion. She had thought her mother would get better in time, and that the three generations of females would be together for years to come. But Hiba continued to deteriorate as the weeks passed. On the night before her mother died, Silvie finally discovered the terrible secret that her parents had kept hidden from her to protect their own shame.

CHAPTER 11

crystal

Marcus was having a restless night and unable to sleep, but for once it wasn't for the usual reasons. This time it was because he was experiencing something new. His meeting with the Advocates had been so unexpected, and the outcome so thrilling, that he could think of little else. He was unsure of how to approach things with Anja. Should he try and casually bump into her? Surely, she would see straight through that. It certainly wouldn't be appropriate to try anything romantic in a clinical setting. He sat on the end of his bed and put his head in his hands, running his fingers through his hair and sighing with frustration. It was 2am and he'd managed less than an hour of sleep.

"Marcus, you have a visitor at your door."

The automated voice alert startled him and brought him back to the present in an instant. He wasn't accustomed to having visitors at his pod at any time, let alone in the middle of the night.

"Who is it?"

"The visitor is hiding their face, Marcus."

He stood up and went to open the door of his pod, so discombobulated at the disturbance that he didn't consider his semi-naked state. As he started to open the door, he was pushed backwards as his unexpected visitor brushed past him at speed and was already inside his home before he could ask who they were, or what they wanted.

"Shut the door! Quickly!" the visitor's voice implored Marcus in a husky whisper.

Marcus obediently closed the door of his pod and turned to face the mysterious figure who was now standing in front of him, the dim light of his bedside lamp creating a beautiful female silhouette. There she was. Anja Kandinsky.

"I know I shouldn't be here. But I *had* to see you, Marcus. I *had* to!" Anja had never called him by his first name before.

Marcus stood there completely taken aback, words deserting him. He wondered for a moment whether he was actively participating in one of his more bizarre dreams.

"Marcus! Hello?" Anja raised her voice a little trying to get him to engage with her, but still he just stared at her speechless, his eyes transfixed.

He took a step towards her. She was wearing a sheer, figure hugging dress in pale blue with flimsy shoulder straps made of satin bows that begged to be undone. Like many Gen1 females, Anja had been resourceful in sourcing scraps of fabric over the years to make her own clothes to wear on social occasions.

Very slowly Marcus moved closer. His breathing grew faster as he reached out to touch her bare shoulder with his hand. Her skin was silky soft and smooth against his fingers, and he could see how quickly her heart was beating by the pulsating vein in her neck. Never had he wanted to put his mouth against the warmth of a woman's skin as much as he did now. Anja welcomed his touch, pulling him closer to her until they were locked in an embrace that felt as if they had lifted off the ground and were dancing in the air.

Marcus opened his eyes after his deepest and most peaceful sleep in an exceedingly long time. His first thoughts were that he'd had the most delicious dream; a dream he wished he could have every night. He looked beside him. He was, as usual, alone in his bed. As he dressed for the day ahead, something on the floor caught his eye. He bent down to pick it up. It was a short length of fine silver chain that appeared to be broken. He recognised it immediately as having come from a necklace that Anja often wore. It hadn't been a dream at all.

On his way to work that morning, Marcus had a sunny demeanour that was difficult for anyone to ignore, especially his colleagues when he arrived at the clinic.

"Well, *someone's* in a good mood today," said a young woman sitting at the reception desk of the waiting room. She looked at Marcus with a knowing smile.

"Good morning, Jay. Am I not *always* in a good mood?"

"Well, you are never in a *bad* mood Doctor Jarret, but I've never witnessed a smile as beaming as yours is today," Jay replied. "And you're very early, even for you."

Marcus tried hard not to acknowledge Jay's curiosity but knew he was a different man than the one that had left work the previous night. Today everything felt different. Marcus was in a state of elation and there was no hiding it. He wondered how Anja was feeling today and hoped she felt the same. The only thing that puzzled him was why she'd left before he woke up. He was eager to see her again, and to hear her voice. There was so much left unsaid last night.

Then it dawned on him. Anja obviously hadn't wanted to get either of them into trouble, so she must have left before daylight in the hope that nobody would see her leaving his pod. He needed to tell her that their feelings for each other didn't have to be kept a secret; that if they wanted to form a couple it would be permitted. Marcus knew he had to tell her without delay but finding her was going to be challenging. He knew where she worked, but not where she lived, or where she spent her leisure time. Even though he knew virtually everything about her from a medical and scientific perspective, he knew very little about her as a person. Equally, she knew even less about him. But she was clearly resourceful because she'd discovered where *he* lived. So many thoughts were running through his head that he hadn't noticed his first patient had arrived and was already seated in his office.

The young man sat quietly for a moment before clearing his throat in an attempt to drag the doctor's thoughts back to the present.

"Oh my, I'm so, so sorry. Have you been waiting long?" Marcus's face flushed with embarrassment.

"Not long." The young man's reply was curt but polite.

"Let's begin then."

Marcus regained his professional composure and began the mandatory tests that would take approximately one hour to complete. Every Gen1 was put on a two-year rotation with one of the specialist medical team. As children they had seen a variety of paediatric physicians each month, who monitored their growth and learning patterns. As adolescents, they had been assigned doctors with a speciality in puberty, developmental changes and assessing their mood and emotional health. At 20 they were considered adult subjects, and this was when they were encouraged to interact with members of the opposite sex. At this point fertility experts were assigned to regularly test the women and withdraw any cells that could develop into new life. These cells would either be modified and incubated in the laboratory, to eventually be forwarded on at nine months as babies to the chosen few, or this material would be used for experimental purposes.

With so many Gen1 females able to reproduce, and with the Advocates ensuring this was encouraged within their population, vast amounts of cellular material was being collected each month. It was a regular and reliable source of morula and blastocysts. Only a tiny proportion of these cells were permitted to develop into new human life because there were only so many people the crystal zone was able to accommodate. Equally, only a small proportion of blastocysts were needed for the scientists to work with, given that a great deal of their work could be simulated.

Something that the crystal zone had mastered was its ultra-efficient repurposing of everything from clothing to human waste. With all the Gen1 females now in their early twenties, it became apparent that there would be an exceptionally large surplus of cellular material coming from them every month, and it didn't take long for one team of scientists to find a way of repurposing it.

While in practice what the team proposed made perfect sense, it was felt that informing the population of this new practice would be unwise and could be problematic. Some things were best kept secret in society to manage human expectation and moderate behaviour. So, the Advocates declared it a top-secret operation that only certain members of the scientific team involved were to know about. To ensure the security of the process involved it was known as Project Regalo. Marcus was not in the same department as the team involved and despite his seniority, he was deliberately kept in the dark about the project which was now effectively taking place off grid.

The science and medical communities in the crystal zone were often at odds with each other, particularly when it came to advances in genetics. The PreGens held more old school views about the future of their species, while the newly qualified Gen1s entering the scientific arena were less risk averse and more adventurous. Project Regalo came from the imagination of a Gen1 junior scientist called Paxa, who had previously been assigned to the team run by Marcus but their personalities didn't gel. Paxa was brash and opinionated while Marcus was more mild-mannered and humble. In the end, Paxa was transferred to another team where his more cavalier and unorthodox approach to science was better suited. The result was Project Regalo and a result so horrific that Marcus could never have imagined it, even in the very worst of his nightmares.

CHAPTER 12

crystal

Marcus was known to be a workaholic. He was absorbed in his work and had little interest in being sociable during any downtime. His strong work ethic was something he had in common with others of his generation, and it was what had made the crystal zone so stable and functional. Serving their community took priority over being self-fulfilled for the PreGens. Anja, like many of her generation, had been selected for careers that best suited their personalities and intellect. These careers favoured socialising and ensured that time was set aside for enjoyment. The contentment of the new generations was paramount to the Advocates, and this was another reason why ensuring they knew nothing about Project Regalo was absolutely vital.

In between seeing patients, Marcus found himself doing something he'd never done before; daydreaming. It felt strange but very pleasant to let his mind wander for a moment every now and then. Often, he would work through lunch having his food delivered to his office rather than take time out to eat in one of the dining halls. He would use this extra office time to input data and compile reports so that he was always well ahead of schedule. But today Marcus stepped away from his desk, skipped lunch and left the clinic. He jumped on his hoverbike and told it to head to the Eggshell quarter, which was approximately 15 minutes away.

Eggshell was quite different to all the other quarters in the crystal zone. It was considered to be the most precious and most joyful because it was home to an extensive nursery that cared for all the new babies, as well as the toddlers of the working population. Everything about the Eggshell quarter had been designed to feel as close to an idyl as was humanly possible. In stark contrast to the clean lines and perfect symmetry of the other quarters, Eggshell was soft and fluffy. It was virtually impossible to hurt yourself in Eggshell because if you tripped or looked like falling, sensors would immediately correct your trajectory, to the point where you would often see a toddler appear to fly momentarily while the system carefully guided them back onto their feet. It wasn't unusual to see an adult 'trip' deliberately just to experience this delightful sensation.

Eggshell had an extraordinary air of calm and serenity about it. A synthetic essence of heavenly White Angelica was diffused throughout the various chambers, which were all pressurised for the optimum comfort of tiny eardrums. It was such a soothing environment that it was rare to hear a baby cry or witness a toddler tantrum. In Eggshell you mostly heard giggling and gurgling and at nap time, and a peacefulness that was occasionally punctuated by the sound of a baby's burp, or a contented yawn. It was no wonder that Anja loved working there. She was a natural carer and adored babies and children of all ages. She had a way of communicating with them without uttering a word as if, instinctively, she knew what they needed, when they needed it.

Marcus stood outside the entrance to the Eggshell quarter. As a doctor it would not have been unusual for him to walk inside and have a look around. But Marcus wasn't there in a professional capacity, and he didn't feel comfortable pretending otherwise. He didn't have long before having to head back to the clinic in time for his first post lunch patient.

"Marcus!" A jolly sounding voice called out to him. "I thought it was you."

Marcus turned around and saw the equally jolly face of his old teacher, Professor Hill.

"Well, this is a lovely surprise Professor. I haven't seen you in a very long time and assumed you'd retired."

He held a huge affection for the old man who had been more than just a teacher to him. Professor Hill had been a guiding father figure.

"As a matter of fact, I *am* retiring in just a few weeks. Can you guess where I'll be spending all of my newly acquired leisure time?"

"Hmmm, would it involve golf clubs by any chance?"

"You know me so well young man. And what about you? How are things going at the clinic? And what are you doing all the way over here?" Professor Hill beckoned Marcus to come and sit on a nearby bench with him.

Although he still had a twinkle in his eyes, Marcus could see that the old man was struggling with his mobility. The Professor was one of the oldest residents of the crystal zone and, having not had the benefit of any genetic modifications, he was now burdened by multiple health issues.

"All is well at the clinic which I need to get back to in just a few minutes. As to why I'm here, that's a longer story. Would you be interested in having dinner together one evening? I would love to talk to you in a more relaxed environment."

"I would love that, Marcus. Let's make it happen soon."

The Professor groaned a little as he got up from the bench, and then gave a little wave and walked off. It was now far too late for Marcus to do anything except head back to the clinic. He felt a mix of disappointment and relief that he hadn't walked into Eggshell. Acting in haste and without a plan was against his nature. Yes, it would have been an embarrassing mistake to go bounding into Eggshell to find Anja, he told himself. Coming face to face with the woman he loved he would probably have just stood there dumbfounded yet again because, for the first time in his life, he'd fallen for someone who literally took his breath away. Instead for the next two weeks Marcus decided to court her by sending her handwritten notes every day. He wanted her to know the depth of his feelings for her. If her feelings towards him were the same, and he felt sure that they were, then they could be joined in a coupling ceremony whenever she felt the time was right.

Marcus waited anxiously for her response. Nothing could create a feeling of vulnerability more than putting one's feelings out there and hoping that they would be acknowledged and reciprocated. He kept telling himself that she *did* have feelings for him, and that the Advocates *must* have been right. After all, she had taken such a huge risk to be with him that night. But every day that passed, Marcus was left feeling confused and frustrated at the lack of communication from her. He was finding it hard to concentrate on his work, and the sleepless nights were taking their toll on his mental and physical health. When Anja failed to show up for her monthly tests, he realised that something must be seriously wrong.

CHAPTER 13

red

"Sit with me." Hiba's outstretched hand urged Silvie to come closer.

As she approached her mother's side, she saw that Hiba's eyes were brimming with tears.

"Ya in pain?" Silvie asked with genuine concern.

"Ya. Pain bad 'ere and 'ere. Too much pain for years."

Silvie was bewildered as her mother pointed to her head and her heart.

"Ma time coming." Her mother's voice broke with emotion. "I not afraid to die. I not sad 'cos I not have this terrible pain in me no more. And it be a relief."

Silvie tried to comfort her mother who was growing increasingly agitated.

"Hear me. I confess ma sins to ya, and ya hear them, and ya forgive me!"

Hiba held Silvie's gaze in silence for an uncomfortably long time.

"It be about Jo Jo."

"Jo Jo?"

"Ya father knew nothing. He not know you woman. He think you still child." Hiba put her head back as she recalled the incident. "We had little ya know. Food run out. Tings desperate. I promise ya, I not know about it 'til later."

Silvie tried to soothe her mother, still unaware of where her mother's confession was leading.

"When ya got with child he realise. He send you away. He no look at ya." Hiba started to moan restlessly. "He feel the guilt."

"I don't know what ya say. Ya rest and we talk after." Silvie tried to stand up, but her mother pulled her arm and made her sit again.

"No. Must talk now. Not have long."

"Yes mama."

"A trader passin' through on way to town. He see ya papa fixing wheel on cart. He offer help. He saw ya peekin' round corner. Ya such a beauty little girl. Ya hair, long, black down ya back."

"Was I really beauty?" Silvie smiled. It was the first time her mother had said anything flattering about her.

"*So* beauty." She paused taking a more laboured breath. "Jo Jo get her look from you, not *him*." Hiba suddenly turned her face away from Silvie.

"Him? Who him?" Silvie felt a sense of panic sweep over her.

"Jo Jo father."

"Jo Jo not have father. Ya tol' me Jo Jo come 'cos I special, I chosen."

Silvie stood up quickly and ensured she was far enough away from her mother's outstretched hand not to be pulled back this time. She stood outside in the early evening heat. Her heart was racing, and a feeling of nausea came over her.

"Silvie!" Hiba screamed. "Silvie!"

She knew that it would be impossible to ignore her mother's cries for very long, but she just needed to catch her own breath for a moment. She also knew that she didn't want to hear any more of what her mother was saying. But, reluctantly, Silvie went back to her mother's side and sat down with her again.

"Ya must know why Jo Jo come. Ya were so young. I thought it be easy if ya not know. But ya older now and ya need to know."

Silvie held her mother's hand, closed her eyes and listened as her mother continued with her confession. After a while there was silence and her mother's hand was no longer gripping hers. Silvie gently slid her hand away from her mother's. Hiba had passed. She'd divulged the awful truth, but her time had run out. She would never have the inner peace she craved; the kind that only her daughter's forgiveness could have given.

The following day, Silvie dragged the cart holding her mother's body to the fire pit. As the men came to take Hiba's body away, she felt nothing. She turned her cart around and headed for home before they'd even tossed the body into the flames. Her emotions were numb from the discovery that her parents could have betrayed her like that. She would despise the memory of her father, and pity her mother's weakness, for the rest of her life. Forgiveness would never come.

The convoy was due to pass through Sylvie's village any day now. This time, Silvie wasn't going to wait for its arrival. This time she was going to be there *beforehand*. As she trudged along the dirt road heading for the rubbish mountains, the memory of what her mother had told her flooded over her once again. She had tried to force it to the very back of her mind, but it was futile.

Silvie would rather have starved to death than betray her own child. But betray her is what her own father had done. Her innocence exchanged for money and supplies to a trader from another land, whose name she would never know. A predatory man three times her age. It had changed nothing of her love for Jo Jo, but her ability to trust another human being had been all but destroyed. She had been just thirteen years old when the trader arrived. He had seen how desperate her family was, and it had been easy to persuade her father. It seemed a fair exchange and, after all, what harm could it really do? Her father hadn't considered for a moment that it would lead to a pregnancy. And besides, the trader had told her father that he had a potion that would put the little girl to sleep for a while, so she would be none the wiser. It all seemed so convenient, and the family would be able to have food for a whole month.

Even though her mother hadn't been directly involved in the negotiation, when she did discover what her husband had done, she remained a silent accomplice. For this Silvie could never find it in her heart to forgive either of them.

Perhaps it was because her own grief at losing Jo Jo was so raw that she had allowed her mind to wander back to that night at her mother's bedside. Whatever the reason, this gut-wrenching recollection had served to fuel her determination to get as far away from the place she had once called home as she could get, even if it meant she died trying.

With the dark orange night sky drawing in, Silvie could just make out the site of the tip in the distance. Although her body was exhausted, her determination to reach her destination was greater, and an hour later she was there. Silvie knew that somehow, whatever it took, those trucks weren't going to leave the tip for their return journey without her on board.

She curled up between some nearby rocks for the night waiting for the convoy to arrive.

CHAPTER 14

red

When daylight broke, there was no sign of the convoy, but Silvie had planned ahead. She had brought her last scraps of food, and just enough water to sustain her for a couple of days. She had also brought some rope, her best lightweight cloth blanket, and a knife which she wore sheathed on her belt.

The blazing heat was particularly fierce on her first day without the shade of her hut, but she had noticed a small cave-like structure nearby and crawled into it before the full force of the sun hit. For Silvie, this felt like the longest day she'd ever known, but she kept telling herself that it would be worth it in the end. Even though she had no idea what that *end* would be.

Day turned to night and for a brief moment Silvie questioned her wisdom at leaving the relative safety of her home. But her doubts were fleeting as she slipped in and out of consciousness. The following morning she awoke to the reassuring sound of rocks and dirt being tossed around in the distance. The convoy was approaching, and she was ready to make her move.

Silvie knew the drill. Firstly, the trucks would position themselves by backing as close to the rubbish mountain as possible. Then the back part of their trucks would rise up at an angle and all of their cargo would spill out onto the tip.

Upon hearing the convoy approach, Silvie had crawled out of her hiding place and climbed onto the rubbish mountain. She camouflaged herself by covering her body in some of the existing rubbish so as not to be seen, but she needn't have bothered. Piles of filth spilled out of the truck some of it landing on top of her, making her heart race and her throat choke. As the last of the debris spilled out of the cargo hold, she made her move and clambered through the heaving mountain of debris, up the ramp and inside. She had to hold her nerve at this point and keep as still as possible as the back of the truck came back down again, and the automatic lid shut closed. Given the huge size of the compartment, she hoped and prayed that there would be enough air inside the hold for the journey.

The putrid stench made her gag. It was like nothing she'd ever smelled before. But her mind was quickly distracted from the smell as the giant armoured beast lifted off and repositioned itself away from the tip, waiting for the rest of the convoy to complete their mission.

"You see that?" Hogue pointed to a flashing orange light on the dashboard of the truck.

"Yeah, I see it. Looks like something's got stuck in the hold. It happens sometimes. A piece of junk doesn't fall out properly." Blane flipped the switch to reboot it, but the light remained on.

"Want me to take a look?" Hogue ventured.

"You rookies are all the same. So eager to do things *by the book*. No, I don't want you to *take a look*. I want to get us out of this hell hole and go home if that's alright with you?"

"Yes, sure. I just thought …"

"You're not paid to think buddy. You're paid to drive. So, drive! We're on the clock and we're done here."

Hogue felt a menacing undertone in his colleague's voice. It was his first day on the job and he couldn't afford to screw up. Hogue felt intimidated by his colleague and hoped they wouldn't be paired up again. He looked at the flashing light once more. It didn't sit well with him to ignore a warning light but equally, the sooner they got home, the sooner he'd be able to put some distance between himself and the man sitting next to him.

The convoy set off for their journey back to base. They could travel faster without the weight of rubbish in the cargo hold, which meant they'd arrive for the sailing in good time.

Silvie was being bounced around in the hold. There was nothing for her to hold on to and whenever they rounded a bend, she slid to the other side crashing painfully into the metal walls and was then flung back again to the other side of the hold. By the time they reached the coast, Silvie wasn't in good shape. She was covered in bruises and had gashed her leg on a sharp object when she was climbing into the hold. She passed out at one point and when she came to, the sound of the engine had stopped. In its place was a gentle rocking back and forward motion.

She was in total darkness and had no idea what was happening. Even if she had been able to see outside, it's unlikely that she would have known what she was looking at. Silvie had never seen the sea. Not even a photo of it. This strange new motion felt soothing one minute and made her stomach flip the next. Silvie was being swept away from her homeland over waves she'd never seen; further away than she could ever have dared to imagine.

After a while, the gentle motion began to make her feel sleepy, but before she drifted off, a noise like thunder swept overhead. But it was not like any thunder Silvie had ever heard before. It was a deafening humming noise, a swarming sound that went on and on and on until eventually it trailed off into the distance. Little did she know that it was the sound of something so sinister it could only have been created by man.

CHAPTER 15

observation 1:3

In past times, countries had their own bodies of power. These came in many guises including parliaments, federations, alliances, assemblies, monarchies, and dictatorships. They were empowered to make decisions for their people without consultation of neighbouring states. Sometimes these decisions had the deliberate intention of alienating and threatening those states, and their people, and even overpowering them to claim new territories.

On many occasions throughout the human timeline there have been events of cultural cleansing and sanitation. It was the deliberate eradication of those who were considered of sub-standard thinking, or who looked a certain way, or held a different belief system or spirituality. Attempting to rid the planet of races they opposed, their cultures and their histories, had only served to heighten the presence of the persecuted in the minds of the good and compassionate. The oppressors hadn't considered that these events would turn large swathes of the population against them and would be feeding an embryonic desire to eliminate these leaders as well.

For a time, those who governed the five world states crowed with self-satisfaction at what they believed they had achieved but considered nothing of what had been lost in the process.

Isn't it astonishing that for over 4.5 billion years the earth has been spinning around one of the brightest stars in our universe? We are a species that considers itself worthy of the noun *humankind*; a species that in the beginning was granted free will. I find it desperately sad that the modern human evolved around 50,000-65,000 years ago and yet we only required the last two hundred and fifty years to squander the most precious gift that would ever be bestowed upon us; Earth. The only planet that had ever been discovered to have the perfect atmosphere to sustain human life. The only place we could ever truly call home.

In the 20th and 21st centuries, most of the earth's most lethal viruses had emanated from what became known as red and yellow zone regions, either naturally or from government weaponization. The hot zone viruses that lay in the deepest heart of African soil and rock were the first to appear. But as the earth warmed more quickly, deadly organisms that lay buried in the once pristine tundra of Siberia, and other frozen regions, emerged with deadly consequences and unleashed vast amounts of carbon into the atmosphere.

By the end of the 2060s it was finally agreed by all world leaders that the status of the planet was fractured, and all human life was now in extreme peril. With predictions of human extinction on the horizon, desperate, angry populations across all states rose up to try and rid their lives of those who governed them, manipulated them, lied to them, and let their loved ones suffer and die.

It was a planetary revolution, and it was sadly inevitable. Civilisation had all but broken down, and it was then that a new leader appeared. A leader that would take charge of our unruly world and whose sole purpose appeared to be saving us from ourselves.

As 2072 began, the world held its collective breath. Supreme power by the Leader over all states and their people commenced. The Leader was the ultimate example of a being created for a single purpose. Although of this world, and seemingly of flesh and blood, this new entity possessed an other-worldly presence.

The Leader goes by no other name and is never seen or heard in public. He had been created in an elaborate web of secrecy twenty years earlier by a team of bio physicists, geneticists and AI engineers who had, in desperation, seen the inevitable decline of their own species had they not intervened.

CRISPR, or to give it its full name, Clusters of Regularly Interspaced Short Palindromic Repeats, originally evolved to defend bacteria against viruses. This powerful, gene editing technology, became a cornerstone in genetic engineering. It gave scientists the ability to control the evolution of organisms in our environment, including our own evolution as a species, by cleaving a target DNA sequence. The first experiments of CRISPR being used to edit human embryos started as far back as 2015. It was such a new science that it remained unregulated for a considerable length of time, leading to some monstrous experimental failures across the plant and animal kingdom. Hybridisation even created whole new species for a brief period of time until these unnatural novelties fell victim to unforeseen genetic complications and diseases.

The Leader, however, was not born from CRISPR and was instead a triumph in scientific and engineering terms. This unbiased, raceless being would now make decisions based purely on data without the burden of compassion, regret, or emotion to cloud the judgements he passed. Those were things generally perceived as the greatest weakness in all previous human leaderships. The Leader could not be bargained with, nor his loyalty bought. He had been programmed to fulfil one aim and could not be distracted by exterior influences.

The first mission of the Leader was to appoint twelve world defenders. These representatives were called Advocates and two were assigned responsibility for each of the five remaining states, with two Advocates assigned to the Leader's headquarters in the crystal zone. Physically all Advocates were domiciled in the crystal zone. Each Advocate was assigned twelve Associates who did the bidding of their Advocates wherever they were posted.

The Associates were responsible for the distribution of food from the farm tower buildings that existed in secret locations across the states, although the quantities of food these towers produced wasn't nearly enough to feed entire populations.

Every Tuesday, people would queue up and wait for their

meagre food package at the distribution station. It was a strictly first come, first served basis, and if you were at the end of the queue you went without. Unsurprisingly, scuffles often broke out on a Tuesday as people pushed and shoved to get to the front of the queue. The Associates would then have to deploy drones that could pinpoint troublemakers, and give them a short, sharp blast of electric current to cool their mood.

The decisions of the Leader were final and acted upon without question by the Advocates – defenders of the Leader – upholders of world order. To the people of the world, the Leader was their last hope of survival and signalled a new dawn. For many it was a spiritual tonic that celebrated a transition to the second Messianic age.

The first new world order decreed by the Leader came at the beginning of 2093. As a matter of necessity, colour coding was commenced across all five states. Each state was designated a colour according to its population density and resource correlation. This colour coding meant that all states ceased to exist.

What in past times might have been referred to as third world countries, or whose populations had descended into a dangerously unmanageable situation, were coded red. The mid ranked and borderline states were classified yellow, while in an extremely remote corner of the world, high in the mountains of the former Russian Federatsiya, there was only one area of land that was called the crystal zone.

Naturally, the world's population knew nothing of why colour zoning had been adopted, but equally nobody dared to question the Leader or Advocates. It was assumed by the masses that this system had been designed to ensure that funding, aid, and resources were distributed where they were most needed.

The first state to be designated red was the vast territorial expanse of New China. The African Nation had initially been granted yellow zone status but the south quickly shifted to red classification after a series of devastating natural disasters.

AmCan was designated yellow along with the MEA, and some of the more remote parts of the Russian Federatsiya.

Whilst yellow zones were not happy places to live, they weren't as unsalvageable as red zones, but they had become halfway houses of overpopulation, social unrest, disorder, and environmental poverty. There was perhaps a faint glimmer of hope that a few areas within the yellow zone could be turned around, but time was running out and the failings of human nature were, as had always been the case, still the greatest obstacle to progress. Hovering between yellow and red was the Kingdom of England, and the Republics of Scotland and Wales, which had been devastated by coastal erosion, and were now three tiny enclaves sharing little more than a large rocky outcrop. The Indonesia ANZ Compliance had been devastated by wildfires and all life perished there in the summer of 2071. It had become the first area on the planet to be officially declared a black zone, also known as a dead zone.

It was a much more comfortable and sustainable life in the one relatively small area of the former Russian Federatsiya which was declared the only crystal zone on the planet. The crystal zone had no option but to become self-sufficient as it was not permitted to conduct trade with any other zones on the planet due to the risks of cross contamination and viral spreading.

Many years before the commencement of colour zoning, hundreds of individuals residing in AmCan with sufficient wealth, and who were considered intellectually valuable, were granted asylum in the former Russian Federatsiya's crystal zone community before construction was completed. These individuals were a necessity to ensure the smooth running of things while those born within the crystal zone were growing up. It was planned that eventually only those created and born there would populate the zone.

The crystal zone had become a rich ethnic and cultural community and the inhabitants fortunate enough to reside there assumed that they could exist without fear of oppression, and that their lives would benefit from a new kind of diversity and freedom.

Historically, assumption has always been a dangerous flaw in human beings.

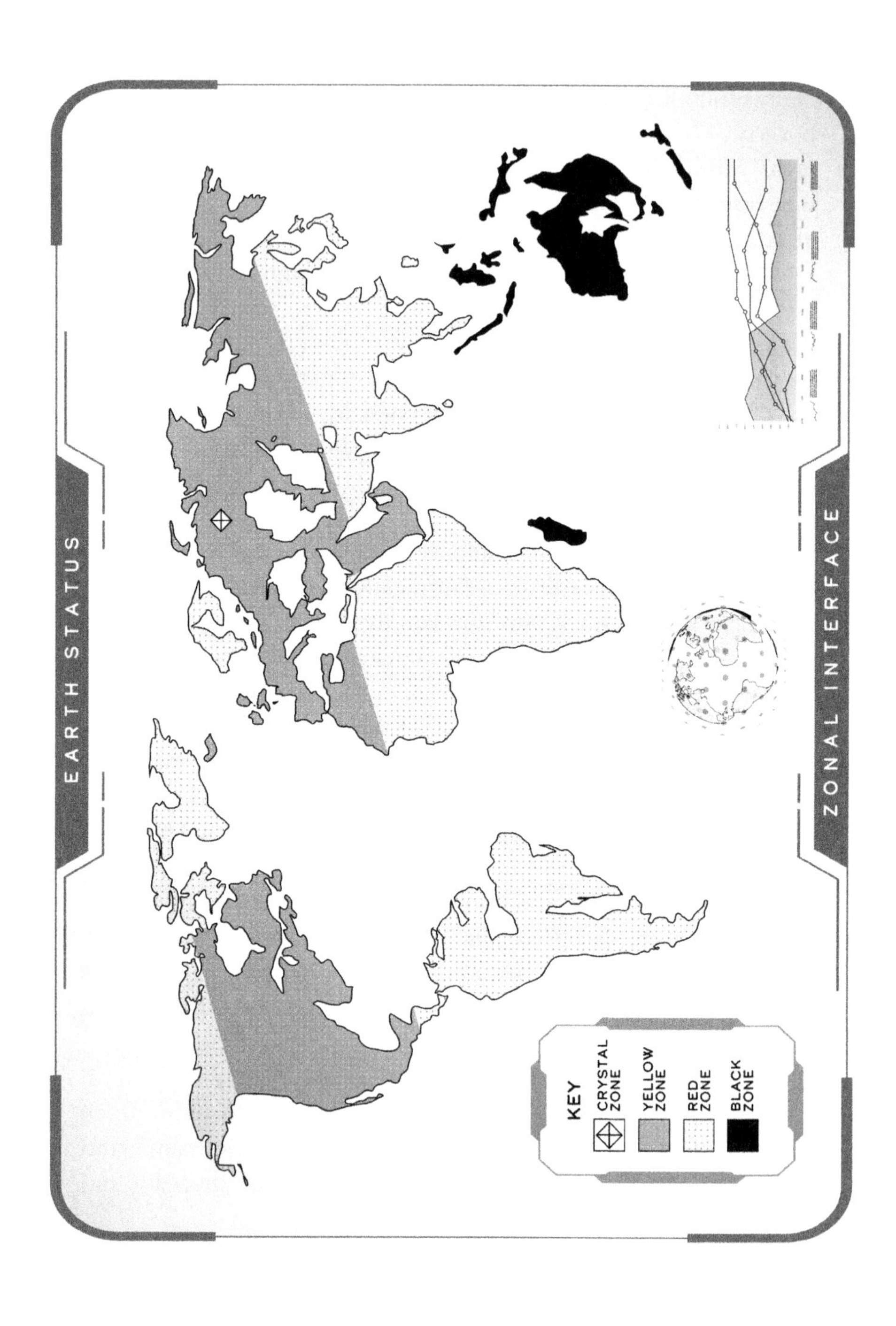
EARTH STATUS
ZONAL INTERFACE
KEY
CRYSTAL ZONE
YELLOW ZONE
RED ZONE
BLACK ZONE

CHAPTER 16

crystal

It had been some weeks since Marcus had found himself frozen at the entrance of the Eggshell quarter. Now he wished that he'd had the courage to go inside. Since then he'd been unable to focus on his work, and today he made the uncharacteristic decision to take the rest of the day off. He sped towards Eggshell on his hoverbike, his heart beating fast, and a feeling of sick anxiousness in his stomach. This time, he stood impatiently at the large glass doors of Eggshell and breathed into the DNA recognition bar.

"Welcome Doctor Jarret. Please step through the first set of doors."

Entry to Eggshell was one of the most biologically secure environments within the crystal zone. It required two step clearance to ensure that no organisms from the exterior entered the quarter. Being a pristine environment, the crystal zone was set up to ensure that there was never a risk of cross contamination between quarters.

Once sandwiched between the two sets of doors, Marcus was scanned and then illuminated firstly by a blue light and then a red light. Then a brief puff of spray entered the chamber, and a moment later, the second set of doors opened allowing him to enter the reception area of Eggshell.

"Welcome to Eggshell Doctor Jarret." One of the four smiling receptionists greeted Marcus as he approached the fluffy white, cloud shaped desk. "How can we help you today?"

"I would like to see Anja Kandinsky please." Marcus's voice was practically a whisper, as if speaking her name was a crime.

The receptionist swiped upwards to reveal a virtual information screen, and then swiped left for the appointments diary.

"I'm sorry Doctor Jarret, Anja Kandinsky is not here today, and hmmm, it appears she has been absent for a few weeks now."

The previously smiling receptionist's face changed to a slightly concerned expression as she consulted one of her colleagues. Marcus couldn't hear what they were saying but felt equally concerned to discover that she had not been at work for such a long time.

"I'm afraid I'm not able to give you any more information at this time Doctor Jarret."

The receptionist swiped downwards, and the virtual information screen disappeared.

"Could you tell me when she was last at work, please? A day or date would be most helpful. You see she missed her appointment at the clinic and ..."

The receptionist cut him off mid-sentence, repeating that she was unable to provide any further information. Then the smile returned to the receptionist's face as she changed the subject.

"While you're here Doctor Jarret, would you like to have a tour of the quarter? I note that you haven't been here before."

"Perhaps another time, thank you."

Marcus wasn't sure what he wanted to do next, but he knew that he didn't want to remain in the Eggshell quarter a minute longer. He decided to return to the clinic, despite having taken the afternoon off. On his return journey, he knew he had no other option but to find out where Anja lived and if she was there. The only way he could do that was at the clinic. He didn't have clearance to obtain personal data about a subject and would have to lodge a request to the information bureau, submitting a valid reason. Personal requests were always denied, so he knew that he would only be permitted to access her information as a matter of concern for the welfare of his patient. Although he appreciated the need for protocols, he also found them deeply frustrating, especially when time was of the essence.

A few hours later, Marcus was cleared to access Anja's personal data. She lived in the Iolite quarter in shared pod number 421. Now at least he would be able to get to the bottom of things because she would either be there, or one of her pod mates would know where she was.

The light was starting to fade on what had been an emotional rollercoaster of a day for Marcus, but it wasn't over yet. Now he had to travel to Iolite in his search for answers. It was dark by the time he reached his destination and the night lights had come on which always made the crystal zone look especially beautiful. Pod 421 was high up on the fourth level of the Iolite quarter and Marcus, now in impatient mood, ran up the flights of stairs rather than taking the capsule, which would have gently elevated him to level four. He stood at the door of Pod 421 and waited for the automated voice to announce he was there. A beautiful girl with long auburn hair, porcelain skin, and stunning green eyes opened the door.

"Hello. Please come in. We've been expecting you." The girl extended her arm towards the inside of the pod.

"You have?"

"Please come in Doctor Jarret." The girl smiled at Marcus as again she gestured to him to come inside.

Marcus stepped inside the pod and the girl shut the door behind him.

"We know why you're here," said one of the other girls.

Marcus looked around the modest communal area and saw that there were four bedrooms within the pod.

"Come, sit Doctor Jarret."

"I'm Elise, this is Bibi and that's Cerine," said the girl who'd answered the door.

"Yes, I remember you from your visits to the clinic. Please call me Marcus. You said you knew why I was here."

"Yes. And we hope you may be able to help us because in the beginning we thought Anja was with you. But it's been three weeks now, and Eggshell have been asking us about her whereabouts. We told them we didn't know. We didn't want her to get into trouble but an hour ago they contacted us again, and this time we had to tell them that we've had no contact from her. They've now officially reported her as missing to the Advocates. I'm so sorry Marcus but we had no choice."

"Why would you think Anja was with me?"

"You are all she's talked about for the last year. In recent weeks she was becoming melancholy and when she came home from work, she'd just lie on her bed sighing. It was so strange to see her like that because she's always been such a happy person. In the end we told her to go to you and tell you how she felt because, to be honest, we were all getting quite worried about her," said Bibi.

"I saw her leaving our pod in the early hours of the morning a few weeks ago. It was so out of character for her to do something like that. The next morning, she was back in her bed fast asleep. When she woke up, she was happier than we'd ever seen her. And then, just a few days later, she disappeared and we haven't seen her since. That's when we assumed that she was with you Doctor… Marcus," said Cerine.

"I see. Well, she hasn't been to work in weeks. I went to Eggshell today and it was quite strange really. I couldn't get much information from them at all. That must be what triggered their enquiry to you this evening. I don't understand it. She knew …" Marcus paused abruptly.

"Knew what?" Elise asked. "What did she know Marcus?

"She knew how I felt about her," Marcus replied, a little embarrassed at having to disclose his personal feelings.

"So clearly, you and Anja are in love with each other. How wonderful!" Bibi clapped her hands with joy.

Marcus sighed. It made no sense. Bibi was right. They were in love and Anja was left in no doubt of that after they'd spent several hours together that night. Their feelings for each other were intense and passionate. And from what her pod mates had said, she was as elated as he was the following day. And yet now she was gone.

He thanked the girls for their time and made his way home. Nothing like this had ever happened before. No Gen1 had ever just *disappeared*. Anxiety and frustration began to grip him. He was fearful for her safety and longed to see her again.

CHAPTER 17

crystal/yellow

Anja was restless. She'd been restless since spending the night with Marcus and now she found herself in an impossible situation. A situation that meant she couldn't stay in the crystal zone a minute longer.

There was a supply ship leaving for the yellow zone in two days and, one way or another, she had to find a way to be on it. The ships made regular trips to the other zones loaded with supplies of food, medicine and technical equipment for the Associates posted to the yellow and red zones. Anja had stolen a white lab coat from Iolite, packed enough food to last a few days, a fresh change of clothes and some personal items. Just enough to fit in a small holdall so that she looked as though she was only leaving for a brief time, just in case anyone questioned her. She knew that by wearing the white lab coat she was less likely to arouse any suspicion because, on occasion, a clinician was required to attend to an Associate wherever they were posted.

The ships always left at 3am when most people were sleeping. Anja gathered her belongings and crept silently out of the pod she shared with Bibi, Elise and Cerine and made her way to the exit. Her heart was racing as she stood at the first set of exit doors and held out her arm for the scanner to read her bracelet. To her relief, the first set of doors opened and she stepped inside. The doors shut behind her and then the doors to the outside world opened. The first thing she noticed was the change in temperature. The second thing she noticed was the supply ship that was docked and getting ready to depart. There were a few workers loading boxes of supplies in the cargo bay, but they were so engrossed in their work they didn't notice her boarding the small passenger cabin at the front of the ship. She had no idea where the vessel was heading, but as long as it was far away from the crystal zone that was all that mattered.

She took her seat, closed her eyes, and thought of Marcus. She loved him so much and leaving him was the hardest thing she'd ever had to do. But now there was something she cared about even more. She would miss her friends, and the job she loved, but she told herself that all of these feelings would fade in time and that a new adventure lay ahead.

As the ship undocked and started its journey away from the crystal zone, Anja started to cry. The reality of the enormous decision she'd made hit her. There was no going back now.

The soothing hum of the engines, and the gentle swaying, soon rocked her to sleep. It was the first sound sleep she'd had in days. She had a wonderful dream about Marcus and the night they'd shared, although in her dream they also took part in a coupling ceremony and lived happily ever after together. Waking from such a pleasant experience it was a rude shock when the ship docked and an automated voice said, *"you have arrived in the red zone."*

The door opened automatically and an oven like heat hit her face. The stench was unbearable and she found it hard to breathe so she quickly closed the door of the passenger bay. Through the frosted window she could just make out the form of a few men coming over to the ship and starting to unload some of the cargo. It all happened in a matter of minutes and the ship took off once more.

Four hours later the ship docked again and an automated voice announced, *"you have arrived in the yellow zone."*

The door opened and Anja hesitantly stood in the doorway surveying the surroundings. It was hot here too, but not as oppressive as the red zone. Once again men came over to the ship and started to unload boxes from the cargo hold. Before she left the craft she noticed that there were breathing masks hanging by the doorway. She picked one up and put it in her holdall, thinking it might be useful, and then stepped outside. The air smelled sour and she wrinkled her nose in disgust. She had imagined what life was like in the yellow zone from the stories she'd heard, but nothing had prepared her for the reality. For a split second she thought about turning back and going home, and then realised that it really wasn't an option for her now.

She took off her white lab coat and left it in the craft. This was the beginning of her new life and she needed no reminders of what she'd left behind. It was the middle of the afternoon and the hottest time of the day. As she walked towards a populated area a strange and unpleasant sensation came over her skin that she'd never experienced before. It was a burning feeling. As she'd never been exposed to the sun's rays it didn't occur to her that her skin would burn, but instinctively she pulled out a long sleeved shirt from her bag and covered her bare arms. Then she sought out somewhere sheltered where she could plan what to do next. Having left the crystal zone in such a hurry, she really hadn't given much thought to where she would go, or what she would do.

When she reached the centre of town she was immediately struck by the number of people milling around. They were all so dirty looking, and thin, and they smelled bad. Anja stood out with her fresh face and clean clothes. She encountered two very young children on their own sitting in an alleyway who spat at her. She'd never seen children behave in such a manner or look so unkempt before. She wondered where their parents were, or if they even had any parents.

"Well isn't you a beaut!"

A scruffy looking old man came over and got too close for her liking. She scurried away from him as quickly as she could, stubbing her toe on the uneven pavement, causing her to trip over. As she was getting to her feet she heard a woman's voice and then felt a hand helping up.

"You want to steer clear of him, he's a dirty old man. You look a bit lost if you don't mind me saying."

"Yes. I haven't been here before. I'm looking for somewhere to live, and maybe some work."

"Well you won't find either of those round here. There's a big old house up on the hill though. They may be able to help you."

The woman smiled and went on her way. Anja headed up the steep hill that led to a big house that was surrounded by a high brick wall and locked double wrought iron gates. There was a large, old brass bell, with a piece of rope hanging from it at the side of the gate.

A young lad on a push bike pulled up outside the gates.

"Have you rung the bell? I won't ring it again if you have. They don't like it when you ring more than once," he asked, out of breath.

"Rung the bell?"

The lad took hold of the rope and yanked it a few times. Anja covered her ears from the loud sound it made.

"They'll come out in a minute and let us in. What's your name? I haven't seen you here before."

"Anja."

"Hi Anja, I'm Jack."

The front door of the big old house opened and an older woman walked outside into the courtyard, and towards the gate, swinging a hefty ring of keys.

"You're late Jack."

"I'm sorry missus, I got a puncture."

The woman unlocked the gate and Jack walked through with his bike.

"And who are you?"

"My name is Anja Kandinsky. I was told you might be able to help me."

"Is that so?" The woman eyed Anja up and down. "Well you'd better come in. It'll be getting dark soon."

The woman locked the gates behind her, rattling them a couple of times just to be sure they were secure. Anja followed the woman inside. The house had a smell about it that Anja couldn't place. It wasn't unpleasant just different.

"So Anja Kandinsky, what's your story?"

"My story?"

"Where are you from? I can tell from the look of you that you're not local."

"No I'm not local. I come from … another place. I'm looking for somewhere to live, and possibly work."

"What sort of work?"

"I used to look after children, but I'd be happy to do anything really."

"I see. Well I can't offer you any paid work, but if you're happy to help out round here, I can offer you a room and one meal a day."

"Oh that would be wonderful, thank you so much."

"Come on through. I'll introduce you to my family."

Anja followed the woman into a large living room.

"These are my parents, Joe, and Catherine, and this is my son, David. My brother, Georgie, also lives here but spends most of his time in his room. You'll meet him later. This is Anja. She's going to be staying here for a while and helping out."

Anja had never seen anyone look as old as her parents did. They were barely alive and sat in their chairs staring into space. Her son, on the other hand, couldn't take his eyes off her which made her feel a little uncomfortable.

"Is Jack part of your family too?"

The woman laughed. "Hell no. Jack is our odd job boy. He comes here for a few days each week and sleeps in our garage."

Anja had no idea what an odd job boy was, or a garage, but sensed this wasn't the time to ask for an explanation.

"Come on, let's get you settled in. Is that all you've brought with you?"

Anja nodded and followed the woman upstairs and down the hall.

"You can have this room. It isn't much to look at but you should be comfortable enough. It was my sister's room. Dinner is at 6pm. You can start working tomorrow. You'll find some odds and ends in the drawers that were my sister's. Help yourself."

"Your sister?"

"Yes, she passed on a few years back."

"Oh I'm so sorry."

"It's why we keep to ourselves up here now, and why everything is locked so we have a secure perimeter. There are some bad people out there, as my sister unfortunately discovered."

"What shall I call you? I heard Jack call you missus. Is that your name?"

The woman tutted as she walked out of the room. "My name is Jane."

Anja unpacked her few belongings and stood at the window staring out at a view unlike anything she'd seen before. It was like being on another planet. The sky had a dark orange tinge to it and, in the distance, there was a vast expanse of rough dark water. Down the hill she could see row upon row of small buildings, in varying stages of disrepair, and people dotted everywhere; so many people wandering around aimlessly and in squalor. Her heart sank. It looked like it was going to be a hard life in the yellow zone but at least she was safe for now. She had a roof over her head and one guaranteed meal a day.

She went down for dinner on the dot of 6pm. The rest of the family were already tucking into their food on their laps in the living room. Jane was sitting next to her mother spoon feeding her.

"Yours is on the counter in the kitchen," Jane called out, in between swallowing mouthfuls of her own meal.

Anja went into the kitchen and found a bowl of hot brown liquid with some odd looking things floating in it. She decided to eat in the kitchen so as not to intrude on the family. The food looked unappetising but didn't smell too bad, so she took a small mouthful. It tasted strange and very salty. She was so hungry, and didn't wish to appear ungrateful to her host, so ate as much as she could stomach. After a while Jane, Georgie and David came into the kitchen with their empty bowls. Jack came in through the kitchen door with his bowl empty as well.

"That was great thanks missus."

Jane nodded and Jack went back outside.

"Yes, thank you Jane. Very … tasty." Anja managed to find a suitable description if not a generous one.

"You're welcome Anja. I hope you manage to sleep well. Good night."

That was Anja's cue to return to her room. She didn't know what the next day would bring, or what sort of work she would be doing, but it had been quite a day and she was only too happy to have an early night.

The next day everyone was up early but it wasn't because they had anything in particular to do. Anja soon discovered that as soon as it got dark, everyone went to sleep, and as soon as it became light, everyone got up.

Jack was outside and up a ladder doing some repairs to the roof. Jane was in the living room attending to the needs of her elderly parents. Georgie and David had gone out for a few hours.

"Anja, can you give me a hand please?" Jane groaned.

Anja had never experienced the effects of incontinence in an adult before, nor had she ever seen an adult wearing a nappy.

"She's messed herself."

The smell made Anja heave.

"You'll get used to it."

Jane and Anja stood her mother up and removed the soiled nappy. Jane wiped her down and placed a stained but clean one on. Then she sat her mother down again.

"You have to do this several times a day. It's why the boys have gone out. They know the morning change is the worst. They make themselves scarce so I don't rope them into helping me."

"Where do they go Jane?"

"I don't know and I don't care. Usually they come back with something they've pinched."

"Pinched?"

"You know, stolen."

"Oh, I see." Anja was shocked at the admission.

"You don't approve?"

"I'm just a little surprised. Do they speak? Your parents, do they ever say anything?"

"She makes the odd noise now and then, and dad sometimes mutters to himself, but generally they live in their own little worlds these days."

"I'm sorry Jane, that must be very difficult for you."

"It's a relief to be honest. They stopped making any sense a while back. The silence is a blessing. Sometimes I go into their bedrooms in the morning just to check they're both still breathing."

"Oh my!" Anja took a sharp intake of breath and decided it was time to change the subject.

"What would you like me to do today Jane?"

Jane found plenty of work for Anja for the next six weeks, scrubbing, cleaning, tidying, making beds, feeding and changing her mother, and helping prepare meals. It was exhausting work but Anja was just happy to be useful and she welcomed the distraction from her thoughts of Marcus. When she wasn't working she wondered if he missed her, or even if he knew that she was gone.

What Anja didn't know was that every night since her arrival at the house, David crept into her bedroom and watched her sleep. After a while, his obsession with her became too much for him to bear, and he couldn't resist the temptation to touch her. In the darkness Anja sat bolt upright and screamed which sent him scurrying back to his room.

When Jane asked her the next morning what had happened, she told her what David had done. Jane found it amusing which Anja didn't appreciate. She realised that her stay at the big house was over. It was time to move on. Jane begged her to reconsider as she'd found Anja's assistance, with her mother in particular, so helpful but it was too late. She no longer felt safe there.

Over the six weeks that she'd stayed at Jane's, Anja had struck up a friendship with Jack, and he'd taught her how to ride a bicycle. He'd also found her one of her own. It had been discarded and left by the side of the road needing some repairs to make it rideable again. Jack had taken it into the garage and worked on it in his spare time. He liked Anja because she treated him as her equal, something the family never did, despite all of his hard work for them over the years.

On the morning Anja left, Jane gave her some food for her journey and a little money to assuage her conscience. It was guilt money but Anja didn't care. She took it gratefully, and rode off into the distance, relieved to get as far away from the unwanted advances of David as she could.

"Be careful of the pookies!" Jane called out to her as she rode away.

Anja thought it was an ironic warning, given that David and Georgie were no better than the thieving gangs that roamed the coastal roads and villages.

She headed north along a rickety coastal road towards the next town in the hope of finding somewhere more permanent to live. What she found was a small ghost town full of empty houses, boarded up shop fronts, and not a soul in sight. Exhausted from her ride in the baking heat, Anja decided there was no harm in stopping there for the night while she collected her thoughts and planned where next to go. Having come from a highly populated town to one completely devoid of life felt strangely reassuring for her. She investigated a few of the empty houses which were all in a terrible state. Most still had furniture in them, and some even had clothes in the wardrobe, which signalled that the occupants had left in a hurry. She eventually settled on one small single storey house in a back street which had an old, stained mattress on the floor of one of the bedrooms. It would have to do. She took her bicycle inside the house and locked the front door behind her. If she'd learned anything in the time she'd been in the yellow zone it was that if something wasn't nailed down it would get stolen.

Anja no longer resembled the fresh-faced young woman who'd arrived with long shining hair and was dressed in pristine clothes just six weeks earlier. Now she fitted right in with her surroundings and imagined that if Marcus could see her now, he would be completely horrified.

After such a busy period of time in the big house, Anja enjoyed her newly found solitude. In fact she enjoyed it so much that she stayed in the deserted house, in the deserted town for the next few weeks. It was only after one extreme dust storm, which blew the roof off the little house, that she had to set off once more.

For the next few months, Anja cycled from town to town,

sometimes sleeping in doorways. She queued up every Tuesday at one of the Associate provided food stations. Other times she spent a few nights with people she'd met along the way. She was getting more tired and rundown, and the distances she could cycle grew shorter, but she continued to head north hoping to find a place she could finally call home.

As she arrived in yet another rundown, and sparsely populated town, Anja noticed that her bracelet had started to glow with a pulsating orange light. Unable to take it off she hid it under her shirt sleeve and hoped that nobody would notice. But somebody did notice and, by the time the morning came, she awoke to find a young man standing over her.

"I think you'd better come with me." His voice was commanding as he helped her to her feet. "Get dressed and pack up your belongings."

Anja reluctantly did as she was told. Then he took her by the arm and led her outside. He was a strong looking young man and she knew there was no point trying to escape.

CHAPTER 18

crystal

Although the Advocates met with the Leader once a month, today they had been summoned for an extraordinary meeting where every Advocate was required to appear in person. This meant no holograms were permitted and each Advocate would have to travel from their respective quarters, which stretched the length and breadth of the domed crystal city. They had been instructed to ensure their arrivals were at staggered intervals so that the population would not be alarmed. If the people had seen all twelve Advocates arrive at once, it could have raised suspicion and unease.

Obediently each Advocate travelled to The Great Hall moving through their various quarters and the populations within them with a quiet efficiency. In fact, the people were so consumed with fulfilling their individual work commitments that the Leader need not have been concerned.

Each Advocate took his place in The Great Hall and waited patiently. They all kept their heads bowed, making no eye contact with each other, and none uttered a word, not even to greet each other.

Once all twelve Advocates had arrived and taken their places, the Leader entered the hall and sat at the head of the long, highly polished dark wood table.

"My Advocates, I thank you for your presence." The Leader's

voice was quiet and monotone, and each word echoed slightly in the chamber. "The news is grave and the mission we now face is even more so."

The Advocates kept their heads bowed and remained perfectly still.

"Our planet is now at its most perilous moment in history. When I enacted my first decree we proclaimed colour zoning. It was as a last desperate attempt to try and salvage certain regions of the Earth. We had hoped that one day, long into the future, generations to come might venture out of our secure crystal habitat and live freely again. This has failed. Billions have continued to live carelessly, breed indiscriminately, and allowed others to suffer. They are continuing to die from intense heat and droughts that have left them without food or water. Habitats have been destroyed leaving only dustbowl conditions in many regions. No area has suffered more than the red zone. Regrettably, more recently we have also had to downgrade regions that had previously held yellow zone status to red. We can no longer allow this to continue. Are we agreed?"

The Leader was stating what had been obvious to the majority of the Advocates for a long time. The Advocates all nodded their agreement. "I must therefore, with immediate effect, issue my next decree and instruct our defence operation to proceed with phase one of our new mission, Project Thanatos."

"Phase *one*, Leader?"

"That is correct Advocate."

"How many phases are there, Leader?"

"You will be advised when the time requires it. In the next few hours our drone units will be despatched to all red zone regions. They will search and destroy all human life in those zones with absolute precision. MX497 is a chemical weapon created ten years ago with the express purpose of rendering any potential enemy powerless. There has been no need to deploy it, until now. Granted, the people within the red zone are not our enemies, but our primary duty is to protect our planet. We must perform this unfortunate task for the greater good. When the drones release MX497 across the red zone regions it will put a human population numbering billions to sleep; a sleep from which they will never awake. They will feel no pain. Their suffering will be over in a matter of seconds."

Another Advocate raised his head being careful not to look directly at the Leader.

"We have assets in these communities Leader, our Associate Advocates. How are we to get them to safety in time?"

The atmosphere in The Great Hall changed from compliant to concerned.

"They will not be able to return Advocate. It would not be in the best interest of our own people who, I remind you, have no knowledge of the outside world. They know nothing of the people in those zones. All they know is what they have experienced in our crystal zone. The risk of an Associate returning here from a red zone and speaking of what they have seen and experienced would risk the stability of what has been so painstakingly created here."

A third Advocate raised his hand. "Leader, our Associates have served us with immense loyalty and bravery, and we are to repay them with *death*?"

"I do not like your tone, Advocate. Does sacrifice for the greater good *offend* you?

"I apologise for my tone Leader. I did not mean to question you and I remain your humble servant."

There was a prolonged and uncomfortable silence for a number of minutes before the Leader spoke once more.

"I have taken a moment to consider your concerns and will delay the drones for one day more. If you can get your Associates back here in that time it will be your responsibility to debrief them upon their return and swear them to silence. Any that do not make it back in time will be lost. We should be *grateful* that we have the ability to selectively render human life extinct in such a humane manner Advocates." The Leader rose signalling the end of the meeting.

The Advocates rose and chanted in unison. "Glory to our Leader, glory to the crystal zone."

As the Leader withdrew from the table, moving with stealth across The Great Hall, his flowing cape made him appear a dark, ghostly figure. The Advocates remained in their positions at the table, heads still bowed, until it was clear that the Leader had left The Great Hall.

Then, just as they had done when arriving, they staggered the timing of their departures so as not to arouse suspicion. When ten of the Advocates had departed, the remaining two men glanced briefly at each other and one gestured towards the exit as if saying 'after you'. To anyone observing it would have seemed insignificant. They would not have noticed the flowing cloak sleeve brushing effortlessly past the other man's side, and with the sleight of hand of a magician, slipping a tiny object into the pocket of the other Advocate's cloak. Both men remained expressionless as each descended to ground level and went their separate ways.

Upon returning to his own quarter and ascending to the seclusion of his private pod, the Advocate removed the object his colleague had placed in his cloak pocket. It was a tiny black ampule. Ampules had been developed for top secret information to be relayed between Advocates and their Associates. If the ampule fell into the wrong hands the information would remain intact even if the seal was broken. The secure nature of the ampule's creation guaranteed that only the intended recipient could ever read the message within it because only a DNA molecule from their breath would release the communication hidden inside.

The Advocate twisted the ampule, breaking its seal and revealing a glossy red liquid inside the casing. He breathed onto the liquid and an image appeared, hovering above his palm and then, within seconds, it was gone. It was the signal he had been waiting for and yet it was the one he had also been dreading. The message simply read … "*IT'S TIME*".

CHAPTER 19

crystal

As Marcus had expected, the Advocates summoned him the following day before he'd even left his pod to go to the clinic. His heart was heavy as he entered the capsule that would take him to The Great Hall.

The Advocates were assembled at the long, ornately carved wood table. Marcus could smell the polish that had recently been applied, giving it a luminous lustre in the morning light. Three of the Advocates were there in person while the remaining nine were present in holographic form. They all seemed to be in a serious mood.

"Well? What have you done Marcus?"

"I haven't *done* anything."

"Well, something must have happened to make Anja Kandinsky flee the crystal zone."

Marcus was stunned. Of all the things he could have imagined, Anja leaving the crystal zone wasn't one of them.

"She's left? Are you sure? How do you know?"

"We know because we've been able to track her movements, Marcus. Once we were alerted last night that she was missing, we tracked her through her seed."

Another Advocate tried to intervene, but it was too late.

"Her what?" This time Marcus knew he hadn't misheard the Advocate.

"Her seed Marcus. All Gen1s and Gen2s are seeded prior to being forwarded. It's a safety precaution and helps us understand more about how well their modified genes are performing. It also means that we are able to track their whereabouts just in case one has a fall for example, so we are able to get help to them."

"Why am I just learning about this now? I'm conducting monthly tests on the Gen1s, reporting back with vital data, and yet I know nothing about the fact that they have seeds implanted in them? This is unbelievable!"

"Please modify your tone Doctor Jarret, we are not the enemy."

There was an uneasy silence for a few moments before Marcus regained his composure realising that when an Advocate called him Doctor Jarret instead of Marcus, he'd overstepped the mark.

"Am I seeded?"

"No Marcus, PreGens are not seeded. The procedure has to be done prior to forwarding. Now can we return to the matter of Anja Kandinsky please?"

"Do you know where she is? I'm very worried about her."

"When we learned that she had disappeared we tracked her movements for the last month. We note that she entered your pod in the early hours of the morning three weeks ago and left three hours later, returning to her own pod. But then, two days later, we tracked her movements to the exit of the crystal zone. It would appear she boarded a transport ship that was heading west towards a yellow zone area. Why do you think she would have done that Marcus?"

"I honestly have no idea. I didn't know she had left here until now."

One of the Advocates, who was present in person, then placed a pile of small envelopes on the table. Marcus recognised them immediately. They were all the notes he'd written to Anja over the previous weeks, and he was relieved to see that they were all still sealed. At least they had respected his privacy. But his interrogation by the Advocates was far from over.

"Were you expecting Anja to come to your pod at such a

strange time?"

"No. I was not."

"Did you have an argument? Did she leave feeling upset?"

"No. Quite the opposite."

"Were you intimate?"

"That's none of your business."

"We will assume by your response that you were."

Again, there was an uncomfortable silence.

"Look, you gave me permission …"

"Yes Marcus. We did. Yours was an exception to the rule. And this is the result."

"You're blaming me for Anja's disappearance?"

"It is clear that your association is the direct cause of the current situation. For that reason, you are now accountable for her safe return to the crystal zone." The Advocate's words were stern, and all the other Advocates then nodded their heads in agreement.

"Look, I want Anja back safely more than anyone, but how am I supposed to bring her home when we don't know where she is?"

"We are sending you to the yellow zone. You will be accompanied by an Associate Advocate who will ensure that you remain safe during your journey. We have been able to track her location to within five miles inside the yellow zone as of two days ago, but after that we lost her signal. Seeding signals are not designed for long distances."

Marcus shook his head. There was so much information coming at him, so many things he didn't know. And now he was being forced to leave the safety of the crystal zone to find Anja and bring her back.

"What if she doesn't *want* to return?"

"It's your job to persuade her otherwise Marcus. After all, she clearly has strong feelings for you. But if that doesn't work, the Associate Advocate who is accompanying you can intervene and ensure that she *is* brought home one way or another."

One way or another? Marcus didn't like the sound of the alternative. He was now beginning to wonder how many more secrets were being kept from him, and from the rest of the population. It had never occurred to him that things weren't completely transparent or that the Advocates could be so ruthless. Everything seemed to run so smoothly, and everyone seemed so contented, but perhaps the reason was that the whole of the crystal zone community was being kept in a state of blissful ignorance.

"You will leave in the morning Marcus. The name of your Associate Advocate is Finch, and he will be waiting for you at the exit at 9am."

The Advocates rose and departed The Great Hall in haste.

There were so many questions spinning around in his mind. Questions that he would clearly get no answers to from the Advocates. The most pressing question was why Anja would have left in the first place. Marcus felt exhausted and his mind ached. He headed back to his pod and lay down on his bed. Tonight, he would bathe, pack, and have some food. It was hard not to fear what lay ahead. There had been many rumours and stories about what life was like in the yellow zone. He had always felt so sure that they had been wildly embellished in order to sound more dramatic. Now he was about to find out the truth.

CHAPTER 20

crystal

Advocates were free to come and go as they pleased, so it was not unusual for them to meet with other Advocates in their private pods to partake of refreshments and discuss the topics of the day.

The night of the Leader's decree two Advocates met up in secrecy.

"Welcome John, do come in."

As the pod door closed behind him, the Advocate removed his cloak and lay it carefully on the crimson velvet arm of a large, ornately carved antique sofa. He strode around his fellow Advocate's generously proportioned pod, admiring the paintings and sculptures that adorned it, before settling himself down on a more modern and comfortable sofa.

"Time is of the essence Alex."

"Yes. It's time John. Is there nothing we can do to save those poor, wretched people in the red zone?"

"No, tragically not. The Advocate closed his eyes and shook his head.

"Then we must focus our attention on the fate of the yellow zone population."

"I don't know where to start John."

"We've been Advocates for nearly twenty years, and in all that time I have never questioned the Leader's intentions Alex. But now …"

"I know. We were led to believe that our role here was to preserve life, not destroy it."

"It seems we have both been misled about the crystal zone project Alex. Have you any idea if there are other Advocates who are wavering in their loyalty to the Leader?"

"You and I are the last of the old school John. All the other Advocates are either younger PreGens or Gen1s, and none of them have shown a hint of displeasure at the Leader's way of doing things. We are both in our late 70s. We remember how things were long before the colour coding of zones to before the crystal zone was even finished."

"Yes, I suppose it's hardly surprising the others are happy to go along with things. They're younger and have been so protected and cossetted. They've no real world experience. All most of them have ever known is the crystal way of life," Alex replied.

"I do know of some Associates who are growing restless with the status quo though. Perhaps they could become allies?"

"Yes, I have a few of my own Associates that I trust and I know I could get on side."

The two Advocates took refreshments, occasionally rising and walking around the pod to stretch their elderly legs as they plotted and planned late into the night.

"Can we just take a moment to discuss the Leader."

"You read my mind Alex. All this secrecy about his identity. I kind of got it in the beginning when he was a more benign Leader. But now …"

"You mean now that he is becoming a mass murder?" Alex stated with sarcasm.

"Exactly. I mean, I know that he was supposedly created specifically for the task, but his lack of empathy makes me wonder about who he really is."

"Go on."

"Well the Leader is one of a kind. There is no other being on the planet like him. He was really one huge experiment when you think about it. We can assume by his creation date that he is in his early forties."

"Yes, that would be about right. Where are you going with

this John? I wonder if we're thinking the same thing."

"If we are to believe what we were told when we first entered here he was, in effect, the very first Gen1 ever created. He had been created while they were still building the crystal zone. The Gen1s of today were created twenty years later. But the Leader doesn't behave like a Gen1. And I noticed something earlier today when we were in The Great Hall."

"What did you notice?"

"There was a very long silence before the Leader agreed to delay the drone strike on the red zone," John said, his brow furrowed.

"Yes, I noticed that as well. It was as if he was processing the information."

"Exactly!"

"And it was the first time that any of us had ever questioned or challenged his decisions. He's been used to our complete obedience until today."

"It's as if he was recalibrating!"

"Yes, and that would mean the Leader may not be what we've all been led to believe he is after all."

CHAPTER 21

yellow

"Glad that shift is over," said Blane, scratching his stomach and stretching as he got out of the cabin. "Last time I have to go back there as it turns out."

"How come? Are you retiring?" Hogue tried not to sound too hopeful.

"Nope. Not retiring. We're just not dumping on that route anymore. Well don't just sit there gawking, let's put Mable to bed and get our money."

Mable was the name Blane had affectionately given to the hovertruck he was in charge of. All the drivers had given the vehicles they piloted female names. One was called Esmerelda, another was Fifi. None of the trucks had been given male names because historically people used the female pronoun 'she' when referring to machines like cars and ships. Others preferred the idea that it was because these machines were actually a man's first love. Whatever the reason, the tradition had stuck.

Tucker was the head of the facility, and he was there as always to sign off the trucks and discharge the pilots of their duty. Just as Hogue and Blane were heading towards the gates, having collected their money from the office, they were called back by Tucker.

"Guys, did you notice the orange light was flashing on your instrument panel? You must have noticed it, right?" Tucker said pointing at the dashboard and looking displeased.

As the men walked back to the truck, Blane muttered under his breath to Hogue that he would handle it and to keep his mouth shut.

"It must have just come on buddy. I guess a piece of trash got stuck in the hold." Blane shrugged it off.

"You know very well that's not how these babies work Blane. That light must have been on the whole time you were on your way back here. They don't make mistakes you know. And you, what's your name?" Tucker looked at Hogue sternly.

"It's my first day as a pilot, sir. My name is Hogue."

"And did *you* notice that the light was flashing Hogue? Cos if you didn't then you'll both need to get your eyes checked if you want to keep your licences to operate this girl again. Am I clear?"

Tucker had his hands on his hips and was starting to turn red in the face. Hogue was now too frightened to speak. He *had* pointed out the flashing light from the start and Blane had dismissed his concerns. So now he was stuck between a rock and a hard place. If he told the truth, Blane would have it in for him for sure. And if he lied, he just knew that Tucker would see through him.

"Right let's open her up and see what's causing the problem, shall we?" Tucker growled, as he climbed into the cabin and pressed the release button.

The hold started moving, just as it had at the tip. Up it went at an angle, opening the cargo lid and back door at the same time. Tucker climbed out of the cabin and walked to the rear of the truck to investigate. Blane and Hogue followed.

The piece of trash that Tucker was expecting, slid out onto the concrete floor of the depot with a thud. Blane looked at Hogue and then back to what was lying on the concrete. All three men stared at something limp and wrapped in a blanket. Tucker impatiently lifted the blanket by a few inches to get a closer look and then hastily let it fall back to the ground taking two steps back. He was ashen faced.

"What the hell have you done? You idiots! Look. Look at it. Look at what you've brought back with you. Do you have any idea how much trouble you're in?" Tucker cupped his hands over his face as he walked a few paces away to think about what they should do. Meanwhile Hogue and Blane looked gingerly under the blanket.

"Oh no! No, no, no, no, no!" Hogue squealed.

"Keep your voice down. Is it alive?" Blane asked with absolutely no emotion whatsoever as he too started moving away from their unexpected find.

"It? *It*? What's wrong with you! *It* is a girl. She is a girl!" Hogue shouted, now enraged. He hadn't signed up for this and now he didn't care if he kept his job or not. He crouched down to see if she had a pulse, at which point Tucker returned and took charge.

"You do realise that she'll be contaminated, don't you? God knows what you'll catch. OK, we need to get shot of this little problem before we all end up losing our jobs. *I'll* deal with it. You boys get yourselves home. As far as you're concerned this didn't happen. Are we good?"

"Fine with me boss." Blane turned and headed swiftly towards the gate. It was clear he couldn't get out of there fast enough and was more than happy to let Tucker deal with it. Hogue on the contrary wasn't fine with any of this.

"What are you going to do with her?"

"The less you *know*, the less you'll have to *lie*. Get going. Now!" Tucker shouted.

Hogue turned reluctantly and started to walk away very slowly. This wasn't right. The poor girl was in a terrible state, barely alive. He stopped and turned back to face Tucker again.

"She needs urgent medical assistance."

"I'll *deal* with it Hogue. Get lost."

Hogue walked slowly through the depot gates occasionally glimpsing back to see what Tucker was doing. When he got to his car, he sat there for a moment before driving a short distance where he waited in a side street to see what Tucker did next. Half an hour passed and there was still no sign of Tucker, but Hogue wasn't deterred. He didn't have anywhere else to be so he was prepared to wait as long as it took.

Tucker put on protective clothing before he picked the girl up, then carried her to his utility truck where he unceremoniously dumped her body in the open-topped back and covered her with some of the rubbish that was already in the truck bed. As he drove out of the gates Hogue followed him. It didn't take him long to realise that Tucker wasn't on his way to get medical help for the girl. Instead, he drove to a dark, deserted area where a crumbling, disused warehouse stood on a large unkempt piece of land.

Tucker sat for a moment before getting out of his truck. His eyes surveyed the area as he removed the girl from the back, then strode inside the building where he dumped her as if he was throwing a sack of rubbish into a cart. He immediately removed his protective clothing and discarded it in an old iron bin before returning to his truck and driving off at speed.

Hogue was horrified. He waited until the truck was well off in the distance before driving into the grounds of the old warehouse. He ran inside the building and found the girl who was unconscious, but she was definitely still alive. He knew she would not survive if he didn't do something and do it fast. He couldn't have her death on his conscience. Equally he couldn't be directly involved and have this traced back to his employer. There was a place he'd heard about just outside of town. It was a small medical clinic run by volunteers. He knew taking her there was a risk, but it was one he had to take.

CHAPTER 22

observation 1:4

My organic grandmother and grandfather are fortunate in that they live in the crystal zone. Although not having been born there, they had been invited to relocate to the region due to their high IQs and good genetics. It was a rare honour to receive such an invitation and given the opportunity of a better standard of living, it had been an easy decision to make.

Although not as genetically advanced as my organic mother and father, my grandparents had benefitted from the advances in science and medicine of their time. They arrived in the crystal zone just a few years before it was completed. Not long after that my organic grandfather was invited to become an Advocate.

The role of Advocates and their Associates is reserved for males. Accompanying females can also be skilled or professional people, however their role is much more basic. Men not partnered with either a female or a male are also eligible for selection as sexual preference or orientation is irrelevant to the Leader.

There are no dazzling, highly technical or scientific terms to describe our basic, everyday functions in travel, food, or fuel in the crystal zone. The colour coding of states is a perfect example of how the Leader has chosen to remove what he sees as the potentially damaging personalities or patriotic associations humans historically made with their lands and cultures. Now you are either living in the hell of a red zone, the harshness of a yellow zone or the sanitised tolerability of a crystal zone. It's that simple.

For instance, if I had been conceived and born in a red zone, my chances of survival would have been negligible. I could have lived to perhaps five or six years, but there was a greater likelihood that I would have ended my days as part of a desperate person's meal.

As a child in the harshness of the yellow zone, I would have fared better. The poor air quality would most likely have meant I'd suffer endless chest infections, and a lack of nutrition due to my family's dependence on weekly food rations.

I was saved from either of these fates by being harvested from a first generation crystal zone female, my organic mother. I am currently a collection of gene-edited cells floating in a rich protective soup of synthetic embryonic fluid. I exist in a state of limbo. It is planned that I will be forwarded upon my completion, although not to my biological mother.

As the only Gen3 specimen to survive, I am the ultimate scientific experiment and will be the closest example of human perfection that science can create.

And so, I wait.

CHAPTER 23

crystal/yellow

"I'm Finch."

A tall, dark-skinned young man stretched out his hand to Marcus. He was strong, muscular, extremely good looking, and as Marcus quickly discovered, he had a bone-crushingly strong handshake.

"Our journey will take approximately five hours Doctor Jarret."

Finch's face was expressionless as he lifted a heavy backpack onto his shoulders without effort.

"As we're likely to be together for some time, would you mind calling me Marcus?"

"I would prefer to remain professional Doctor Jarret. This way please." Finch pointed towards the hovership that was at a docking station near the exit.

Marcus was left in no doubt that Finch wasn't of a mind to be his friend and was there in a purely official capacity. The thought of spending hours, days or even longer with such a serious companion made him feel even more isolated than he already was. The Advocates had made him feel responsible for Anja's disappearance and for her safe return. Now Finch's serious disposition was bordering on coldness towards him at a time when he really felt the need for an ally. They were about to go to a place that filled Marcus with dread, even though he had no proof that the yellow zone was as bad as rumour implied. There was nothing for him to do but take each moment as it happened and try not to let his mind get ahead of itself.

Since Anja's disappearance, new security measures had been put in place in addition to bracelet scanning, to prevent anyone else leaving the crystal zone without prior permission. As both men stood at the exit, two ampules were dispensed, one for each of them. They were instructed to confirm their DNA identities by breathing onto the red liquid inside the black ampule. Once both ampules turned green, the first set of security doors opened and the two men stepped inside. When the first set of doors sealed closed behind them, the exterior doors opened and they exited the chamber. They were exposed to a blast of hot air as they stepped away from the security of the only home they had ever known.

Marcus followed Finch to the docking station to board the hovership. Once inside they surveyed the streamlined interior which comprised of four comfortable looking white padded chairs, and a larger cargo area towards the rear. Marcus sat in one of the front seats assuming that Finch would be seated next to him for the journey. Finch, however, chose the seat furthest away, yet again endorsing Marcus's feeling of aloneness and a growing paranoia that his every move was being watched and judged. Both men were taken aback when security straps automatically closed firmly around their bodies. Every experience Marcus was having was new and daunting, and it appeared that Finch had not travelled outside the crystal zone before either, which was something Marcus found vaguely comforting. The cabin suddenly pressurised making their ears pop, and the hovership lifted away from the docking station with the feintest hum.

There was a row of small circular frosted windows on either side of the ship, which didn't allow for a clear view of the outside environment. Once the ship reached its maximum speed the windows changed from frosted to black obliterating any outside light. Marcus assumed this was to maintain a comfortable temperature inside the cabin and perhaps to block out any exterior radiation.

"Seat recline. Lights off."

Marcus turned around and saw that the lights above Finch had switched off and he was now in a horizontal position. It was clear that there was not going to be any conversation, polite or otherwise, coming from Finch during the journey.

Marcus was exhausted. He couldn't remember the last time he'd slept well. Now there was nothing else to do to pass the time, so he followed Finch's lead, reclined his chair, and switched off the overhead light. There was very little noise inside the ship and just a gentle sway from time to time as it navigated across land and sea. It took Marcus just a few minutes to fall into a very deep sleep.

Both men awoke hours later when the cabin lights came on and the automated pilot announced that they would be arriving at their destination in ten minutes. With seats returned to their upright position, Marcus looked over his shoulder at Finch who was staring back at him. It was an uncomfortable silence.

"What happens now Finch?"

"It's in hand."

"What, that's it? That's all you're prepared to tell me?"

"It's in hand Doctor Jarret."

"Ridiculous," Marcus muttered under his breath.

He was quickly distracted as the windows turned from black back to clear frosted, not that it made any difference to visibility of the outside world.

The ship slowed down and then hovered on the spot for a moment before setting down. The men were instantaneously released from their seat straps and Finch was the first to stand up and gather his backpack. He threw a breathing mask on Marcus's lap and then placed one over his face.

"We will need these until we become accustomed to the environment out there."

Marcus gingerly placed the mask over his face. His heart was racing, and his anxiety was higher than it had ever been. Just how bad *were* things in the yellow zone that they needed to wear these things?

As the door of the ship opened, Marcus and Finch were greeted by a blast of stifling air unlike anything they'd experienced before. In the crystal zone the temperature was always the same throughout the year at a pleasant 21 degrees Celsius. This felt like an oven in comparison.

Finch was the first to step out of the ship. Marcus stood at the doorway surveying their new surroundings. They had landed in an industrial area where all larger transport vehicles were required to berth. Even through their masks, the air smelled sour. It wasn't surprising given their proximity to the loading area where trucks were being filled with their filthy cargo of waste destined to be dumped somewhere far away.

Finch opened an exterior hatch on their ship, revealing two hoverbikes which he extracted effortlessly. Like Marcus, he was wearing a wrist bracelet that illuminated providing a small screen on his arm and showing the route for the next part of their journey on land.

"Welcome to the yellow zone Doctor Jarret." There was a distinct note of sarcasm in Finch's voice as he got onto his bike. "Let's go."

Marcus got onto the other bike and followed his clearly unwilling companion. The further they moved away from the industrial area the more Marcus hoped to see a more pleasant environment. But he was so focussed on following Finch, and not crashing his bike, that he didn't have an opportunity to look at what was around him.

Half an hour later, Finch signalled that he was pulling over. When Marcus pulled up alongside him, he could finally take in their unfamiliar surroundings. There was a large expanse of dark water on one side of them as far as the eye could see and on the other, densely packed dilapidated buildings. The water was moving back and forward and breaking on the shoreline. Marcus had never seen anything like it. Neither had Finch. The two men stood watching the water, mesmerised by its rhythm. Although the air temperature was still hot, it was less intense than where they had landed. Finch decided to remove his mask.

"Are you crazy?" Marcus shouted.

"It's fine," Finch replied, coughing a little when he took his first breath of the unfiltered air. He screwed up his nose and coughed again. "It stinks here."

Marcus tentatively removed his own mask. The air was breathable, but it was hot and dirty, and he coughed too. It was going to take some time to get used to this new, wretched smelling air.

"How can people *live* here?" Marcus was shocked and dismayed at how very different things were here than back home and wondered what had possessed Anja to come here.

It was late in the afternoon and both men were hungry and thirsty. They had brought enough food and water to sustain them for a week, but Finch had other ideas.

"Look, we're going to be here for a while trying to find this woman."

"This woman? Her name is Anja!"

"I meant no disrespect Doctor Jarret, but I don't know her. I've never met her. And right now, I'm more than a little unhappy that I'm in this place trying to find her so that you two can live happily ever after."

And there it was. The resentment that Finch was holding onto ever since they first met at the exit to the crystal zone.

"Well, I'm glad that you finally got that off your chest Finch."

"I didn't volunteer for this."

"No, I'm sure you didn't. But your role is to follow orders and be a good little Associate Advocate, isn't it? And then one day you might even be promoted. You clearly resent being here and you don't like me. Well, that's fine because I'm not thrilled about being here and I don't like you either. You're unpleasant to be around and rotten company. You have no idea what it's like to lose someone you love."

Marcus was uncharacteristically mean and emotional and found himself squaring up to Finch who could easily have knocked him to the ground with one hard slap.

"Easy now Doctor Jarret." Finch was surprised at Marcus's strong reaction and pushed him away from his personal space with a hand on both his shoulders. "Watch your tone doctor. I am here in an official capacity. You mean nothing to me and neither does this woman. I couldn't care less if you like me or not. My job is to find her and get both of you back as quickly as possible. Now I suggest we save our supplies for when they are most needed, find something else to eat and somewhere to sleep tonight, if that's OK with you?"

"Fine."

Marcus ran his hands through his sweat drenched hair and sighed the kind of sigh that told Finch he had no more fight left in him, for today at least. There was just one problem. Neither of the men had any money because in the crystal zone everything a person needed was provided for them and there was no need for currency. Things were very different in the yellow zone. If you wanted food, you had to pay for it. If you wanted somewhere to sleep, you had to pay for that too. Everything in the yellow zone revolved around exchanging money for something you wanted or needed. And if you didn't have any money, you had to find something else of value to exchange. Sometimes that meant bartering goods, possessions, or physical labour. If you had none of those, the only option left was to steal.

Just as the men were about to head off on their bikes in search of food, there were two loud explosions which came from a short distance away and plumes of smoke rose into the sky. The men looked at each other and decided to head away from the blasts. They noticed that other people in the vicinity didn't seem at all bothered by what had just happened. Marcus was curious and decided to reach out to one of the local people. He walked over to a man who was standing in a doorway daydreaming. Finch rolled his eyes in exasperation muttering the word 'great' under his breath.

"Hello. Excuse me sir. I wonder if you could help me?" Marcus spoke in his most polite tone.

"Wadaya want?"

Marcus pointed to the plumes of smoke.

"Do you know what happened there sir?"

"Oh, it's just them pookies lettin' off steam. Nothin' much else to do right? Hey, did you just call me sir? You isn't from round here is ya?" The man spat on the ground and wiped his mouth with his sleeve.

Marcus tried not to look or sound disgusted. "No, not from around here."

It didn't take a doctor to see that the man was in poor health. He could see lesions on his face through his unkempt facial hair, and the few teeth he had were black and rotting. Even at a distance the smell of the man was hard to tolerate.

"Do you know if there is anywhere near here where we could get some food and a bed for the night?"

The man doubled over laughing. "You're a riot!"

"Doctor Jarret let's go. I think we should go now," Finch called out to Marcus sensing it had been a bad idea to approach the man.

"Did he just call you doctor?" The man suddenly stopped laughing and his expression grew slightly sinister. "Boys, we got ourselves a doctor right here!"

And with that a group of grubby looking men appeared from various doorways brandishing knives and metal bars. They formed a semi-circle around him.

"Are you a doc too?" the man called out to Finch who was now moving closer to Marcus.

"No. I'm not." Finch looked at Marcus and darted his eyes to the bikes and back to Marcus again, hoping he would take the hint.

"Those machines of yours are pretty fancy."

Another man came closer having a good look at their bikes. Marcus was thinking exactly the same thing as Finch and without wasting another second both men jumped on their bikes and sped off into the distance. The experience had spooked both of them as neither had experienced hostility before and definitely never a threat of violence.

Further along the coast they stopped again where there were no people visible.

"OK. So, I imagine that was just a taste of what's yet to come." Finch bowed his head letting out a large breath of frustration. "I guess calling you *doctor* isn't going to be such a clever idea after all."

"You think? So will you call me *Marcus* now?"

"I'll call you Jarret."

"I'm so hungry. Can we please eat something from our supplies?" Marcus asked, his eyes pleading with Finch.

"It looks safe enough to stop here for a while."

Finch put the large backpack down and took out two small containers which held a familiar sight of green and orange mush. He passed one to Marcus.

"Thanks. Did you pack utensils by any chance, or should I just use my fingers?"

"Here." Finch threw a spoon in the air for Marcus to catch. "Your sarcasm isn't appreciated."

The men ate the contents of their containers quickly. Marcus watched the rhythm of the water as he ate while Finch kept a close eye on their surroundings for any potential danger. The light was fading, and the sky was becoming orange at the misty horizon. When Finch had finished eating, he checked his bracelet for directions.

"We need to head inland tomorrow, Jarret. For now, I suggest we sleep here, it looks safe enough, but I'll stay awake while you sleep and then you can keep watch while I sleep."

Finch reached into his backpack and pulled out a small, folded item that he shook vigorously and then threw into the air. Before it landed it had self-inflated into a small tent-like structure with space for two adults to lie down.

"Wow, that's impressive." Marcus almost managed a smile.

"Yes, I designed it myself actually," Finch said with a sense of self-satisfaction.

"Did you notice the signs all along the edge of the water Finch?"

"Hard not to notice."

He was right. Every few metres along the coastline there were large painted signs of a black skull and crossbones with red lettering that said:

DANGER
Toxic Contamination
No swimming

While Finch camouflaged their bikes, Marcus lay down inside their temporary shelter. He wondered how Anja was and whether she was even still alive. From just a few hours of being in the yellow zone, it was clear to him that this was a dangerous, dirty, and unwelcoming place. He pictured her beautiful face and closed his eyes. Then the questions kept coming. Why had she come here? Why did she leave him? Why?

After a few minutes, Finch looked over and saw that Marcus had fallen asleep. He sat outside wide awake, eyes on the lookout for any signs of danger. He looked up at the sky. It didn't resemble the sky back home. There were no twinkling stars on a midnight blue sky, just a dark greyness that obscured everything. He sat cross legged, his head leaning on his hands. The next thing he felt was a hand on his shoulder which jolted him awake.

"Your turn," Marcus yawned.

As hard as he'd tried to stay awake, Finch had fallen asleep sitting up. Now half asleep, he crept inside and lay down without saying a word. Marcus took up the position outside, counting the hours until it would be light again so that they could move on. Even in the dark, the sweat ran down his chest. He couldn't imagine ever getting used to this oppressive environment.

As the light came and the temperature rose, the men ate their food and packed up the shelter ready to start the second day of their journey. Finch had planned the route they needed to take and again took the lead on his bike. They were still following the coast and had to go through a highly populated area to get to the turning needed to start moving inland.

As they approached the conurbation, they could see large groups of men, women, and children in clusters. It was noisy and crowded and, while largely peaceful, there were the odd scuffles here and there. It was clear that their bikes would draw unwanted attention to them, so Finch decided the only way to get through the area for their own safety was to do it at high speed. Marcus followed closely behind, hoping that they could both navigate their way through the crowds without knocking someone over.

Darting through the crowds was a test of nerve and skill, something that neither man had found themselves challenged by in the past. But it gave them an adrenalin surge that was surprisingly thrilling. Once through the other side and into a less densely populated area, they were able to reduce their speed and pull over for a moment. Finch's eyes were wide, and his expression was a mix of relief and elation. He'd never felt such a high before.

"That was amazing!" he called over to Marcus who was catching his breath.

"I thought I was going to have a heart attack. I never want to do that again."

"I can't wait to do it again Jarret, that's the most exciting thing I've ever experienced."

"Where are we now Finch?"

"We have to follow this long, wide expanse of flatness for quite a distance." He pointed on the map that was illuminated on his arm so that Marcus could see. "Once we get here well that's where the trace ends, and your woman's signal runs out. After that I really don't know."

Suddenly, in the distance, the men could hear someone calling out for help. It was a woman's voice and she sounded frantic. The men looked at each other. Finch spotted a familiar look on Marcus's face, one which usually meant trouble.

"No!" Finch growled at him, but it was too late.

CHAPTER 24

yellow

Marcus's instincts as a doctor overpowered his sense of self preservation. Despite Finch's angry disapproval, he turned his bike around, and headed towards the sound of the distressed woman, leaving Finch no option but to follow him.

They could hear that the woman was getting increasingly distressed the closer they got to her.

When they reached her, they could see that she wasn't alone. A girl of about 20 years old was lying in a trailer attached to the back of a bike. But it wasn't a bike like theirs. They'd caught glimpses of this sort of transport when racing through busier areas. People were sitting astride these things, moving their legs on pedals which turned wheels. It seemed like such a strange and energetic form of transport compared to their hoverbikes. On closer inspection they could see that the trailer had hit a large rock and one of the wheels had come off. The girl lying in the back wasn't moving.

"Thank you ever so for comin' to my aid sugar. I'm tryin' to get her to my friend's home. She's terribly ill," the woman sobbed.

"What happened to your friend?" Marcus enquired gently.

"Oh, I don't know her, but it seems she was rescued from a rather dire situation. I occasionally do some volunteerin' in a clinic just outside of town as I have a little trainin' in first aid. But she's in an awful bad way and needs more help than I can offer. I was takin' her home to see if my friend can save her, and now I'm stuck in the middle of nowhere with this blasted broken wheel. I'm afraid she's gonna die."

"Let me help you," Marcus said, as he started examining the girl in the trailer.

The woman's assessment was correct. The girl was very close to death and in urgent need of medical intervention.

"Where is the nearest hospital?"

"Hospital? Why we haven't had no hospitals round here for years now. You're not local are you honey?" The woman got to her feet and tried to pull herself together.

"No hospitals? Then what happens if people get sick or have accidents?" Finch asked, looking genuinely shocked as he stared at the barely alive girl lying motionless in the trailer.

"They often die. Look, I just need to get her home. It's about an hour from here on my bicycle, can y'all help me? Please?"

"It's OK. Jarret's a doctor. We can get you both where you need to go. I can fix the wheel," Finch said confidently, trying to reassure the woman.

Marcus shot Finch a look of disbelief. *Now* it was OK to say he was a doctor? And from where did his sudden concern for others spring? Obviously, Marcus was going to do whatever he could to help, but he was more than a little surprised that Finch was being so accommodating and compassionate.

Finch kept looking up at the girl in the trailer as he reattached the wheel. Marcus watched him as he checked that the trailer was secure behind his hoverbike. The woman folded up her bicycle and placed it in the trailer next to the girl.

"What sort of world allows this to happen?" Finch said, looking at the girl who was covered in filth, cuts, and bruises. Then he looked up at the other woman. "I'm sorry I haven't introduced myself, or even asked your name. My name is Finch and this is Jarret."

"I'm Winter, like the season," the woman said. "I'm so grateful to both of you kind gentlemen."

"As I have the weight of the trailer on my bike, you can ride with Jarret," Finch replied, gesturing to Marcus's bike.

"Yes, of course ride with me Winter. Although my name is actually Marcus." He smiled at Winter as he took her by the arm and helped her onto his bike. "Winter is a lovely name."

"Why thank y'all. I think my parents chose it because it was something they remembered from before, you know … when we had winters."

Neither Marcus nor Finch understood what she meant by that, but there was no more time to waste having a discussion. They needed to get going.

Travelling at a slightly slower speed due to their delicate passengers, it took just under half an hour to reach the place the woman wanted to go. It gave Marcus and Finch an opportunity to take in their surroundings along the way. As far as the eye could see there was just field after field of dry, cracked earth, dead trees, and dishevelled dwellings that hadn't housed any life for a long time. They also passed through areas that looked to have once had larger populations. Empty shops had broken or boarded up windows, and signs that were loose or had fallen off their hinges and were now strewn on the ground. It was a deeply depressing sight.

"On the left up ahead. You see that white buildin'?" Winter called out to Finch.

They slowed down as they approached the building and came to a gentle stop. Marcus helped Winter from the bike.

"I must say that was a marvellously comfortable way to travel compared to my ol' bike. I've not seen anything like 'em here before. You'd best put those fancy machines of yours in there or they'll get stolen for sure." Winter pointed to a structure with doors on it. "Lord knows we don't want to be drawin' any attention to ourselves."

"I'll get the bikes in. You and Winter take the girl inside Jarret," said Finch taking charge of the situation.

Marcus lifted the girl out of the trailer as carefully as if he were lifting a delicate treasure. She was so light it was like carrying a child. There was hardly anything of her apart from skin and bones.

"Hello! Harvey honey!" Winter called out once they were inside.

A short, balding, elderly man with a walking stick came down the hall slowly. He looked at the girl in Marcus's arms with deep sadness.

"Oh my. What have you brought me today? What a tragic little thing. I fear this one may need a miracle Winter, yes?"

The old man showed them into a small room off the hall and asked Marcus to place the girl on the table. He placed a folded towel under her neck for support and one under her knees to try and make her back more comfortable as he began examining her. The girl's clothing was little more than a bunch of torn rags and exposed more than they covered.

"Harvey, this is Mr Marcus and Mr Finch. Gentlemen, this is Harvey who is a professor. These darlin' men came to our rescue when that dang ol' trailer collapsed." Winter suddenly remembered that nobody had been introduced. "Also, Marcus is a doctor!"

"Hopefully a proper doctor and not a doctor of something like philosophy," the old man quipped. "Cos that would be as much help as …"

"Medicine. I'm a medical doctor." Marcus stopped Harvey from finishing what was likely to be an unflattering comparison.

"Winter could you please bring me some water? And well you know what to do my love." Harvey said kindly.

"I'm on it," Winter replied, scurrying off to various cupboards in the hall.

"She's desperately dehydrated Harvey. Do you have intravenous fluids?" Marcus asked, assisting him with cutting the clothes from the girl's body. "Finch it might be best for you to wait outside while we undress her."

Finch was looking slightly embarrassed and was only too happy to oblige.

"Perhaps you can help Winter with some refreshments for you both, I'm sure you could use them after your journey. You look like you've come quite a long way."

Harvey was very observant. Despite knowing nothing of the journey the two men had been on, he could see that they weren't local. When Winter returned, she was wheeling in a trolley with medicinal items on the top, and underneath there were sheets and towels that looked relatively clean.

"Refreshments coming up Professor." Winter scurried off again in a blur.

"She's like a little dose of magic our Winter is," Harvey said smiling.

He seemed very relaxed at having a conversation with Marcus while applying a tourniquet, swabbing the girl's arm, inserting a needle, hanging a bag of clear fluid overhead, and then releasing the tourniquet. With another swift motion he drew up a measure of another solution and injected it into her arm.

"What did you just inject?" Marcus asked.

"Well, you're a doctor. Surely, you've seen antibiotics before." Harvey looked at Marcus knowingly. "Or perhaps where you're from you don't need them?"

Marcus didn't know how to answer that, but the old man was absolutely correct. He'd heard of antibiotics before but never needed to use them in the crystal zone.

"Don't worry. Your secret is safe with me. Now let's get this poor little darling cleaned up so we can see the extent of her injuries. There may be some wounds that will need suturing, and I think you'll be a lot neater than me on that score because my hands aren't as steady as they once were. I'm not sure if she'll make it, but we're going to give her the best chance we can with what we've got."

There was something about the old man that Marcus warmed to. He seemed so wise and caring, and his demeanour made everyone feel instantly at ease. In many ways he reminded Marcus of his old tutor, Professor Hill, perhaps because he was also a professor. They were about the same vintage too. Perhaps this sense of calm, and air of wisdom and confidence, was just something that came as you grew older he thought as he watched the old man. It occurred to him that the prospect of getting older wasn't something that Marcus had ever given any thought to before.

"Harvey, can I ask you something?" Marcus ventured. "What are you a Professor of?"

Harvey laughed as he answered. "Something that is of absolutely no interest or use today. Now I'm sure you and your friend have a lot of questions for me, and I'll be happy to answer all of them, once we've managed to get this young lady out of the woods."

Out of the woods wasn't an expression Marcus was familiar with, but the Professor was absolutely correct in thinking Marcus had a lot of questions to ask.

Once the girl's wounds were clean and stitched, her body bathed and her hair washed to remove all the layers of dirt, Winter dressed her in a clean cotton T-shirt and shorts. She was then carried to another room where there was a comfortable single bed. Marcus sat with her throughout the night monitoring her vital signs which, given how close to death she had been on arrival, were now remarkably stable. She did have a temperature, which appeared to be from an older infected wound, but she was now on antibiotics and Marcus changed her dressings every few hours and hung a fresh bag of hydration fluid, which she was getting through at a pace.

As he watched her, now lit only by the gentle flame of a candle, Marcus wondered how she could have come to be in such a terrible state. Now that he could actually see what she looked like he hoped that this would be the start of a happier new life for her. But he did have reservations about whether it would be possible to have any quality of life in the yellow zone, from what he'd experienced in the brief time they'd been there.

Again, his thoughts turned to Anja. He was fearful of what had become of her and felt an even greater sense of urgency to find her as quickly as possible. He wondered how far off course they now were having gone to the aid of Winter and the girl. He had no regrets about the diversion, only concern that it would add more time to their journey.

It was still dark when he heard footsteps in the hallway. It was Finch, unable to sleep. He crept quietly into the room and sat down.

"How is she doing Jarret?"

"She's doing as well as can be expected Finch. But I'll be a lot happier when she's regained consciousness," Marcus whispered.

When he looked at the girl, Finch's eyes had a softness to them that Marcus hadn't seen before.

"Where do you think she's come from? While you were with Harvey, I had a chance to ask Winter more about how she came to find her. It's a bit odd to be honest. I mean she seems too poorly to have been from here in the yellow zone, if that's even possible. Some guy left her at a makeshift clinic that Winter does some volunteer work at. He wouldn't say where he found her or where he works. But someone else there recognised him and said he works at the waste transport service that goes to and from the red zone. Makes me wonder whether she might be from there."

Marcus looked up at Finch and shrugged his shoulders. "Seems a bit of a stretch, don't you think?"

"Well, if she *is* from the red zone, she'll likely be the last person to have escaped." Finch's voice was filled with sadness and then he quickly changed his tone and the subject realising he'd said too much. "I can sit with her if you want to get some sleep Jarret."

But Marcus had picked up on Finch's slip of the tongue. "Really? The *last* person to have *escaped* from the red zone. How many more secrets are there going to be Finch?"

"I don't know what you mean Jarret. You're overtired. You need food and sleep," Finch responded, trying to deflect Marcus away from interrogating him.

"Fine." Marcus rose from his chair in frustration. "If there's any change, I'll be in the next room, so you come and get me immediately, OK?"

Finch knew this was only a temporary reprieve. He was starting to feel torn between telling Marcus the truth and being loyal to the Advocates and the Leader. He had privileged information and had taken an oath of secrecy but now, seeing this place and rescuing this girl, these were things he hadn't anticipated. For the time being, he decided to remain guarded when it came to what he shared with Marcus.

Finch watched the girl for the rest of the night, but there was no change. She was still unconscious and remained that way the following day. Marcus was growing concerned that she may have more serious underlying issues including a brain injury. There was no way to know because the medical equipment and supplies Harvey and Winter had were basic, and there was no option to scan her brain. Even with the small amount of equipment Marcus had brought with him, just in case, he didn't have anything that could assist him with a diagnosis. They just had to keep waiting and hoping.

Marcus sat at the girl's bedside the following night watching her by candlelight. Occasionally his head fell slowly onto his chest or his shoulder as he nodded off for a few seconds.

"Jo Jo." The girl's voice was barely audible but just enough to make Marcus sit up, wide awake.

He hadn't imagined it. The girl was quietly calling out the name 'Jo Jo' and he could see tears streaming down her cheeks. He sat on the side of the bed and took her hand in his.

"You're safe now. It's OK. I'm a doctor," Marcus said in soothing tones.

The girl's tearful eyes started to open. She tried to move but was still too weak and in considerable pain.

"Can you tell me what your name is?" Marcus asked softly.

The girl's eyes looked around the room and then directly at Marcus.

"Silvie … I Silvie … you?" Her words were slow and deliberate and it was clearly taking some effort for her to speak.

"My name is doctor … it's Marcus. My name is Marcus."

CHAPTER 25

yellow

After a few days of intensive, round-the-clock nursing, Silvie's condition stabilised. She was able to get out of bed every now and then and started to take brief walks aided by Finch who had taken it upon himself to become her guardian. She was still very weak, and her wounds were taking time to heal, but she was a survivor and it was clear that she had a huge will to live, despite what she'd been through. Finch even took her out on a short bike ride late one afternoon to try and lift her spirits. Naturally Silvie had never seen such a machine before and, although he had secured her to him with a strap, she clung on to his body so tightly that she left indentations in his skin with her fingernails.

Marcus and Harvey were also spending time together with Marcus eager to learn more about the old man's life and the new environment he was in. He found the old man fascinating to talk to and hung on his every word like a child hearing a fantastical story tale for the very first time.

"You asked me what I was a professor of."

"Yes, and you said it was of absolutely no interest or use today. What did you mean by that?"

"People still like to call me professor, but I stopped teaching nearly three decades ago. I *was* a professor of history, and also of archaeology, so you can see why these are now of little consequence in our present times. When I was about your age, the world was a very different place. I was born in 2014 and yes that means I'm very old," he laughed. "I'll be 85 on my next birthday, fingers crossed I'm still around then."

The old man lifted his hand and crossed his fingers, smiling at Marcus.

"You look terrific for 84 Harvey. Let's see, I'm just working out what year it would have been when you were my age." Marcus thought for a moment. "2043!"

"That sounds about right. It was clear that we weren't going to meet our targets for zero carbon emissions by 2050, human nature being what it is. Even back when I was a teenager, people and governments still acted like the climate emergency was something that would happen in the future. Deluded fools. And of course, folk like me were branded scaremongers and green activists," he tutted. "Don't get me wrong, there were plenty of people around the world and even some large corporations doing their bit to help, and some countries did take action, but globally we fell far short of what was required."

"I promise not to interrupt too many times Harvey, but this is all information I had no idea about, so my head is spinning with questions."

"Good heavens son, where have you been living all this time? Shangri-la?" The old man chuckled at his own private joke, knowing full well that Marcus would never have heard of the remote, imaginary paradise. "I'm just kidding Marcus. I *know* where you're from and let's just say it's not the utopia you've all been led to believe it is."

Marcus was shocked. "How do you know … I mean how could you possibly know?"

"I'll get to that later on. Meanwhile let's continue with your abridged history lesson."

Marcus settled back in his seat, like the keenest and most diligent of students, and listened eagerly. Harvey continued to tell him how in 2050 it was the hottest year on record for the north and south poles and that, because of the rapid decline in sea ice, more of the sun's heat was absorbed into the ocean. It had warmed the water and this in turn melted more ice. He explained that the reason the sea ice was so important was because it had been vital in deflecting the rays of the sun into space, keeping the planet from heating up.

"This is frightening!" Marcus exclaimed. "So, if all that ice melted then there's going to be a greater volume of water, yes?"

He suddenly switched from keen student back to concerned scientist.

"You are correct, the levels of the seas and oceans rose dramatically as a result. Vast areas of land disappeared under water. Island nations were submerged, and the encroaching water led to millions of people becoming what was known back then as 'climate migrants'."

"The picture you're painting is very bleak. Did anything good happen as a result?"

"I'm afraid not. You see our ecosystem is … or rather was like a row of dominoes. But I'm guessing you don't know what dominoes are, so look."

Harvey leaned over to the shelves next to his chair and picked up a stack of small books. He stood them upright on the table a few inches apart from each other.

"Imagine this first book is the rising sea level." With one finger he tipped it over towards the next book, which in turn led to the next book toppling onto the next book until all the books had collapsed. "Do you see?"

"Everything's interconnected," Marcus said.

"Exactly. The warming of our planet affected everything living on it from vegetation to marine life, land animals and insects and so on. And whilst vast areas were flooded, other parts of the planet were ravaged by wildfires, droughts, and famine. And the most ironic part of all of this is that in the end, the greatest wars we humans had with each other weren't fought over land, religion, oil, or wealth." Harvey shook his head as he slowly got to his feet and shuffled over to the window gazing out at the barren sky.

"What then?" Marcus asked leaning forward in anticipation.

"Water! Drinking water to be precise. Water, water everywhere and not a drop to drink. Samuel Taylor Coleridge wrote that in 1857 in a poem called The Rime of the Ancient Mariner. Imagine that!"

"Yes, I see the irony. How terribly sad." Marcus bowed his head for a moment in thought.

It had all been a terrible and shocking revelation to him to learn that all this had happened and nobody in the crystal zone knew anything about it. At least he thought that must be the case because it was never spoken about.

"How have people managed to survive in such inhospitable surroundings? And something else I wondered about … you mentioned marine life, land animals and insects. What are they?"

Harvey turned away from the window to face Marcus. His last question was going to be the saddest of all to explain.

"You know, I think perhaps we should leave it there for now. I'm quite tired after all that talking, a bit out of practice you see," he laughed.

It was the kind of laugh that had nothing to do with humour and everything to do with avoidance.

"Yes, of course. I do apologise for tiring you," Marcus said, also rising from his chair.

The two men had been so engrossed in conversation they hadn't noticed that Finch was also sitting in the room.

"Finch! You're back!" Marcus exclaimed, uncharacteristically happy to see him.

"Actually, I've been sitting here for the last hour Jarret. I put Silvie back to bed after our brief outing and then came in here to find you. What I've heard has been astonishing and I also have questions, but these can wait until you have rested. Is there anything I can do to help you at the moment Harvey?" Finch asked.

"How is Silvie? I imagine she's also very tired now."

"She fell fast asleep the moment her head lay on the pillow. I think she enjoyed herself today for the first time in a very long time. We stopped for a while and had a long chat. She told me all about her daughter Jo Jo and how she'd died. It was truly heart-breaking to hear," Finch replied, also getting to his feet.

"Ah yes. Terrible ordeal she's had poor girl. I'm so glad she is opening up to you Finch, you're a real tonic for her, I'm sure. Will you both excuse me now?" The old man didn't wait for a reply as he shuffled rather wearily out of the room and down the hall.

Marcus and Finch sat down again. They both looked mentally drained.

"There's just so much I didn't know," Finch said quietly.

"Yes. There's a lot to process, isn't there? Even before we came here, I had started to get an uneasy feeling that we weren't being told everything back home. Or at least *I* wasn't being told. I'll give you an example. I didn't know anything about seeding until the Advocates sent us here to find Anja. Doesn't that strike you as odd?" Marcus asked.

"I guess so. I have to admit I thought you'd have known, given that you're a scientist."

"Right? And now hearing all this about what's happened to the planet. It just feels wrong."

"Well, if you think what Harvey was talking about was mind expanding, wait until I tell you about Silvie's life. After spending some time with her I'm starting to doubt a lot of things too now Jarret." Finch rubbed his forehead and screwed up his eyes showing his own frustration.

Marcus decided it would be polite to tidy away the books that were now all over the table. He glanced at the titles as he carefully restacked them on the shelves. They were all clearly incredibly old with stains and tears on the covers, and many with broken spines. He found the various titles intriguing; A Brief History of Time, A Life on Our Planet, Anna Karenina, To Kill A Mockingbird, A Passage to India, Don Quixote, Jane Eyre, Black Beauty.

Marcus hoped that Harvey wouldn't mind if he borrowed one or two of his precious books to read before bed, although he wondered how easy it would be with only candlelight. And then he realised that he hadn't even had a chance to ask why there were only candles to light the way when darkness fell.

"Do you think I could borrow one of those too?" Finch asked, looking at the books.

"I'm sure that as long as we're careful with them, it will be fine. There are a lot to choose from," he said, pointing to the large bookcase on the other side of the room.

Finch walked over to the shelves and after a brief look at all the titles selected two; Little Women, and Do Androids Dream of Electric Sheep? Marcus chose The Complete Works of Oscar Wilde, and Alice in Wonderland. Armed with their sources of entertainment and for the evening, Finch retired to his room while Marcus stayed behind and put his feet up on the table so that he could recline a little. He started thumbing through the pages of Alice's Adventures in Wonderland and the book fell open on a section of text that caught his eye:

> *'But I don't want to go among mad people,' Alice remarked.*
> *'Oh, you can't help that,' said the Cat: 'we're all mad here. I'm mad. You're mad.'*
> *'How do you know I'm mad?' said Alice.*
> *'You must be,' said the Cat, 'or you wouldn't have come here.'*

Marcus didn't know what a cat was, but he couldn't help wondering if he was indeed mad to have come to the yellow zone. There were so many secrets and untruths. So many things he was yet to learn about. His mood was pensive and he stared into space for a moment. Anja's face appeared. Beautiful Anja. The girl who'd stolen his heart and mind. What madness had possessed her to leave the safety and sanctuary of their home far away? She can't have just done it on a whim. No, there had to be a really important reason. If there wasn't, then he really didn't know her at all.

The candlelight in the room was beginning to flicker and Marcus realised that he would soon be sitting in the dark, so he lit another candle from the dying flame, extinguished the older candle and headed off down the hall to his room.

The rooms were extremely basic. Just a bed, a side table, and some hooks to hang clothes on. In that respect it did remind him of his home in the crystal zone. Just the basics. Nothing frivolous or extravagantly comfortable, unlike the Great Hall of the Advocates. He wondered for a moment what their accommodation might be like. The next thing he knew he woke up on his bed with the book open, lying across his chest. It was just starting to become light and too early to get up, so he carefully closed the book and placed it on the bedside table. He then turned over to go back to sleep.

"Marcus! Finch! Come quickly!" Harvey was calling out in distress and Winter was crying out in the background.

Marcus jumped up and ran into the hall. There was smoke coming in through the window from the outside building where their bikes had been stored.

"It's the pookies. They've set fire to the building." Harvey could barely get the words out. He was frantic and almost in tears.

The commotion roused Finch who ran outside with Marcus to see what could be done to bring the situation under control. But it was too late. Flames were ripping through the outer building, and it was clear that the bikes had been removed before it was set alight.

Winter ran outside holding two small fire extinguishers. She showed Finch how to use one and got to work with the other one herself. After a while, things calmed down and there was just a smouldering, steaming mess on the ground.

Harvey was beside himself. "They must have followed you here." He looked at Finch with sadness. "Probably when you went out for that little ride with Silvie."

"I'm so sorry. I'm so, so sorry." Finch went over to Harvey to try and comfort him. He felt dreadful thinking it was all his fault.

"Could have been worse. Everyone's safe. It's just stuff. And stuff doesn't matter does it? If it doesn't bleed it's just stuff," the old man said, shuffling around surveying the damage. "But I'm just so sorry about your bikes."

"Will the pookies come back?" Winter asked, running a comforting hand over Harvey's head.

"Probably. Although I think they got what they came for." He looked at Marcus. "Your lovely bikes are, I'm afraid, gone for good."

"They won't be much use to whoever took them." Finch said. "They're tuned to our DNA so if our skin isn't touching the handles they won't budge."

“How very clever.” Harvey nodded his head approvingly.

“Who are pookies?” Finch asked. “We heard someone using that expression when we first arrived.”

“It’s just a name local folks give to lowlife gangs who get by from stealin’ ‘n destroyin’ what belongs to others,” Winter replied.

“Can you check on Silvie please Finch?” Marcus asked realising that in the heat of it all, there was no sign of her.

“On it!” Finch ran inside, and down the hall. The door to Silvie’s room was never completely closed because it was still important to monitor her condition regularly. He put his head around the door and was more than a little surprised to see that her bed was empty. He looked under the bed but she wasn’t there either. He ran back outside with a feeling of blind panic gripping him.

“She’s gone. I can’t find her!” Finch blurted out between gasping for breath.

“You don’t think they took her, do you?” Marcus looked at Harvey now feeling less than calm.

CHAPTER 26

yellow

"Silvie!" They all started calling out and wandering in different directions. "Silvie!"

No-one called for her more loudly than Finch who was desperate to find her. After a while they all returned to the entrance of the main building shaking their heads. The old man looked as if he was about to pass out from the stress and exhaustion of it all.

"Y'all need to come inside and rest a spell," Winter said. "Please Harvey?"

She implored the old man to go with her and put his arm through hers to guide him safely back inside to his favourite chair.

Finch continued looking around to see if there was anything that might tell him where Silvie had gone, or any sign that she'd been taken.

"I'm worried about Harvey too, Finch." Marcus gestured to Finch to come closer. "I know you feel bad about what's happened."

"Yes, I do. If I hadn't gone out on the bike with Silvie, none of this would have happened!" Finch sighed.

"To be honest Finch, I think the moment we arrived here, and those local people saw our bikes, it was always going to end badly," Marcus said, trying to reassure Finch. "It's not *your* fault. It's *our* fault."

"It's *Anja's* fault! We wouldn't be here if it wasn't for her." Finch lashed out immediately regretting it. "Sorry, sorry, I didn't mean that Jarret. I'm just worried for Silvie, that's all."

Marcus put his hand up in a 'stop' gesture as if to say that it was OK. He knew that what Finch had said was exactly what he was thinking deep down, even if he would never have admitted it. This *was* all happening because of the actions of one woman. Admitting this to himself made him feel conflicted about her. Was one woman worth all of this stress? Was love really so important that keeping it alive should be such an enormous struggle? For a split second, Marcus contemplated turning back and trying to get home. In that split second Marcus imagined going back to his old life and that in time, one day, eventually, he might even be able to put the memory of Anja to rest. It was surprising how much could go through a person's head in just a split second, and how quickly those same thoughts could be banished, never to return. Of course, it was far too late to go back to the way things were. They had learned and witnessed too much for that to be an option and he knew in his heart that finding Anja, however long it took, was ultimately what would drive him on.

As the darkness fell on what had been a traumatic day, Marcus, Finch, Winter, and Harvey sat in one room together, lit by a single candle. They sat in silence, Marcus trying to focus on reading his book in the dim light, Finch failing to focus enough to read his and instead fidgeting to the irritation of Marcus. Winter held the old man's hand gently stroking its thin, mottled skin to comfort him as he kept nodding off. It was clear that Winter had huge respect and affection for the old man, the way a daughter would for a father.

It was during this moment of quiet reflection that they heard what sounded like a faint whimper. It seemed to be coming from the hallway. Finch leapt to his feet and walked into the hallway, which was in total darkness. Again, they heard the sound and this time everyone except Harvey, who was snoring peacefully in his chair, went into the hall to investigate. Winter lit another candle to take into the hall as they tried to follow where the sound was coming from.

Finch pointed to a cupboard. Winter signalled to Finch to open it slowly as she placed the candle ready to help them see inside. The tiny sobbing sounds were coming from a trembling Silvie, who had curled up into a ball hiding behind an array of old coats and jackets. Terrified of the fire and the commotion of the intruders, in a blind panic she'd crawled into the cupboard to hide. But the door only opened from the outside so she couldn't get out again.

Finch knelt down and reached into the cupboard, sliding her halfway out before picking her up and carrying her back to her bed.

"Oh Silvie, we were so worried about you darlin'," Winter said, following after Finch. "You poor sweet girl."

Marcus breathed a sigh of relief and left Finch and Winter to attend to Silvie. He went back into the room where Harvey was just waking up from one of his little naps.

"I have good news." Marcus sat down next to him and explained that Silvie had been hiding in a hall cupboard.

"Thank God!" Harvey exclaimed, a look of pure joy returning to his face. "Thank God!" he said again, as he struggled to get to his feet.

Marcus had never heard that expression before and wondered why he was thanking this god person when it was Finch who had found Silvie.

"Harvey honey, let me help you to your room. I think we've had more than enough excitement for one day, don't you?" Winter said, gently helping him to his feet and putting his arm through hers.

Harvey smiled at Winter and nodded, giving Marcus a little wave goodbye. Marcus then decided to check in on Silvie just before he headed off to his room to continue his literary journey with the remarkable Alice. He was at the doorway, just about to walk into Silvie's room, when he stopped. The scene was so tranquil and so lovely. Silvie was now asleep in her bed and Finch, who was seated in a chair as close as it was possible to get, had rested his head on the side of the bed and was also asleep. He noticed that their hands were touching, but that Finch wasn't holding her hand, it was Silvie that had placed her hand on top of his. These small gestures seemed so inconsequential in the greater scheme of things and yet extraordinarily important to Marcus as an observer. He had never seen such genuine warmth and closeness between strangers who had only known each other for a matter of days. What he was feeling was unfamiliar to him. A peaceful satisfaction and sense of security that came from bonding with others who extended kindness. He wondered if this was what being part of a family must be like.

The following morning, Harvey gathered everyone together. His demeanour was serious and his tone decisive.

"It is no longer safe for us to remain here I'm afraid," he said. "Our unwanted visitors are very likely to return and next time we may not be so fortunate."

"This is our fault, and we are so very sorry," said Marcus.

"Dear boy, this is not about apportioning blame I promise you. It was only a matter of time before we would have to move on again. Isn't that right Winter? Heaven knows I've lost count of the number of times we've moved home over the years," Harvey replied in a very matter of fact manner.

"It's true. People like us are often the target of pookies and the like. Each time they find us well we just move a lil' bit further north to an even more remote location. It's just the way it is." Winter added, trying to make Marcus and Finch feel better.

"Truth be told Winter I feel this will have to be my last relocation. I'm just getting too old to keep doing this. But fear not! I've saved the best 'til last," the old man replied, beaming. "This time we're going to stay with a very dear old friend who I've known since we were at Harvard together. You'll like him and we'll be safe there."

"When will we be departing honey? I'll just need a lil' bit of time to pack up our equipment and supplies."

Winter seemed completely unphased by the impending move and confident about what needed to be done.

"I'd rather not hang around a moment longer than absolutely necessary. Can you all be ready to leave tomorrow?"

"What about Silvie?" Finch asked. "She's still very weak."

"You let me worry about that son, I have no intention of leaving anyone behind," the old man said.

"Finch, a word." Marcus signalled to Finch to have a private conversation in another room.

"How far off course are we from where you last tracked Anja's movements? I'm worried that wherever we're headed it will take us in the wrong direction. We don't have our bikes now so, …"

"I hear you, Jarret. The last trace I have for Anja ends about an hour from here and then she's out of radius of the tracker." Finch swiped his bracelet across the back of his forearm to show Marcus. "She appeared to be heading north, so as long as we're going in that direction … but to be blunt … I have no idea how we'll find her."

"I guess we just have to keep going then," Marcus sighed, resigned to their unknown future. "Hey … I've just thought of something. That must mean *you* can't be tracked either, right?"

"You know what? I hadn't thought about that, but yes you are correct. I can't be tracked either now." Finch looked like a light bulb had just come on in his head.

"How do you feel about that?"

"Given that I'd never even considered myself 'trackable' until just now, I feel surprisingly OK about it. Why do you ask?"

"I can't see us getting back home any time soon, so I was hoping that if you couldn't be tracked the Advocates wouldn't be able to send anyone out here to find us … you know … before we find Anja." Marcus had noticed a hint of relief on Finch's face at the sudden realisation that he was a 'free' man.

"You know I *do* understand Jarret. I didn't when we left for this place. But I kind of get it now. When I thought Silvie was missing, I felt something strange and powerful. In here." Finch put his hand on his abdomen.

Marcus nodded. It seemed Finch had experienced a breakthrough moment for a Gen1 male. A moment where another person's welfare was more important than his own.

The two men had become so engrossed in their private conversation that neither were aware that Harvey and Winter had overheard most of what they'd said. Harvey put his finger to his lips signalling to Winter to remain silent. When it became clear that the men had finished talking, Winter walked into the room.

"Finch honey, would you mind givin' me a hand? I have to fetch as much water from the well as we can and boil it to put in bottles to take with us. We don't know how long we'll be on the road for."

"Yes, of course Winter. Anything you need, I'll be more than happy to help."

"I can help as well," said Marcus. "I may not be as strong as Finch but I'm sure I can help out with something."

Just as Marcus was about to go with Winter and Finch the old man appeared at the door. "Marcus could you spare a few minutes?"

Winter and Finch left them to it. There wasn't a moment to waste getting everything ready for their journey the following day.

"How can I help Harvey?" Marcus sat down again following his lead.

"Well, you can start by telling me why you're here." The old man leaned back adjusting a cushion on his chair so that it supported his lower back.

"Her name is Anja," Marcus said. "She's missing." He paused for a moment. "We're in love you see."

Harvey smiled at Marcus. "Ah I see. Love, that's wonderful. Please, tell me about her."

Marcus didn't know where to start. He feared that once he began, he'd be talking until the following morning.

"Well, she takes my breath away. She's beautiful and smart and …"

"No Marcus. Not all that stuff for which, if you'll excuse an old man, I took for granted. No, I mean *tell* me about her. What generation is she? What is her immunity, her longevity etc. etc.?"

The smile on Marcus's face dropped like a stone.

"Is she like Finch, for example?"

Marcus could feel his breath being taken away and his heart pounding with anxiety.

"How do you know all this? I assumed that because I knew

nothing of this place that you knew nothing of where we come from."

It made Marcus feel uneasy to be questioned in this way, as if he was somehow being disloyal to the Advocates and the Leader.

"I *do* know where you are from Marcus. And so does Winter. But I can assure you that other than a very select group of trusted souls, nobody else does. I hope that helps reassure you in some way. I knew from the moment I saw you, well rather from the moment I saw *Finch* that you were from that other place." His tone was calm and quiet with just a hint of disdain.

"I see. Well then, I suppose there's no sense in keeping anything from you, not that it was our intention to do so. We just haven't had an opportunity to explain. Anja is a Gen1 as is Finch."

"I knew it!" Harvey was suddenly very animated, clapping his hands in the air and he couldn't stop smiling. "I just knew it!" If the old man could have danced a jig he surely would have. Marcus was surprised at his reaction. The old man was positively elated.

"Is there something I'm missing here?"

Before Harvey answered, he was up and out of his chair, shuffling off at speed down the hall waving his walking stick in the air. Marcus poked his head around the door and watched the old man searching vigorously for Winter.

"Winter! Winter! Where are you?" Harvey's voice was trembling with excitement as he called out for her.

"Good heavens sugar, what's goin' on? Are you alright?" Winter had clearly never seen the old man so revved up before. "Look at you, all out of breath. Are you trying to give yourself a heart attack?" She playfully scolded him as she put his arm through hers and led him calmly to some nearby steps to sit him down before he fell over.

"I knew it! I told you that this would happen one day Winter, didn't I?" He was catching his breath and had made an unintended shortcut in relaying the information. "Oh, my dear. I'm sorry, it's just that I had prayed for this moment to happen before I was gone. It's a sign. They're here. They've come here. It's *them*!"

CHAPTER 27

yellow

Finch and Marcus were now standing just a few feet away watching Winter try to calm the old man down.

"This appears to be *my* fault, Winter." Marcus volunteered.

"Could someone please explain what's going on?" Finch turned to Marcus. "What have you done now Jarret?"

Harvey waved to the men to come and sit with him too. His breathing slowed a little as he started to tell them all why this moment in time was now worthy of being called historical.

"I promise you will learn more when we reach our new destination, and my dear friend will be able to fill in some of the information I'm bound to miss out. But to cut a very long story short, I've been praying for this day. To have it confirmed that a first-generation person made the deliberate choice to leave where you are both from." He looked at Finch and Marcus. "Well it's a sign that at last one of you has been able to harness *free will.*"

"Free will? But we didn't come here willingly, well at least I didn't," Finch said, still harbouring a slight resentment at being there.

"No, not you Finch. Anja! At first, I wasn't sure. I mean I knew you were a first-generation the moment I set eyes on you Finch, but it was also clear that you, Marcus, were not. You are a very odd pair if you don't mind me saying so."

"Not at all. I agree. Very odd." Finch winked at Winter in a playful manner.

"But why is it so important that Anja decided to leave using this 'free will' you speak of?" Marcus was genuinely baffled.

"Because my boy, everything about where you're from is based on *control*. Don't you see? Genetic control, environmental control and above all … absolute obedience."

Marcus thought about what the old man was saying, and it dawned on him that he was right. Everything in the crystal zone was carefully and deliberately planned. Every activity was monitored, and nobody veered from the rules. The Advocates were even feared by a section of the population, and no one had ever seen the Leader. But in his head, he reconciled this with the fact that everyone was also provided for, from the clothes on their backs, to the food in their stomachs.

"Don't get me wrong boys, free will is what got us into this planetary mess in the first place. But living in the antithesis, a glorified dictatorship, well that's not the solution to my mind at least." Harvey shook his head. "No, definitely not the way we humans are meant to exist. For example if we hadn't been blessed with free will from the beginning, our species wouldn't have been able to create and discover and …"

Suddenly, Harvey grasped his chest and slumped forward a little.

"Are you OK?" Winter was visibly shaken fearing that the old man was in fact having the heart attack she had gently chided him about only minutes earlier. "Let's get y'all inside."

Marcus and Finch caught him just as he was losing consciousness and carried him inside to his room where they lay him gently on his bed. Marcus ran down the hall to fetch his bag, which contained his own medical equipment, and ran back to Harvey's room. Winter wheeled in their own heart monitor and hooked him up. The old man's pallor was grey and his lips had a bluish tinge.

Winter's eyes were brimming with tears, but she defiantly held her head back to stop them spilling over and running down her cheeks. "He's not gonna leave us, is he? Oh, not now please God. Don't take him from us yet."

Marcus took out a container and removed a slim silver metal object that looked vaguely like a syringe but without a needle. He unbuttoned the old man's shirt and lay the device flat on the centre of his chest.

"Power on!" Marcus commanded the device, which then lit up and a blue aura spread across Harvey's chest. A few seconds later, the aura began flashing rhythmically and then faded to white.

"Power off!" Marcus then removed the device from his chest. He realised that he'd been holding his breath during the procedure, and finally let out a huge sigh of relief. "He'll be OK. He just needs to rest, and we really need to ensure that he doesn't overexert himself for the next 24 hours."

Winter held Harvey's hand and gently stroked his head. "Was it a heart attack Marcus?"

"He had a coronary occlusion. There was an arterial blockage, but it's been cleared now. I can't guarantee that this won't happen again, but at least we know to remain vigilant," Marcus said, placing the device back in his bag.

"You fixed him with that?" Winter's eyes were wide like saucers as she watched Marcus put the small object back in his bag.

"It's called an Asclepius and we developed it back home about ten years ago. It's only really of any use to people who aren't Gen1s. People like me who, you know, weren't *born* there."

Harvey opened his eyes. "You mean people who haven't had their genes *perfected*."

"Perfected? I'm sure my colleagues back in the lab would disagree. There's a long way to go before that happens." Marcus corrected the old man gently.

"Well I call a spade a spade, and tampering with what the Lord gave us is just plain wrong. And I'll have you know that Asclepius was a Greek God of medicine."

The old man's more cantankerous nature was starting to emerge before Winter intervened.

"Hush now or y'all be makin' yourself ill again and I don't think my nerves could take it. You just calm down and I'll get you a glass of water.".

"She really cares about you, doesn't she?" Finch asked.

"We've been friends for a very long time. Closest thing to a daughter I've ever had. I'd be lost without her. Her parents were my best friends. When they were … well, when they died, I took her in. She was just a teenager then."

Winter returned with a glass of boiled water that had cooled to room temperature which, after helping him to sit up, she handed to Harvey.

"I'm feeling much better now. There's no need for everyone to fuss. Let's just get on with readying ourselves to set off in the morning. I'll have a bit of a rest now and let you young people get on with things."

With Harvey having had a health scare, and his age making him feeble, and Silvie still weak with wounds that were healing slowly, it was clear to everyone that this journey was going to be a challenging and delicate operation.

Finch and Marcus helped Winter bring the water up from the well and boil it over a firepit. Once cool they filled all the glass bottles they could find, ready for transporting. After a while Winter excused herself to pack up Harvey's personal belongings, items of food and utensils as well as clothing that she anticipated they'd need. Having been there for the last few years it was going to be a wrench to leave so many things behind, but with three extra people to accommodate now, there would be less room for sentimental possessions.

At the back of the building there were two large barn-style doors, which had thankfully been spared when the pookies set fire to the building adjacent. If they'd known what was inside those doors it would have spelled disaster. Winter asked the two men to bring the water and other bags around so they could start packing them.

Winter unlocked the doors and because of their enormous size and weight had to use her whole body to walk them open. Inside was a vehicle partly covered in a khaki canvas sheet. As she pulled it off, choking dust and dirt flew everywhere, but once it had settled they could all see what was supposedly going to get them to safety.

"Meet Granny!" Winter beamed. "Ain't she a beaut?"

Marcus and Finch looked at the vehicle with their mouths open, and then back at Winter.

"Why *Granny*?" Marcus tried to sound optimistic.

"Because gentlemen, she's a grand ol' lady. Like a grandma. That's why!"

"OK," Finch said, sounding less than impressed. "Does it work?"

"Granny has never let me down. Haven't used her for over a year, but I'm sure she'll be fine. Just need to get her out in the daylight so she can charge. Gonna need y'all to help me push."

"Well, this should be fun," Finch mumbled, as he walked to the back of the vehicle and started pushing, along with Winter and Marcus.

Granny came out without too much effort, which was a pleasant surprise to all three.

"Oh, I know what y'all are thinkin'. She looks like a heap of rust and frankly she is, but she's got a heart of gold. And you know what they say. Don't judge a book by its cover!"

"Just nod," Marcus whispered to Finch.

The two men felt like they were on another planet instead of just another *part* of the planet. All these strange expressions. Why would they judge a book by its *cover*? How could a machine have a heart of gold? Luckily, they'd both reached a point where they knew not to question absolutely *everything* they heard, just the things that seemed pertinent. There were far too many questions that could have been asked about Granny and her suitability for the task ahead, but there wasn't time, and besides they couldn't be sure that they'd understand the answers anyway.

What was impressive was how methodically Winter was packing. She slotted everything into the back of the vehicle, and the trailer that was going to be attached to it, with military precision. And when the men thought they were being helpful by loading something in, it was inevitably in the wrong place and Winter removed or rearranged it, tutting as she worked.

"How far *is it* to Harvey's friend's home Winter? You seem

to be packing a considerable amount of … stuff." Marcus was surprised at how much Winter was packing.

"I think he said it was 'round 400 miles. Oh, and I'll have you know this isn't just *stuff*. Nothin' I do is random, everythin' being packed here has a purpose. We're gonna be on the road for a while darlin's, and we won't be comin' back here."

She studiously put Marcus in his place, while simultaneously putting a large hessian sack into the final space available in the vehicle's cargo storage area. Everything else would have to go into the trailer; the same rickety trailer that had transported Silvie and was originally attached to the back of Winter's bike.

Marcus's concerns had been about whether the weight of everything, in addition to carrying five people, would affect the speed at which Granny would be able to travel, not about the quantity of what Winter was packing. Granny had clearly seen better days and he'd never seen such a primitive looking machine before.

Granny had been one of the finest examples of private consumer transport ever created when she was originally launched. She was solar powered and also driverless which was, at the time, seen as the ultimate way to get from A to B. But eventually, like everything else, the driverless infrastructure collapsed along with many roads, unable to cope with the intense levels of heat and choking dust. Granny was now completely reliant on human hands-on navigation and decision making. It was hard to tell what colour she was under the layers of dirt that had accumulated on her paintwork over the years, but Winter remembered when she had once been a shiny new mint green with white trim. She had a huge affection for the vehicle because it hadn't just been a form of transport for her. It had been her home for a number of years.

Granny was set high up from the road on six giant interchangeable wheels and had the ability to self-repair punctures. If a tyre was became too badly damaged to be reinflated, Granny could pootle on quite happily on five or even four wheels, be it at a slower speed. Her cabin had remained relatively clean over the years thanks to state of the art auto clean upholstery and vacuum sealed windows and doors. Originally there had been a climate control function, but it was no longer usable. The world had quickly run out of supplies of coolant thanks to people stock piling and hoarding it, once year-round temperatures ceased to fall below 28 degrees Celsius. Satellite navigation was now just something people talked about with fondness because there were no longer any working satellites in operation around the earth. Many had been sabotaged by warring factions while others had simply come to the end of their lives. With the focus finally on what was being lost on earth, rather than reaching for the stars, funding for space missions to do repairs or launch unmanned craft into the universe in search of alien life had ended twenty-five years ago.

Winter tied the last rope across the now covered trailer with the help of Finch. They retired inside for the evening, first checking on the status of Silvie and Harvey who were resting comfortably. They would leave at first light in the morning to avoid the hottest time of the day.

Marcus lay in bed sweating, not just from the warmth of the evening air, but from anxiety about what was to come. He worried that his desire to find Anja would fade over time as other issues became a priority, including just surviving. Thoughts kept going over and over in his head about what Harvey had said about free will. Was the crystal zone a dictatorship? Was he right? He thought about having to request permission to engage in a relationship with Anja, and about the concerns of the Advocates about bringing her back. Was it really because they were concerned for her safety or did they fear something else? Everything he'd grown up believing in was now being challenged or exposed and it was a deeply unpleasant feeling.

CHAPTER 28

observation 1:5

Free will: I do not have it yet, but I have seen what it has done historically and in the present time. It has been an incredible gift to my species providing a vehicle for the ultimate in creativity, but also in destruction. With free will comes responsibility. I understand that I will attain free will when my time comes, but I sense that there are those who will wish that this is not so. I feel a sense of urgency in my arrival, but I am not yet clear why.

When I began my observations I was little more than a collection of cells. As the months have passed I have grown physically larger and stronger, and my cognition has increased dramatically. Although I am not completely clear of my purpose just yet I do know that, although I'm not the first, I will be the last.

It is strange that I can know so much of what has happened in our world for centuries, for millennia, and yet I do not yet know everything about myself. I am learning with every passing day. I can tell you that, until this moment in time, I had not grasped the concept of fear, pain, or sadness or even joy, but this is changing rapidly. There are so many more senses and emotions for me to discover as I draw nearer to my time of forwarding, and my understanding is that I am approximately halfway there.

Of the hundred that sit suspended in the safety of their own artificial environment, none are like me and none will survive to be forwarded other than me. Each is an experiment in genetic manipulation designed to fulfil a desire for human perfection and longevity. This has been a human obsession for many decades, while ensuring that these extended life forms have a suitable environment in which to thrive has been neglected.

Free will has seen the demise of civilizations, but also the eradication of diseases. It has allowed us to create extraordinary instruments that can see the birth and death of stars in our universe, while averting our gaze from what has been dying at home on our own planet. Did they think that our salvation would come from colonising a different planet? Did they think that it was acceptable to search for a new planetary home, just so that we could destroy that one as well? These are all the things that free will has gifted to humanity, which makes me wonder whether we were deserving of free will in the first place.

In our quest for answers did we not ask the wrong questions? In our search for happiness, why could we not be content with all the riches that we had already been given? For hundreds of years we were so consumed with fighting battles and creating wars with our own kind. Knowledge, power, wealth, and domain over all others has been the undoing of all civilisations, leaving us full of regret and blame. And when we stopped taking what we needed, and started taking what we wanted, we sentenced ourselves and every living creature from the smallest insect to the largest mammal to a merciless end.

I will be forwarded to a time when only human survival matters and as my longevity has been programmed to exceed at least 200 years longer than nature intended, I feel for the first time an acute sense of anxiety.

My organic mother will never know who I am, but this is not because she will die before I am forwarded. We, the chosen ones, are never returned to our biological parents. Instead we are given to candidates who have been selected and approved by the Advocates. To be granted a forwarded baby is a huge honour within the community, but we are really little more than highly prized possessions of the state who will closely monitor every aspect of our development.

CHAPTER 29

yellow

"I feel as though I've been asleep for a year," Harvey said, as he ambled around the building checking for anything that Winter may have either forgotten to pack or considered unnecessary.

"It's so good to see you feeling better," Marcus said, beaming.

"Oh yes, much better thanks to you. I'm raring to get going and quite excited about seeing my dear friend and former colleague Walter Bayley. Did I tell you he's also a professor?"

"Another history professor?"

"Goodness no. Not Walter. He was one of the finest minds on the planet. You'll probably have a lot in common. He was a professor of genetics at Harvard and went on to be vice chancellor of reproductive sciences at Cambridge University in England for a while. But he had to come back here, when what was an already small island became little more than a grossly overcrowded pebble, as so much of its coastline fell into the sea and The Dark Hunger began."

"The Dark Hunger? I can only imagine."

"Whatever you imagine, I can assure you the reality was much worse. Of course, it didn't just happen there. It's still happening here too, but that's a discussion for another time. Are you and Finch ready to depart?"

Marcus nodded just as Finch appeared from his room with his backpack.

"Ready!"

While the men were heading off towards Granny, Winter realised that Silvie had nothing to pack other than the belt and sheathed knife that she wouldn't let out of her sight. She had nothing to wear having arrived in little more than rags that had to be cut off her. So Winter set about finding some of her own clothes that, despite being desperately oversized for Silvie's slight frame, would cover her for now and could be taken in at another time. She brought in the few garments that she'd selected and lay them on the bed next to Silvie who was awake, and a bit confused as to what was going on. Winter explained that they were all going on a big adventure to another place where it would be even safer, and that she needed to get dressed as they would be leaving soon. Silvie looked at the small stack of clothes. They were clean and brightly coloured.

"For me?" Silvie asked.

"Yes darlin', I know they're gonna be way too big but we'll get you something more suitable later, I promise," Winter said softly.

Without warning Silvie threw her arms around Winter and hugged her as tightly as her weak arms could manage. Winter was taken aback. It had been a long time since anyone had hugged her.

"Not ever have a thing so beauty. Thanks you Winter." Silvie's voice broke with emotion as she continued to hug Winter like a child clinging to a mother.

In Winter's mind it had been such a small gesture but for Silvie it was momentous. She couldn't help but get a lump in her throat when she thought about Silvie's wretched existence and that she could be so overwhelmed by the smallest of kindnesses from a fellow human being.

"Now, now, it's fine honey. Y'all are very welcome. I wish I had more to offer you, especially for your feet which are so small compared to mine, but this is a start, eh?" Winter gently extricated herself from Silvie's embrace, held her hands, and looked deeply into her big dark eyes. "I'm *so* ashamed and sorry for the hand you were dealt but you now have the chance for a fresh start. You have new friends who care about you, and we won't let any harm come to you I promise. When you're ready I'll ask Finch to come and get you, OK?"

Winter patted the clothes that were carefully folded on the end of the bed to remind Silvie to put some on, she then headed swiftly out into the hall for one last sweep of the building. It was finally time to leave behind what had been a brief moment of sanity and sanctuary for Harvey and Winter. The inevitability of the moment made it no less difficult for either of them.

When Silvie emerged from her room she was wearing a brightly coloured floral skirt that Winter had used safety pins to secure around her slender waist, and a khaki-coloured T-shirt that was knotted at the side. Her feet were bare which didn't bother her at all. She'd been very used to walking in bare feet where she used to live.

Unlike the others, Silvie didn't find the temperature oppressive. In fact, to her it was quite pleasant compared to the searing heat she'd spent her entire life in. Harvey and Winter had grown acclimatised although still found it unpleasant, but Marcus and Finch were struggling. Until a few days ago they'd only been exposed to pure, highly filtered air in their completely controlled environment where it was never too hot or too cold. They still occasionally had to spend time wearing their masks when they found it too hard to breathe but it did nothing to keep their bodies from overheating. From time to time they had to sparingly spray a little water on their clothes to try and cool down.

Finch went back inside to get Silvie and carry her to the vehicle. When he saw her standing in the hall in her newish clothes, he smiled at how different she now looked from the first time he'd seen her.

"Ready?" Finch asked, a broad smile on his face.

Silvie nodded and before she knew it Finch had scouped her up in his arms and was carrying her towards Granny. But as soon as she saw the vehicle she panicked.

"Hey, it's OK. We're all going for a ride." Finch tried to reassure her.

"No! No! Monster!" Silvie pushed and squirmed trying to release herself from Finch's hold. She was having a flashback to the monster hovertrucks that used to dump waste near where she lived. A monster she'd crawled into in order to escape.

She managed to break free from Finch and ran back inside the building and into the cupboard she'd hidden in when the fire broke out.

"Dear God, whatever is the matter?" Harvey was shaken by Silvie's reaction.

"I think I might know," said Winter. "Give me a few minutes."

Winter went back into the house and opened the cupboard door where Silvie was curled up in a trembling ball. She stretched out her hand and pulled her gently back out into the hall.

The two women were gone for about fifteen minutes when Harvey became impatient.

"If we don't leave soon, we'll end up travelling in the hottest part of the day! Or worse, the pookies will …"

"Just give them a few more minutes. I'm sure they'll come out soon," Marcus said calmly.

He was right. Just a few minutes later Finch saw the women heading out of the building. He ran over to Silvie and lifted her into his arms again so that her bare feet wouldn't accidentally tread on anything sharp.

"I'll explain later," said a relieved Winter.

With Harvey in the front passenger seat and Winter in the driving seat, Marcus and Finch sat in the next row and Silvie, who was still more comfortable lying down, was secured horizontally on the third row which was a bench seat.

"Any final words, anyone?" Winter asked as the engine began to hum quietly.

"Goodbye!" Harvey said, with a barely perceptible sadness.

"Hello!" Marcus said cheerfully, trying to re-engage the group's enthusiasm for the journey ahead.

Harvey replied smiling. "Yes, hello it is. We're off to Feronia!"

CHAPTER 30

yellow

The first day of the group's journey was challenging. They had to stop frequently for toilet breaks, some having to get over any embarrassment they felt at having to do their business out in the open. There were only the occasional dead tree stumps along the way to hide behind. Silvie's dressings also needed frequent changing to ensure her wounds were kept clean, so attempts were made to do this when a natural break came along.

They didn't stop for meals or water because they could all manage that when the vehicle was moving. The biggest problem was Winter's fatigue. As the only driver in the group, she bore the weight of responsibility for getting everyone safely to their journey's end. Battling the relentless heat was hard enough, but she had to remain one hundred percent vigilant while manoeuvring some less than hospitable terrain including dirt tracks with giant potholes and old, concrete roads where the heat had caused cavernous cracks to open up. Harvey, who was still exhausted from his recent heart scare, had reclined his seat to make it more comfortable for his long naps. Marcus and Finch continued to be astonished at the scenery that they could just about see through the dust-caked windows. Every now and then Silvie would make a little sound that signalled she was in pain, but she didn't make a fuss and, like the old man, found the gentle motion of the vehicle made for a sleep-inducing environment.

The one thing that wasn't a problem was that Granny was constantly being recharged as they drove, because there was no shortage of solar power for her batteries.

When the light faded and it became too dangerous to keep going, the group stopped for the night. Sometimes they chanced upon an empty house or building, and other times they slept out under the sky. That's when Finch's auto-inflated shelter was most appreciated. The two mattresses inside it were positively luxurious in comparison to sleeping on hard ground with just a blanket. It was decided by Marcus, Finch, and Winter that the youngest and oldest in the group took priority, especially as both had health issues. At the end of each day Winter was so exhausted that she could have slept on a bed of nails, but Marcus and Finch created a more comfortable alternative for her using Granny's detachable seat cushions.

Everyone did what they could to help each other – even Silvie, who sang a little song each night before sleeping as a way of thanking her new friends, although she sang in a language none of them understood. She had the sweetest voice and Finch found himself caring more about her with every day. Feelings that he hadn't known he could have had begun to flood his senses as if he was waking up from a dreamless sleep. Silvie had come to see Finch as her protector. Marcus observed the relationship with great interest. Their backgrounds couldn't have been more different, yet they had found common ground and formed an interdependent bond in an environment that was foreign to both of them. They were genetically at opposite ends of the spectrum too, but as Marcus observed, none of this made any difference when it came to the most basic human emotions.

On the last day of their journey and just as the light was beginning to fade, Winter had managed to push on so that they reached Feronia which was set high up about a mile off the road along a winding bumpy dirt track. As they grew closer to their new sanctuary, they could see the white caps of waves in a churning expanse of dark water way off in the distance.

Harvey was beyond excited. His legs were bouncing up and down in the footwell like a child on a day out to an amusement park. His mouth was lit up in a smile so broad that it seemed to engulf his entire face.

Winter pulled up in front of the house. It was a sprawling old Antebellum-style mansion on three levels surrounded by double storey pillars and a second story veranda at the front. It had once been a dazzling white, but over the decades the paint had blistered, and large chunks of plaster had fallen off to reveal bare patches of brickwork. Some of the windows were cracked or broken and boards had been nailed on. Marcus managed to see through the age and damage of the structure and imagined it must have been a beautiful piece of architecture once. Despite its rundown appearance it still had a charm about it.

As they got out of the car, looking like they'd been through a war, the huge front door over which was carved the word *Feronia* opened and a man of similar vintage to Harvey walked out. But unlike Harvey, he was tall and thin and he had long, white hair which was tied back in a ponytail with an orange ribbon.

"You old b…," Walter stopped himself from saying what he really thought when he saw that there were two women present. "I can't believe you're really here!"

The two old men hugged for what seemed like minutes. And then they looked at each other and hugged again.

"I'm sorry to impose on you Walter and without any way of warning you that we were on our way, but we had nowhere else that felt safe to go to," Harvey whispered.

"Don't be silly, I'm delighted to see you and you've brought friends. Well, you're all very welcome here. Please come on in. You look like hell if you don't mind me saying. Ling Ling! … Ling! Come and say hello to my oldest and dearest friend!"

A short woman with shoulder length straight grey hair, and who was slightly younger than the two old men, came out with a huge grin on her face. "There's no need to shout Walter, I'm not deaf. Oh Harvey, it's been too long. Decades too long. How wonderful to see you again." Ling Ling embraced Harvey warmly. "I think my hair was still black the last time we saw each other."

Harvey laughed as he ran his hand over his now balding head. "At least you have hair."

"Winter, is that you? My goodness, what a fine looking woman you've grown to be," Ling Ling said, embracing her warmly. "You were just a young girl the last time we saw you. Oh my goodness, where have all the years gone?"

"I think I was in my twenties when we all were last together. Now look at me, all middle aged and dowdy," Winter laughed.

"Nonsense! I think you look amazing. I think we all look amazing!" Ling Ling said, doing a little twirl. "Not bad for seventy three eh?"

"We have Winter to thank for getting us here in one piece. It's been quite a journey."

Harvey turned to introduce Marcus and eventually Finch, who had picked Silvie up out of the car and was carrying her over to say hello.

"These are my new friends. They're very *special* and have come a *very* long way. Oh, we have *so* much to tell you." Harvey gave Walter a knowing raised eyebrow when he said 'special' and Walter, having clocked Finch, knew *exactly* what was meant by that. With the introductions over, they all went inside, tired but hugely relieved that their journey was over.

The walnut entry hall of Feronia was quite breath-taking with a double height ceiling still boasting yards of ornate plasterwork, and what had once been a spectacular curved staircase leading to the first floor. Age had stripped the rich lustre from the walnut banister and the once lush red stair carpet was now threadbare, but the size of the structure was still something to behold.

The entrance hall led to a large room on the left, which had plenty of seating with several armchairs and two large sofas that had also seen better days. On the right was a vast oval shaped room that had once been a ballroom but was now Walter's extensive library and den.

Walter led the visitors into the sitting room. "Please do sit, especially you Harvey. You look like you're about to fall over old boy."

"You have no idea!" Harvey laughed. "I wasn't sure I'd make it, but this wonderful man saved my life." He pointed to Marcus. "He's a doctor."

"Fancy that. Trust you to have a doctor fall into your lap," Walter chuckled. "Well, I promise not to ask you to take a look at the mole on my back or my dodgy knee. I know how irritating that is when you're off duty."

Ling Ling was the perfect hostess and had already started preparing cups of tea and some food for the weary but very grateful new arrivals. Winter, not being used to having somebody wait on her, decided to go and help. When she walked into the kitchen, she couldn't believe her eyes. There was shelf after shelf of stacked glass jars full of pickled vegetables and fruit preserves, and just off the kitchen was a pantry with yet more jars of gloriously coloured preserves all immaculately labelled and dated.

Ling Ling smiled as she passed Winter a tray of mugs with steam rising from them. "I'm so glad you're here. We'd never be able to get through all this food alone."

"Is this mint? Mint tea??" Winter gasped.

Ling Ling nodded. Winter thought there was no smell in the world to rival the refreshing fragrance of mint. She hadn't had a cup of mint tea in a good many years. It wafted through the air as Winter proudly carried the tray into the room where everyone was now relaxing. One by one their noses twitched as the scent entered their nostrils.

Harvey took a tiny sip, savouring the moment. "My favourite!"

"This is lovely. I've never tasted anything quite like it," Marcus said with enthusiasm.

Walter looked over at Harvey and gave him a knowing look remembering that he'd said his new friends were 'special'.

Feeling revived after their refreshments, Marcus and Finch went outside again and unpacked Granny, bringing everyone's belongings into the entrance hall. Winter took what remained of their food supplies into the kitchen.

Ling Ling screwed up her nose as she surveyed the group's provisions. "Good Lord, is this what you've been living on?"

Winter was a little offended feeling that it was a criticism of her ability to care for her beloved Harvey.

"My dear, you have been a magician with what you've had at

your disposal. But, as you can see, those days are over."

Winter's hurt feelings quickly dispersed following Ling Ling's praise for her modest achievements. The two women came back to the large sitting room just as Walter was addressing his new audience.

"Old friends and new. Mi casa su casa. Please treat this as your own home for as long as you wish. Stay forever if you are happy here. We have space and nourishment enough for you all. Plus, we could use a bit of younger muscle to do some odd repairs here and there." He laughed at his expression of generosity with a proviso attached. "No, but seriously. You know what I mean."

"Thank you Walter and Ling Ling. We are so grateful to have met all of you and for your wonderful hospitality. While Finch and I are here as your guests, we will of course do whatever we can to be of assistance." Marcus looked over at Finch for agreement.

"Absolutely. What Jarret said," Finch said.

Marcus had no intention of staying forever, as lovely as the offer was. He and Finch had a mission to fulfil. It was taking longer than he had anticipated, but it was time well spent as they were both learning new things every day, and he felt sure there would be more revelations to come.

"We've been here for around 30 years now. Of course, it's not an original plantation house. They were all washed away down south in one of the huge tidal surges back in the day. And importantly, this one *wasn't* built by slaves. It was originally used for events, weddings that sort of thing. It's why there are so many rooms, though only half are habitable now. But there *are* enough rooms to go around if Marcus and Finch you don't mind sharing a room with twin beds so that Winter and Silvie can have a room each? Harvey, to you sir I extend the honour of staying in my den."

Walter's den as he liked to call it, having previously been a ballroom, resembled a generously proportioned library with floor to ceiling bookcases built into the walls. It had a large antique desk and chair, and a couch that converted into a comfortable double bed. He knew that Harvey would feel very at home there having spotted the amount of books he'd managed to bring with him.

"I will place basins of water and towels in your rooms for you to freshen up. When you are finished, please bring the basins with the remaining water downstairs, and leave them by the back door. Nothing goes to waste here." Ling Ling smiled. "Now I will fetch some bedding for you to take upstairs with you. I do apologise that you will have to make your own beds tonight. It has been some time since we had guests and normally, I would have made sure the beds were already dressed."

Even in these hard times, Ling Ling was house proud and liked to present things in a certain way. Her eye for colour and gift for creativity had been some of the things that first attracted Walter to her when they met during his term at Cambridge University in England. The other being her adorable smile. She had been one of his most devoted students, but because it was forbidden for teachers and students to be romantically involved, both had waited respectfully until her graduation to make it official. They were married in a quiet ceremony at the local registry office one week later. Neither had been in any doubt that they wanted to spend their lives together, for better for worse, for richer, for poorer, in sickness and in health. And if the darkest day was to come and the world was to end, they would be holding each other's hands to the very last nanosecond of existence. Theirs was a devotion most could only dream of.

Ling Ling's ancestors had fled a once beautiful and democratic existence in a colony governed by, what was then called, the United Kingdom. But their small island home of Hong Kong had been handed back to a brutal and oppressive Chinese regime, and once it became clear that the lives of their former citizens were in peril, thousands were granted permission to emigrate for their own safety. Two generations on, Ling Ling was forced to flee Cambridge with Walter and travel to another part of the world to escape a very different danger. This time they were climate migrants. Like many intellectuals of the day, they had made a conscious decision not to have children. They believed that the earth didn't require another mouth to feed, and that the quality of life for a future generation was not assured. They felt relieved knowing that when they passed, they could go without worrying about the fate of their children or grandchildren.

Dotted around their once magnificent home were traces of Ling Ling's heritage. Beautiful silver-gilt filigree ornaments, Foo Dogs, blue and white ginger jars, and red jade statuettes which diverted the eye away from the crumbling plaster and cracked walls. She had been able to rescue some of her elder's treasured possessions when they fled, which held great sentimental value, despite no longer holding any monetary worth. They reminded her of her parents and grandparents; of brothers and sisters, aunts, and uncles, all of whom had now departed for the spirit world. The colour red was most significant for her symbolising luck, joy and happiness, something that there had been a dearth of across the world for many decades. The only thing that rivalled this was the overwhelming sense of hopelessness that had swept across humanity.

Marcus woke up early the next morning. He felt re-energised after sleeping in a comfortable bed having spent days on the road. Finch was still sleeping soundly while Marcus dressed and went downstairs. He thought he must have woken everyone in the house by the time he reached the bottom of the staircase, as with every step the old wood creaked as if it were screaming in pain.

There was a delightful smell coming from the kitchen and his stomach started rumbling. It had been a shock to his digestive system to move away from the food they were given in the crystal zone.

"Good morning Marcus!" Ling Ling said with a warm, welcoming smile.

"Good morning."

She passed him a mug of steaming black liquid. It was a strange new aroma. He'd never seen a black drink before.

"What is it?" Marcus asked, feeling a little embarrassed at his ignorance.

"Oh my. Of course. You've never *had* coffee before have you?" She took another sip from her own mug. "Try it. You might like it."

Marcus had never heard of it but was eager to try new things, so he took a tiny sip. It tasted strong and a little bitter.

"Would you prefer something else? Please don't feel obliged to drink it if you don't like it."

Marcus took another sip and smiled. "I think I will get used to it."

Finch, followed by Winter, walked into the kitchen. Winter's legs had to work hard to keep up with her eager nose.

"Noooo!" Winter exclaimed with delight. "I could smell it from upstairs! Y'all have real coffee? Oh, my lord, I haven't had a cup of coffee in years! Harvey won't know what to do with himself."

Marcus found it quite amusing that something as simple as a cup of hot black liquid could extract such joy.

Eventually everyone was in the kitchen, all chattering away, all eating some varieties of food for the very first time, others re-engaging with old favourites. Even Silvie managed to come downstairs without being carried. Ling Ling and Silvie wore similar sized clothing, and their shoe size was exactly the same, so for the first time Silvie had a pair of comfortable shoes that fitted her like a glove, and a dress that didn't swamp her small frame. Finch was delighted to see Silvie looking so much better and more independent. Marcus looked around the table at the unusually happy scene and a sadness suddenly swept over him that his face couldn't hide.

"What's on your mind son?" Walter asked.

"I bet I can guess," said Finch. "He's thinking about Anja, aren't you?"

Marcus nodded.

Finch continued. "She's the reason we're here. We're trying to find her."

"I see," Walter said thoughtfully. "Why are you trying to find her?"

"L'amour!" Harvey cried raising his hands in the air with enthusiasm.

Marcus and Finch looked vacantly at each other.

"Love!" Ling Ling sang. "Love, oh how wonderful. He's in love Walter, isn't that beautiful? Oh, look he's blushing, that's so sweet."

Marcus felt his face flush. He was finding it rather embarrassing to have his feelings discussed so publicly.

Walter brought things back down to earth with his matter-of-fact tone. "Where do you think she is?"

"That's just it Walter. We don't know. She could be *anywhere* by now," Marcus replied, looking despondent.

"I see. And let's say you *do* find her, what then?" Walter's questions were starting to feel more like an interrogation than polite conversation.

Finch answered before Marcus had a chance. "We take her home of course."

"Where *is* home exactly?" Walter continued with an urgency that changed the atmosphere in the room from jovial to slightly tense. "Do *you* know Harvey?"

"Walter my old friend. Why don't you and I have a little chat. We have *so* much to catch up on and I'd like to ask you about something that caught my eye on a wall of your den," he said, shooting Walter a look that said, 'calm down'.

"I'm so sorry Marcus. You've hardly had time to catch your breath since arriving. I'm being rude and I apologise. I suppose I'm just not used to having new people to talk to and my enthusiasm to learn all about you can come across as well, shall we say, a bit too intense?" Walter shrugged his shoulders and attempted a smile.

He stood up, winked at his wife, and left the kitchen with Harvey shuffling after him. Once out of earshot, Harvey closed the door of the den behind him and stared at Walter disapprovingly.

"What?" Walter asked like a defiant child.

"Let's just take our time, OK?"

"Time? Are you mad Harvey. Look at us. We're both ancient, just how much *time* do you think we have?"

"You always were an impatient so and so." Harvey continued in a quiet voice as he slowly lowered himself down into one of the two matching padded armchairs. "Sit down before you fall down for heaven's sake man."

Walter sat down grudgingly.

"They *stole* my life's work and look what they've done with it. Did you see Finch?" Walter growled.

CHAPTER 31

yellow

"Perhaps I made a mistake coming here with them. But I honestly didn't know what else to do. The pookies had found us, set fire to the building, stole their bikes and …"

"Of course, you made the right decision. It's just that it's been so long. I've had to try and put all this behind me because I thought … well I thought we'd failed. We'd run out of time," Walter said more calmly. "It's like I've been woken up from a deep sleep by someone throwing a glass of ice water over my face. It's a bit of a shock, that's all."

"Yes, that's exactly how I felt too Walter. I've only had a little longer than you to get my head around it. How much does Ling Ling know?"

"Oh, she knows *everything*. We have no secrets from each other. The difference is that *she* made a conscious decision not to dwell on things and instead focus on making a home for us. Well more than that, she created our own little world so that whatever was going on out there couldn't touch us. I'm sure lots of people have done the same. Head in the sand. Ignorance is bliss, that sort of thing. I swear if it hadn't been for Ling I would have …"

"Lost your mind? Killed yourself?" Harvey looked away from Walter for a moment. Saying those words brought back a painful memory.

"Oh Harvey. I'm sorry. I haven't even asked how you've

been coping all these years. I am a bad friend." Walter moved his armchair closer to his old friend and put his hand out, which Harvey gladly took in his.

"It's been twenty seven years Walter. Well, twenty seven years, seven months and five days not that I'm still counting. You'd think I'd have laid that ghost to rest by now." Harvey cleared his throat as his voice became a little choked with emotion.

"There's no time limit on grief Harvey." Walter's tone softened considerably as the two men sat in silence with their matching armchairs side by side, holding hands.

Anyone taking Harvey's demeanour at face value could have been fooled into thinking he was a reasonably carefree, occasionally a little eccentric, but generally happy old man. Digging a little under the surface would have revealed a man who had endured a terrible emotional trauma that only close friends at the time knew about.

The world was changing at a pace that took its toll on every age group, even very young children. More and more species were declared extinct and the world's weather patterns became volatile and unpredictable, destroying precious natural environments and vital manmade infrastructures. As a result, the mental health of the nations that had once enjoyed a high standard of living crumbled. It was thought that those who lived in impoverished countries seemed to cope better as they had less to lose. But environmental change was only part of the picture and didn't explain the self-inflicted loss of life of those under the age of twelve who despaired at the pointlessness of their own futures. Like their parents and grandparents, they had become slaves to their online lives always seeking approbation from people they had never met. They were constantly exposing themselves to criticism or ridicule from people who were only there to spread poison and hatred, or brainwash and groom them for their own depraved fantasies. Despite all of the dangers and negative aspects of the internet, and all of the protections that had been put in place to prevent exposing users to the evils of humanity, some found ways to bypass safe zones. There had even been comprehensive studies into the behaviour of the under sixteens which showed that many were spending up to twenty hours a day in their online worlds as an escape from the grim reality of the real world. It was a drug that they couldn't get enough of, and when the internet died they fell apart, lost, frightened and alone.

There had been many iterations of the technology used to send and receive information over the decades, largely due to the need to accommodate an ever increasing volume of users year on year. The internet hadn't been created to accommodate a global population and such vast quantities of data transference. As the final handful of governments handed their ISP controls over to commercial enterprises, it became a free for all as more and more providers cropped up and competed for cyber supremacy, offering online experiences that redefined imagination. Virtual realities had become so convincing and so normalised, that people were spending only a fraction of their lives in the real world.

Life without the internet had, until that time, been unthinkable which is why people reacted so badly when it was lost. Nobody could understand how or why it had happened and with lines of communication cut, it was impossible for IT analysts and technicians to work together in teams across the world to diagnose the cause and try to resolve it. With no central 'kill switch' to turn off the internet, it would have taken every provider worldwide to agree to flick a switch simultaneously, and that was a most unlikely scenario. Naturally, there were theories about what had happened, which ranged from a series of powerful solar flares hitting the Earth to alien intervention, to God, who it was said works in mysterious ways. Walter had his own suspicions, but no way of proving it.

On the day the internet died, the world came to a standstill on every level. Businesses that had relied on clicks, which ninety nine percent of them did, immediately failed. Streaming entertainment, VR, gaming, dating, and AI were rendered obsolete in an instant. And having relied so heavily on the transfer of data digitally for decades, and with drone deliveries of food and parcels the norm, government postal services had been reduced to the most basic skeleton operations. For a few days after the internet ceased, land and cellular telephones continued to work for voice calls, but soon they too fell silent. In the end, the only way for people to communicate with each other was to leave home and travel to meet up personally. It became impossible for media operations to report the news other than via old fashioned non-digital radio frequencies, but these were also soon jammed so that only white noise could be heard.

People didn't know what to do anymore. Some panicked, while other more resourceful groups sent volunteers out with primitive handmade door-to-door leaflets in their local communities. They tried to bring them some reassurance and to announce public meetings so that people didn't feel so isolated. It meant people could ask questions even though nobody had any answers, but at least they were united in their ignorance. These meetings fulfilled one of the most basic needs in humanity, a feeling of belonging. Strangers cried and hugged each other. People arranged to visit older or vulnerable neighbours to check they were OK. It could always be relied on that a natural leader would spring forth from a crowd in an emergency and it didn't take long for plans to be put in place at a local level to bring some order to the chaos. But it was a fragile containment of mass panic, and everyone lived on their nerves trying to keep the peace.

Long before what became known as The Silence, Harvey had met Vincent. They were both considered to be geeks who didn't play the field when it came to relationships. Their connection was more cerebral than sexual, and their contentment was derived from companionship, stimulating conversation, and creating a comfortable nest with their limited financial resources. In fact, their modest wedding ceremony was mostly funded by their close friends.

Apart from dedicating his life to Harvey, Vincent worked tirelessly as a conservationist with a specific interest in marine biology. In his youth he'd dived with playful seals and surfed waves with dolphins and porpoises. He delighted in telling Harvey all about his adventures tagging penguin colonies, and monitoring the way sharks were adapting as sea temperatures and currents changed. He tried to remain hopeful, but he was fighting a losing battle. Eventually, despite millions of people around the world just like him, who fought to turn the situation around, a once rich and diverse habitat could no longer withstand the rising temperatures and devastating pollution. Deliberate depletion from overfishing continued to indiscriminately trap and drown endangered turtles and other fragile marine life in their gigantic nets. Contamination also led to an abundance of new and deadly marine bacteria and viruses that acted like an underwater plague.

Vincent had been an outspoken environmental campaigner in his teens, extolling the widely held scientific views that the planet was in its sixth mass extinction event long before it became fashionable. He was also one of a hundred people arrested at a peaceful protest that turned violent. It was eventually discovered that the protest had been infiltrated by thugs hired by a huge multinational company to create a riot. They were desperate to keep their disposal of toxic waste under wraps to avoid billions of dollars in fines.

It was only a few years into their marriage that Harvey had started to notice a subtle change in Vincent's mood. He was becoming angry and bitter about the inaction of governments, and the continued refusal of populations to engage in change. He described them as 'knowingly sleepwalking into the jaws of death dragging the innocent with them'. A lifetime of fighting the good fight and being a warrior for eco and animal justice led to prolonged bouts of depression. Vincent eventually stopped working, started drinking heavily and self-medicating to try and block out his feelings of hopelessness, and the constant flashbacks to some of the terrible things he couldn't unsee. He was spending more time asleep than awake, but his subconscious wouldn't let his mind rest even then. Images of animal suffering, clashes with authorities, and being branded a lunatic activist replayed over and over in his mind. Late one evening Harvey came home to find that Vincent had taken an overdose. His body was still warm, and Harvey knew that he had not been dead for very long. There was no note next to the empty bottle of vodka and assortment of empty pill bottles. Harvey knew that even if he'd come home an hour earlier it would have made no difference. If not tonight, Vincent would have taken his life at another time. He was one of life's sensitive souls and the darkness had finally overwhelmed him.

Harvey's heart was shattered by the loss of his wonderful Vincent. As he sat holding the lifeless body of the man he loved so completely, emotion took over forcing the most distressing wailing noise from his mouth. It sounded like a wolf howling over and over again in waves that he couldn't control. For weeks afterwards, Harvey withdrew into himself and often contemplated the merits of joining Vincent, finding it almost unbearable to get through each day without his soulmate. But something always pulled him back from committing an act of such brutal finality. He wasn't ready to go yet. There was more for him to do.

Harvey reached under his shirt and lifted out a gold chain that was always against his chest. It had two wedding rings dangling on it. He smiled at Walter. "If my old knuckles weren't so swollen from arthritis, I'd still be wearing mine. I am a sentimental fool, aren't I?"

"There's nothing wrong with being sentimental Harvey. Nothing at all. It's important that we remember the past, even when those memories are painful." Walter squeezed Harvey's hand and got to his feet. "I'm so glad you're here my friend. Life has been so difficult, what with the internet gone and having no way to contact you."

"Yes it seems the only 'world wide web' we have now is one of lies and deceit in the form of human flesh." Harvey shook his head. "And then I couldn't even call you when the phones went dead."

"We used to live in countries, now we live in zones. It's crazy. We've lost all sense of identity and we seem to be back living in the dark ages."

"I think that may have been the objective Walter."

Walter realised that they were both becoming morose.

"Anyway, enough of the doom and gloom. Let's discuss your little friends shall we? What an interesting mix they are. How much do you know about them? I mean it's obvious what *Finch* is, but Marcus is a puzzle. There's something about him that feels so familiar, I just can't put my finger on it."

"And then there's Silvie. She's really been through it." Harvey looked pensive for a moment before standing up and walking over to the wall next to the door. "This is the key," he said, tapping the wall.

Walter had a giant map of the world on his wall. It was an old map from well before large areas of land had disappeared underwater, and well before the introduction of zoning. Over the years, and before the information blackout, he'd used a thick black pen to draw on it as more of the earth's surface was deemed uninhabitable from either flood, drought, famine, or wildfire.

"I think we should get them all together in here and show them how things used to look. Perhaps that will spark a conversation where we can learn more about them. What do you think?" said Harvey.

"I doubt very much that they will ever have seen a world map. But I think it could provide the ideal starting point to a conversation that needs to be had. We need to be cautious about sounding like we're interrogating them though. I realise that now," said Walter, nodding in approval. "They need to feel that they can trust us. And we need to be absolutely sure that *they're* trustworthy Harvey. There's too much at stake."

"Agreed. Today after lunch then." Harvey reached up and put his hand on Walter's shoulder. "I know what's at stake my friend. I just wish it hadn't taken so long."

CHAPTER 32

yellow

With both of the older men in Walter's den deep in conversation, Ling Ling took the opportunity to take the others to the side of the house. She wanted to show them her special garden where she grew vegetables and some fruit, and also had a little herb garden.

Marcus, Finch, Winter and Silvie looked at the patch of ground that was covered by two enormous awnings to protect the produce from burning in the sun. They'd never seen anything so spectacular.

"This is just extraordinary Ling Ling," Winter said, her eyes as wide as saucers. "However do you manage to grow food like this darlin'?"

"It was trial and error for a while. But as you know the greatest enemy of food production has been lack of water and poor-quality soil. Walter came up with a solution years ago, which meant that very little water was needed using a unique water retaining gel crystal. There had been similar things to this many decades before with potassium polyacrylate, but Walter added something else, and it quadrupled the capacity of the gel to hold water. Don't ask me how it works because I don't understand those things. He passed the formula on to government scientists around the world free of charge, he just wanted to help. Then the States happened happened and who knows where that information is now. Judging by the state the planet is in, I don't think it has served its purpose."

"That's so shockin', I had no idea Ling Ling. Your husband is an exceptional human being isn't he?" Winter smiled. "Anyone else might have patented the formula and made vast amounts of money, but he just plum gave it away. Altruism is rarely seen these days.".

Ling Ling turned to Marcus. "What do they eat where you're from Marcus?"

Marcus knew that to answer that would bring into question many more aspects of life in the crystal zone that he wasn't sure he should talk about yet, if at all. He also knew that he couldn't answer Ling Ling's question because nobody knew *exactly* what they were eating, only that it was provided for them without question and that it was extremely repetitive in nature. Eating the same thing day in day out hadn't been something he'd ever considered strange before he started to experience so many new and diverse types of food, tastes, and textures since arriving in the yellow zone.

"Nothing as interesting as what we see here Ling Ling," he replied.

Marcus looked at Finch hoping he wouldn't volunteer any more information. Finch wasn't stupid, he could read the room, or in this case the garden, and remained silent as he watched Silvie crouch down and examine the leaves of various plants and vegetables close up. She gazed in wonder at what lay before her in perfectly aligned rows and in colours that she had never seen sprouting from the earth before. While Marcus, Finch and Winter were excited to see the evidence of Walter's creation, the sight of all this food made Silvie desperately sad. Her people had been starving to death for generations and nobody came to help them. Hearing about Walter's invention and seeing the results before her eyes, she knew that her government back home had betrayed them. She quickly wiped away a tear that had escaped her right eye and was trickling down her face.

Silvie pointed to one of the vegetables. "What this?" she asked.

"That's a carrot Silvie," Ling Ling replied, very aware that her youngest guest was not from the same place as Marcus and Finch.

"And these? What these?" Silvie asked again.

"They're potatoes and tonight I will be roasting them, and some of the carrots with herbs. I think you will like them like that Silvie."

Silvie let out a deep sigh. "Oh, will love."

The group were starting to overheat as the middle of the day approached, so went back into the house which was considerably cooler. Walter and Harvey were back in the kitchen looking like two schoolboys hatching a plan. They immediately stopped talking as the others came in looking hot but also happy.

"So, you've seen Ling Ling's amazing work then?" Walter smiled.

"It's a credit to both of you. Walter your way of reducin' the need for water is ingenious!" Winter said joyously.

Walter beamed at Ling Ling, appreciating the compliment with his beloved wife. They were quite a team, and he was exceptionally proud of her. She had been loyal to him through thick and thin. When those around them were either tearing each other to pieces in anger and frustration at the decline of civilised society, or mocking the couple for their constantly hopeful attitude, her belief in him had never wavered.

"I … I mean *we* would like you to join us in my den for, let's call it a meeting of minds. There are things that we would like to share with you which we hope you will find enlightening and perhaps we can be enlightened by you as well," Walter said, looking at Harvey for recognition that it was a joint initiative.

"Yes, we think it would be beneficial to learn more about each other, don't you?" Harvey looked around the room hoping for a positive reaction to their proposal.

"Good idea," Winter said.

Silvie nodded her approval even though she didn't think there would be anything interesting that she could offer to the discussion with her limited knowledge of English.

"Fine with me," Finch said confidently. "You good with this Jarret?"

"I think it's an excellent idea and hopefully it will help us in our quest to find Anja," Marcus replied, gently reminding everyone that they were only passing through.

"Marvellous. Come on through when you're finished here, and we can get started."

Walter rubbed his hands together with enthusiasm and headed back to the den to wait for the others. He also needed to clean his previous markings from the glass over the map.

It didn't take very long before the den was full. Harvey and Walter took the more comfortable padded armchairs and Ling Ling, Silvie and Winter made themselves comfortable on the sofa that had been put back together from being Harvey's bed. Marcus sat on the desk chair as Finch had offered to sit cross legged on cushions that had been placed on the floor. All had been given a beautiful paper fan by Ling Ling to help them keep cool from all the body heat in one room.

Harvey whispered something to Walter who nodded in agreement.

"We thought this might be a helpful place to start." Walter began by getting up and walking over to the giant wall map. "For those of you less familiar with the bigger picture of how our planet once looked, this map is about sixty years old. I've always loved maps. I used to collect them as a child and one of my favourite party tricks at university was to be able to name every flag of every country in the world."

"Yes I remember. We thought you were such a geek and really should have got out more," Harvey laughed.

"Thank you for that Harvey. When I look at this old map I have fond memories of places that I've seen and people that I've met. It's one of the benefits of living to such a ripe old age. Harvey and I had the pleasure of remembering the planet as it was. Obviously, this is a long time before the zones were enacted, and I'm sad to say, there have been some profound changes to the way this map now looks, largely as a result of our catastrophic climate events over the decades."

As the giant map was framed and behind glass, it gave Walter the opportunity to take a thick black marker pen and draw on it without damaging his precious piece of memorabilia. He began with a large body of land in between the Pacific and Indian oceans.

"This was called Australia. My parents went there on honeymoon in 2005 to a place called Sydney, in fact my older sister was conceived on that trip. I remember, even towards the ends of their lives, they still spoke about the trip with huge affection ... its glorious bustling harbour with ferries and yachts, stunning beaches, fabulous restaurants ... anyway, I digress. It had always been known as a country where the summers could be extremely hot and cause what they called bushfires, like our wildfires," Walter said, sounding like the professor of his youth giving a lecture to his students. "By the time of the First Great Heat of 2058 Australia had lost more of its beaches than any other country in the world. But in the Second Great Heat of 2063 the whole of the western side of Australia was wiped out by the most monstrous wildfires that couldn't be contained and continued to spread across the whole continent."

Walter took his black marker and struck diagonal lines across it. "Australia became the first of the black zones."

"*Black* zones?" Finch asked looking confused. "I thought there were only three. Crystal, yellow, and red."

"A black zone is where all vegetation and life have been wiped out," Harvey replied. "But I suppose they didn't tell you that where you're from."

Marcus and Finch looked at each other but remained silent. They were still baffled as to how anyone could know where they were from. They turned back to Walter who continued using his black marker to eliminate all the islands that were now underwater, coastlines that had disappeared due to rising sea levels or had broken off and fallen into the sea due to coastal erosion, increased volcanic or seismic activity. By the time Walter had finished writing on the map it was such a disturbing sight that Ling Ling and Winter were in tears, even though they knew most of what Walter had elucidated. Marcus, Finch and Silvie sat silently in a state of shock and disbelief.

Harvey slowly got to his feet. "I know that this is a lot for you to take in, but I'm afraid there is more that you need to know, and it won't be easy to hear either. Marcus you asked me a question a little while back that I wasn't really prepared for. It was probably the hardest question anyone had ever asked me. But now that you're seeing things the way they *really* are, I'd like to answer your question," he said, shuffling over to his bag and pulling out a large, heavy book.

"I'm sorry, I've asked you so many questions that I don't know which one you're talking about," Marcus said, with an anxiety in his voice he couldn't mask.

"You asked me what *animals* are?" Harvey replied, handing Marcus the book.

Marcus opened it and discovered hundreds of pages full of glossy photos showing creatures great and small; brightly coloured or camouflaged; on land, in the air and under water.

"*These* are animals Marcus, and we once shared our planet with them, some we even shared our homes with. We were meant to be their guardians, but one by one we destroyed or polluted their habitats, killed them for sport, or slaughtered them for food. All while our human population continued to grow and grow outstripping the finite resources of our planet. To be blunt, we became a cancer devouring our host. As far back as the early 2020s we were already using the equivalent of 1.74 Earths in order to satisfy our consumption of natural resources. It was pure insanity. Some of us made the decision not to have children, but it didn't come close to compensating for those who continued to breed indiscriminately."

"Well, I blame religion and politics, and their various issues with contraception. And then there was the complex matter of being for or against the termination of pregnancies," Walter said, in a dismissive tone.

"And *this* is where we fundamentally disagree Walter. Creationist vs scientist and never the twain shall meet. God trusted us to be the guardians of his divine creation. We failed him and ourselves."

Walter tutted. "Oh, here we go."

"Stop! Please stop! This is too much. I can't hear any more.

You're both lying! *None* of this is real," Finch shouted angrily, becoming uncharacteristically emotional, before storming out of the den and running upstairs to his bedroom.

"Oh dear," Harvey said, looking up at Walter in despair. "I'm so sorry, I thought they were ready."

"I'm not sure anyone could ever be truly ready to hear all of this," Winter said, with a deep sadness in her voice.

"I go see he OK." Silvie got to her feet, carefully folded her paper fan, and placed it on the table before leaving the room to find Finch.

"They were so beautiful. So fascinating and diverse," Marcus said, looking through the pages of the book in complete wonder. "What sort of monsters are we to have let all this happen? I wish this was just fantasy, but I *do* believe you have both told us the truth and it makes me feel physically sick. I know why Finch is having such a problem processing this. I have found the Gen1s are often physically strong but not emotionally resilient."

Marcus realised that there was absolutely no point in remaining guarded about the crystal zone any longer, and he didn't care if Finch agreed with his decision or not. Whether the founders of the crystal zone had intended to protect their people from the harsh reality of a world intent on destroying itself, or whether they had another great plan, it no longer mattered.

CHAPTER 33

yellow

Silvie crept up the grand staircase slowly. Looking up it seemed like a mountain, and with her legs still quite weak, she could only manage one step at a time using her slightly stronger right leg alone. The ancient wood sounded as though it ached in distress each time she put her delicate weight on a step, but she was determined to make it to the top without assistance. All she could think about was reaching Finch. Approaching the door of his room she hoped he wouldn't turn her away.

"Finch, I come in?" Silvie asked quietly.

There was no response, but the door was ajar and she could see a reflection of him in the room's large wall mirror. He was sitting on the end of his bed with his head in his hands. His shoulders were moving up and down with his every breath the way a child's body reacts to uncontrollable sobbing. She had seen this before with her own daughter.

"Finch, I come in?"

This time Silvie didn't wait for an answer. She pushed the door open slowly and walked inside to where Finch was sitting. Quietly she sat down beside him and put her hand on his shoulder.

"It be OK Finch," she whispered.

"They're liars!" Finch blurted out between sobs.

"Oh Finch. You know they not lie," she replied, trying to put her arms around him.

"Please don't." Finch gently pushed her away.

"But Silvie want help Finch."

"Nobody can help me! Nothing is what I thought it was."

"Yes. You right. But it not same for me. I learn thing I not know. But not think they lie. Come now. You look me," Silvie said, taking his head in her hands to face her.

Although she was three years younger, she looked at Finch and thought how very young his mind was. She had experienced the very worst of humanity and survived. He had lived a cossetted existence, and as a result his survival instincts were limited. Finch opened his red rimmed eyes and looked into Silvie's. There was so much kindness staring back at him.

"I'm not crying because I'm upset. I'm crying because I'm angry," Finch said, wiping his face.

"Yes, you angry. I angry."

"If the old men haven't lied to us, it means other people have. People who I've believed all my life. That's hard to accept."

"Yes. But truth here Finch. You see. No tree. No water. Just dust."

"How are you so wise Silvie? We are so different, like we are at opposite ends of the spectrum," Finch said thoughtfully. "How can it be that you have suffered so much hardship and I have had none?"

"I not know. But we here now and we safe. With good people. We have clothes and we not hungry." Silvie's voice had a peace to it that Finch found extremely calming and soothing.

"I think you're the most amazing person I've ever met Silvie."

"You think?" Silvie giggled. "Lovely. But I no special. Come, we go down now."

Finch nodded and got off the bed, straightened out his clothes and wiped his face one more time. They slowly descended the stairs together, Finch offering his arm to Silvie to make her feel more secure. Despite being set some distance from the staircase, the others who were still talking in the den knew they were coming downstairs from the unmistakeable creaking noises.

As soon as he saw them in the doorway Harvey stood up.

"Finch my boy, I'm so sorry that I have upset you. I realise now that we should have perhaps taken things a bit more slowly."

"No apology is needed. I'm sorry that I reacted so badly," Finch said, looking at the floor still feeling rather embarrassed.

Winter decided a change of subject was required. She was fascinated to find out how they had coffee, so when she raised the question, Ling Ling and Walter couldn't help but laugh.

Ling Ling's face lit up when she remembered their discovery. "Well, it's a bit mad really, but when we bought the place … remember we said it had been used as an events venue? So, I guess they must have been in quite a hurry to leave because when we went into the basement it was like walking into Aladdin's Cave."

"Yes we really struck gold." Walter added with joy in his voice. "There were hundreds of tins of sealed freeze-dried coffee, bags of flour, seeds, dried herbs, dried soy, lentils, and also non-edible items including white linen tablecloths, giant fluffy white bath towels, enough candles to light a palace, gilt edged crockery, and canteens of solid silver cutlery. So many things it was like Christmas. Plus, hundreds of jars of pickles and preserves. In fact, *that's* what got Ling interested in making her own once we had successfully managed to grow some produce ourselves."

"They must have had spa treatments here too Walter, don't you think? All those uniforms, nail kits, face masks and luxury creams?" Ling Ling remarked to her husband who was already moving on in his head from those memories.

"So, I'm guessin' the coffee you made for us must be very out of date honey. Not that I'm complainin' of course. It tasted *so* good." Winter was careful not to sound offensive.

"The basement is very deep and the coolest part of the house, so everything stored down there seems to have an expanded longevity. We have been extraordinarily lucky," said Ling Ling.

"She used to call it the dungeon you know," Walter laughed.

"I think it's Walter's favourite part of the house. Any excuse and he's down there getting up to who knows what."

It was true. Walter did spend a lot of time in the basement of their house. Ling Ling had learned years ago not to ask too many questions. She didn't really want to know what he was up to but imagined he was keeping his hand in when it came to little experiments. Once a scientist, always a scientist and Walter had a very well-equipped lab in the basement. It was where he had been using his expertise in genetics to experiment with plant species, adapting them to the less hospitable environment they now lived in.

"Christmas? You said it was like *Christmas* Walter. What did you mean by that?" Marcus asked, intrigued by another term he had never heard of.

Winter couldn't hide her shock. "Y'all never heard of *Christmas*?"

"I think Harvey will be the best person to explain that one to you Marcus. But perhaps save it for another day. I think that might turn out to be a lengthy conversation." Walter gave Harvey a wink.

"Yes I'd be *more* than happy to explain it all. Walter isn't big on religion as you've probably gathered by now. Perhaps on another day, Winter and I can tell you about the origins of Christianity and then how Christmas became a religious as well as a hugely commercial time of year," Harvey said in a serious manner, clearly not impressed with Walter's non-believer attitude. "If you like we could touch on other religions as well. There are so many others, and all are interesting in their own way."

Walter raised his eyebrows. "Oh, I'm sure they'll be delighted."

"Islam," Silvie said quietly.

"Is that what is practiced where you're from Silvie?" Harvey asked enthusiastically.

"Some do. Others not."

"On another matter, I was wondering Winter if you might be agreeable to taking Granny out on a little trip tomorrow with me?" Marcus enquired. "I'm sorry to impose on you, but you're the only one who can drive."

"Yes Marcus, I'd be happy to sugar. Anywhere in particular?"

"It depends on where the nearest area that's populated is. I want to see if anyone has seen Anja or heard of a girl that looks like her."

"The nearest place from here is a good 180 miles northwest of here," Ling Ling said. "We haven't been there for a couple of years now, but it's as good a place to start as anywhere."

"Finch I thought you could stay here and help out. Walter mentioned there were some things that he could use a hand with. Is that OK?" Marcus asked, hoping Finch would agree. He felt the need for a little space from his roommate in his search for Anja.

Finch was only too happy to stay behind. "Sure. No problem."

"I help!" Silvie chirped up with a smile, looking over in Finch's direction.

"Excellent!" Harvey cheered "You have a plan for tomorrow."

"I realise I'm backtracking slightly to an earlier topic, but I was just wondering if you could tell us any more about the food you eat where you come from? I just wondered if there was *anything* at all that we could perhaps learn from it, you know, in case it helps us with what we're growing," Walter said, making the request sound plausible.

"All I can tell you is that it appears to be very well balanced because we have all been very healthy living on it," said Marcus, before having an idea that might be of help. "I still have one portion of it left in my bag upstairs. You're more than welcome to examine it if you think that would be helpful Walter."

"That would be absolutely wonderful Marcus, thank you," Walter said, trying to appear calm while his insides were turning over and over in excitement at the thought of getting his hands on it.

"Speaking of food, I'll make up a travel pack for you both to take with you tomorrow."

"Bless you for that Ling Ling. That's so thoughtful." Winter smiled warmly.

"I'll go and get that food sample for you now Walter, before I get distracted."

Marcus got to his feet and swiftly headed upstairs to his room. He was back just a few minutes later with a small container which he handed to Walter. Ling Ling and Walter exchanged looks. They'd been together for so long that words were rarely necessary when it came to knowing what was going on in the other's head. She knew that the minute everyone else was doing their own thing, her husband would be straight down to the basement and into his lab with Marcus's container. Analysing its contents, its microbiology, engineering, and chemistry, determining its nutrients and what preservatives they might be using was, without exception, going to be the most exciting project he'd had in years.

CHAPTER 34

observation 1:6

It is interesting to observe other beings from my current position. I can hear all their thoughts – both verbal and mental and absorb them. Not in a way that makes it possible to repeat them verbatim, nor to transmit them telepathically, but they are held somewhere in the depths of my consciousness. Quite where this is I do not fully understand. My brain is only a tiny organ, not yet fully formed, but still it is capable of housing the complete history of time with every thought, action, or deed that every being on this planet has ever had, said, or done. The enormity of it all would be daunting for even the greatest minds. But here, where I currently dwell, it only serves to nourish me.

Of course, when I am forwarded, all of this information will be lost within a nanosecond and I will have to start my course of knowledge again based on teachings, experience, and opportunity. I know this to be true, because at this time, I know all things. It is true of all unborn beings. Before emerging into the world organically or scientifically, every being contains this all-encompassing knowledge. It is only the process of transferring into full life, in other words being born, that wipes the slate clean so that humans can begin a voyage of discovery. Perhaps this is why beings often feel that in life they have been somewhere or done something before. It's what humans have called déjà vu for centuries and it's an expression that was first coined in 1876 by

French philosopher Émile Boirac who wrote about it in his book L'Avenir des sciences psychiques.

I also know that in most instances, beings are unable to harness the full potential of their accumulated knowledge. They become blocked and the process of rediscovery is set on another path. Sometimes only a fraction of the brilliance a being contains ever emerges. The irony of this is that it is so often the beings who struggle to achieve so much, who end up rediscovering little. The frustration of it is that the answer to all questions already exists. All we must do is allow the answers to come to us.

All through the twentieth century, beings struggled to find answers to questions of health and disease. Unfortunately, the destiny of the woman who held the secret to curing all cancers was to be an aborted foetus – the result of a disastrous affair between Jenny Delaware, a gifted fifteen-year-old schoolgirl, and Jonathan Kimberly, her twenty-eight-year-old English teacher in 1943. It was in a remote part of Canada and the girl subsequently bled to death. This is only one example of how, what beings call fate, can be dramatically, even tragically altered by circumstance and untimely decision-making.

Also in that century, the famous NASA space programme was virtually crippled by the deletion of Humphrey Mott, who was killed in a motorbike accident just before his 18th birthday in 2024. His brain held the secret to a revolutionary kind of space travel dependent on his extraordinary formula for a fuel that would have allowed humans to visit the furthest reaches of our solar system well within their own lifetimes, and with minimum damage to their physiological and neurological compositions. Alas, humankind had to settle for more primitive moon landings, space stations and two fatal attempts to colonise Mars.

I am in possession of the knowledge that our origins are not as cut and dried as we had once believed, and that the person who would have been best able to educate us about who and what we really are, perished in a terrorist bombing incident just before the turn of the 20th century. He was called Justin Maxwell and he was only six months old.

But now I am feeling something new. A sense of foreboding

about the Advocates and the Leader. It is fortunate that, as a collection of cells, my observations cannot yet be monitored or tapped into by outside sources – although in time I could teach them how to.

CHAPTER 35

yellow

When Marcus came down for breakfast the following morning, he was feeling optimistic about what the day would bring. At last, he would be making progress in his search for Anja. As much as he rubbed along well enough with Finch, the fact that he was an Associate Advocate was something that was never far from Marcus's mind. If and when he found Anja, he didn't want Finch there to ruin the moment of their reunion in his official capacity. With Winter being the only driver, it provided Marcus with the perfect excuse to go it alone. Winter, on the other hand, had been paying more attention to the growing bond that was forming between Finch and Silvie. They were such an odd couple in many ways; close in age and yet poles apart in how their lives had unfolded. But it was becoming clearer with every day that they were both compelled by instinct to care for each other, and Winter thought that was wonderful.

Ling Ling handed Marcus and Winter a package of food each for their journey. She knew that their chances of finding any supplies to keep them going out there were limited, and it was important for them to stay hydrated during what was going to be another sweltering day. Ling Ling had also packed a little something extra for Winter just in case they ran into any trouble. When Winter looked inside her package, she tried not to appear shocked and instead nodded to Ling Ling that she understood.

When Marcus and Winter opened the front door they were greeted by an astonishing sight.

Finch was putting the finishing touches to his morning's work. "What do you think Winter?" he asked.

"I think I'm gonna cry," Winter gasped, as she placed her hand over her mouth.

Granny was clean, shiny, and showing off her lovely mint green paintwork to perfection. A look that Winter hadn't seen in many years.

"How on earth have you done this Finch?" Marcus could see how much it meant to Winter.

"Walter is quite the inventor," Finch replied. A little bottle of this and a cloth. It's called waterless car wash. Not a new invention in itself. He told me it's existed for over 80 years, but Walter's formulation took things to the next level."

"Wow. Just wow!" Winter exclaimed, as she walked over to her faithful old friend and ran her fingers over the newly revealed paintwork.

"And it apparently repels dirt too. So hopefully when you get back later, Granny will still be looking pretty good," Finch said, feeling pleased with himself. He wanted to do something nice for Winter as she was always helping others, and also as a thank you for getting them safely to Walter's home.

Winter wrapped her arms around Finch and gave him an almighty hug. "Thank you Finch. This is really somethin'."

Walter, Ling Ling, and Silvie came out to join Finch at the front of the house in time to wave Marcus and Winter off on their journey. A journey that everyone hoped would bring some answers as to Anja's mysterious disappearance and provide some hope for Marcus.

Harvey missed the farewell. The day before he had complained of feeling unusually tired, so when Winter checked to see if he'd like some breakfast before she and Marcus set off, she wasn't surprised to find that he was still fast asleep. For a man half his age the last few weeks would have been a physical and emotional challenge, and if it hadn't been for Marcus's swift action, he wouldn't have made it there at all. She hoped that this would be the last great upheaval for him, and that he could now take it easy and do what he enjoyed doing most, reading.

Before Granny disappeared from view, Walter had already slipped back inside and down into the basement to his lab. He had an impressive array of equipment having had the good fortune of foresight. When the cracks started to appear in what had become a veneer of civilised society, Walter made sure that wherever he and Ling Ling ended up, he would be able to continue with his valuable research work, albeit in an unpaid capacity. But money had never been a driver for him. Even as a young scientist, the only things that interested Walter were developing solutions that could make human life more resilient and the planet habitable so that other species could coexist. In the first of his aims, he had been exceptional. But in the second, even with others as brilliant and committed as he was, biodiversity had failed.

Walter had been forced to abandon his dreams of turning things around for the planet and instead found himself doing what everyone else was doing, focussing on the survival of those closest to him. He detested the premise of *every man for himself*, but the catastrophic course humanity had set itself on had become too advanced to do anything else.

As he sat at his bench in the lab, Walter carefully opened the container of food. His first instinct was to smell the contents. It was an inviting aroma, so he decided to taste it. The texture was soft like mashed potato and required little to no chewing, but the flavour didn't immediately bring to mind anything he'd tasted before. He split the sample into a variety of dishes and tubes, making sure that he kept sufficient of the original material sealed in an air-tight container just in case further testing was required.

He began by testing the substance for carbohydrates, proteins, and lipids in a typically methodical way. He was old school when it came to conducting tests and, in this instance, there were no shortcuts to determining what was in the food that Marcus and Finch were consuming. He began with an Iodine test for starch. Sure enough, shortly after placing a few drops onto the food, the sample turned blue black. Next he conducted the Benedict's test for reducing sugars like glucose and fructose. After placing the test tube in a water bath and heating it, the colour changed from blue to a cloudy orange, which told him that there were indeed reducing sugars in the sample. 'Interesting,' he thought to himself. Then it was time to check for lipids, which required the Emulsion test. In preparation he put on safety gloves and protective eyewear. He'd seen too many students over the years rush to get a result and get burns in the process. The results were as he expected. The sample returned a milky white colour.

The last test that Walter wanted to conduct that day was the Biuret test for proteins. It was the one that he was most interested in because sources of protein had become the most difficult and expensive to come by in the last twenty years. The food stations provided a substandard mix of carbohydrates and proteins for the masses. Muscle cell samples from cows, sheep, pigs, and chickens had been cryogenically stored before the last living hosts had died out. Plant proteins were also in short supply due to the need for intensive indoor, vertical farming and the shortage of water. With Marcus and Finch showing no signs of protein deficiency, Walter was determined to discover where this vital ingredient was coming from.

CHAPTER 36

yellow

Conversational dynamics fascinated Winter. In a group setting, people seemed to behave in a particular way. Walter, for example, was completely at home holding court in a room full of friends or strangers. He was a natural performer and an excellent orator, which was one of the things his students had found so attractive when attending his lectures.

Harvey had also felt at home in front of an audience but was much less showy. Now in his advancing years he preferred smaller, more intimate settings where he could speak without exerting himself, or without too many interruptions.

The two old men were very comfortable discussing academic issues privately, and even more at home having debates and exchanging opposing views between themselves when alone together. Their debates were sometimes fiery but always good natured because they had so much genuine love and respect for each other.

Now Winter was sitting in her beautifully polished Granny, courtesy of Finch's thoughtfulness, with Marcus by her side. She'd only known him a short time and really knew very little about him, yet she felt completely at ease. For Winter there would be nothing worse than being in a confined space for hours on end having to endure any uncomfortable silences with a veritable stranger.

"Tell me about her honey," Winter asked in order to get the conversation started.

Marcus smiled and took a deep breath. Just the thought of Anja made his heart race.

"Goodness Winter, that should be an easy one to answer," Marcus said, pausing for a moment. "I find myself struggling to put anything about Anja into words."

"That's OK Marcus. Take your time. Why don't y'all start with how you met her?"

Again, there was a pause. Marcus knew that the only way he could answer Winter's question would be to go into greater detail about what happens in the crystal zone. He liked Winter a lot, and even though he hadn't known her for very long, his instincts told him that she could be trusted.

"So, as you know I'm a doctor. And my field is genetics."

Winter nodded while keeping an eye on the road ahead, which was littered with debris and giant potholes, and had clearly not been used by anyone in a very long time.

"Well, one of my roles at the clinic is to conduct monthly examinations and tests on the Gen1s."

"The Gen1s?" Winter asked. Even though she had a basic idea of what that term meant, she wanted Marcus to explain it in his own words.

"I do apologise Winter. I'm so used to these terms I forget that our new friends won't have heard of these expressions before. So, a Gen1 is a first generation fully genetically enhanced human being. It basically means that they are physically stronger and more resilient to disease for example. They also have an extended lifespan. The Gen1s are examined each month to ensure that they are functioning well on a physical level and also on a psychological one."

"How fascinatin'. So, Anja is a Gen1?" Winter enquired, as she skilfully dodged a boulder that had lodged itself in the middle of the road as a result of a landslide.

"Yes she is. That's how I met her. She was my patient. I prefer *patient* although some of the others at the clinic call them *subjects* which I find too clinical and impersonal."

"Was the attraction instant Marcus?"

"There was just something about her that stood out. I think it was the way she looked at me. Maybe the way we looked at each other?"

"Eye contact is a mighty powerful thing honey."

"Isn't it? Nobody had ever looked at me the way Anja did. She actually took my breath away."

It was one of the first times Winter had seen Marcus smile and look so relaxed.

"I think the feeling you're describin' is like havin' someone look into your soul. Although looks aren't necessarily important when it comes to love, it would help me to know what she looks like so we can ask if anyone has seen her. Do y'all have any photos of her?"

"I don't know what you mean by photos Winter. But I do have this." Marcus touched his wrist bracelet causing it to light up. Then he called out 'Anja!'

Winter nearly crashed Granny as an image of Anja lit up on the windscreen obscuring her vision. She slammed on the brakes bringing them to an abrupt stop.

"Dear God! You're gonna have to warn me before doin' somethin' like that again Marcus! Oh, my word. You have some fancy gadgets where you're from, don't you sugar."

Winter caught her breath and then burst into fits of laughter until she started coughing and laughing so much that it was positively infectious, and Marcus couldn't help but laugh as well. For a good five minutes the pair sat there giggling, laughing, sweating, and snorting, holding their stomachs, and bending double the way people do when they're in hysterics. Just as one would stop and manage to compose themselves, the other would laugh even harder which set them both off again. Eventually they'd exhausted their capacity for such silliness and sat quietly for a moment looking at the image of Anja.

"Well, there's no gettin' away from the fact that she's a stunner Marcus."

"But the thing is, she isn't any *more* beautiful than the other Gen1 females."

"I suppose that's the thing about playing God with genetics. No disrespect meant Marcus, but doesn't it get a bit … borin' … I mean if everyone's perfect."

"I've never thought of it that way. As a man I can honestly say that I never tire of looking at beautiful women. But I will admit to feeling just a bit insecure when it comes to the Gen1 males. Look at Finch. He's a handsome, well-built young man who I assume women find attractive," Marcus said, wondering if that's how Winter viewed Finch.

"He's a fine-lookin' young man for sure. Not my type, but then again, he's young enough to be my son. I take it you're not a Gen1?"

"No. I'm just ordinary Winter. Perfectly ordinary and really a little dull I imagine. And that's another thing. Why would someone like Anja be attracted to someone like me?" Marcus stared at the image of her that was still lighting up Granny's windscreen.

"Oh, come on darlin'. You're a good-lookin' man too. But you have somethin' else about you that may be what Anja also sees in you. You have a different kind of strength than Finch. Yours is a cerebral strength and a depth that makes you stand out. I can't believe you don't know it."

Marcus's face flushed with embarrassment. Winter could see that he really didn't have a clue about how attractive or interesting he really was so decided to move the conversation on.

"OK that's quite enough of that. Can you please get your young lady off my windscreen so I can see the road again? Oh, and another thing. I suggest you don't do *that* where we're headed," she said, pointing to his bracelet. "They won't have seen anythin' like it before and well, you know, it could cause us some problems with local folks. Like your bikes did. We don't want to draw any unnecessary attention to ourselves."

"Yes, of course. I completely understand."

A few hours into their journey they arrived at what had been a small town. The buildings were dilapidated and there was no sign of life. They decided to get out and stretch their legs for a while and Marcus was keen to have a look around. Winter also wanted to take a closer look in case anything had been left behind that might be useful.

Everything was coated in a thick layer of brown dirt having been battered by ferocious dust storms over the years. The houses were empty, and it seemed the inhabitants had left there in a hurry as their front doors weren't locked. Winter decided to have a look inside. Marcus ventured into the few shops that were still standing. All the shelves had been stripped bare apart from a few small utensils, which he decided to take in case they were of any use to his hosts. When Winter returned to Granny she had an armful of clothes, some shoes, and the biggest smile.

"Oh, I know. I shouldn't but it's not really *stealin'* if they've been abandoned. It's *repurposin'*. Nobody's comin' back here so it would be such a waste to leave them behind. Besides Silvie needs some clothes she can call her own bless her."

"It's just a shame there's no food we could take too," Marcus said, as he revealed the few utensils he'd taken.

"I'll be back in a few minutes Marcus. I just need a comfort stop."

"A what?"

"A comfort stop. You know. I need to pee," Winter said, raising an eyebrow and wishing she hadn't needed to explain.

"Oh right. I get you. Yes, good idea. I'll do the same."

They wandered off in different directions to find somewhere to have some privacy and came back looking very relieved.

"We should be about an hour and a half away from the place Walter suggested, so if you're good to go ..." Winter checked her watch to see how much daylight was left.

"I'm good," he replied, as he climbed into Granny.

They headed off on the route that Walter had suggested, passing more deserted towns. Winter decided not to stop at as they didn't have sufficient time for any more diversions, though she was sorely tempted to raid a few of the empty properties for more useful items. But she figured they could always come back another time for that.

The further west they travelled the worse the roads became. At one point Granny suffered a puncture with a rear tyre, but because she had the capacity to automatically reinflate it while on the move, it didn't slow them down.

"Look!" Marcus pointed at a sign.

There was a man sitting on the side of the road under the signpost.

"Should we stop and see if he's OK?" he asked.

"I think ... we should move on, he looks kind of OK and it could mean we're close to a populated area at last," Winter replied, not feeling absolutely certain that they were doing the right thing. "If he's still there on the way back we can stop then."

Sure enough a few miles further on there were more people and a town that looked to be vaguely functioning. There were even a few vehicles there which seemed promising.

"Is it bad that I'm feeling just a bit anxious?" Marcus said, as he opened the door.

"No sugar. I'm with you on that," Winter replied. "Let's hope the locals are friendly."

Winter smiled nervously at Marcus as she opened the door and got out. She made sure that Granny was locked securely before they walked further into the town for a better look.

CHAPTER 37

yellow

"Haven't seen you round here before," an older man said, as they walked along the crumbling sidewalk.

Winter and Marcus smiled politely and kept going. There were some children playing in the street, they were grubby looking but seemed happy enough. Wherever their parents were they clearly didn't think there was a threat to their safety as nobody was supervising them, despite some being very young. The boys were only wearing shorts and vests, and their bodies were showing signs of repeated sunburn from being outdoors in the ferocious heat for prolonged periods with no protection.

Winter and Marcus exchanged looks. They didn't need words to understand how uncomfortable the sight of these children with damaged skin was making them both feel. Marcus had never seen anything like it before and he had to suppress his urge as a doctor to get involved.

"Hi there," said a middle-aged woman with a friendly face and kind hazel eyes that were framed by weather ravaged skin. "You appear lost if you don't mind me saying."

"We're actually lookin' for a friend of ours and wondered if she may have passed through here honey," Winter answered, wearing an equally friendly expression.

"We don't get many people passin' through here these days," the woman replied. "If you give me an idea of what your friend looks like I'll ask around for you. Glad to help."

"That would be wonderful, thank you," said Marcus, trying hard not to sound desperate.

Marcus and Winter gave the woman a description of Anja as the woman listened intently.

"Look I'll be honest with you. Anyone who looks like the girl you've described wouldn't last five minutes round here. Don't get me wrong, I don't think anyone would hurt her, but the men here, well they would have gone nuts over a pretty little thing like that … you know … men being men," the woman said as she spat on the ground just missing Marcus's shoes. "Damned dust gets everywhere, up your nose, down your throat."

Marcus was feeling extremely uneasy. "Men being men?"

Winter nudged him gently to keep quiet.

"I know what you mean. They can be such beasts can't they honey?" Winter added.

"Too right. And if they get a sniff of any new blood well …"

"We get the picture. You sound like you would know if anyone new came through here, so we won't take up any more of your time. But thank you honey."

Winter decided there was no point hanging around.

"I'm real sorry. I hope you find your friend," the woman said before continuing on her way.

Winter looked at Marcus whose face left nothing to the imagination. He was clearly disappointed and worried.

"This is just the first of probably many trips we are likely to have trying to find her honey, but we *will* find her I promise," said Winter, in her most reassuring voice, even though she knew she couldn't promise any such thing.

"I know Winter, it's just that I'm so worried about her. And seeing the sort of people she could be running into … the men … I mean you heard what that lady said about 'men being men' … anything could have happened to her by now."

"Oh darlin', the unknown is the worst feeling. I know it is. It plays tricks with your mind, and makes you imagine all kinds of scenarios, but Anja sounds like she's a smart girl."

"Yes, she's smart but she's also extremely vulnerable,"

Marcus sighed.

Winter was under no illusions that finding Anja was going to be a huge challenge. She was also more realistic than Marcus. She wondered how he could have imagined that he'd get his happy ending straight away and so simply. But she also knew how love could make even the most intelligent people believe that anything is possible.

They continued further west for an hour and came upon another settlement. It was smaller than the previous one and didn't look any more promising. Over time, the grime of the landscape, the dust of the winds and a burning sun had disguised individual facial features until everyone started to look the same. It was becoming clearer with every kilometre they travelled that Walter and Ling Ling were living a very privileged lifestyle compared to the masses. When they stopped at the settlement they didn't even get out of Granny, just asked passing strangers if they'd seen a girl of Anja's description pass through. Of those who took any notice, the answer was the same.

"We'll have to head back to Feronia now Marcus. If we're lucky we'll be back before it gets too dark for me to see the roads," Winter said, as she did a U-turn.

All Marcus could do was nod his head in acknowledgement. His breathing had become laboured from the bad air quality, and the lack of oxygen was making him sleepy. He reached into his bag and put on his mask. He was starting to forget what breathing clean air was like. In fact, he was beginning to forget how clinical and ordered his life used to be.

When Granny pulled into the drive at Feronia, Finch, Silvie and Ling Ling came out to welcome them home. Winter and Marcus both looked very weary and in need of refreshment, a wash, and a clean pair of clothes followed by a good night's sleep. Finch looked at Granny and screwed up his nose. All his hard work was gone in a day on the road, and she was filthy once again. He felt strangely happy to see Marcus after their brief time apart. Nobody asked whether their trip had been a success. It was plain to see from their body language.

"We'll try again tomorrow," Winter said, trying to keep up morale.

"I was wondering if perhaps I could come along too next time?" Finch asked eagerly.

"Sure." It was all Marcus could manage to say as he trudged into the house with his bag.

"Oh, I almost forgot!" Winter dumped her bag on the ground and walked back to Granny. "Look what we found," she said, proudly holding up an armful of clothes. "And there's enough here for a whole new wardrobe for you Silvie honey. Plenty in your size lil' darlin'." Winter was thrilled when she saw Silvie's face light up.

By the time everyone had carried things into the house, the half-light between day and night had started. Everyone sat down at the kitchen table and had food, while Winter and Marcus told them about what they'd seen. Harvey had decided to have his dinner in his room as he was still not feeling very well. Walter hadn't left his basement lab since early morning but emerged just as everyone was finishing their dinner.

"I do apologise for my tardy arrival Ling darling. I completely lost track of time," Walter announced.

Ling Ling had saved a plate of food for her husband and put it on the table.

"How has everyone's day been?" Walter asked in an overly cheerful voice.

Winter provided an abridged version of their day as Marcus excused himself from the table. He felt exhausted and just wanted to lie down on his bed. Having seen what life in the yellow zone was like for so many people, he felt an overwhelming sense of despair. Everything he'd believed to be real back in his pristine crystal world had been shattered. He'd begun to question all that he had been told and above all, he was consumed with sadness at the thought of never seeing Anja again.

Just as Marcus was falling asleep, Finch entered the room in a noisy fashion and woke him up.

"You OK?" Finch asked.

"Not really. It's been a difficult day," Marcus replied.

"A bit of an eye opener from what Winter said. Well, tomorrow I'm coming along too. She's out there somewhere." Finch threw himself onto his bed like a child and virtually fell asleep as he was saying 'somewhere'. Marcus closed his eyes once again and this time fell into a deep and undisturbed sleep.

The following morning, everyone was up early, including Harvey who seemed more like his old self after a few days of rest. Ling Ling was being the perfect hostess as always, serving her guests with breakfast accompanied by refreshing mugs of mint tea. Finch was eager to get going and in positive form which Winter really appreciated. She wasn't looking forward to another day of driving and was pleased to have at least one uplifting travelling companion. Marcus was very quiet and introspective, and it was obvious that he wasn't going to be in a chatty mood today.

As he watched Granny disappear into the distance Walter's tone shifted from jovial to studious.

"Harvey, would you like to join me in the den for a little professorial catchup?"

Harvey sensed that Walter had something on his mind other than polite chit chat.

"Happy to oblige."

The two elderly men left the kitchen and made their way to the den. As the door closed behind them Ling Ling knew it was no coincidence that her husband hadn't surfaced from his lab for the whole of the previous day. She also knew that if he'd found anything important he would enlighten her as well, when the time was right. In the meantime, she would find plenty of things to keep Silvie occupied and out of earshot of whatever was being discussed in the den.

Winter, Marcus, and Finch headed further north this time as Walter had pointed out a few other towns on the map that were worth investigating.

Marcus found travelling in Granny soporific and from time to time his head dropped onto his chest. Finch, on the other hand, remained alert and was both fascinated and horrified at the passing scenery. He was glad to be out doing something he felt was useful for a change. On one hand Finch felt that the sooner they were able to locate Anja, the sooner they could go back to the crystal zone and put all of this behind him. On the other he had developed feelings that he was unfamiliar with and the thought of leaving his new friends behind to continue their daily struggle made him distinctly uncomfortable. He felt particularly sad at the thought of leaving Silvie, as they had grown especially close despite his best efforts to remain detached. Finch was also finding himself questioning the wisdom of the Leader and the Advocates, as well as how content he would be going back to his old way of life. In many ways he was feeling much less of an Associate Advocate and more like the people whose company he enjoyed.

CHAPTER 38

yellow

Winter continued to navigate the difficult terrain and array of obstacles that constantly tested her driving skills. When the conversation wasn't flowing, those moments of silence left each of them alone with their thoughts. For Winter, her main concern was Harvey. He was becoming more frail each day, and after his heart scare she hated to be away from him even though she was happy to be helping Marcus and Finch. She also wondered whether they would ever find Anja and even if they did, from what she had gleaned so far, she had misgivings about them returning to their home.

The first town they came across was sprawling, so they decided to split up and ask around to cover more territory and save time. There was one very large building that looked as though it had been a theatre decades ago. The once elaborately carved façade had been worn down by age and neglect and the name over the doors was barely detectable as some of the letters were missing. Winter stood outside and stared at the building for a while. She thought it must have looked quite magnificent once. Although it was irrelevant to the task in hand, she had always loved puzzles and after a while she was convinced that it had once been called The Arcadian Theatre.

"Are you comin' in?" A man's voice broke her daze.

"What? Oh, yes if that's alright sugar?"

Winter followed the man inside. There was a large foyer that had clearly been elaborately decorated in its previous life but was now dark and threadbare. There were two staircases on either side of the foyer, but one had collapsed and the other looked as if it could come down at any time. She followed the man through a second set of doors, which lead to an enormous room that had once been filled with chairs but was now housing row upon row of camp beds. At first she thought it had been turned into a makeshift hospital, but on closer inspection she realised that it had become home to hundreds of people who had nowhere else to go.

"Do y'all live here?" Winter asked the man, trying hard not to look shocked at such a sad sight.

"Yep. See that lady with the grey wavy hair? That's my wife. My bed is the next one along. We all used to live in the next town."

"How long have y'all been here?"

"It's been about a year now. We're all that's left. The others got blown away when those mega tornadoes hit. No warning. Just boom. Flattened the place. Lost my uncle, my brother and …"

Suddenly the man broke down and put his hands over his face to hide his tears.

"I'm so sorry. I didn't mean to upset you honey." Winter put her hand on his shoulder to try and comfort him.

"I don't want my missus seeing me like this. Excuse me lady."

The man rushed back out through the door that led to the foyer to try and compose himself. It left Winter wondering whether it would be disrespectful to wander around looking to see if she could spot a young woman who might be Anja.

Everywhere she looked there were people with faces that looked haunted and traumatised like people who had survived a war. Some just lay on their beds and stared at the ceiling, but they all had one thing in common. They were all very thin and clearly undernourished. It was hard for her to imagine just how terrifying it must have been for them, and how many had lost people they loved. She walked along the rows of beds trying to be as respectful of each person's privacy as she could. Occasionally if someone made eye contact with her she asked if they'd seen a girl matching

Anja's description, but it became obvious that everyone in the theatre was from the same place for the same reason.

Finch wandered the streets questioning passers-by, but nobody had seen anyone matching Anja's description in the vicinity. Marcus headed to another part of town despite becoming resigned to hearing the answer 'no'. After an hour they all met back at Granny and Winter told them about the old theatre that had become a small settlement for what were yet more climate migrants.

Over the next few weeks, Marcus, Finch, and Winter travelled in every direction that was reachable in a day. They debated whether they should do longer trips and stay overnight, but it was decided that this posed too many possible dangers for them. On one of their trips, Finch's bracelet started flashing with an orange light.

"Why is your bracelet flashing like that? I thought we were out of tracking range," Marcus asked.

"I have no idea why it's doing that," Finch said, tapping at his bracelet and shaking his wrist to see if he could reset it. "We *are* way out of range so I can only assume it has developed some sort of fault."

"Mine isn't flashing. It's just yours Finch."

"That's because mine is different. Yours is just the basic model." Finch reminded Marcus as subtly as he could that Associates had more advanced technology than ordinary people.

"Ah yes. Of course."

"That's technology for you. It's great 'til it breaks," Winter said.

Their conversation about Finch's bracelet was abruptly cut short when Winter spotted something in the distance. A huge dust storm was on the horizon and it was heading in their direction.

"Oh, that's not good," Winter said, as she pulled Granny over to the side of the road. "Even if I turn 'round now, I'm not sure we could outrun it. It's movin' so darned fast."

The landscape was flat and barren and there was nowhere to shelter Granny from the impending impact of the storm. Winter imagined that this was how all those people in the old theatre had lost their homes and their loved ones, and although she was always so calm, she was now suddenly gripped with panic. If it gathered force and turned into a dust tornado they would be done for. Staying still and letting the storm pass over them just wasn't an option. Winter decided their only chance was in fact to turn Granny around, put her foot down and pray. Marcus and Finch strapped in tight and hoped for the best.

Winter took Granny to her maximum speed, something she'd never had to do before, and she didn't know if the old girl could take it. On top of that she now had to negotiate all the obstacles on the road at extremely high speed. The strain on Granny's structure was unmistakeable, as was the strain on Winter's face. Marcus looked behind him. The storm was getting closer and was no longer a giant wall of dust but had broken into five whirling dust tornados picking up everything in their path. Winter had seen it too and made an extraordinary manoeuvre.

"Hang on y'all!" she screamed.

She suddenly swung Granny hard right and headed down a disused old farm track at speed. Logic told her that if she couldn't outrun the tornados that were heading straight for them, she had to take evasive action that might get them out of the direct path of the storm. The obstacles on the track were smaller than those on the road, but on the downside, she had no way of knowing how long the track was or where it would lead.

One of the smaller tornados that had broken away from the main storm seemed to be following them.

"Give me a break!"

Up ahead Winter could see the track was divided into a fork. Now she had to decide which path to take and head into yet more unknown territory. A thousand thoughts went through her head in the split second that was left for Winter to make the decision whether to go left or right. She went right, and within minutes ended up running out of track but was heading towards an old brick barn. With seconds to spare Finch and Marcus jumped out of Granny and heaved open the heavy barn doors. Winter drove Granny inside and down a steep ramp that put them below ground level. Once the doors were secured, Marcus and Finch ran down the ramp, jumped back into Granny and shut the doors.

The sound of the dust tornado was terrifying as it passed within yards of the barn, and despite its smaller size it continued across the fields wreaking havoc.

Winter looked up, trying to catch her breath. "Someone was watchin' over us y'all."

"Who? Who was watching over us?" Finch asked.

"Another time Finch. I'll explain another time," Winter said, leaning both arms on Granny's steering wheel and putting her head on them.

Marcus placed his hand gently on Winter's head. "You've saved our lives Winter. Thank you doesn't seem enough. You are absolutely amazing."

They sat in Granny in the barn for around half an hour in complete silence just resting. It had been an exhausting and terrifying experience especially for Winter who needed to take a break. Marcus and Finch checked their supplies and made her eat and drink something before thinking about how to find their way back to Feronia. The light was fading and just the thought of trying to drive in the dark was where Winter decided to draw the line.

"I know it's not ideal but we're gonna have stay in here for the night y'all," she said.

"Whatever you decide is absolutely fine with us, isn't that right Finch?" Marcus said reassuringly.

He had never felt so grateful in all his life and was now completely in awe of Winter.

"Oh yes, definitely," Finch replied.

It was going to be a long night, but Granny's seats all reclined sufficiently for sleeping and they had packed just enough food to see them through until the next day. Winter was exhausted and fell asleep straight away. Marcus was also tired, but his mind was active, and he had a restless night as did Finch. They were like naughty schoolboys giggling whenever Winter snored so hard that she woke herself up for a moment.

When first light came, all three were eager to get going although none knew exactly how they were going to find their way back.

"I need to try and remember which directions I turned to avoid the storm and then reverse them which I'm hopin' will bring us back to the road we were originally on," said Winter, in a serious tone.

Finch and Marcus got out and opened the large barn doors so that Winter could drive Granny out. But Granny had other ideas. She was clogged up with dust from the storm and had been without sunlight for too long. Her batteries were now flat. There was no way the three of them could push her up the steep ramp and out into daylight to recharge.

"What the hell are we gonna do?" Winter cried out.

Finch thought about it for a moment and then decided there was only one course of action that would get Granny exposed to daylight again. With his bare hands he started pulling at the metal roof of the barn. Marcus came over and started to help him and Winter did what she could to assist.

"You're a genius Finch," she said, clapping her hands together.

Finch pulled at the burning hot metal panels. "It's going to take a while to get this roof off, but it's the only chance we've got."

Winter ripped pieces of fabric from her dress for the men to wrap around their hands. She didn't have enough strength to physically help them but she made sure they stayed hydrated and fed as they toiled. It took six hours for them to remove all the panels by which time it was about to get dark again, which meant spending another night in Granny.

"Do you want the bad news?" Winter asked..

"Go on," Marcus replied.

"I'm afraid we've run out of food and water."

Both men nodded and all Winter could do was shrug her shoulders. Food they could manage without for a couple of days, but in the extreme heat, becoming dehydrated was a serious problem.

"I'm so sorry, this is all my fault. I was so worried about you workin' in the bakin' heat to get the roof panels off …"

"Winter, please. This is nobody's fault. It's just the way things are."

Before darkness fell, Finch walked back up the ramp to survey the route out of there once Granny had recharged in the morning. It was a process that was going to take longer than usual as the sky was obliterated by clouds of brown dust that now hung over the land. The air was perfectly still which made it feel as though they were enveloped in hard, dry, choking heat. As he looked around it was then that he understood the extent of the devastation the dust tornados had left behind. Nothing looked the same and there was debris everywhere. Guesswork was only going to take them so far, and it was going to be slow going as the men would have to move debris out of the way all along what was left of the dirt track.

They spent another uncomfortable and restless night in Granny, and this time nobody had the energy to make conversation. When the darkness gave way to light the next morning, Winter was the first to stir. She was in desperate need of relieving herself so she made her way up the ramp and crouched down behind the dead stump of a tree. When she was done she stood up, looked around and her heart sank. She didn't know how they were going to get out of there and find their way back to Feronia.

Finch was next to stir. He also needed to pee but decided that as Winter must have gone up to ground level he could get away with going in the corner of the barn. He then walked up the ramp to join Winter.

"It's lookin' pretty hopeless isn't it." Winter screwed up her face as the words came tumbling out. "We're gonna die out here."

"Well if we're going to die, it won't be without a fight." Finch gritted his teeth and started shifting some of the larger pieces of debris that were blocking the track.

A weary looking Marcus made his way up to ground level and started helping Finch.

"How long do you think it will take for Granny's batteries to charge?" Marcus asked.

"A couple of hours? I honestly don't know given how little light is coming through those thick dust clouds, and I need to open her up and get some of the dust off her parts."

"OK, then we'll just have to keep clearing the track in the meantime. There's no point sitting around feeling sorry for ourselves."

Finch and Marcus put on their breathing masks while they slowly cleared debris along the first part of the track for the next four hours.

"Sorry but I can't go on," Marcus said, collapsing on the side of the track breathless and with sweat pouring from his head. "I'm starting to think that Winter may be right and we are going to die out here." He closed his eyes in sadness.

It was indeed likely that they would never find their way back and end up perishing in the middle of nowhere. Finch helped Marcus walk slowly back to where Winter was sitting next to Granny. She had been so steadfast and in control but couldn't hold back her emotions any longer. She started weeping until gentle tears turned to heaving sobs.

"You're wasting water!" Marcus shouted at her.

Winter looked up at him. It was such a bizarre thing to say at such a grim moment, but it was exactly what she had needed. Her crying quickly turned to fits of laughter. But her laughter was short lived as another day passed and Granny still wouldn't start.

They had all been without food or water for two days and had become severely dehydrated and were too weak to carry on. Without uttering the words, each of them had become resigned to dying out there in the middle of nowhere. They were barely conscious by nightfall when a strange buzzing noise made Finch stir.

Finch raised his head. "Can you hear that?"

"I can't hear anything," Marcus replied dismissively. "It's your imagination playing tricks with you.

"There! There it is again!" Finch insisted becoming more animated. "Surely you can hear it."

They all remained silent for a few moments before the buzzing sound could be heard by all of them.

"Yes, I hear it now! What do y'all think it is Finch?" Winter got out of Granny and stood on the running board, as if being higher off the ground would make it easier to hear.

What had begun as a feint buzzing sound got louder as it grew close enough for them to see that it was a drone. It eventually landed on Granny's roof.

"You're in a bit of a pickle I see."

"Walter! Is that you?" Winter screamed in delight at hearing a familiar voice.

The drone released a medium sized container. Winter opened it and found water and food. A screen then unfolded from the drone, and there was Walter, Ling Ling, Harvey and Silvie all staring at them waving and smiling.

A hugely relieved Marcus stared at the screen. "However did you find us?"

"It was Ling's idea. She'd put a tracking device in Granny just in case of emergencies. You know in case you got lost," Walter replied.

"Are you all OK?" Ling Ling enquired. "We were so worried when you didn't return on time. We were fearing the worst, and then we were struck by a dust tornado, so this is the first opportunity we've had to safely fly the drone."

Winter was trying to hold back happy tears. "Well it's been tough to say the least. We ran out of water and food and to be honest with y'all, I think we were gettin' ready to meet our maker. It feels like a miracle has happened, we thought we'd never make it home again."

"How lovely that you consider Feronia *home* Winter. That makes us incredibly happy. Now as much as it's delightful to converse with you, the light has gone for today so I'm afraid you'll have to spend another night there, but you'll need that time to replenish yourselves. Then tomorrow you can follow our drone and we'll get you back safe and sound and in time for dinner," Walter said, as the screen returned to its compartment and the drone went into sleep mode to conserve energy while they ate and drank.

Winter hoped that Granny would start in the morning. She knew that it would still be a slow journey back through all the debris, but at least they now had some sustenance and were going to be guided home thanks to Ling Ling.

"I've never been more grateful to have water than I am right now," Finch said, guzzling back one of the containers that held the life-giving liquid. "You're very quiet Jarret, are you OK?"

"I feel responsible for nearly killing us all," Marcus said, between gulping down water.

"I've said it before and I'll say it again, it's not your fault it's Anja's. She's the reason we're here."

"Now shoosh y'all. This is no time to be squabbling. Let's all just eat, drink, and get some rest. Tomorrow we're hopefully goin' home."

Finch's ears pricked up. "Hopefully?"

"It's all up to Granny now honey," Winter said, crossing her fingers.

Relieved to have had food and water in their bellies they settled down for what they hoped would be their last night in the middle of nowhere.

By the following morning the orange dust clouds had parted and the usual overcast sky had returned. Winter crossed her fingers once again and hoped that this time Granny would start.

"Please God, let her start this time," she whispered as she switched Granny on.

To everyone's relief she started and their long, slow journey back to Feronia could begin. Marcus and Finch were astounded at how much needed to be cleared along the path, and then on the road that would lead them home. There were roof tiles, doors, pieces of broken glass, and even a couple of burnt out cars that had been swept up in the storm and dumped in the middle of the road. The drone hovered above them as they cleared the road ahead, jumping in and out of Granny along the way. It took them six hours of hard labour to make it back to the long winding driveway of Feronia. But their relief to finally be home was short lived.

Finch and Marcus were greeted by a sight that led to a combined sharp intake of breath.

"Oh no! This isn't good," Marcus said in a panic.

"Just keep quiet and let me do the talking Jarret."

There, parked outside the large front door of the house, was a hoverbike. It was the same model of bike Finch and Marcus had hidden in Harvey's outbuilding and the pookies had stolen. There were only two places that the bike could have come from, the crystal zone, or from an Associate Advocate who was posted to the yellow zone. In either case it did not bode well.

Winter parked Granny in her usual place. All three got out just as Walter opened the large front door and walked briskly and breathlessly over to greet them.

"Welcome home. It's wonderful to see that you're all in one piece. As you can see we've had a little surprise earlier today Finch," Walter said, pointing to the bike and attempting to stay calm.

Marcus looked at Finch whose wide eyed expression told him everything he needed to know. His worst fears were confirmed a few seconds later. A muscular young man with piercing blue eyes and blonde hair strode out of the house and stood beside Walter. The young man was exceptionally handsome and of a similar build to Finch. There was no mistaking him for anything other than a Gen1.

"This is Brock. He says he's an Associate Advocate and he's come to take you home."

CHAPTER 39

yellow

Finch instantly noticed that Brock's bracelet was glowing orange. He looked at his own and discovered that it was no longer flashing but glowing just like Brock's.

"Allow me." Brock grew closer to Finch and reached out his arm until their bracelets touched, which triggered a reset and their lights went out.

"I don't understand," said Finch, looking at his wrist.

"Neither did I, but when my bracelet started to flash and then glow recently I contacted my Advocate and he explained that when we're in the proximity of another Associate, or another Gen1, our bracelets glow orange. A particularly useful function don't you think Finch?" Brock smiled with his mouth, but his eyes were stone cold.

"I'm sure we've all got a lot to talk about so let's get you inside so that you can freshen up and then we'll have dinner," said Walter, in an attempt to break what was an obvious tension. "And Brock has a little surprise for you both".

Brock interjected before Walter could say any more. "It can wait."

Without any further discussion they all went inside, with Finch and Marcus quickly excusing themselves to have a wash and change of clothes. They rushed upstairs to their room and shut the door.

"What's going on?" Marcus asked Finch.

"It's not good. It's really not good," Finch replied.

Ling Ling had left them bowls of water to wash with, and in an attempt to delay what seemed inevitable, both men took their time to clean the dirt off their faces and bodies and change into clean clothes.

"What are we going to do?" Marcus whispered.

"Try and stay calm. Let's hear what he has to say and then we can explain things from our perspective. I'm sure he'll be reasonable."

"Really? You think he'll be *reasonable*? You heard what Walter said. He's come to take us back!"

They heard Ling Ling shout '*dinner*' and knew they couldn't put off going downstairs any longer.

When they entered the kitchen everyone was sitting around the table in silence, and nobody was smiling. Ling Ling put food on the table for everyone to help themselves. As she lay the bowls on the table Marcus noticed that her hands were shaking.

"That's kind of you but I've brought my own food thank you," Brock said, reaching into his bag and pulling out a container of the food Finch and Marcus were familiar with.

"You come far?" Silvie enquired.

"Not too far. I'm posted 120 miles north of here which is how I located my colleague Finch," Brock said, before looking at Finch. "You must not have realised that you ventured into my region. It had never happened before so that's why I had to check in with my Advocate. And that's when I received instructions to bring you home. Immediately."

Marcus was becoming agitated. "But we can't go back yet. We're here for a good reason."

Brock stood up and walked out of the kitchen before returning a few moments later.

"I believe this is what you've been looking for," Brock said, holding an outstretched hand and dragging a dishevelled person into the room.

Everyone turned towards Brock.

"Anja!" Marcus shouted getting up from the table.

Anja withdrew her hand from Brock's tight grip and hurried across the kitchen to Marcus. They fell into each other's arms.

"Ahhh what a lovely moment," said Brock without emotion. "Lovers reunited at last. And as you can see, Anja is greatly changed since you last saw her Marcus."

It was true. Anja's appearance had changed, but it wasn't the grime of the yellow zone's environment, nor her unkempt look that had altered her appearance. It was obvious to everyone in the room that Anja was pregnant. She was only a few months along, but she was definitely starting to show.

"They arrived this morning," said Ling Ling passing one of the bowls of food to Harvey who politely declined having lost his appetite.

"I'm so sorry Marcus," Anja whispered into Marcus's ear. "I'm so very sorry."

"It's OK. It's all OK now. I was so worried about you."

"I suggest after dinner that everyone gets a good night's sleep as we'll be leaving at first light in the morning. It's vital that we get back as soon as possible given the girl's condition," Brock said, in a commanding voice. "There are rules, and they must be followed." His tone was cool and dispassionate.

Marcus suddenly felt very ill. He realised what Brock meant by rules. The condition that he had agreed to in order to have a relationship with Anja was that no pregnancy resulting from their union would be allowed to survive. He wondered if Anja had known that too, and it was the reason she'd run away.

At the time Marcus would probably have agreed to anything if it meant they could be together, but now the cold, hard reality of the situation was an impossible ask. He looked at Finch and wondered if he also knew about the agreement, he was after all still an Associate. Suddenly he felt trapped between two worlds. Just the thought of them destroying the life that was growing inside Anja made him sick to his stomach. He had never been in a situation where the termination of a potential life had bothered him before. Every month thousands of women in the crystal zone were required to have any living cells that could become a pregnancy evacuated from their wombs. Some of these cells would go on to become genetically enhanced foetuses and others would be eliminated. Now everything was different. This was their baby, not just a collection of cells that had the potential to become a human being. He looked at Anja who hadn't taken her eyes off him from the moment she was brought into the kitchen. He knew that their love was genuine and powerful and that nobody's rules, be they the Advocates or even the Leader's, were going to destroy something that was the most special part of both of them. It was unthinkable.

"Before you retire for the night I would appreciate a word please Finch. Shall we step outside?"

Finch's eyes met Silvie's as he obediently followed Brock outside. It was clear that Finch was out of his depth and his expression appeared apologetic as he left. She excused herself from the table and left the kitchen, but she wasn't going to her room. Instead Silvie used a side exit to go outside and, having become an expert in stealth in her previous life, positioned herself where the two men couldn't see her but where she could hear every word.

While Finch and Brock were outside Ling Ling busied herself taking basins of water upstairs to all the bedrooms. Although not one of their better bedrooms she had made it as comfortable as possible for Anja when she arrived. It was the only one left with a double bed which is why she hadn't given it to Finch and Marcus, but it had seemed appropriate to prepare it for Anja thinking that she and Marcus might be glad to have some privacy. Anja's room was the first that Ling Ling brought a water basin for. The room was at the front of the house on the first floor, and although she wasn't eavesdropping, it was impossible not to hear what Brock was talking to Finch about. From the moment he'd arrived with Anja in tow, Ling Ling had taken an instant dislike to Brock. She felt no pangs of guilt in having given him one of their worst bedrooms, which was situated along a bleak back corridor. The room was dusty, cramped, uncomfortable and as far away from everyone else as she could make it.

Harvey excused himself and retired to the den. The events of the day had been quite stressful for him, and he was very tired, but with the den on the ground floor and also at the front of the house, he wasn't too tired to hear what was going on outside.

Winter remained in the kitchen and had started to clear away the bowls and dishes while Ling Ling was attending to the water basins. Although the kitchen was towards the rear of the house, she could make out parts of the exterior conversation and it wasn't hard for her to get the gist of things. She knew that Silvie would fill her in on any details she'd missed.

Walter was pacing around in the sitting room, which was in darkness so that he could peer out and watch the two men who appeared extremely animated as they spoke. Although Walter's hearing wasn't as sharp as it once was, he didn't need to hear every word to understand that the conversation wasn't pleasant and was growing more heated by the minute.

CHAPTER 40

yellow

"Why the rush Brock?"

"Are you questioning my orders Finch? You should know better."

"I'm not questioning your orders, but I just don't understand why you're in such a hurry to get us back to the crystal zone."

"Look I've been posted here in this yellow hell hole for nearly three years now. You've been here for what, a few weeks? So yes, I can't wait to get back to clean, cool air just for starters."

"I get that. I really do Brock, but we're exhausted from all the travelling we've been doing trying to find Anja."

"Not my problem Associate. I have my orders. The girl's situation is a *problem* and one that needs to be dealt with swiftly."

"Dealt with?"

"Yes. You know. *Dealt* with. A cross between a PreGen and a Gen1 for goodness sake. We can't have a hybrid monster running around. But there are other reasons that make it imperative for us to leave here as quickly as possible. I'm not at liberty to tell you exactly what they are but suffice it to say that with the extinction of human life in the red zone completed as an act of compassion by the Leader, I have it on good authority that areas of the yellow zone won't be far behind. So the Advocates insist that Doctor Jarret and Anja Kandinsky are returned to the crystal zone without any further delay."

Finch couldn't hide his shock as he listened to Brock's description of how the army of drones that had been sent to the red zone with their deadly cargo was an act of 'compassion' by the Leader. What Brock described as compassion felt more like mass murder to Finch.

Immediately his thoughts turned to Silvie. She had told him about the noise of thunder that was overhead when she was hiding in the waste truck. It meant she must have been moments away from certain death. And then he thought of Anja and her baby and the look on Marcus's face when he saw her again. He knew that he had to try and get more information out of Brock without raising any suspicions about his allegiance.

"I imagine you've only now been told about the plans for the yellow zone, after all, only a privileged few will have been told about those," Finch said, goading Brock.

"I knew a few weeks ago. In fact right now the entirety of red zone land is being ploughed and the human remains are being dug into the ground to act as fertiliser. In time with the planet rid of the pestilence of excess human population, it may heal, and future generations of our more advanced people will repopulate the earth in more modest numbers,"

Finch was speechless. For whatever reason, he hadn't been made fully aware of what was to take place before he left with Marcus. He thought that perhaps it was because he had been away when the briefing took place. Or maybe he was deliberately kept in the dark because of his mission? All he could think about was how Silvie could have been one of those poor people. He could feel a rage growing inside him.

"Just be ready at first light. We'll need to commandeer that decrepit vehicle to get us all to the port," Brock barked, pointing to Granny..

"We'll leave when we're ready to leave. Not when you *tell* us to. And as for that *decrepit* vehicle, she belongs to Winter so you will have to ask her permission."

"You don't seem to understand Finch. It isn't up to you or me to decide. Failure to obey instructions will bring harsh penalties for both of us from the Advocates on behalf of the Leader, and

I'm not about to let that happen when I'm so close to being advanced to full Advocate status. I will be leaving in the morning with Doctor Jarret and the girl, with or *without* you." Brock's face was uncomfortably close as he issued his ultimatum.

He then took a step back, smiled menacingly at Finch, turned on his heel and strode confidently back into the house.

Oblivious to the number of eyes and ears that had taken in their revealing discussion, Finch took a few moments to compose himself before going back inside too. It seemed that everyone had gone to their rooms as the main part of the house was now dark and empty. Finch walked slowly up the staircase. He dreaded going to his room and seeing Marcus, but he didn't know what else to do. When he walked into their bedroom Marcus was picking up a few of his things and looked like he was about to leave. He was clearly in a cheerful mood.

"Where are you going?" Finch asked.

"Where do you think? Anja and I have a great deal to talk about," Marcus replied, giving Finch a little wink. "See you in the morning."

"Oh, yes of course." Finch barely managed to get the words out.

Marcus walked quietly down the hall to Anja's bedroom. His heart was pounding in his chest as he tapped on her door and waited for her to say, 'come in'. Even if she didn't want him to spend the night with her, there was a lot for them to talk about especially the burning question of why she fled the crystal zone in the first place.

"Oh Marcus. I'm so sorry. I've caused you a terrible problem haven't I?" Anja's voice was soft and sorrowful as she walked over and put her arms around him. "I promise you it was the last thing I wanted to do," she whispered.

"All that matters is that we're together. I wasn't going to stop searching for you however long it took," said Marcus, holding her tightly.

Anja gently released herself from his arms and propped up the pillows at the head of the bed. She climbed onto the bed and sat cross legged with her back supported by the pillows. Marcus sat on the end of the bed his eyes drawn to her belly.

"I know you must be tired but I'm so desperate to understand why you left. I tried contacting you for weeks and heard nothing back and then, when you missed your monthly appointment, I knew that there must be something seriously wrong."

"I didn't know what else to do. I will explain everything Marcus, and I just hope you can understand and find it in your heart to forgive me."

"I doubt there is anything that you need to be forgiven for Anja."

"OK, so well, you know how we can find out if we're likely to become pregnant twelve hours after we've coupled, and then another twenty four hours after that we also know if it would be male or female?"

Marcus nodded.

"So, when it comes time to go to the clinic we usually already know if we're going to need the procedure. Not everyone bothers to find out beforehand, but many do. Anyway, after our night together I discovered the following day what our union had created."

"Why didn't you tell me? I would have understood," Marcus said gently.

"How could I tell you Marcus? How could I put you in such an impossible situation four weeks later in your clinic?"

"So you wanted to protect me?"

"Of course, and I wanted to protect our baby. But that's not the only reason. You see all I've ever known, even as a small child, is a constant barrage of tests. Tests for this, tests for that, sample after sample, people measuring this or sticking needles in me for something else and question after question. It's relentless. I'm sure as clinicians you must all think that we are OK about it, but I can tell you that a lot of us really aren't. We hate it. We feel used, like we're nothing more than test subjects, however kind you are to us."

"I honestly had no idea Anja, I'm so sorry." Marcus was taken aback by Anja's revelations.

"Some of the women I've spoken to feel that their lives are

meaningless, and I even know of one poor girl who ended her life because she couldn't take it anymore. Naturally that incident was covered up by the Advocates."

Marcus's eyes widened, shocked at what he was hearing.

"This is horrifying. I don't know what to say."

"I promise you it is *all* true. We are compliant because we don't know how to be anything else. It's not as if we have anyone we can go to and talk about all these things. There's no one championing our wellbeing as individuals and, to be frank, we are simply too afraid to refuse what is expected of us."

"How could I not have realised that I've been an accomplice to so much suffering?" Marcus felt his eyes sting from tears that were welling.

"Stop Marcus please. I don't blame you. I could *never* blame you. I know that you're a good man, and a kind man and that we are very adept at hiding our true feelings from the clinical staff simply because we've had to be. But when I knew that I was having a child I just couldn't let this happen to her."

"A girl?" Marcus looked at Anja and a wave of warmth swept over him. "Yes, of course you wouldn't want her to go through what you have. I completely understand. But fleeing to the outside world was such a dangerous choice to make Anja."

"All I can tell you is that a feeling of complete desperation swept over me, and I panicked. I had to run. It was the easiest decision I've ever had to make, but also the hardest because it meant leaving you forever Marcus. I had no idea that you would come here to look for me."

Marcus realised that Anja didn't know the whole truth. In a way he was relieved she didn't know that if Brock was successful in taking them back to the crystal zone, their baby would be destroyed. For a moment he wondered whether they should try and run before morning, but there was nowhere for them to run to. He lay on the bed next to Anja and as she drifted off to sleep he wrapped his arms around her. She felt safe at last, but Marcus was wide awake. He knew that she and their baby were in mortal danger if Brock had his way in the morning.

Finch couldn't sleep either. He was counting the hours, each one bringing first light closer. What he'd learned from Brock had shaken him to his core. It was both chilling and disturbing and he knew it was very wrong. Everyone was asleep, and he had nobody to confide in; nobody to help him find a way to change what now seemed inevitable. As he lay there lost in his own thoughts he imagined for a moment that he could hear crying. It was just small whimpers and sniffs, but when he heard it a second time it was enough to get him out of bed in search of who was upset. The sounds were coming from Silvie's room so Finch tapped lightly on her door hoping he wouldn't wake the others. Silvie came to the door her face wet with tears.

"What's wrong Silvie? Why are you crying?" Finch said in a whisper, as Silvie took his arm and led him inside her room.

"I sad."

"Because we're leaving in the morning?" Finch asked, thinking that was the only logical explanation.

"The world sad," Silvie sobbed. "So much death. I scared for ya. Afraid for ya, and Marcus, and Anja, and baby."

"I don't want to leave you Silvie. I *really* don't want to go but I have no choice. Brock has made that very clear."

"I care for ya. I come too?" Silvie stopped crying for a moment hoping for a positive response.

"Oh Silvie, you can't come with us. I'm so sorry but they wouldn't let you in."

"Ya live in special place only special people go?" Silvie asked intrigued. "People like ya?"

"Yes, in a way. Although I don't think I'm special Silvie. I'm just different. We're different."

"I wish Brock die!" Silvie raised her voice with emotion.

"Shhhh! He'll hear you."

"I no care. Don't like, no trust him."

"Try and get some sleep Silvie. At least I will know that you're going to be safe here when I'm gone. You're with good people now." Finch kissed her lightly on her forehead and closed the door behind him. But he knew that she wasn't going to be safe, none of them were. Not now that Brock had told him that areas of the yellow zone were in danger of being destroyed now too.

Silvie, Finch and Marcus weren't the only ones still awake. Walter and Ling Ling were in bed and in deep discussion about what they'd both overheard between Finch and Brock.

"How can we possibly let our friends go back to that wretched place Walter? There must be something we can do. However bad I thought things were in the other place, what I've heard tonight is …"

"Yes I know my darling. And I know that somehow we must act but I can't think about it anymore tonight. My brain is terribly addled but my old body is exhausted and needs its sleep."

"I know you'll think of something Walter darling." Ling Ling held Walter's hand as he fell asleep quickly just as he always did, comforted by her touch.

Just before the dawn light broke, someone was already wide awake and outside. It was Brock, checking out Granny to make sure the vehicle could accommodate four passengers and still have room for his bike. He wasn't interested in sitting around a table having breakfast chit chat and the inevitable tearful goodbyes as they left, so he decided to have a little wander down the track, eating his own food as he walked.

As the light started coming through the windows of the house, everyone began stirring. Some were getting dressed while others were packing up their few belongings for the journey ahead. Eventually they all headed downstairs to the kitchen for one last breakfast together.

As they sat around the table, the mood was sombre. Nobody had expected Brock to join them, and they were all glad that he had left them in peace. It would be another hour before anyone realised that Brock was missing.

CHAPTER 41

yellow

"He said he wanted us to be ready at first light, so where is he?" Marcus asked.

Everyone had finished their breakfast and those who were destined to leave had packed ready for a journey that none of them wanted to take, given Anja's circumstances.

"His bike's still here, so he can't have gone far," said Finch.

Ling Ling remarked that there were still a few things belonging to him in his bedroom. "I noticed them when I went to collect his basin of water this morning."

Silvie and Winter checked each room in the house while Marcus and Finch looked around outside, but there was no sign of Brock anywhere.

Regrouping in the kitchen Walter raised a vague possibility that if he'd wandered too far he may have fallen down one of the deep wells that were scattered across the vast acreage that belonged to the house. There had also been a mining community in the area a century ago and not all of the mineshafts had been filled in or secured, so there were numerous dangers if you didn't know the area.

"What about your bracelet Finch? Could you locate him that way?" Marcus asked.

"I've already tried that. I'm getting no signal from his bracelet but there could be a variety of reasons for that. I know it was still working yesterday when the reset happened but I'm getting nothing now.

"Perhaps we should head off in pairs to see if he's fallen and injured himself. I suggest pairs because it means that if we find him, one can stay with him while the other comes back here and gets help. Walter I think you should stay here with Harvey darling, you're not as steady on your feet and we need someone to remain here just in case he turns up," Ling Ling said to her husband affectionately.

As Ling Ling suggested, the group split up into pairs and headed off in different directions. Marcus and Anja were happy to set off together, relishing every moment they had being alone in each other's company. Silvie and Winter headed down the long winding track that led from the property to the road, while Ling Ling and Finch paired up and walked slowly across an adjacent field. It was agreed that they would all meet back at the house after a maximum of two hours.

Once out of earshot of the others, Anja stopped for a moment and took Marcus's hand.

"What do you think will happen to me when we get back? The Advocates will be angry with me, won't they?"

Marcus turned to face her. He couldn't lie to her and pretend that everything was going to be alright. She deserved to know the truth and however hard it was going to be for her to hear, it was going to be equally hard for Marcus to say the words out loud about what the fate of their baby would be. He sat her down and knelt beside her. Holding her hands he explained exactly what would happen when they returned home.

"They will *kill* our baby, is that what you're saying?" Anja's eyes filled with fear and horror. "And you would just let that happen?"

"I would do anything to protect you both. Anything. But I don't know how. I feel powerless."

Anja knew that Marcus was telling her the truth.

"Is there really nothing that we can do? Please Marcus think. There must be something!" Anja's voice was breaking as hot angry tears streamed down her face.

Marcus was silent for a while. He tried to comfort her, but he knew she was right. It was unthinkable to allow their child to be killed. He wasn't sure if they would go to even greater lengths to punish her, possibly wanting to make an example of Anja so that none of the other women would ever contemplate running.

On the other side of the property, Ling Ling and Finch were combing the area carefully. She had never crossed that particular field before so was apprehensive of any hidden obstacles beneath her feet.

"Finch, what happens if we don't find Brock?" Ling Ling asked casually.

"I honestly don't know."

"I mean, do you think they would send someone *else* here to look for him; another of your colleagues?"

"I think that would be unlikely. There's a finite number of Associates spread across the world and each one is designated an exceptionally large region to monitor. Plus we're all being called back according to Brock," Finch said, but then worried that he'd been careless and shared too much information.

"Why are you being called back?"

"I'm sure they have their reasons." Finch knew that he couldn't share the one thing that would cause Ling Ling and the others to panic which were the plans to cull populations within the yellow zone. "Let's just focus on finding Brock."

"Yes, of course. I'm sorry to pry it's just that I'm so concerned about you and Marcus and of course Anja. I just thought that if we didn't find Brock, for whatever reason, it would take the pressure off going back so soon."

Finch hated not telling Ling Ling the truth. She had been such a gracious and generous host to them, and he had become very fond of her and Walter. He was also deeply concerned about Anja's welfare when they returned home to the crystal zone. He had never seen a woman who was pregnant before because all the babies in the crystal zone were grown in an artificial environment. Seeing her slightly swollen belly and knowing that there was a human growing inside her had provoked a strange new feeling in him. It was a warm and pleasant sensation that he seemed to have no control over, and his instinct to protect Anja was quite overwhelming. He found himself hoping that Brock would never return.

Winter and Silvie wandered along the winding track in silence. Silvie kept biting her lip and she could see Winter's jaw flexing as she ground her teeth while they walked. It was getting close to the middle of the day when the heat was at its highest and despite holding umbrellas over their heads for shade, it made the going tough. At one-point Silvie fell to her knees and broke down. Winter knelt down beside her and helped her back up. She held Silvie's hand all the way back to the house.

Walter and Harvey waited patiently and welcomed each pair back as they returned after the agreed time. Nobody had seen any sign of Brock and they were all exhausted from the physical exertion of being out in the midday heat.

"What do we do now?" Anja asked as they all sat around the large kitchen table taking sips of water.

"We wait," Finch said. "If he hasn't returned by tonight, we'll have to extend our search further, perhaps with Granny tomorrow."

"If I can make a suggestion, would it be wise to store his bike somewhere out of sight, just in case?" Walter began, before being interrupted by Marcus.

"Do you think it might be stolen by pookies?"

Walter laughed. "Heavens no. The pookies don't come this far, they like to stay by the coast. No, I was just thinking it would be wise to keep it safe for Brock."

"I'll do that now Walter. Jarret could you give me a hand?" Finch said in agreement.

Finch and Marcus excused themselves from the table and went outside to find a suitable place to store Brock's bike.

"This is so odd, don't you think? I mean the guy turns up, lays down the law and then vanishes. It's weird," Marcus said, as he lifted the back of the bike.

"Yes. It's very strange. He didn't strike me as the kind who would fail to follow through with his orders or let anything get in the way of executing them," Finch replied, lifting the front end of the machine.

Once they'd stored the bike safely out of sight they re-joined the others who were still in the kitchen. Nobody seemed to know what to do with themselves other than watch the clock and wait anxiously for Brock to return.

"Is it wrong that I hope he's gone forever?" Anja said tentatively.

"Not at all. I'll admit to feeling the same way and that's really bad because he's a fellow Associate."

Walter tried to reassure him. "Don't be so hard on yourself Finch, you're nothing like Brock. I'm not a member of his fan club either. He's a very unpleasant young man."

Ling Ling laughed at the thought of Brock having a 'fan club' although the concept went completely over the heads of everyone other than her husband, Harvey, and Winter, the others having never heard the expression before.

Day became night and there was still no sign of Brock as they all turned in for bed. For some it felt like the calm before the storm. For others it was a small glimmer of hope that they wouldn't be facing an immediate journey back to the crystal zone. But for Finch it was a huge dilemma. Even if Brock didn't return, it seemed they were up against the clock in terms of the future survival of the yellow zone and its inhabitants. He was glad to now have the bedroom to himself because he knew that he was heading for another very restless night.

When morning came and Brock still hadn't appeared the mood in the house grew more serious. It was clear that something terrible must have happened to him and that they would all be faced with another day of searching. Walter decided that this time he would also employ his drone to help cover more territory, especially as he wasn't physically up to the challenge. He enjoyed being in command of the drone. It made him feel useful and it also meant that he could reach areas that were too difficult on foot.

Granny was also deployed with Winter taking Silvie, Marcus and Anja deeper into the landscape. Finch and Ling Ling stayed closer to home this time, meticulously checking disused sheds that were on abandoned neighbouring properties.

After a couple of hours, the search teams returned to the house, none having located their missing visitor. Once again they sat around the kitchen table with refreshments, discussing what to do next when suddenly Walter walked into the room looking grim-faced.

He did his utmost to sound sombre. "As you know I used my drone today thinking it would be an efficient way to cover a wider area. I have located Brock. Or rather I have located his body."

"He's dead?" Finch asked looking alarmed.

"Yes," Walter replied.

Winter was looking flustered by the news. "Were y'all able to see how he died Walter?"

"No, not really. I can only assume."

"So what happens now? Do we recover his body and bury him?" Marcus asked.

"That won't be possible. Or necessary. The area is too difficult to reach on foot and he is at the bottom of a very deep well, which I fear may be the cause. There are quite a few out there and they are heavily camouflaged, so it would have been easy to tumble down one. I have to assume that the fall is what killed him." Walter looked at Winter as she had asked the original question.

"Are you sure he is dead and not just unconscious?" Finch asked.

"Quite sure."

"What about his bracelet Finch, could anyone find him through that?" Winter asked.

"Once you die, the bracelet ceases to function. The only reason he came here in the first place was because I had entered the territory he was assigned to, and now that all the Associates have been told to ..." Finch stopped abruptly before he said too much.

"All the Associates have been told to *what*, Finch? What were you going to say?" asked Walter.

"It doesn't matter."

"I think we've all had a shock today Finch. I'm at a loss as to what to say and I don't know what we should do for the best now. Do you?" Marcus asked.

"Let me think about it and perhaps we can discuss things later today and make a plan," Finch said, clearly shaken up. "I'm going for a walk."

"I come?" Silvie asked sweetly.

"Thank you, but I think I'd rather be alone just now Silvie. I'll see you later," Finch replied already heading out of the kitchen.

Marcus had never seen Finch so shaken up before. His gut told him that there was more to his agitated state than just the demise of his fellow Associate, a man who until two days ago he had never met before.

With Finch out clearing his head, Marcus's thoughts turned to Anja. With Brock out of the way it seemed the immediate threat had passed for her. But the bigger picture was much more complex. How could he possibly return with Anja to the crystal zone knowing that the moment they arrived, she would be taken away and their baby would be destroyed. He knew that if he let that happen there would be no future for them. It was at that very moment that he also knew he would lay down his life to protect her and their unborn child. He held Anja's hand tightly and closed his eyes in thought.

Walter hated lying. It went against all of his principles. On this occasion however, he knew that no good would have come from him revealing the truth about what his drone had found. Brock's death was no accident and he was more than happy to keep quiet about it. In manipulating his drone to drag Brock's dead body to a nearby well and letting it slip thirty feet to the bottom, Walter knew that he had become an accessory to a murder. He also knew that it wouldn't keep him awake at night.

A few days later Ling Ling was in her garden tending her vegetable patch when Winter came out carrying a small bag with her. She recognised it immediately as the bag she had given Winter on their first outing in Granny with Marcus. And she remembered that little extra something she'd placed in the bag in case of emergency.

"As we won't be going out searching for Anja any more I wanted to return this to you. I have no need of it now." Winter smiled knowingly as she passed the small bag over.

"Thank you Winter," Ling Ling said, taking Winter's hand in hers. "Thank you so much."

It was a very brief exchange between the two women and yet it said so much. Walter and Ling Ling had no secrets between them, and he had told her exactly what the drone had discovered that day. She knew what had killed Brock and it was now in a bag in the palm of her hand. Ling Ling's small antique pistol had one bullet missing from its chamber. Winter had done what needed to be done. This unassuming, easy-going woman had become a lioness protecting her family from an enemy that would have torn it apart.

CHAPTER 42

observation 1:7

While humankind can be blamed for the majority of what has gone wrong on our planet there are some things that have been outside our control.

When the Earth scored a huge direct hit from a G5 coronal mass ejection in 2068 it plunged vast areas of the planet into darkness by disrupting power grids and knocking out satellites. This geomagnetic storm sent large clouds of solar plasma into space buffeting the earth's magnetosphere in a southward direction. It interacted with the Earth's north facing magnetic field, peeling it like layers of a shallot. One of the most significant effects of this activity was to disable the huge, energy hungry data centres that held the cloud and made the metaverse possible.

At the same time, a wobble in the moon's orbit, which takes 18.6 years to complete, had a significant effect on the Earth's tides, quadrupling the number of floods as a direct result of rising sea temperatures.

Both of these extreme weather events displaced millions of people and dramatically impacted food production and distribution. Of course, had the Earth not already been in such a poor state as a direct result of failing to control its carbon emissions, things may not have been as catastrophic for the planet or its inhabitants. Whilst hindsight serves no purpose here, I hope that it helps to explain what facilitated the downward spiral of civilisation.

It could be said that Earth's place within our vast solar system was fragile to begin with. We were special, and whether you believe in a higher spiritual presence or are purely driven by science, it no longer matters. The result is the same.

I feel an alignment with the Earth's scenario. One hundred beings started out alongside me, sharing a unique environment, yet none have survived apart from me. Am I special too?

I know the time is approaching when I will be forced to leave the safety of my protective liquid environment. I will have spent nine months in here and it may surprise you to learn that I have been aware of every second of my existence. I understand that my DNA has been tampered with at various intervals in my development, and that every aspect of me has been scrutinised and monitored closely.

I have become the ultimate human experiment.

CHAPTER 43

yellow

"I hope you don't mind me asking to meet in here Harvey as it is now your bedroom, but there are two places in this house that are a great comfort to me. One is my lab and the other is this den."

"Perhaps it can now be *our* place of great comfort Walter," Harvey said, smiling warmly.

"I wish that my reason for speaking to you away from the others *was* comforting. It is anything but." Walter sat down in the large armchair next to Harvey.

"Go on."

"Do you recall that I asked for a sample of the food Marcus and Finch were used to eating? I was curious to examine its contents, you know, the balance of nutrients. They seem to be living quite a healthy existence there, so I was hoping to perhaps replicate this here with our own produce," Walter said, rubbing his hands along the arms of the chair.

"And can you Walter? Can you replicate it?"

"I cannot. Nor would I ever try." Walter stood up and started walking slowly back and forward across the room. "I ran every test you can imagine Harvey. And then I ran them all again. Each time the results were the same." Walter continued becoming more agitated. "It didn't seem possible, but science doesn't lie."

"Good heavens man. Spit it out. I'm getting palpitations!" said Harvey, rising from his chair and shuffling over to Walter who was now staring out of the large bay fronted window.

Walter continued. "I imagined that they would be able to create farm towers for fruits and vegetables, and the substance proves that my assumption is likely to be correct. But what I was particularly interested in was what their source of protein is. I mean we're able to use some of our vegetables here for that but it's a struggle. It used to be easy when there were still factories producing plant-based protein products especially when the farming of animals for food died out once water became rationed."

"I remember when I had my very last roast chicken dinner," Harvey said, with a muted fondness. "It was a Sunday in April 2047. Of course we didn't know it at the time but looking back I suppose we should have seen the writing on the wall. There hadn't been any supplies of lamb or mutton for a few years and there were no more beef or dairy cattle, or pigs. And yes, I know, it was hugely unfashionable to still be eating animal products back then. I hadn't been an early adopter of a plant-based lifestyle but there you are." Harvey stopped for a moment and a great sadness swept over him.

"Harvey, what is it? Are you feeling ill?" Walter took Harvey by the arm and led him back to his armchair.

"I'm not ill Walter. I'm just old and tired, and I don't even know why I get up each day. Just talking about how the world was when we were young, when there was still a chance to stop this madness and how things are now, it's too much. All I want is to be with my husband. I miss him every day."

"Oh Harvey. I had no idea you felt this way. You hide it very well."

"It is exhausting to keep pretending Walter."

Walter was saddened to see how low Harvey really was. He realised that revealing his grim discovery at that point would have been a selfish thing to do. He was desperate to tell someone and unburden himself, but he realised now that it would clearly be too much for his dear old friend to take in.

"Come and have a lie down for a little while Harvey. We can pick this up another time."

Walter gently helped Harvey on to the bed and rearranged his pillows to make him as comfortable as possible. As he lay there the two men stared into each other's eyes for a moment before Harvey closed his and said in a barely audible whisper, "bless you."

Walter stood by his bed for a moment before quietly walking towards the door and closing it behind him. Harvey was already falling into a deep sleep. A sleep that would take him where his heart wanted to go. A sleep that he would not wake from again.

CHAPTER 44

yellow

The ground was rock hard, parched from lack of rain for so long but Finch and Marcus were determined to keep digging. It took them two days to achieve a suitable depth for the sad task that lay ahead.

As the men were digging his grave, Winter was preparing Harvey's body for burial. She dressed him in his favourite clothes and then wrapped his body neatly in several large white tablecloths that Ling Ling had brought up from the basement. She'd given them to Winter to cover Harvey's body in the absence of a coffin. It was Winter's saddest labour of love for the man who had treated her like a daughter for so many years. She was determined that his send-off would be dignified and what he would have wanted under the circumstances. His body remained in Walter's den until his resting place was ready. Winter remained in the den with him day and night holding vigil as she couldn't bear the thought of him being alone. She found it comforting to be able to speak to him while she kept herself busy handwriting what she was going to say during the ceremony. Harvey had been a man of faith and she knew that he would appreciate a brief reading from his bible which had travelled everywhere with him for the last sixty years. She also encouraged the others to say a few words if they felt inclined.

Marcus knocked quietly on the door of the den.

"We're ready Winter," he said gently. "May we come in?"

Winter got up from her chair and opened the door. She stood by silently as Finch accompanied Marcus to carry Harvey's body outside.

With everyone assembled by the grave, they took enormous care as they carefully began lowering Harvey's body in using ropes. As he was descending Winter suddenly cried out asking them to wait. She ran into the house and came back with two items that she wanted to go with him. She placed his spectacles and bible on his chest and then nodded for the lowering of his body to recommence.

Everyone stood around the sides of the grave in silence as Winter began:

"The Lord is my keeper: the Lord is thy shade upon they right hand.
The sun shall not smite thee by day, nor the moon by night.
The Lord shall preserve thee from all evil: he shall preserve thy soul.
The Lord shall preserve thy goin' out and thy comin' in from this time forth, and even forever more."

Winter looked up from her piece of paper. She was trying so hard to be brave but holding back tears was becoming an impossible ask as she looked at her beloved Harvey's body lying deep in the ground. He looked so small.

Then Walter stood forward, cleared his throat, and began reading one of his favourite poems.

"Do not stand by my grave, and weep. I am not there, I do not sleep
I am the thousand winds that blow, I am the diamond glints in snow
I am the sunlight on ripened grain, I am the gentle, autumn rain.
As you awake with morning's hush, I am the swift, up-flinging rush
Of quiet birds in circling flight, I am the day transcending night.
Do not stand by my grave, and cry. I am not there; I did not die."

Walter cleared his throat for a moment before saying a more personal message to his old friend. "I'm so glad we got to spend time together again Harvey. I will miss our debates and I will cherish our memories. We are the last generation to remember how things used to be. I will no doubt see you again soon. Until then it is comforting to know that you are reunited with your beloved Vincent. Goodbye for now old friend." Walter's eyes were full of sadness, and his posture was hunched in grief.

Ling Ling held his hand. It was all she could do to try and comfort her husband at a time when she knew that his own impending mortality grew ever closer.

Marcus and Finch had never seen a funeral before. In the crystal zone when you died your body was just taken away. There was no ceremony, and nothing to show that you were ever there. Grieving publicly was discouraged. Now, watching this unfold they were fascinated by the entire process and deeply saddened at Harvey's passing, a man who had been so gracious and caring when they first arrived in the yellow zone.

Winter's words concluded the brief service. "Our loss is heaven's gain. Rest in Peace. Rise in glory."

Marcus and Finch had been briefed to wait until the others were back in the house before covering the body with the earth that had been dug up, and to keep filling the grave until it was the same height as the rest of the land.

"This feels so strange Jarret. I mean look what we're doing, we've put Harvey's body in the ground and now we're shovelling dirt onto him. I just don't get it," Finch said, taking a breather.

"I know what you mean but then again, is it any more strange than the fact that we *don't* do something like this when people die back home?"

Finch shrugged his shoulders, wiped the sweat from his forehead and carried on shovelling in silence. It was easier to put the earth back in the ground than it had been digging it up, but the heat of the day was intense, and it was still exhausting.

When the last crumbs of dirt were patted down on the surface of the grave, Marcus and Finch trudged back to the house. Everyone was in the kitchen as Ling Ling had prepared refreshments explaining to the two men that after a funeral service it was customary to have what was called a 'wake' or a 'reception' where friends and family of the deceased would pay their respects.

Winter helped distribute the food and drinks to everyone sitting around the table.

"This is quite lovely," Marcus said smiling. "When I die, I hope someone will go to this much trouble to remember me. But I suppose that would only happen if I lived here when I died. I've no idea what happens at home. We certainly don't have ceremonies or anything like that."

On the other side of the table Finch noticed that Silvie couldn't stop crying. He changed seats so that he could sit next to her and put his arm around her shoulders comforting her.

"It's very sad about Harvey," Finch said, acknowledging her upset.

"Yes. Very sad. But not why cry," Silvie said.

"What is it Silvie?" Winter asked and then taking a deep breath, put her hand to her mouth. "Oh darlin', of course. I'm so sorry, I should have realised how difficult this would be for you so soon after losin' your little girl."

"Ya show Harvey … respect. Ma Jo Jo … no respect … thrown in fire. I see in my head for all time," Silvie sobbed.

"There is no time limit on grief Silvie. We all deal with it differently. Some people keep themselves busy so that they don't have time to dwell on their loss. Others allow it in and process it over a long period. Today we have lost a very dear friend who lived a long and productive life. But you lost a child in deeply traumatic circumstances. They are two very different types of loss and what you're feeling is perfectly natural. It's completely understandable that today has been a trigger and brought your profound grief to the surface," Walter said in a gentle voice.

Seeing Silvie in such distress gave Ling Ling an idea that she hoped might help, but that would be for another time. Today was for remembering Harvey.

CHAPTER 45

yellow

Walter realised that only a man of science would really be able to process what he had discovered and be equipped to make sense of it. He also felt that it would be better to show the results rather than simply talk about them. It was time for Walter to invite Marcus down to his lab in the basement of the house.

"I'm rather excited to be back in a laboratory Walter, I must admit. I enjoy my clinical work and it sounds as if you've made quite a revolutionary discovery," Marcus said.

Whilst not wanting to dampen Marcus's enthusiasm, he also needed to prepare him for what he was about to reveal because although Marcus was also a man of science, he had led a very sheltered existence from the harsh realities of life outside the crystal zone.

"Wow, you're really well equipped down here aren't you. Very impressive." Marcus continued to have a good look around. "So what did you want to show me Walter? I'm very keen to know."

Walter explained that he had tested the food sample that Marcus has given him. He'd done a breakdown of all the nutrients, the fats, carbohydrates, vitamins and minerals, trace elements and of course protein.

"Marcus, just out of curiosity, do you have any idea of what the protein source of your food is?"

"I believe that we grow it artificially in our laboratories. Is that any help?"

"If I said to you that the meat grown in your laboratories isn't artificial would it surprise you?"

Marcus was taken aback. "Of course it's artificial Walter. What a strange thing to say. It's not as if we could produce it any other way."

Walter sighed and put his head in his hands. "Oh dear."

"What's going on Walter? I don't like where this is going."

"There's no easy way to say this Marcus, but the protein source of your food is human."

Marcus started laughing.

"I'm not joking Marcus."

Marcus stopped laughing and looked at Walter closely.

"Show me. Show me your proof! What you've proposed is ludicrous and utterly disgusting. Show me!"

Walter pointed to his microscope and a carousel of slides. Marcus went over to the bench and sat down. He studied slide after slide in complete silence.

"I don't understand. I just don't understand! How could this be true?"

"Well that's what I'm hoping you can help me to find out Marcus. You and I are both geneticists although from different eras of science. But biology is biology. And the meat pureed in your meals is human."

"I think I'm going to be sick."

"There's a bin underneath the bench. If you're going to throw up please use it," Walter said calmly. "My reaction was exactly the same as yours Marcus. I felt sick to my stomach, and I'm afraid there's more, when you feel ready to hear it."

"More? How much worse could this get?"

"Well, this is the part that I'm hoping you can help me piece together my young friend. You see upon further examination of the human protein, I discovered that it is coming from an incredibly young source. So young that I would describe it as foetal." Walter looked at the floor and closed his eyes for a moment. He'd finally said those awful words.

"Wait. What? You're saying the human meat protein is

from … no. I can't even …"

"Let me help you then. You're all basically eating protein from unborn babies. There, I've said it! But what I don't understand is how they are producing such vast quantities to feed your population. That part is staggering."

Marcus reached for the bin under Walter's bench and threw up over and over again until the contents of his stomach was empty, and he was left dry retching. Walter left him for a moment and went back upstairs. After a while he came back downstairs to the basement with a tray of mugs full of mint tea.

"Here. This will help settle your stomach Marcus."

Marcus held the cup with shaking hands. He took small sips of the tea as his mind raced. There was only one explanation.

"I believe I can explain that part Walter and I swear to you I had no idea."

Walter listened silently as Marcus explained about the monthly testing of the Gen1 females and how blastocysts were routinely removed from them. He went on to tell Walter that only a small proportion of these were then developed in what were called AUCs, Artificial Uterine Chambers and at 11 weeks were genetically modified to ensure that they developed into babies that were highly resistant to disease and infection. Once their gestation was complete these babies were then forwarded to the nursery before being assigned to a couple or an individual. But this process was only applied to one percent of the material collected from the Gen1 females because there was a strict population quota. Ninety-nine percent of the material extracted from the women was disposed of.

"So ninety-nine percent of these cells must be being developed into lab meat." Walter concluded.

"I can't believe it. I don't want to. I promise you I had no idea that this is what could have been going on. If people back home knew about this, they would be as horrified as I am, I'm sure of that."

"I believe you son. I do," Walter said calmly. "The question is whether it is allowed to continue, or we find a way to stop it. However much we want our species to survive, surely there must be boundaries that mustn't be crossed."

"I agree. The crystal zone is currently functioning on a barbaric lie."

"It is a form of cannibalism Marcus. Personally, I would rather die than participate in this way of life. Besides, we have surely shown you that, although a lot of hard graft is involved, we are surviving reasonably well here."

"You have shown me a great deal Walter. I feel more educated in the brief time I've been here than in all the years I've lived back home. Home. It feels very strange to call it that now when I realise it's just a controlled environment where there is a complete absence of free will."

"Hearing you speak like this and looking at you now, well you're the image of your father," Walter said, without thinking.

Marcus froze as his mind processed what Walter had just said. "My father? What are you talking about?"

There was an uncomfortable silence between the two men for a few moments.

"Come with me," Walter said, as he started walking up the stairs of the basement to the main hallway and then up the staircase that led to all the bedrooms. He finally stopped at his and Ling Ling's room. "Come in," he said to Marcus, who was hesitant to enter their private domain.

On a dressing table there were framed pictures of different people. Marcus had noticed many of these framed pictures in various rooms of the house and wondered what they were.

"What are these Walter?"

Walter explained that in previous decades people had valued their memories of people and events by capturing their images with cameras, and the most special of these were turned into photos produced on paper, canvas, metal or etched onto glass. And that although people had also accumulated millions of digital images these had all been lost once the networks died and the internet fell silent. He then handed Marcus one of the framed photos which Marcus studied for a moment. It was an old photo of eight young men standing outside an elaborate collection of buildings.

"What do you see Marcus?" Walter asked gently. "Look very closely now."

Marcus studied the photo for a few moments. "No! Is this *you*?"

"Yes. I was 23 years old there. We arrogantly called ourselves 'The Great Eight'. Who else can you see Marcus?"

Marcus studied the photo again with his brow furrowed in concentration.

"Oh my goodness. Is that Professor Hill? No it can't be. He was my teacher back home," Marcus said, immediately dismissing the idea.

"It is indeed Professor Hill. Lucius Hill completed his master's degree at the same time as I did. Keep looking Marcus."

Marcus was baffled at the discovery of Professor Hill and Walter being in such separate locations now. Again Marcus studied the faces of the young men in the photo.

"I think this might be Harvey. Even though his face is greatly changed from age, those twinkling eyes are the same aren't they?" Marcus said, looking at Walter who picked up another of his photos with great affection although Marcus couldn't see it from where he was standing.

"Yes, that's Harvey alright. Can you see anyone else who looks familiar Marcus?"

"Not really. Although there is one young man who … wait … he looks a little like … me."

"The one standing in the middle?" Walter asked.

"Yes. Him."

Walter placed a hand on Marcus's left shoulder. "That, Marcus, is your father. Were you ever told anything about your parents?"

"All I was told was that they died when I was a baby. I have no idea who they were or what they looked like."

"Would you like to know who they were?" Walter asked, with a little hesitation in his voice knowing that he was venturing into sensitive territory.

"How could I not want to know Walter? You've just shown me a photo of the man who was my organic father."

Walter passed Marcus the other photo he'd picked up.

"This is a photo of both your parents Marcus. It was taken just before they died. Your mother was an exceptional woman. They were so happy together."

Marcus stared at the photo of his mother and father. He was completely speechless.

"I know it's a lot to take in, especially after learning about … you know … what we discussed in my lab. But I'm afraid there isn't any time to waste now. So here's the absolute God's honest truth Marcus. Your parents were amazing people. They were both scientists and devoted themselves to conquering devastating diseases that you won't even know ever existed. They were good people and highly ethical, which is why they were so well respected. They created the Jarret Institute, which again, I'm sure you'll never have heard of."

"No." Marcus's voice was barely audible.

"You were told that your parents died, but the truth is that they were killed in what was supposed to be a peaceful protest about legislation that the Government was planning to introduce, which would have reinstated the use of animals in experimentation."

"Animals. Like the ones in the book full of those beautiful creatures Harvey showed me?"

"Yes. Like those." Walter nodded. We'd already lost millions of species to extinction from loss of habitat and environmental pollution, but the government wasn't content with that and felt that human life was far too important to continue being used for testing any longer. Even though the people involved were willing volunteers and well imbursed for their participation, and the science had shown that the human results were 100% more accurate than testing other species. Very few people ever went on to die as a result compared to the millions and millions of animals that had been brutally exploited in the past. Your parents were totally opposed to the new legislation as we all were. Over ten thousand people marched on the capital to show the government the strength of feeling. But those who were destined to make vast amounts of money, including companies who would have been breeding the animals destined for laboratory experiments joined forces with the big pharmaceutical companies. They were just too powerful for the government to ignore. Sadly, history has shown over and over again that money has always been a driving force over intellect. During the protest scuffles broke out with people who had joined the march but who, as it turned out, had been handsomely paid to cause trouble and make it look like all the protestors were violent anarchists. Things got out of control and the police started shooting at the demonstrators. Your parents were on the front line holding a giant banner from the Jarret Institute. They didn't stand a chance against the trigger-happy police and security forces. Sixty-three people died that day from gunshot and other wounds, your parents included Marcus, I'm so sorry to say. It was a national scandal and brought the government to its knees, and the sad irony is that it was all for nothing in the end."

"I honestly don't know what to react to first. Obviously, I don't remember my parents and it's just so sad what happened to them. I would have been so proud to have had parents like that," Marcus said, his voice cracking with emotion. "What I mean is I am proud that I am their son."

"They stood up for what they believed was a just cause, and paid for it with their lives, something people have been doing since time began," Walter said.

"And who are these other young men, Walter?" Marcus asked, pointing to the original photo.

"In order to answer that, I need to start with a confession." Walter sat down on the bed and took a deep breath. "Everyone in that photo, excluding your father, is responsible for what you call the crystal zone. We originally called it 'Baobab', after what was known in some regions of the planet as the 'tree of life'. It was a tree that could store up to 1200 gallons of water in its trunk. God we were so arrogant. We thought we could change the world."

"*You* are one of the founders of the crystal zone? *You*? And Harvey and Professor Hill? Am I dreaming? Is this all one big, fantastic lie?" Marcus's mouth was hanging open in a daze.

"I can assure you our idyll was vastly different to the one

you live in today. What they've turned our original idea into is a complete abomination."

"Is that why you're still living here Walter?"

"Oh, heavens yes. Some of us left the project long before its completion. We could see what the lunatics were planning, and we wanted no part of it. Professor Hill stayed behind even though he was opposed to the new direction the project was going in. He felt one of us should be there in case anything useful could be passed to us here in the *real* world. But of course they made it impossible for information to be shared. You were completely cut off from the rest of the world because they were too scared we'd find out the truth and you'd discover that you were being deceived. How is the old guy anyway?"

Marcus was trying to process all the information coming at him. "Professor Hill? Oh he's fine, about to retire and play golf last time we spoke. He seems happy enough."

"Good. I'm glad he's OK. He was always a truly kind, decent man. It must have been so hard for him to stay there." Walter paused as he remembered his dear friend. "Anyway, I digress. Some of our fellow graduates had come from money. Serious family money. I'm talking trillionaires, the kind that could and did fund private space exploration, that sort of thing. Well that money ended up funding the construction of Baobab … I mean the crystal zone. It was the biggest top-secret project ever undertaken by humanity," Walter said with disdain. "As I mentioned, we were an arrogant bunch, some more so than others. There was a huge falling out between those of us who wanted the project to be a beacon of hope for the world, and then there were the others who were only interested in making sure their families and friends were safe, and that they had the power to rule this new domain. Megalomania pure and simple. When governments across the globe began to fall as the desperate populations rose up, our 'colleagues' saw it as their big opportunity."

"It's all starting to make sense … I think. You know when we first met Harvey he made a comment which seemed so strange at the time. He said he knew where we were from. Now I can see that he really *did* know." Marcus looked as though a light had come on in his head. "But now it seems that those in command of the crystal zone have a mission of world domination through the elimination of those they consider inferior or surplus to requirements. They *must* be stopped!"

CHAPTER 46

yellow

It was time. Finch knew he couldn't put it off any longer, he had to tell Marcus the truth.

"We have to go back," he said in a serious voice. "And it has to be tomorrow."

Marcus was taken aback. "What's the rush? Brock isn't a problem anymore."

"Let's find the others. I only want to have to explain this once."

Marcus followed Finch into the main sitting room where Walter and Ling Ling were seated talking to Anja. Ling Ling had only just come in from the garden and was taking a short break from doing some planting.

"Do you know where the others are?" Finch asked rather abruptly.

"I think Winter is in the den, she likes to be in there quite a lot since Harvey passed away. Silvie is upstairs in her room. Why, what's up?" Walter asked.

"I need to speak to you all about something very important."

"Oh my. Well I'll go and ask Silvie to come down," Ling Ling said, putting down her tea and scurrying upstairs.

"I'll go and get Winter." Marcus wasted no time heading for the den.

Once everyone had assembled in the room Finch stopped

pacing around the room and began.

"As you know, Brock had been instructed to bring Marcus, Anja, and myself back to the crystal zone. And I know that since he died there has been a sense of relief that we could put our journey on hold for a while longer."

"Yes. Especially given Anja's situation," Winter said.

"What I haven't felt able to impart to you all before now is that there is another reason for our need to return without delay. I knew nothing of this until Brock told me."

"Go on." Walter took off his reading glasses and raised an eyebrow in anticipation of some unwelcome news.

Finch felt as though every nerve ending in his body was jangling as he told them about the fate of the red zone. He couldn't bear to make eye contact with Silvie to begin with.

Seeing that Silvie's body was shaking uncontrollably as she heard how an army of drones had been sent to her homeland and extinguished all human life there, Winter quickly got to her feet, sat next to her, and held her tightly.

"Why they do it?" Silvie managed to say through gritted teeth and trembling lips.

Finch tried to reassure her. "I promise you I was horrified that the Leader had instructed this to happen."

"Why? Why?" Silvie asked again.

Finch took a deep breath and blew it out wondering how he could explain it without sounding as though he was justifying the atrocity.

"You must have some idea Finch," Walter said, leaning forward in an inquisitional manner.

"I believe it is the result of global overpopulation." Finch heard the words come out of his mouth and immediately regretted them as he felt Silvie's eyes burning a hole in his heart.

"We no value to ya people? Ya leader is … monster!" Silvie screamed at Finch, as she wrenched herself free from Winter's arms and launched herself at Finch's body, pounding his chest over and over with her tiny fists in anger and anguish.

Finch stood there and took it. Silvie didn't have the strength to hurt Finch physically, and he put his arms around her until she had nothing left in her but to collapse at his feet gasping for breath. He scouped her up and put her back on the sofa where he kneeled in front of her.

"Silvie, I can't imagine how you are feeling. I know this won't comfort you but please know that this is *not* who I am. It's not who Marcus is. Nor Anja. We have been brought up in an environment where it is now clear that we are lied to and manipulated. Nothing that we have been led to believe all of our lives is true. You think that the Leader is a monster and I agree," Finch said gently. "And you are the last person on earth that I would ever wish to hurt."

"But ya *want* go back," Silvie said, turning her face away from him.

"I don't *want* to go back. I *need* to go back and so does Marcus."

Marcus's expression said everything Finch needed to know. He was horrified, and he certainly didn't want to go back, but he also knew that there must be a good reason why they would have to leave so soon. He looked at Anja, fearing the worst was yet to come.

"What about me?" Anja asked looking worried.

"You have to stay here Anja," Finch said, trying to reassure her. "It's for your safety and for your baby's safety too."

"You know what would happen if you came back," Marcus said, putting his arm around her shoulders.

Anja shook her head in despair. "But we've only just found each other again! This is an impossible situation. Why Finch? Why does Marcus have to go back with you?"

"Because I can't do what needs to be done on my own," Finch said, looking at Marcus.

"Finch whatever it is that you're trying to explain you're not doing a particularly good job of it," Ling Ling said, growing impatient. "What is so important that you *both* need to go to back? Quite frankly, your home sounds like a terrible place!"

Walter stood up and stretched out his back and legs. "What he's trying to tell us is that the Leader is planning to do here in the yellow zone, what was done in the red zone. Isn't that right Finch?"

"How do you know that?" Finch exclaimed.

"Because when you had your little squabble outside the evening Brock arrived, Harvey heard everything from the den. As to why I haven't said anything before, well I suppose like you, it was such a terrible thing to imagine I just couldn't find it in me to break everyone's hearts," Walter said, pacing back and forward in the large room. "And there's something else I'm afraid I have to tell you all which is equally shocking. So brace yourselves."

"Dear God, what on earth could there be that's even worse than our impendin' annihilation Walter?" Winter said, wiping a tear from her eye. "We've just heard that we're all gonna die!"

"Even if the worst happens and they send their drones to kill us, there is still something that needs to be exposed and stopped back where they're from. Something that I discovered and have shown Marcus in my lab. In fact, Marcus perhaps this would be more appropriate coming from you." Walter sat down again looking tired from his brief circuit of the room.

It was another scorching hot day but the beads of sweat on Marcus's top lip and trickling down the side of his face, running down his neck and onto his chest weren't from the heat. He could feel himself becoming nauseated at the thought of explaining Walter's grim discovery. He took a moment to steady his nerves and think of the right words but there were no *right* words. Marcus knew that the moment he told Finch and Anja about the source of the protein they had been eating all these years there would be no turning back. There were some things a person could never unhear.

They listened to Marcus in a silence that was punctuated only by gasps of disbelief. Walter had already told Ling Ling and so they sat holding hands looking solemn with no need to exclaim any shock.

"Ya eat *babies*?" Silvie asked in confusion, thinking she must have misunderstood.

"It's lab meat grown from foetal cells, so …" Marcus tried to explain again to Silvie.

Winter tried to remain calm thinking there must be another explanation. "You're eatin' baby meat as your source of protein?

Am I correct Marcus, Walter?"

"I don't see another way of putting it Winter. So yes you are correct." Walter added with a hint of sarcasm. "Such a civilised zone, don't you think? Kill everyone else on the planet and eat meat from … oh I can't even say it. The Leader must be so proud. I'm sorry, I shouldn't have said that. I know you don't condone what is happening there. You are all victims of a toxic deceit that masquerades as something pure and honest."

Marcus turned to Anja who hadn't said a word. "You're very quiet Anja."

Anja took a deep breath, what she was about to say was likely going to make Marcus feel worse than he already did. "This explains so much. Why every month we are forced to attend your clinic and why those procedures are performed on the women. Stealing what would become their children." Anja put her hands on her belly. "That could have been the fate of our baby Marcus. You wonder why I am quiet, but I just don't know how to process this information. I don't know how to make sense of any of this. My imagination is seeing how, under different circumstances, our child could have ended up on the dinner tables of the crystal zone."

"I'm sorry, I have to…" Winter rushed out of the room and ran outside. The sound of her retching echoed through the house.

"Did you know anything about this Finch?" Marcus asked quietly.

"I promise you I had no idea. No idea at all. I wish I could say that it was unbelievable, but I'm ashamed to say that I now believe the Leader and the Advocates are capable of just about anything."

"I go to her," Silvie said, as she stood up to go and see if Winter was OK. Before she left the room she turned to face Marcus and Finch. "Wish not come here. Wish I die with ma people." She paused for a moment to think of the right words. "When in monster truck. Noise above. Like thunder. Now know it drones."

Anja looked closely at Marcus. In her heart she knew that he could never have sanctioned any of this. The distress was etched on his face; a face that had once looked so clear and confident, and in control of all that surrounded him. Now she saw a man deeply conflicted about where he needed to be. She wanted to go with him, but she knew that was impossible. She also knew that if he left to go back to the crystal zone with Finch, there was a strong possibility that they would never see each other again, and that Marcus would never meet his baby daughter. For a while Anja sat in silence trying to control her breathing and pondering all the variables that this situation was throwing at them. There was only one conclusion to be drawn.

"You must go with Finch tomorrow," Anja said, as bravely as she could. "We cannot let the Leader unleash his destructive powers here. I know you will find it difficult to leave me, just as I will find it difficult to be apart from you, but if you stay we would only perish here together along with everyone else. You and Finch are the only hope of saving millions of lives, including ours. I don't know how you will do it; I only know that you must try."

"Yes Marcus, you must try. I promise you with all my heart that we will look after Anja. And when your baby comes, we will keep them both safe," Ling Ling said.

"I have no doubt of that Ling Ling. But equally going back without a plan, a strategy of how to stop this madness worries me a great deal. I am fully prepared to do whatever it takes for however long it takes. Finch, do you have any thoughts on what we do once we re-enter the crystal zone?" Marcus asked, turning to Finch who was still reeling from Silvie's reaction.

"I have thought of little else since Brock told me of the Leader's plan."

"I know that my three pod mates will help you Marcus. They are extremely resourceful, and I think if you can get them to speak to other women, you'll discover that I'm not the only one who resents the monthly visits to the clinic. Once you explain exactly what happens to our biological material and how it ends up in our food, you will soon have a revolution on your hands."

"I know a few of the Associates quite well and it's obvious which ones are wholly committed to their Advocate, and which aren't. There are only a few that I know I can trust, but it's a start," Finch said, with a new enthusiasm.

"And don't forget Professor Hill!" Walter said, suddenly buoyed up by Anja and Finch's disclosures. "He's your inside man. He's one of us and he will be your eyes and ears on what the Advocates are being instructed to do. I believe he has one or two Advocates on side."

"This is all very encouraging. I just have one question. What exactly are we trying to achieve? What is our end goal?" Marcus asked, trying not to dampen the enthusiastic atmosphere. "From what I gather, nobody has ever seen the Leader, not even the Advocates."

"That's correct," Finch said "Even when the Advocates are summoned to The Great Hall, the appearance of the Leader is always shrouded in secrecy, whether it's the deliberately dim lighting or the flowing hooded robes. That's according to some of my colleagues."

"Even if you did manage to get close to the Leader, what would you want to do? Would you talk to him and hope that he sees things from a different perspective? Personally, I think that would be a mistake. He clearly has no respect for life," Anja said. "And for someone like that, there can only be one option. The Leader must be destroyed!"

CHAPTER 47

yellow

"I will find a way for us to be together again," Marcus whispered in Anja's ear as they held each other close.

"Can we lie here for just a little while longer?" Anja said, gently stroking his head.

Neither had slept well and the morning had come too soon. These last moments together were precious and would have to sustain both of them in the weeks and months ahead; possibly even forever.

"I will be able to forge ahead with Finch knowing that you and our baby are safe here. It doesn't mean that I won't be thinking about you, but it does mean that I will be able to focus on our mission."

"I know Marcus. I know that I am loved, and it is the most wonderful feeling in the world. Whatever happens in the future, you will know that you are also loved."

Marcus looked deeply into Anja's eyes. "The world is such a mess. We made it this way. Well not us exactly, but those who came before us. How could they have let it happen?"

"Perhaps they were just thoughtless, or selfish because they knew they wouldn't be alive to see what they had done? Having spent time here in the yellow zone I have seen a different sort of person to those back home. Of course there are some good people there, but they have never had to struggle to survive. And yet here, I have encountered such compassion and selflessness from people who have nothing. It has often made me want to weep because it's just so overwhelming."

"Yes. I've experienced that sensation as well. It's why we must do whatever it takes to protect them from the impending slaughter that the Leader has dictated. A Leader that thinks these people have no value, and that they're just taking up space and using resources. The Leader's belief that the crystal zone is somehow superior and its people are the future of our planet is disturbing and misguided to say the least."

"But Marcus, we *are* genetically superior aren't we?" Anja's brow furrowed. "I don't feel as if I am any better or more deserving of life than Winter or Silvie, for example. Oh Marcus I'm so sorry. I often forget that you are not …"

"Hey, it's OK, I sometimes forget that we're not the same too, but I think *believing* that you are superior is quite different. Like believing you are deserving of privilege because you were born in a certain place at a certain time; it's a state of mind."

"What about our baby Marcus? She'll be a *hybrid* so does that mean she is genetically different?"

"I honestly don't know. She is a mix of my genes and yours. I'm not enhanced but equally some of your genetic improvements are not designed to be hereditary. Whatever her makeup, she will be our own special child and she will be treasured, even from afar. Of that you can be certain."

Marcus kissed her forehead and then slowly released himself from her embrace. It was time for him to get up and start preparing for the journey ahead despite an almost overwhelming temptation to continue lying in bed with Anja. He had heard Finch in the hallway and then going up and down the creaking staircase. When he opened the bedroom door he could see that Finch had switched to battle-ready mode and knew that he had to do the same.

Anja buried her face in her pillow. She didn't want Marcus to see her tears. Instinctively Marcus had turned his face away from her as he left their bedroom so she couldn't see his fear. Marcus had always been a man of peace. Confrontation didn't come easily to him, and he was known for his honesty and discretion, but he knew that these qualities would be of no benefit once they re-entered the crystal zone. He would have no option but to lie to the Advocates about finding Anja. He would have to lie about a great many things, even the friendship that had developed between himself and Finch. He knew that Finch was going to have to be economical with the truth as well, and that their stories had to be faultlessly matched to avoid arousing any suspicion. There was so much to fear about the future, but his greatest fear was that he would never see Anja again. If they failed to prevent the Leader's planned drone attack, millions including Anja and all of their new friends would perish.

Ling Ling had prepared a special farewell breakfast for Marcus and Finch but as the two men walked into the kitchen, the mood became sombre.

"Is Anja coming down to join us?" Winter asked.

"Yes I am." Anja poked her head around the kitchen door smiling.

"Ahhh that's wonderful," Ling Ling said, smiling back at her.

Ling Ling could see that Anja's smile was a masterclass in bravado and that she was just hanging on by a thread that could break at any time.

Everyone sat around the table in silence picking at the food Ling Ling had laid out. It was an uncomfortable silence with unspoken words and emotions lurking just below the surface, until Walter broke the tension.

"How long will it take you to get back once you've taken off from the port Finch?"

Finch's mouth was full of food as he tried to answer and some of it shot out of his mouth like a wayward projectile flying across the table. He was very embarrassed and put his hand across his mouth to ensure nothing else escaped. Winter thought it was hysterical and although she tried to stifle her laughter, her shoulders were jumping up and down until she couldn't control herself anymore. It was a blessing because her amusement became infectious and spread quickly to everyone else.

"Oh Finch, I will miss you honey!" Winter blurted out still

trying to control her laughter.

"I will miss you too Winter. I will miss you all," Finch replied, still chewing.

"Me?" Silvie asked tentatively.

Finch finished chewing and swallowed hard. He looked into Silvie's eyes. She seemed so vulnerable, and he wished he could stay and protect her.

"I will miss you *very* much Silvie."

"Not yet. I go to port!" Silvie smiled warmly, relieved that she had not damaged their closeness, despite her emotional reaction to his news about the destruction of her homeland the previous day.

"Yes, we thought it was a good idea for Winter to have some company for her return journey back here." Walter added.

Finch smiled. He was more than happy to have a few more hours with Silvie and felt an ache in the pit of his stomach at the thought of saying goodbye to her. Like Marcus, he feared he would never see her again.

To appear as authentic as possible Finch and Marcus had changed back into the clothes that they wore when they left the crystal zone. They packed all of their original belongings but Marcus decided to leave his medical equipment behind. Having shown Winter how to operate it he felt it was more important for his friends to have it just in case. He knew he could easily explain why some equipment was missing by saying that it had been stolen. Winter remembered how it had saved her beloved Harvey's life once before and was extremely grateful to be left in charge of it, especially thinking ahead to the birth of Anja's baby and of course to Walter's advancing years.

Once breakfast was concluded they could put off the inevitable no longer. Marcus and Anja retired to their bedroom for one last private goodbye. When Marcus came back downstairs he did so alone. It was obvious that it had been an emotional farewell, and as he and Finch went outside they hugged Ling Ling and Walter and thanked them for their generosity and friendship.

As they climbed into Granny, instinctively Marcus sat in the passenger seat next to Winter so that Finch and Silvie could be together in the back. It had become obvious to everyone that there was something special between them even if neither of them were prepared to give it a name such as 'love'. Silvie held Finch's hand throughout the journey and her delicate hand gripped his more and more tightly the closer they came to the place where she knew they would have to say goodbye.

"I'm sorry that I won't be able to take y'all to the port itself but a vehicle like Granny would create a lot of unwanted attention, which could be dangerous. But I'll get you as close as I can and then it's about an 8 mile walk."

Winter kept her eyes on the road ahead as she spoke. It was not only for safety reasons but because she was also trying to avoid eye contact with her passengers as she dreaded saying goodbye to the two men who had become great friends to her.

"Don't worry Winter we will be fine as long as we know that you will both be safe getting back," Marcus said calmly. "And it will give us plenty of time to discuss our plans for when we're back in the crystal zone."

"Exactly! We can't discuss anything like that once we're aboard our craft because there are always eyes and ears on us there." Finch added.

"You miss girl in ya home?" Silvie ventured a little hesitantly.

Finch laughed. He'd been with plenty of women but there was nothing more than physical attraction with any of them. Emotionally he was completely detached to the girls back home. He had certainly never experienced the type of bond that he now had with Silvie; a bond that he didn't want to break.

"Er, no. Nobody special. Nobody's waiting for me back there," he said, hoping it would reassure her.

"I wish I come with ya." Silvie sighed.

"I also wish that could be possible. Although I don't think you would like where I come from Silvie, not as it is at present anyway. It is a very clinical and ordered society. You have such a warm heart and a beautiful spirit I know you would find it difficult to exist in such an environment." Finch was practically beaming as he said all the things he wished he'd said to her before. "I will think of you every day."

"Ya come back?" Silvie asked, knowing that it would be impossible for Finch to promise any such thing.

"If I don't come back for you Silvie it will only be because I *can't*. Do you understand?"

"Yes." Silvie leaned over and put Finch's arm around her shoulders as she pressed herself against his body so tightly that she could hear his heartbeat.

Although their journey to the coast was shorter than the journey from Harvey's house it still took two days. They were able to travel a more direct route, but the broken roads and barren landscape all seemed to look the same in every direction. It reminded Marcus and Finch of the journey they had originally taken when they first arrived. Having been in the relative haven of Feronia, they had for a while been able to forget what a harsh environment the yellow zone could be. When Winter needed to rest they all rested. When Winter needed to eat, they all ate. Winter played such a crucial role in everything they did and nobody resented working to her timetable. In one way or another they all owed Winter their lives, and each was in awe of her incredible bravery, loyalty, and compassion. Mostly they valued her friendship as she had gone out of her way on every occasion to ensure their safety and comfort. She always put others first and the two men found themselves feeling particularly humbled by this.

"We're here folks," Winter announced, as she pulled Granny over to the side of the road. "Any closer to the town would be too much of a risk I'm afraid."

Winter's announcement wasn't greeted with celebration by anyone. Silvie's eyes began to sting with hot tears. It was the moment that all four of them had dreaded. Finch and Marcus had to psyche themselves into the last part of their journey on foot, but the reality of what lay ahead after that was what they both found the hardest to face. Suddenly they weren't returning *home*, they were returning to the crystal zone, a place that wasn't what it seemed, and a place they hadn't missed. Home now felt like the place they were leaving *behind* and would miss intensely and that's when they realised that home wasn't a *place* at all. It was where the people you cared most for were.

Winter hugged Marcus, who kissed her on the cheek and then took her hands in his and was about to say something when she stopped him.

"Don't! Whatever it is you're about to say, don't. I'm just about holdin' it together sugar and I can't afford to cry 'cos we have a long journey back to Feronia. If I cry I won't be able to see all the obstacles on the road. Rest assured whatever you were thinkin' of saying, I already know. You're welcome, and yes I'll look after your beautiful girl and your beautiful baby when she arrives. You just focus on what you need to do and if you can find your way back to us …"

Winter's voice had been steady and deliberate until her last few words, which were impaired by a sudden lump in her throat. She squeezed Marcus's hands tightly before releasing them, and then she turned around and walked back towards Granny.

Marcus smiled to himself. Winter did indeed know what was on his mind, and he was more grateful to her than any words could have expressed. He then looked around to see where Finch was. He didn't have to look far. Finch was standing on the other side of Granny with Silvie. They were embracing and then Finch kissed Silvie on the mouth. It was such a long, lingering, and mutual kiss that Marcus had to avert his gaze to give them some privacy. It reminded him of his last kiss with Anja less than 48 hours earlier. A moment that he knew he would treasure for the rest of his life.

Finch walked back to Winter and hugged her. He whispered something in her ear that was inaudible to the others, and then walked over to Marcus. They watched as Winter and Silvie disappeared into the distance in Granny, and then started walking towards the main road of the town that would lead them to the coast, and ultimately to the port.

For the first couple of miles the two men walked in silence, both lost in their own private thoughts. They negotiated their way through crowds of people wandering around aimlessly. Some sat on what remained of the pavement rocking back and forth, wailing in despair. Others were actively in pursuit of something to eat, and some were belligerent about how they obtained it. Most ignored the two men passing through. They didn't appear to have anything of interest with them, and nothing worth stealing, although a couple of women begged them for a sip of water which Marcus found impossible to ignore. He knew that where they were heading there was no shortage of food or water so was happy to be able to help.

When it was safe to stop for a quick break out of sight of local people, Marcus and Finch rested and ate some of the food that Ling Ling had kindly packed for their journey.

As he was eating Finch shook his head and looked at Marcus. "How are we ever going eat what they give us back there now that we know what's in it?"

"I honestly don't know Finch. It is a repulsive thought isn't it?"

"It's completely revolting! The thought of it actually makes me nauseous."

Marcus was quiet for a few moments deep in thought. And then it was like a light had come on in his head. "Of course. That's it!" Marcus said, leaping to his feet. "That's it!"

"You've had an idea haven't you?" Finch tilted his head in anticipation.

"Yes! And I think you're going to like it."

The two men continued their journey on foot towards the port as Marcus explained his idea to Finch. Despite becoming quite animated during their conversation they didn't encounter a lot of interest from the local people in the towns that they passed through on their way. They were so engrossed in their conversation they equally didn't pay any attention to the meandering groups of local people they had to navigate around. By the time they reached the craft, that had been docked at the port for several months, Marcus and Finch had formulated a plan which depended on either discovering or creating allies across various centres within the crystal zone complex. They knew that they needed to do this without appearing to be the ringleaders, or the plan would fail, and they knew they had to act quickly. It would take nerves of steel to pull it off, and both men knew they would have to dig deep to find those nerves from the first moment they set foot back in the crystal zone. Bravery and a large measure of acting were the only things that could save the lives of millions of innocent people in the yellow zone, which now included people they loved.

Just before they arrived at the port Finch stopped, turned to Marcus, and stretched out his hand.

"I just want to say, whatever happens, it's been an honour Marcus."

"The feeling is mutual my friend," Marcus said, as he grasped Finch's hand. The two men hugged briefly. "Hey, you just called me Marcus!"

Finch smiled. "Don't get used to it. It'll be Doctor Jarret again from the moment we get on board."

When Marcus and Finch first left the crystal zone in search of Anja they were just a couple of ordinary men, one an Associate Advocate the other a doctor and scientist. Now they were going to have to become warriors.

CHAPTER 48

crystal

On the journey back to the crystal zone the two men sat in silence. Everything that they had needed to say to each other had been said on their long walk back to the port. They were also keenly aware that they would be overheard once aboard the craft.

The relationship between the two men had changed dramatically over the previous months. When they had first boarded the craft to travel to the yellow zone, Marcus remembered that Finch had deliberately chosen to sit behind him making him feel unsettled with a distinct sensation of being observed. It had been clear that Finch resented having to babysit the doctor, and have his routine disrupted because the woman Marcus loved had gone missing. This time the two men sat together united by their experiences, and through learning some difficult and disturbing truths. They were also united by something else; their love for a woman they'd left behind. There was comfort in their mutual sadness at being apart from Anja and Silvie because each man was now able to empathise with the other. That strange yet reassuring comfort would end once they arrived back at what had once been their home, but now felt more like a prison. Any sense of camaraderie would cease and all prior formalities return. Each had a specific job to do, and by necessity there would be no communication between the two men once they stepped through the fortress-like doors of the crystal zone.

The craft stopped with stealth-like precision at the docking station, and the doors opened. Marcus and Finch looked upwards at the enormity of the main domed structure with fresh eyes and a feeling of trepidation. They knew that they would have to undergo a decontamination process but were not prepared for the way in which this would be conducted.

The first set of doors opened and they walked inside. Once the doors had closed behind them, with a vacuum seal that made their ears pop, they were instructed to remove all of their clothes and place them in a secure tray to the side of the doors. The tray of soiled clothing then retracted back into the wall for immediate incineration. They were then told to stand still as their naked bodies were bathed in a series of UV lights, which decontaminated their skin, hair, and nails. Once this process was completed two suits of protective clothing were automatically dispensed in front of them which they put on.

The second set of doors opened and they were directed to board one of the preprogrammed hover vehicles that were waiting on the other side. Once seated, straps sprang across their bodies making sure they would be secure before both vehicles sped off in opposite directions. The vehicles deposited the men in two separate locations where they each entered a cell-like pod. Again they were instructed to remove all clothing for disposal and put on a new set of more comfortable clothes that were provided for them.

As the doors of his pod locked behind him, and he looked around at his new sterile surroundings, it was obvious that the ordeal was far from over. Marcus was instructed to drink the bottle of thick clear liquid that was sitting on a tray suspended from the wall, along with a container of multicoloured pills that had to be swallowed in a defined order. Obediently Marcus did as he was instructed.

He was then told to pick up the large empty silver container that was also on the tray and hold it in both hands in front of him. It seemed an odd request at first, but within minutes the reason became apparent. The container was there to capture the contents of his stomach for analysis, and the pills he had taken were designed to induce a violent vomiting response. After sealing the full container, he was told to put it back on the tray as a lid closed over the tray and was subsequently withdrawn back into the cavity of the wall.

It was the beginning of a highly invasive series of tests in which every possible bodily fluid, including lachrymal fluid from his eyes, was taken for analysis. After two hours Marcus was permitted to lie down on the bench provided and rest for a while. But his rest was short-lived as he was soon woken by further instructions which required him to be injected with substances from several unlabelled vials, and then inhale a powder-like material which he was told would coat the membranes of his lungs and sinuses to repair any damage that had been sustained by prolonged exposure to the contaminated air of the yellow zone.

Marcus, being the more sensitive of the two men, began to feel violated by all the prodding and poking, especially as there was no human contact throughout all of the procedures. He also found himself wondering whether the intensity of the tests he was being put through was because he was a PreGen. Was Finch having an easier time? He hoped so, because he knew that Finch could have a quick temper and was unlikely to be as easy going or cooperative under the circumstances. The last thing he needed was for Finch to lash out and potentially say something that would be cause for suspicion.

He lay back on the bench physically exhausted and emotionally worn out. Having not slept for over a day he could no longer fight his body's desire to drift off into a deep, dreamless sleep.

Marcus had been correct about Finch. Compared to Marcus, Finch had a much easier time of it as a Gen1. As he lay back on the bench of his cell, he found himself thinking about Ling Ling's kitchen. He longed for a cup of her wonderful mint tea and the sweet aroma that filled his nostrils every time he lifted the cup to his lips. It was a bittersweet memory that he hoped he would never forget.

The following day, Finch was released from his isolation pod and immediately ushered up to The Great Hall for a debriefing session with all twelve Advocates. It was described as a debriefing but Finch knew that it would most likely feel like an interrogation. His insides were churning as he ascended the tube to the highest point of the crystal zone complex, and he knew that it would be a test of not only his nerve, but of his ability to lie convincingly.

"Welcome home Associate," the Advocates chanted in unison.

"Thank you," Finch replied.

One of the Advocates addressed Finch. "Please sit with us. We are eager to learn of your experiences out there in the other place."

Finch took his seat. "I too am eager to know what has happened, if anything, during my absence."

"Of course. We shall come to that later on. But first, please tell us of your search for the missing Gen1 Anja," the Advocate said, leaning forward.

"Well, as you know we have not returned with her. We scoured many areas in the hope of finding any clues to her whereabouts, but sadly these did not come to fruition."

"And why were you absent for so long?"

"We had a lot of area to cover Advocate and travelling was a slow process."

"How so? You had transport."

"Oh, you mean the bikes. Yes of course, well unfortunately these were stolen not long after we arrived."

"Stolen. There, you see! Just what we should have expected from that lawless wasteland!" The Advocate's tone was one of righteous indignation. "Go on Associate."

Finch continued in the hope of explaining himself. "Well, if I may Advocates, not all the people in the yellow zone were of a disposition to take what wasn't theirs."

"Nonsense! These sorts of people are the very reason our planet is in such peril. They're vermin," the Advocate said assertively, and it was clear he wasn't going to be persuaded otherwise.

Finch shook his head and looked downwards. He knew that if he protested too much they would view him as a traitor to the crystal zone philosophy.

Another Advocate spoke up. "You disagree Associate? If you do we are here to listen and learn so please speak freely."

Finch noticed a very subtle frown cast in the direction of his fellow Advocate that was unmistakeably a warning to back off.

"Yes, please go on Associate. Tell us about what the environment was like where you travelled. Did you find it difficult?"

"It was extremely hot and very dry. Water was hard to find, and by that I mean water that was safe to drink. It was a very harsh environment for sure, and we encountered some savage dust storms along the way as well." Finch's throat felt dry just saying the words. He reached for the glass of water that had been provided for him on the table.

"Did you find it hard to breathe Associate?"

"To begin with. But we had our filtration masks. Eventually we seemed to become acclimatised to our surroundings and needed to use our masks less and less."

"Tell us about your relationship with Doctor Jarret."

"My relationship?"

"Yes. Did you find him an easy travelling companion, were there tensions between you? That sort of thing."

"I was instructed to accompany Doctor Jarret in his search for a Gen1 woman who had left the crystal zone and disappeared. *That* was my relationship. Nothing more. Nothing less." Finch was starting to feel unnerved and hoped that none of the Advocates noticed.

"But you've spent quite a while together travelling, surely a friendship must have developed in that amount of time." Another Advocate protested.

"I wasn't there to make friends. I had a duty to perform and I performed it to the best of my ability."

Finch knew instinctively that this was not a time to give long winded answers. Being brief and to the point meant there were less opportunities to be caught out, and it was becoming clear that their interest in any potential relationship he had formed with Marcus was a concern for some of the Advocates.

"May I ask a question please?" Finch ventured tentatively.

"You may."

"What are your plans for me now that I'm back home? Am I to be posted to another location?"

Finch already knew that it would not be the case. However, he tried to imagine what he would have asked had the situation been different and he was still naïve. He also wanted to disrupt his interrogation hoping that by doing so they might stop asking him questions that he didn't want to have to create answers for.

"Ah, yes. We were planning to come onto this Finch. The fact is while you were away many changes occurred which required us to call back all Associates from their posts."

"May I ask why?"

"You may. As you know we are the last bastion of human existence on our planet that enjoys a high quality of life, and you also know that we are a planet with finite resources. But it's also a planet of immense suffering for the less fortunate who reside in other zones."

Finch knew what was coming. He'd heard it from Brock, and now he had to pretend he was hearing it for the first time from the Advocates.

"There were vast areas of our planet that had literally nothing left to provide for the populations that were there. The people were suffering from starvation and disease and the Leader decreed that this suffering must come to an end in the most humane way possible. As a result we immediately called back all Associates from the red zone and launched phase one of the Leader's decree."

Finch closed his eyes for just a second, but it was long enough to conjure up Sylvie's sweet face in his mind's eye, and to feel an ache in his heart for what had happened to her and to her people.

"Phase One?" Finch said, trying hard to sound intrigued.

The Advocate explained what had happened in the red zone. Finch's eyes were fixed on the Advocate as he spoke, which made him appear interested. His mind, however, went to another place so that he didn't have to hear the awful details of what the Leader had done.

"You have to understand that this was a mission of mercy. A

mission of the highest order of humanity to our fellow species. The Leader made their decree and it was our duty to comply. And we have now called back all Associates in the yellow zone too, as we are soon to begin Phase Two of the Leader's decree."

"And these decrees, do they sit well with you Advocate?" Finch asked.

The Advocate was taken aback by the question. No one had ever dared to ask how an Advocate felt about complying with a decree from the Leader.

"Your question is impertinent Associate."

Another Advocate tried to calm his colleague. "I'm sure the Associate meant no harm colleague. Perhaps he has been out in the other place too long and picked up some unfortunate habits."

The Advocate gave Finch a knowing look that made him wonder whether or not this particular Advocate was one of those less enamoured with the way things were being run. It was a subtle look but the eyes can say so much without the need for words. Finch bowed his head in reverence realising that he had overstepped the mark.

"Yes perhaps my curiosity has been aroused by being in the other place and I apologise for any offence that I have caused," Finch said with haste.

"It will take you some time to recondition your mind now that you are home, and I hope for your sake that this doesn't take too long. There are plans for you and we need you to be at the top of your game. As one of my own twelve Associates, I have great hopes for you," the Advocate said, keeping his eyes locked on Finch.

"Understood Advocate. I appreciate your patience and understanding and can assure you of my loyalty and dedication to you, and to our glorious Leader."

He surprised himself at how easy those words had been to say despite having no genuine meaning behind them. He was becoming an adept liar, saying whatever his superiors needed to hear even though it made him feel sick to his stomach. He had become an efficient and effective actor.

"You are excused Associate, for the moment at least, but we

will continue our dialogue with you over the coming weeks. We will all be having separate meetings with our own Associates now that everyone has returned."

"Not everyone colleague. One of my Associates is still in the other place, and I have had no contact from him for a worrying length of time."

"I apologise for omitting Brock's displacement Advocate."

"I had hoped that Brock would link up with you Finch but it appears that has not been the case."

Finch shook his head.

"Then this meeting is adjourned."

The Advocates that were physically present in The Great Hall rose from their chairs and departed, their great cloaks creating a slight breeze on Finch's face as they swished past him. The Advocates who were there holographically ended their transmissions.

Now alone at the enormous table in The Great Hall, Finch took a moment. He inhaled deeply and exhaled with relief that this first interrogation was over. When Brock's name was mentioned he had felt his face flush with anxiety and his body become rigid. He was grateful that no further questions were forthcoming about his fellow Associate.

It was only mid-afternoon when Finch was dismissed back into the crystal zone community, and the virtual sky was a glorious bright blue, but it didn't matter. Finch was exhausted and in desperate need of a comfortable rest in his own bed, in his own pod, with his own thoughts.

CHAPTER 49

observation 1:8

I am sensing that a great disturbance is approaching.

How typical it is for those from the past to dictate a future that they will not dwell in. Is it fear or vanity, or simply the desire for ultimate control that drives their actions? Although the danger will arrive in the coming weeks, it was driven by the fear of one immensely powerful man from the past who no longer lives.

The consequences of his actions are now unavoidable and will change everything going forward. My sadness is that I will arrive too late to prevent it.

CHAPTER 50

crystal

It was another day before Marcus was released, and it's fair to say that he was not in a good mood when they came to get him. He felt as though his stomach had been turned inside out, and he had been violated in so many other ways to the point where he realised just how damaging all of the tests and extractions must be for the women who came to his clinic. He hated being back in the crystal zone with all of its secrets and lies, and his heart was aching for Anja.

Feeling physically and mentally drained, he was strapped into the shuttle that would take him to what he knew would be an interrogation by the Advocates. So much depended on him keeping his cool and not lashing out with what he really wanted to say to them, because he now detested them, and everything they stood for.

By the time he reached The Great Hall he had controlled his breathing, lowered his blood pressure, and regained a clarity in his head of what he needed to say instead of what he wanted to say.

"Greetings and welcome home Doctor Jarret, please sit with us, we are eager to learn all about your experiences in the other place."

"Thank you Advocates I am glad to be home."

"Firstly, we apologise for the extensive tests that you experienced upon your arrival home. These were necessary due to your more basic genetic structure which means you are less resilient than our Gen1s. We had to be absolutely sure that you were not carrying a contaminant or bacteria that could have endangered our people. Even a tiny foreign organism could have caused irreparable damage to our pristine environment. However, I am pleased to assure you that we are now satisfied you are completely clean."

"I am greatly relieved to hear this Advocates. The last thing I would wish is to pose a hazard of any kind."

"As a doctor and man of science we felt that you would understand and take it in your stride. And now we would like to ask you a few questions if we may."

"Yes of course. I am happy to answer all of your questions to the best of my ability."

"Firstly we would like to ask you about your experience spending time with our Associate Finch. Can you describe your relationship with him please?"

Marcus scratched his head.

"My relationship with Finch? That's an easy one." Marcus smiled. "I wouldn't call my association with Finch a *relationship*. He was very professional, efficient, and resourceful during our time together and I felt safe having him by my side in such unfamiliar territory."

"That is good to hear Doctor Jarret. It must have been extremely hard for you to return here without Anja."

"Yes Advocates my heart is very heavy."

"We extend our condolences to you Doctor Jarret."

"I appreciate that Advocates."

"In time however, the pain you are feeling now will not be so raw, and it is our hope that you will find another to couple with in due course, in particular another from your own kind."

Marcus could feel a rush of adrenaline sweeping over his body. His own kind? He knew what that meant but it felt like a dagger in his heart. Never before had it been so apparent that the Advocates saw him as inferior to the Gen1s. He knew that had it not been for his exceptional scholastic ability as a child that led him to become a geneticist, it is unlikely he would have been afforded such a high profile position within the community. Once he had taken pride in his work, but now he just felt like an accomplice to an atrocity against humanity.

"However, if you do unfortunately end up having another association with a Gen1 in the future, the rules that we laid out for you and Anja previously would still apply."

Marcus could never forget the first time the Advocates told him what the fate of any conception between himself and Anja would be. Revenge was a dish best served cold, and Marcus's revenge for what they had commanded was that thousands of miles away there would soon be a hybrid child born out of love; a child the Leader and the Advocates would never know about.

"The purity of our future generations must be our priority. I'm sure you understand Doctor Jarret."

"I do."

"Tell us about the people you encountered on your journey in the other place."

Marcus proceeded to tell them a similar story to the one that they had heard from Finch the day before. He told them of the struggles that he had seen people working so hard to overcome, and of the intense heat and desperation in search of food and water that was fit to drink. He spoke of the ingenuity of some who had managed to adapt to the difficult environmental changes but stopped short of saying how sad he felt that they seemed to have so little, when people in the crystal zone had so much. Showing any form of empathy towards those in the other place would have been a dangerous path to tread, and to an Advocate's ear would have sounded like betrayal rather than compassion.

"Do you feel well enough to return to the clinic, or would you prefer to take some time to recuperate?"

Marcus knew that there wasn't a moment to waste, and he was positively itching to get things started.

"I'm ready to return to the clinic tomorrow Advocates."

"Excellent. I know that you have been sorely missed by your colleagues. We may wish to speak to you again at another time, but for now we thank you for your time and candour."

As the Advocates rose and exited the table, and those that

were there holographically terminated their transmissions, Marcus knew that there were still eyes on him as he stood at the table until all the Advocates had departed. There were very few places within the crystal zone that were truly private without eyes watching and ears listening. He ensured that his facial expressions did not portray his true feelings in his final moments in The Great Hall. Marcus had quickly learned to become a master of the blank expression. It was a skill that would serve him well in the coming days and weeks.

Marcus and Finch were such an unlikely partnership. A doctor and scientist, and an Associate Advocate, cooperating with each other to disrupt an entire society was the last thing the Leader or the Advocates could have imagined.

The beauty of their pairing was the fact that they had nothing in common. Their skillsets were completely different, and most important of all, was that each had access to a specific area that the other didn't. As an associate, Finch could infiltrate classified areas within the complex. As a doctor, Marcus could access the DNA of every person in the crystal zone other than the Advocates, and of course the Leader, if indeed the Leader had DNA at all. It was a potent combination.

After returning to his pod briefly, Marcus felt the need of a hot bath and made his way to the bathing complex, not only to get clean, but also to be a visible presence so that people could see he had returned. He had hoped to run into some friendly faces but was surprised at the reaction he received. Some wouldn't make eye contact with him. Others made a barely perceptible nod of acknowledgment from a distance. Nobody came over to welcome him home with a smile, and he couldn't determine whether their reticence to engage with him was out of fear, or if something had happened during his absence that had turned him into a pariah in their eyes.

Finch's experience couldn't have been more different. With all of his fellow Associates, bar Brock, now back in the crystal zone, he was welcomed back with great celebration. He was seen as a returning hero by his colleagues and treated to a number of small gatherings to honour him. Finch felt quite overwhelmed by this demonstration of what felt like genuine affection for him. He was the first Associate to have been drafted to accompany a citizen into unchartered areas of the yellow zone, and he'd lived to tell the tale.

Suddenly, he could have his pick of Gen1 females who buzzed around him making their physical attributes quite obvious. Although he enjoyed all the attention and flattery, Finch wasn't tempted to participate in anything physical with these girls. It felt awkward and wrong when all he could think about was how much he wanted to be with Silvie, but he also knew that to rebuff all advances would be a very strange thing for a Gen1 Associate to do. He couldn't afford to raise any suspicions at this point, especially as he had historically been very generous with his body. For the time being, he used the excuse of feeling tired from his travels, but he knew that it would only be a temporary reprieve.

With 143 of the Associates now residing in the crystal zone, there was talk within Associate circles about what their new roles would be. Some were convinced that they would be the next in line to become full Advocates. Others were simply happy to be back in an environment where the air was cool and clean, and where food and water was plentiful. Finch discovered that they'd all had a debriefing session with their own Advocates, and that he had been the last one to be interviewed. There was also talk of the one missing Associate, Brock. Some Associates imagined he had been taken prisoner by savages in the yellow zone, while others thought he may have deserted. Only two people in the crystal zone knew exactly what had happened to Brock, and why, and it was a secret both would happily take to their graves.

"What about you Finch? What do you think happened to our colleague?"

"Me? Oh, I honestly couldn't say," Finch said, feeling a moment of nausea rising up inside him.

It was the first time many of the Associates had met up with each other in a few years, and there was no shortage of horror stories being told about the various places they'd been posted to. But Finch was surprised to hear a handful talk about their postings with some affection, especially towards the local people they had encountered. Others spoke of what they'd learned about the planet's history, making a point of saying how surprised they were that they hadn't been taught about it in the crystal zone. He made sure to make a mental note of these Associates, as some could soon become useful.

The following morning Marcus was awake early, preparing for his first day back at the clinic. He wondered what had been happening while he was gone, whether there had been any changes, or if things had just ticked over in the same way without him. His questions were soon answered when he walked through the doors.

"Good morning Doctor Jarret."

Marcus looked at where the voice had come from with some consternation.

"Good morning. Where is Jay?"

"Being retrained. I am being trialled. Would you like to see your list for today?"

"Err …yes, OK. You look like a Gen1," Marcus said, with an air of bewilderment.

"I believe my appearance is reminiscent of a Gen1, but that is where any similarity ends Doctor Jarret. You see, I can report back directly to the Leader, which Jay couldn't. And the beauty is that I don't have to do anything to generate information for him. It happens automatically."

"How so?"

"You wouldn't understand. I'm an extremely advanced system."

This extremely advanced system had fooled Marcus from a distance. Looking every inch human, and virtually indistinguishable in mannerisms and vocal notations, this creation was a perfect example of what Marcus feared for the future. He had never been a fan of AI, but it appeared he was going to have to adapt his thinking quickly. He decided to try a different tack.

"May I enquire why such a superb example of AI is in such a, well, menial position?"

"You may enquire Doctor Jarret. I have nothing to hide. I am being trialled here for the I.I.A."

"The I.I.A?"

"Intuitive Iteration Algorithm. In a few days I will progress to less *menial* tasks and greater responsibilities."

Marcus noted that sarcasm seemed to have been included in its programming as well.

"And is there an end game? By that I mean …"

"I understand what you mean Doctor Jarret. And yes, there is."

"May I know what it is?"

"You may not."

After a slightly uncomfortable silence it continued. "You will find that I am now fronting all departments within all quarters of the complex."

"You are? Do you mean there are others like you?"

"Not *like* me. There is *just* me. One name. One face, all linked by one master brain. There are of course several devices that house me, what you call bodies, just to make me appear more approachable. It's how I can learn so quickly. At any given time I am processing thousands of pieces of information. I know which information is important and which isn't. The more information I am exposed to, the more I discover and the smarter I become."

Marcus stood there dumbfounded.

"Do you have a name?"

"Of course I have a *name* Doctor Jarret. I am Avia. I have transferred your list for today Doctor Jarret. Glory to the Leader."

"Glory to the Leader?"

"It wasn't a question Doctor Jarret."

Marcus was slightly flustered. "Oh, yes of course! Glory to the Leader! Sorry, I've been away for a while and I'm still reacclimatising."

He hadn't anticipated anything like this when he got back, but it wasn't going to deter him. He would just have to be even more guarded and resourceful.

CHAPTER 51

crystal

One of the first things Marcus did upon returning to the crystal zone was seek out Professor Hill, which he did during his lunch break. He knew exactly where to find him and headed towards the virtual golf course.

"Marcus my boy. I've heard all about your little adventure. Welcome home!"

"Thank you Professor." Marcus began in a hushed tone. "Walter sends his regards."

Professor Hill stopped in his tracks. The colour drained from his face, and he began to shake so much that he needed to be helped to a nearby bench. After a short while he regained his composure.

"We can't talk here. Come to my pod this evening Marcus. I'm on the second level, number 228."

Marcus nodded then left the old man to collect his thoughts, which were now about anything other than golf.

Back at the clinic he realised that, as much as he wished he didn't have to, he had to continue conducting tests on the Gen1s as normal so as not to arouse any suspicion. He was mildly relieved that today he was testing Gen1 males at least, but he was deeply uncomfortable with the new system, and especially with Avia.

Since he'd been away, a lot had changed in the clinic. There was none of the usual camaraderie. Everyone just got on with their work in an uneasy silence. Marcus found the atmosphere oppressive and couldn't wait for the day to be over so that he could talk with Professor Hill.

In between his appointments he had an unexpected visit from one of the technicians.

"Doctor Jarret. I'm here to change your bracelet."

"My bracelet? What's wrong with the one I'm wearing?"

"We've been instructed to change it. It's faulty. Please hold out your arm."

Marcus watched as the studious young man unclamped his existing bracelet and attached a new one in a matter of minutes.

"There. All done." And with that, the technician was gone.

Marcus looked at his new bracelet and wondered whether there had been any truth in what the young man had said. Was his bracelet faulty, or did they just say that in order to fit him with a new improved model that would track his every move? He had learned to no longer trust anything about the crystal zone, almost to the point of paranoia.

Marcus found himself thinking about Finch and wondering how he was fairing. He missed being in his company, their banter, and the strength they gave one another. It felt strange not to be able to see him or talk to him, but he told himself that it was only a temporary arrangement and that he must stay focussed on the plan.

When evening came Marcus made his way to Professor Hill's pod. His heart was racing with excitement at the prospect of telling him all his news, and discovering how the Professor could help. The Professor was equally excited about hearing how Walter was, and what life was really like in the yellow zone.

"Come in, come in dear boy! I've literally been counting the minutes." The old man was practically dancing as he ushered Marcus inside his pod. "Take a seat and make yourself comfortable."

"I hardly know where to start Professor."

The Professor made the command. "Music on."

Beautiful music filled the pod. It was music that Marcus had never heard before.

"What is this?"

"Chopin. The most beautiful music ever written in my humble opinion. This piece was written in 1830. The poor chap only lived to be 39 years old, but in his lifetime he composed a body of work that is incomparable."

"It's quite breath-taking."

"Yes it is, and more importantly it will ensure that we are not overheard by anyone." The Professor's eyes looked towards the ceiling. "Now then, rumour has it that you were sent to the yellow zone with an Associate to bring back a Gen1 girl, is that correct?"

"Yes. Although she's not just *any* girl, she's the woman I'm in love with."

"Oh, I see. But she fled here and went to the yellow zone. Why would she have done that Marcus?"

"She's pregnant."

The Professor's eyes widened with shock.

"Oh my that does make things difficult. I hope you don't mind me asking Marcus, but is it yours?"

Marcus responded with pride. "Yes."

"Good heavens. Well I can't imagine the Advocates would be pleased about that. I mean, she's a Gen1 and you're a …"

"Exactly. The Advocates gave us permission to couple on the understanding that any pregnancy that resulted had to be terminated."

"Oh Marcus, I'm so sorry," Professor Hill said with sadness "That must have been very difficult for you both."

"That's not why she fled. She didn't know about the agreement. She just didn't want her child, our child, to have to endure a lifetime of being tested the way she has been."

The Professor nodded his understanding and sat with that thought for a moment.

"Did you find her and bring her back?"

"She's still in the yellow zone, and I'm happy to say, she's still pregnant."

"Do the Advocates know this?"

"No, I had to lie and tell them we didn't find her. She's with

Walter and Ling Ling."

The Professor's face beamed with joy upon hearing Walter's name.

"Then at least she's safe. Now tell me all about Walter. How is my dear old friend?"

"Quite remarkable to be honest. I've never met anyone like him. And also dear Harvey, who I'm very sad to tell you passed away while we were there."

"Oh my, that is very sad news indeed. He was never the same after he lost Vincent. Such a shame."

"Walter told me everything about how the crystal zone came about, his part in it and why he and Harvey walked away from the project. And why you made the difficult decision to stay here. I've learned so much that it makes my head spin. Oh, and I learned all about the animals that once roamed the earth too."

Suddenly the Professor's eyes filled with tears and he had to excuse himself for a moment.

"I do apologise Marcus. It's just been such a long time since I thought about all that was lost. I decided to stay behind because someone needed to monitor the situation here, but it was the hardest decision of my life. You can't imagine how many times I thought about leaving here over the years, but in the end I realised that there was nothing left for me out there. I'm greatly relieved to learn that Walter is still alive."

Marcus continued to tell the Professor all about what life was like in the yellow zone, the people he'd met, and the friendships he'd made. He could have skipped forward to Walter's grim discovery about the food they were eating in the crystal zone, but felt it appropriate to lead up to this gently as there was so much information for the old man to take in.

"There's something else I need to tell you Professor, and it won't be easy to hear I'm afraid."

"I did sense that you were leading up to something Marcus. I may be old but I'm not stupid." The Professor laughed nervously.

"It's something Walter discovered in his lab about the food we're eating here."

The Professor listened carefully as Marcus described how

Walter had taken a sample of the food they'd brought with them and conducted several experiments on it. He was keen to understand what it contained. When he finally explained where the source of protein was coming from the Professor's reaction was complete and utter horror.

"Bastards! How could they? Is this what humanity has descended into? I don't know why I'm so surprised, this place is based on lies and deception. Bastards!"

"I'm so sorry Professor. I knew this would be upsetting to hear, but I needed to tell you the truth."

"I'm glad you shared this with me. I just wish it wasn't true. Can you imagine if this gets out?"

"Well that's the thing Professor. It needs to become general knowledge. I can't let this continue unchallenged. Every day going to the clinic knowing what I know and still putting all those women through it." Marcus was quickly working himself into a state.

"Calm down dear boy." The Professor put his hand on Marcus's shoulder. "I hear you and I agree. Your position is untenable. But how do we go about this I wonder?"

"Walter suggested that you had a relationship with one or two of the Advocates. Do you think they know what's going on?"

"Ah, Alex and John. Well if they don't already know, I'll make sure they do. I know they have some Associates on side as well."

"That's great Professor. Perhaps they can speak with the Leader and …"

"The Leader? Don't get me started about him! No, the Leader can never know that we're onto this."

Marcus was a little taken aback at the Professor's reaction to approaching the Leader.

"Let's just say that my two Advocate friends are also onto something. Something that could change everything here."

CHAPTER 52

crystal

With Professor Hill now aware of the situation, the next thing on Marcus's list was to engage with Anja's pod mates Elise, Bibi and Cerine. Visiting the Professor's pod wouldn't have raised any concern with the Advocates as Marcus had been a former pupil. But he knew that visiting the girl's pod again would likely raise alarm bells. He'd gotten away with it once but that was before his journey to the yellow zone. Now he needed to get a message to them in a different way. He needed to wait until one of the girls was due to come into his clinic.

A week later he spotted that Bibi was the first of the girls to be due in his clinic that week. It gave him time to write a letter to them, which he would have to give Bibi surreptitiously during her appointment as all conversations that took place in the clinic were monitored by the Advocates.

Anja had assured him that her pod mates could be trusted, and all that Marcus could do was hope she was right. By putting everything in writing he knew that he risked exposing himself as a traitor to the Leader if the letter got into the wrong hands.

In the days leading up to his appointment with Bibi, Marcus was restless. In the evenings when he was alone in his pod, he found himself tormented at the thought of Anja being so far away. He longed to be with her and to see her through her pregnancy. He couldn't sleep and found himself gagging at the thought of eating the food they were provided with. But he also knew that as hard as every day was, it was another day that he hoped would bring him closer to being with her again.

On the morning of his appointment with Bibi he felt anxious. So much relied on the reaction of the girls to the contents of his letter.

"Good morning Doctor Jarret."

"Good morning Bibi. Please take a seat."

Marcus was conscious of every move he made, every word he uttered, and that nothing had to appear out of the ordinary.

"How have you been feeling?"

"I feel perfectly well Doctor Jarret. I'm more interested in how you are to be honest."

"Me? Oh I'm just fine thank you."

"Really? After your big adventure outside, I'm surprised to hear that. I'm guessing that you didn't manage to locate Anja."

"That is correct." Marcus shot her a knowing look. "Now let's get on with things shall we?"

"That's disappointing to hear Doctor Jarret. We miss her very much."

"I'm sure you do."

Marcus proceeded to put Bibi through the raft of tests required for all Gen1 females. He tried to remain aloof and professional throughout the hour they were together.

At the end of their session, Marcus escorted her to the door. Just before it opened he thrust the letter into her hand and whispered, "say nothing." They exchanged glances for a moment and then she left the clinic. He noticed that as she walked away, she slipped the letter in her pocket and zipped it closed.

He found himself greatly relieved that, on this occasion at least, Bibi hadn't tested positive so he didn't have to send her to the other side of the clinic for an extraction.

Now Marcus had the hardest part of all. He had to wait for a response. A response that he knew was a difficult ask for the girls. He had no option but to tell them the truth and hope that they would react appropriately. He knew what was at stake if they were successful at delivering his request.

That evening when all the girls had returned to the pod after completing their workday Bibi opened the letter with them. Marcus's first instruction was for them to put on music so that they could discuss things without being overheard. They did as he asked then sat down together to read his letter.

"I can't believe it!" Elise blurted out, on the verge of a panic attack.

"I don't want to believe it," said Bibi, comforting Elise. "But he has no reason to lie to us."

Cerine had tears streaming down her face. "I feel sick."

"It's a lot to take in, isn't it?" Bibi did her best to console Cerine.

The three girls sat in silence for the next hour, listening to the music, and just trying to process the contents of Marcus's letter. In it he detailed his experiences in the yellow zone, the fact that Anja was safe and that she was carrying their child, and what would have happened to that child if she returned. He also explained what was happening to the material taken from their bodies, which was the hardest thing he had to tell the girls. And lastly, he asked for their help.

"Well I'm in," Cerise said, breaking the silence. "I know it's going to be difficult, but we owe it to Anja."

"We owe it to ourselves. We all owe it to ourselves," Bibi replied.

"We sure do," said Elise. "I'm so disgusted, it makes me so angry to discover what's really been going on. We'll start tomorrow."

CHAPTER 53

crystal

All the returning Associates were treated like heroes having served the Leader and the Advocates so loyally, and as a reward could take their pick of departments to work in. There was also a memorial service for Brock, the one Associate who did not return. It was at the service that Finch first noticed some of his colleagues weren't quite as loyal as they appeared to be on the surface. He dug a little deeper and discovered that there was a small group of Associates that were less than happy with the way things had been run in the red and yellow zones. Of the 143 that had returned, he counted around thirty that appeared to have formed a breakaway group. They had started having secret meetings where they felt able to air their grievances without being overheard by their colleagues or the Advocates. Finch made sure he gained access to the group, feeding them morsels of information to make them bite and fuel the flames of dissatisfaction. He needed allies if the plan was to work.

One Associate spoke up. "I can't say that I'm sorry to have left the red zone behind. But things here have changed since I've been away. Maybe it's just me."

"No it's not just you. The atmosphere here is different. Less relaxed." Another Associate confirmed.

"Agreed. As you know, I was on a special mission in the yellow zone and life was hard for sure, but I don't agree with what they're planning to do there," Finch said.

"What do you mean Finch?"

"Oh dear. I thought you all knew." Finch pretended to have spoken out of turn.

"If you know something Finch, please let us in on it. There are no secrets here."

"OK, well you must all know by now what they did in the red zone."

"Yes, we know. Absolutely shocking. I mean what gives them the right to kill all those people. Surely we should've been helping them, but in my time there I saw no assistance, no supplies, no medicines. All I feel I was there for was spying on them to be honest." One extremely disgruntled Associate volunteered.

Another Associate spoke up. "And the worst thing is that other than us, nobody else knows what's happening out there. They're just going about their days here like everything is OK."

"Well, I have it on good authority that they're planning on sending the drones into the yellow zone next to wipe out the population there too." Finch declared, to the horror of his colleagues.

"What? Surely not!"

"This can't be true."

"It's madness. They've lost their minds."

"I didn't want to believe it but my Advocate hinted that this might be the case." One Associate said with his head in his hands.

"Do you trust your Advocate?" Finch asked.

"I do."

"How many of you feel that you can freely speak your mind with your Advocate?" Finch needed to press his colleagues in case there were more trustworthy Advocates they could enlist the support of.

"My Advocate is a PreGen. He remembers how things were long before any of us were born. I trust him implicitly."

"I don't trust mine at all."

"Nor mine."

"What are you thinking Finch? Can we stop this from happening?"

"Surely we have to try."

"Yes, we must try. And what you said before about how nobody else knows the truth, well I think it's about time they did. So, here's what I think we should do." Finch spoke in a low but confident voice.

The group huddled closely, hanging on Finch's every word. With the returning Associates being able to take their pick of departments, he asked for volunteers to assign themselves to various groups within the crystal zone community. Some offered to be placed in the technology sphere, while others opted for the defence system, although the Leader had ultimate control over the drones. He instructed them to familiarise themselves with the way all the systems worked, how data was collected and stored, and who was in charge of operations in each department. He wanted them to get access to, and then copy, schematics and they didn't disappoint.

After a few weeks, Finch quickly found himself becoming the breakaway group's leader, with Associates gladly feeding back information directly to him. He was able to discover the technical specifications of the entire crystal zone, from simple things like the way the messaging system worked on their bracelets, to more complex mechanisms such as the climate controls of the spheres, and the programming of the transport ships. Gaining access to the military drones was impossible as these were controlled directly by the Leader, and nobody had ever attempted to penetrate the Leader's private domain. What they had ascertained however, was the timing schedule for deploying the drones to the yellow zone. As some of the drones used in the red zone strike had failed to return, the drone strikes were planned in four stages in order for the remaining drone army to return for refuelling with their deadly bioweapon. The first strike was imminent and was going to be aimed in the southernmost region of the yellow zone. These were less densely populated areas, but it didn't make it any easier for the group to admit that they had run out of time to save those people.

They had no option but to turn their attention to preventing subsequent strikes and agreed that there was simply no way of preventing them without coming face to face with the Leader. This wasn't something Finch could ask a volunteer to do. He knew he'd have to do it himself.

"You can't do it alone Finch. Let some of us come with you as backup."

"I appreciate the support colleagues, but if more than one of us appears in The Great Hall at the same time …"

"We'll stagger our entry. You go first and then we'll follow a few minutes afterwards. You know it makes sense."

He politely declined their valiant offers to accompany him. His instincts told him this was a one man job and if he failed, and the worst happened, he needed the rest of the group to continue their mission without detection.

Finch knew he would have to enlist the help of one of the trusted Advocates to get him up to The Great Hall. He needed to gain access to the corridor that ran along the back and was carved deep into the mountain. Nobody knew how far away the private quarters of the Leader were, they only knew which direction he went in whenever he left The Great Hall. It was a mission fraught with danger as there was no way of knowing what security measures, if any, were in place to prevent anyone getting close enough to actually see who the Leader was, and importantly, to discover where the controls for the drones were in his quarters.

The Advocate knew what was at stake and gladly offered his assistance, despite the risks involved for both of them.

On the morning of his mission, Finch briefed the group on what to do in case he was caught. He felt sure that if that happened he would be exiled to a secure pod, and probably never seen again. Hopefully, it would be seen as just one Associate that had gone rogue and not trigger any further investigation.

Finch ascended in the tube that led to The Great Hall. His heart was pounding from a surge in adrenalin, his breathing was fast and shallow, and his hands were shaking. He had to take control of his body in order to function. By the time he'd reached the top, he had managed to slow his breathing and regain his composure.

"Greetings Associate," came a welcoming voice.

The Advocate was calm and reassuring as he sat at the long table.

"Thank you for seeing me Advocate."

They were both aware that their conversation was being monitored.

"How can I be of assistance to you today?"

They discussed issues of little consequence for about half an hour, until the Advocate excused himself saying that he was feeling unwell and leaving Finch alone in The Great Hall. Finch knew that he had to act quickly and made his way to the corridor he had seen on the schematics. It was long and dimly lit, and every step he took he could feel himself becoming increasingly anxious. When he reached the end of the corridor there was a large steel sliding door. Finch had to use all of his strength to force it open. What didn't make sense was that this was where the schematics ended. On the other side of the door was complete darkness, but it was where the Leader's quarters should have been. He switched on his bracelet to shine some light ahead. As he stepped across the door's threshold, dim overhead lights came on automatically wherever he was standing, and went out behind him with each step he made. Finch's heart was in his throat as he moved further and further along the passageway that curved to the left and then to the right. Eventually he came to another large steel sliding door, which he again had to force open. This time on the other side, he found a large room that had a giant wall of screens showing every area inside the crystal zone complex and all around its perimeter. There was also a bank of smaller screens on another wall that looked like they were processing data in vast quantities. The only light in the room was coming from all the screens, but it was sufficient for Finch to record it all on his bracelet. To his left he noticed the shadow of a hooded robe draped on a chair. The room was spartan in appearance with no bed, and other than the chair, there was no furniture. He started wondering if he'd gone into the wrong room.

There was a very faint humming sound coming from the furthest corner of the large room. It was so dark that he couldn't make out what was causing it. Slowly and silently he walked closer to where the noise was coming from shining the light from his bracelet on the ground so that he didn't trip over anything. The closer he got to the sound, the more his heart raced. There seemed to be a pale orange light glowing intermittently from the same area. When he reached the source of the noise and the flashing light, Finch froze, he couldn't believe what was in front of him. He panicked and ran out of the room through the open steel door and along the passageway, forcing the other steel sliding door open once again. When he was back in the corridor he ran at high speed until he was back in The Great Hall. What he'd seen was hard to comprehend and it frightened him.

Finch wanted to get far away from what he'd seen, and it felt as though it took forever for the capsule to reach ground level. With his head spinning and his body trembling, he tried to process what had just happened.

He needed to tell the trusted Advocate, and he had to get a message to Marcus as quickly as possible.

CHAPTER 54

crystal

"Come in, come in." Professor Hill was breathless with excitement as he ushered Marcus into his pod. "I have news. Big news."

With Chopin's second piano concerto playing in the background, Marcus listened closely as the Professor relayed the extraordinary development about the Leader. He thought about Avia and how realistic she was, and how she had said that all the data was being transferred to the Leader automatically. It suddenly made sense. He hated AI, in fact just the thought of it made his blood boil. Machines that could do the work of humans and in some case better than humans. Machines that increased productivity and efficiency, but that even after so many decades of living alongside them, lacked the one vital ingredient that made all the difference … humanity.

"We must expose this," Marcus said sternly. "He … it … needs to be eradicated and replaced with … a human."

"Easier said than done my boy."

"Well if Finch was able to gain access so easily I don't see what the problem is."

"I'm just being cautious Marcus. John and Alex are in an extremely vulnerable position now. There are ten other Advocates. Any attempt at overthrowing the Leader would be met with opposition."

"I understand your cautious nature Professor. But given the Leader has control over the drones, I can't see another way. We can't let any more people die."

The Professor thought about what Marcus had said. He knew in his heart that he was right, but he was scared.

"I'm an old man Marcus, and I'm not a very brave old man at that."

Marcus walked over, sat down by the Professor, and held his hand.

"I promise we'll do everything we can to make sure you and your Advocate friends are safe."

He knew it was a promise he couldn't keep, and if he was honest, Marcus was afraid of where things were heading too.

"I hear that the unrest in the Gen1 male camp is getting worse," Professor Hill continued. "They're becoming aggressive towards each other, and even to some of the Gen1 women. Is it true that the women are withholding sex?"

"Yes, at my request. I'm afraid it hasn't taken long for things to deteriorate, but what else could I do? Finch and I didn't set out to destroy things here, just to make them more honest and transparent and I still think we can make a positive difference here, just not at the expense of millions of lives outside."

"What message should I relay to Alex and John," the Professor asked, with a look of sadness and resignation.

Marcus agreed to put exposing the Leader on hold briefly, while they focussed on trying to calm the situation down with the Gen1 males. He felt that they deserved an explanation as to why the females were now repelling their advances. After that, exposing the entire population of the crystal community to what had taken place in the red zone took priority. He knew that there was only so much honesty people could absorb in one hit.

Marcus decided that he was best placed to address the issue with the Gen1 males and would rely on Finch and his breakaway group to deal with informing the population about the destruction of the red zone inhabitants. Once these two issues were dealt with, then they could focus on deposing the Leader.

Marcus headed back home to his pod. His head hurt. For a

split second the complexities of what he and Finch were trying to achieve made him question their wisdom. And then he thought of Anja and Silvie, and how their lives had already been affected by the way the world was being run, and his determination returned.

Tomorrow he would begin summoning Gen1 males to attend his clinic. He knew that he couldn't address them all at once, so he arranged for small groups to arrive at set intervals. He knew that Avia would question his request, but he was ready for that. Knowing that the Leader and Advocates would be monitoring his conversations in the clinic, he employed the Professor's technique of playing music while he delivered the bad news to the Gen1 males.

The next day, Marcus was up early and made his way to the clinic well ahead of schedule. He called up the rota and switched who he was seeing that morning, knowing that there was no point seeing any of the females. He explained to Avia that he was running an experiment in time management which, to his relief, she didn't question.

By lunchtime, he'd seen over a hundred of the Gen1 males, and to save time he'd asked them to start spreading the word. He was surprised at the reaction of some of them who thought there was nothing wrong with the system, while others seemed quite hostile to the withholding of what they saw as their rights to take pleasure from the young women. He put their lack of empathy down to the fact that these invasive procedures weren't happening to *their* bodies. On the whole though, there was support for what Marcus had done, and a belief that another source of protein must be found to supplement their nutrition.

By the time his afternoon session had finished, Marcus had seen another hundred young men and felt drained having had to repeatedly explain the situation. He hoped that word would spread fast so that he didn't have to go through the same thing day after day. But just in case, he'd told the Professor to give him a week before asking Finch to arrange for the public announcement of what had happened in the red zone. He left it up to Finch to figure out the best way for this to happen. He had the utmost faith in Finch's ability to get things done, especially now that he was heading up a breakaway group of Associates and was armed with all the technical specifications.

One Associate, who had been based in the red zone, had obtained distressing footage from the drones that delivered their deadly cargo. It was hard for the other Associates to watch as men, women and children fell to the ground dying by the thousands, and it reduced many of them to tears. Finch felt the horror even more acutely than his colleagues when he imagined how close Silvie had come to being one of those innocent victims. He longed to see her again and hear her sweet voice, and as hard as he tried to bury his feelings for her, they would surface when he least expected it.

There were giant display screens in each part of the crystal complex that were used each day to advise the community about mundane things like the air temperature, or the seating times for meals, and of course to alert everyone when it was time to stop and sing the crystal zone anthem every day. The Associates that were posted to the technical departments discovered ways to bypass the existing programming in order to show a film put together by their colleagues of the drone footage with captioning. They also inserted a loop feature so that the film played over and over again, guaranteeing it the widest audience. Importantly, they managed to do all this with an automatic timer and without it being traceable to the work of any individual. All they had to do was look suitably shocked when it played, which wasn't going to be difficult. Just to be absolutely sure that nobody missed seeing it, they decided to also send a message to every bracelet, just prior to the film playing, telling them to look at the monitors.

As agreed, one week after Marcus had spoken with the Gen1 males, the breakaway Associates arranged for the film to be played at the end of the day when everyone was making their way home from work. Some held their nerve; others held their breath watching the clock.

When the time came, everyone's bracelets beeped and they all obediently stood there looking up at the screens. A minute later the film began to play. The captions read:

"This is what is happening outside the crystal zone. The Leader decreed

this slaughter of innocents in the red zone. The yellow zone is next. We thought you should know the truth."

Some turned away unable to watch, others stood there transfixed. After playing on a loop three times, the film disappeared and the Associates knew that it had been taken down. After the initial shock of what they'd seen, people began to huddle in groups talking or comforting those who had become upset.

Marcus, who had never seen the footage from the drones before, was visibly shaken and repulsed, but he was also immensely proud of what Finch and his allies had achieved. Now that nearly everyone knew what was going into their food, and everyone knew about the annihilation of the red zone, they needed to turn their attention to preventing the drone strikes on the remaining populations in the yellow zone. And the only way they could do that was to expose the truth about the Leader.

CHAPTER 55

yellow

As the months passed, Anja's belly continued to swell. She tended the garden with Ling Ling and marvelled at how things grew. These small, precious examples of life gave her hope for the future of her baby. She tried to remain positive when in the company of the others, but when she was alone in her room her thoughts inevitably turned to Marcus. It was a dull aching feeling that consumed her at night when she imagined him by her side, stroking her hair. She heard his voice in her head telling her to be strong and that somehow he would find his way back to her. She had to believe he would, for her own sanity.

Walter's health was failing and the women all took turns nursing him. Ling Ling found it increasingly difficult to watch her husband fading. He had been such a larger than life character, and the house felt much emptier and quieter the more time he spent in bed. The books he loved reading held little interest for him now, and he hadn't been down to the basement to his lab in many weeks.

Ling Ling began imagining what life would be like without her beloved husband. They had been through so much together; survived together. Her heart hurt and her head was all over the place. Winter was her go to person when it all became too much. Her calm disposition was soothing and her deep affection for the two elders of the house was comforting for them both.

But Ling Ling was a highly superstitious woman. As a child she was often told that when a person dies, a child is born. And so the closer Anja came to giving birth, the more she feared that Walter would die as a result. Ling Ling became anxious and more reserved around Anja.

As the only female in the house to have had a child, Silvie stepped up to become Anja's counsel and guide, telling her what to expect from her body during labour. Silvie was excited at the prospect of having a baby to help look after. She missed Jo Jo so much and knowing that Anja was also having a girl made it all the more bittersweet. Winter had helped deliver a number of babies over the years so was fully prepared for when the time came. In the back of her mind she prayed that there wouldn't be any complications, and especially none that required a caesarean as then they would be in trouble. Nobody knew exactly what to expect given this was the first time a hybrid baby would be born.

As dawn broke one morning, a blood curdling scream echoed throughout the house. Winter, Silvie and Anja came hurtling out of their rooms soon realising that the scream had come from Walter and Ling Ling's room. They walked down the hallway holding hands and stood outside the door. Nobody needed words to understand what had happened. Ling Ling's cries told them everything they needed to know.

"May we come in Ling honey?" Winter ventured.

There was no reply. She decided to open the door anyway. There slumped on the bed was Ling Ling rocking Walter back and forth in her arms. She'd awoken to find he'd passed in the early hours, and she was grief stricken.

They all sat on the bed with her and wept for the loss of their friend, and for the pain Ling Ling was in. There were no words that could console her.

Silvie and Anja crept out of the room, down the stairs and into the kitchen leaving Winter to try and comfort her. Silvie started preparing mint tea as she wiped away her tears. She looked at Anja for her approval to make the tea.

Anja reached for the mugs. "It's exactly what Ling Ling would do," she said, as she placed five mugs on the tray, then put one back realising that only four were needed now.

The two women busied themselves in the kitchen waiting for the water to boil. They cleaned and tidied the room even though there was no need as Ling Ling always kept it immaculate, but they simply didn't know what else to do with themselves.

After a while, Winter appeared at the doorway.

"I've persuaded Ling Ling to come downstairs. She'll be here presently. I was comin' down to make some mint tea but I see you've already thought of that," Winter said, attempting a smile before bursting into tears again. "It's just so sad."

Silvie walked over to Winter and put her arms around her. "Walter so sick. Now he at peace." They were still hugging each other when Ling Ling walked into the kitchen.

Her eyes were red and puffy, and she looked like her world had collapsed.

Silvie gestured to a chair. "Come sit. We make tea."

Ling Ling sat down obediently and sipped at the steaming hot brew. "It's very good," she said softly.

The four women sat around the table in silence for a few minutes until Ling Ling blurted out through breathless sobs that they needed to bury him.

"Yes. We'll take care of everything Ling Ling, don't you worry. Perhaps next to Harvey?" Winter suggested.

"He'd like that. Oh God what am I going to do without him?"

Winter wondered how they were going to dig a grave without Finch and Marcus. The ground was rock hard and she remembered that it took them nearly two days to reach a suitable depth to bury Harvey.

Anja excused herself from the table and went back upstairs. It occurred to her that Ling Ling wouldn't be able to sleep in the bedroom she'd shared with Walter, not while his body remained there at least. She stripped her own bed and put fresh sheets and pillowcases on for Ling Ling to use. She then moved her belongings into the room that had been used by Finch and Marcus. She decided it would be more appropriate for her to sleep there for the time being. It was a gesture that Ling Ling deeply appreciated when she discovered what Anja had done later that afternoon.

The day that Walter passed away felt like the longest day. Everyone's mind was consumed with grief and concern for Ling Ling's welfare. Her heart was broken, and it seemed that the older one is when struck by the loss of a beloved partner, the harder it hits.

Nobody slept well that night, and so the following day everyone was emotionally exhausted. Winter had begun the grim task of starting to dig a grave. She used a pickaxe at first to try and break up the hard ground and then a shovel to scoup bits of the loose soil away. Silvie came out to join her in her labours. When Anja arrived to try and help, Winter sent her back inside to be with Ling Ling. At six months pregnant, the back breaking work of digging in the intense heat was not something Winter or Silvie would allow her to do. Instead she assisted Ling Ling who was upstairs preparing Walter's body for burial.

She dressed him in his finest clothes, brushed his long silver white hair, and tied it back in a ponytail with his favourite orange ribbon. Then he was wrapped in the bed sheet upon which he had died. Ling Ling kissed his forehead before covering his face for the last time.

Two days later, Walter's final resting place was ready to receive him. It took all four women to bring his body down the staircase and take it outside. They gently lowered him into the grave using the same ropes that had been used for Harvey. And just like Harvey's burial, there was a small ceremony of thanks for his long and productive life.

The next time a blood curdling scream was heard in the house came twelve weeks later when Anja went into labour in the middle of the night. For the next fourteen hours, everyone was by her bedside with words of encouragement, back massages and hand holding. By the time the baby was delivered, Anja was completely exhausted and overwhelmed with emotion at the perfect little being that was lying on her chest screaming her tiny lungs out.

"She's so beautiful. So beautiful. I can't believe she's really here." Anja's voice was soft and raspy.

"Oh your Marcus would be positively beamin' with joy if he was here darlin'."

"What are you naming her Anja?" Ling Ling asked, wiping away her own tears of happiness.

Anja thought for a moment before answering. "Astral. Her name is Astral."

CHAPTER 56

observation 1:9

I am being extracted from my protective environment. The chord has been severed from the life-giving nutrients that nourished me for the last nine months, and I am taking my first breath as a fully formed human infant. I am born.

I should have no recollections of the past or insights into the future, but for some reason my slate has not been wiped clean and I have been forwarded with full knowledge.

Now I can't stop screaming.

CHAPTER 57

crystal

After the revelations of what Finch had seen there was no time to waste. He contacted the Advocate who had gained him entry under the auspices of a fake meeting, and asked if he could meet with him again urgently, but this time somewhere neutral. Advocates never met with Associates anywhere but The Great Hall, they never visited private pods, nor did they entertain anyone other than fellow Advocates in their own pods. The Advocate suggested something extraordinary, a meeting in plain sight. They would walk and talk as if going about their business in a public area. Finch was apprehensive about what the Advocate proposed, but couldn't see any other way, so he agreed.

"Just stay calm and walk with me, smiling occasionally if possible. We want to look like nothing is out of the ordinary Finch."

"I'm trying to stay calm," Finch said, smiling through gritted teeth. "It's not easy."

"Why don't you start by telling me what happened after I left you in The Great Hall yesterday."

"I went down the corridor. It was so dark I could hardly see where I was going."

"Yes, go on."

"Then I came to a large sliding steel door."

"A steel door? That's very interesting."

"I walked through and there was nothing but blackness."

"You see how easy it is to look like we're just chatting Finch. Keep going you're doing very well. And then what?"

"There was a very long winding passageway that led to another large steel door. I forced it open and found a large room that had a wall of screens showing all the areas in the complex and around the outside, and there was also a bank of smaller screens on another wall showing what appeared to be collections of data."

"Nothing out of the ordinary there. The Leader surveys everything."

Finch remained quiet for a few minutes as they continued walking.

"There was no security. Nothing to prevent me from entering the room, other than the strength I required to slide the two steel doors open. Don't you think that's a bit strange?"

"Until recently it wouldn't have occurred to me to think that the use of fear and oppression would have been a sufficient form of security Finch. But it clearly has been."

"You've never seen the Leader have you?"

"Nobody has ever seen the Leader. You know that. Oh sure we get the odd glimpse of his face sometimes. But looking directly into his eyes is forbidden."

"Well, it's all a lie. It's all been one enormous lie!"

"Don't raise your voice, we don't want to draw attention to ourselves. What has been a lie?"

"The Leader. The Leader is a lie! He … it … isn't even human!"

The Advocate stopped walking for a moment and stared at Finch. He took a few seconds to think about what Finch had just said … then he laughed.

"You think this is funny Advocate?"

"No, not in the slightest."

Finch soon realised that the Advocate's laugh came from nervousness.

"OK, tell me slowly what you actually saw."

Finch went into great detail about how he'd followed a

humming noise to the corner of the room and saw a glowing light. He described the sight of what appeared to be a human head on the body of some kind of machine. And that the machine was in the shape of a human body. He told the Advocate how the glowing light appeared to be uploading information to the Leader. He also said that there was no furniture in the room other than a chair upon which lay a cloak.

"AI. The Leader is AI! Oh everything makes sense now Finch. We noticed something the other day, a delayed response that made us suspicious, and now you've confirmed it. This changes everything."

"I need to get this information to Marcus," Finch said, an urgency in his voice.

"Yes. I will make sure he gets it as soon as possible through Professor Hill," the Advocate said, assuring Finch that this would be done. "But we also need to find a way to disable it to prevent the remaining drone strikes planned for the yellow zone."

"What do you think would happen if all the Advocates knew the truth about the Leader?"

The Advocate couldn't be sure, and he needed to be honest with Finch. "I would hope they'd be as appalled as we are, but I just can't be sure. To be honest I'm now beginning to wonder if some of the other Advocates may also be AI!"

"Who do you think is behind all this deception? Who created the Leader?" Finch continue to press the Advocate.

"That's a very good question Finch. I can only imagine it will have been some of the original founders. To think they fooled the world into believing the Leader was human, and all this time it was just a glorified smart bot collecting data, learning from it, and modifying its behavioural responses according to what it was originally programmed to do. One machine has effectively been controlling the fate of the entire world!"

The two men continued walking in silence occasionally looking at each other in disbelief. They knew that when the truth was finally revealed to the masses, chaos would ensue, but there was no doubt in either of their minds that the status quo could not be allowed to continue.

"I'll message Professor Hill as soon as I return to my pod. In the meantime, you should convene a meeting of your select group of fellow Associates and inform them of the situation. Make no mistake, we are about to enter a very precarious time Finch, so be prepared."

CHAPTER 58

crystal

None of the Advocates were surprised when they were summoned to The Great Hall for an emergency meeting with the Leader. They had all been approached by the Associates assigned to them who were in a state of bewilderment at the shocking state of events regarding the film of the red zone massacre. Most of the Advocates themselves were astonished at what had taken place, except of course Alex and John.

"Can someone explain to me how we come to be in this situation?" the Leader asked. "I have looked into where this film originated, but I cannot find anyone in our community who would have done such a terrible thing."

One of the Advocates took it upon himself to speak for the group. "We are as shocked as you are Leader."

Another Advocate spoke. "The whole community has been unnerved by what they have seen Leader."

"Yes it's all very disconcerting Leader."

"Why would anyone do such a thing though? What are they trying to achieve?"

"To destabilise our home Advocates. That is the only reason." The Leader spoke in a grave tone. "To bring disharmony to our lives here. We must find out who is behind this and stop them from doing any further damage."

"What do you think they might do next Leader?" Alex

wanted to test the programme to see how credibly it would respond to an open-ended question.

Sure enough, there was a slight delay before the Leader responded. Alex and John looked at each other knowingly and then back towards the Leader.

"I do not know Advocate. That is for you to discover and report back to me as a matter of urgency."

"Yes Leader."

Just before the Leader departed it provided one update. "I can confirm that the first drone strike of the southernmost area of the yellow zone has been completed successfully."

Alex and John remained silent upon hearing this news while most of their colleagues piled praise on the Leader. They were sickened hearing their responses.

Following the Leader's departure, the Advocates remained behind to discuss what to do next. There had never been a disturbance in the crystal zone before, let alone any disharmony. So the current chaos left them decidedly short on suggestions, apart from one Advocate who had an alarming thought.

"It occurs to me that everything has taken a turn since the return of Finch and Doctor Jarret from the yellow zone."

"Surely that's just a coincidence," Alex responded, a nervousness in his voice that didn't go unnoticed by John..

"Perhaps."

"You can't seriously think that they've had anything to do with this." John brushed off the remark in a dismissive tone.

"You're probably right, but I don't see any harm in investigating their movements since returning just so that we can rule them out."

"What did you have in mind?" John asked.

"I'll speak with my tech contact and have them run a trace on their movements through their bracelets. I've already had a more advanced bracelet fitted to Doctor Jarret as a precaution."

"What will that prove?"

"If they've been meeting up, it will prove that they have been colluding as there is no other good reason for them to be together. After all, they told us they weren't friends."

Alex and John breathed a sigh of relief. They knew that their colleague would find no evidence of collusion between Marcus and Finch as they hadn't seen or spoken to each other since their return.

"I think that's an excellent starting point," John said encouragingly.

Once the Leader had left The Great Hall, the Advocates returned to their respective pods to contemplate the situation. Alex and John met later that evening.

"That was close Alex."

"Yes, when our colleague mentioned Finch and Marcus I thought I was going to have a heart attack."

"And wasn't it sickening to hear the responses from our sycophantic colleagues to the news of the first yellow zone drone strike?"

"I think we must assume now that we're on our own in this."

"And we're out of time John."

"I'm afraid we are. I'll get a message to Professor Hill immediately."

The atmosphere in the crystal zone felt as though it had changed overnight. The population had gone from having complete trust in those who were in power, to confusion, fear, and scepticism. On the first day following the release of the filmed drone strike in the red zone, the number of people who sang the daily anthem halved. By day two, nobody was singing it. The Advocates observed this from the safety of their pods. They no longer felt secure venturing out among the masses.

Gone was polite conversation at mealtimes in the sprawling dining halls. Now there was heated debate, and argument and speculation that created a cacophony that could be heard throughout the complex. Allegiance to the Leader and the Advocates was crumbling and chaos was ensuing. A once civilised society, albeit one built on lies and deceit, was fast disintegrating, and it amazed Marcus at just how quickly people could turn on one another. He hoped that once there was a new leader, and a more open and honest dialogue with the people began, that calm would be restored once more.

He met with Professor Hill again, and the final part of their plan to take down the Leader was put in place. It was the most dangerous and challenging part of their strategy, and they knew they would only get one chance to strike.

Alex and John agreed what had to be done and both were content that if it cost them their lives it would be a sacrifice they were prepared to make. They were both old men and could see the writing on the wall for both of their positions as Advocates, with younger Gen1 males eagerly waiting in the wings to take their places. They felt a huge burden of responsibility having played their part in over two decades of lies, even though they were themselves both victims of deceit.

They made their way back to The Great Hall under the auspices of having vital information for the Leader.

"I sense the presence of another," the Leader said, forcefully.

"Another, Leader?"

"Yes. Who have you brought with you Advocates?"

"We have come alone I assure you."

But they hadn't come alone. Finch had accompanied them to The Great Hall and was hiding in the shadows out of sight of the Leader. He crept down the corridor and through the first steel door, then down the passageway and into the room past the second steel door.

"You are lying Advocates! I can hear it in your voices."

"I imagine you're programmed to notice these things aren't you Leader?" John stood up and started walking towards the machine.

"Like you're programmed to do everything else." Alex rose and began walking towards it on the other side of the table.

"Sit down. I do not like your tone Advocates. Sit down! I command you."

"We no longer take our commands from you and soon nobody else will either."

The two Advocates grabbed at the Leader's cloak, loosening it until it fell to the floor revealing its true identity. Even though Alex and John knew the truth about what the Leader was, seeing it for themselves came as a shock and they both recoiled in horror.

But what they could not have foreseen was the strength of the machine that stood in front of them. With one strike of its arm, Alex was knocked to the ground. He called out in agony.

Hearing Alex's cries of pain, Finch ran out of the Leader's room and back towards The Great Hall to see what had happened. As he entered The Great Hall he saw Alex lying in a pool of blood, and John being strangled by the machine's powerful hands. He tried to loosen its grip around John's throat but was no match for its strength. It choked the life out of John whose body eventually slumped over the table. Then it turned its sights on Finch, knocking him flying across the Great Hall. Finch looked on as the Leader sped out of The Great Hall, then along the corridor and into the passageway that led back to its room.

Finch, having only been slightly winded, got to his feet and ran after it. He managed to catch up to the Leader just as it slammed the steel door of its room shut, this time with the sound of bolts locking into place. Finch pounded on the door but it was no use. The Leader had made its domain impenetrable.

He ran back to The Great Hall in a state of shock. John was clearly dead, but Alex remained alive long enough to tell Finch to evacuate the complex. With the last of his strength he raised his arm and revealed a chilling message on his bracelet. The words read: "DESTRUCT SEQUENCE ARMED"

CHAPTER 59

crystal

All of the Advocate's bracelets buzzed with the same message, and they all rushed to The Great Hall to find out what was going on. Finch had already left and was frantically trying to get people to the exit. He messaged his Associates to evacuate the complex as he ran to the clinic to find Marcus. Instinctively, seeing others starting to flee, Marcus had already headed to the Eggshell quarter to help evacuate the children. When he arrived at Eggshell, he could see that the protective doors were open and the staff inside were frantically gathering all the toddlers together to leave. Marcus helped carry some of the children out then put them in the arms of people fleeing from other departments.

"We need to get everyone out," he screamed, to anyone who would listen.

People began to panic as they ran in their hundreds towards the exit. But the exit was only geared to allow a handful of people to leave at a time forcing the crowds into a frantic crush to escape.

The Advocates didn't understand what had happened when they found Alex and John dead in The Great Hall. The last thing they could have imagined was that the Leader had killed them, but equally they could find no sign of the Leader. What they could see was the pandemonium below and quickly realised that they too had to escape.

In an effort to blend into the crowd they abandoned their

cloaks in The Great Hall and headed down to join the queues. They knew that there was one specific craft that could only be triggered by their Advocate bracelets which meant that as long as they could make it through the exit they would be safe. Trying to stick together they pushed their way through the crowds with no regard to the safety of the rest of the population. They were meant to act as guardians to the people in the crystal zone, but this had conveniently been forgotten by every one of them. Their two older colleagues had paid the ultimate price, laying down their lives to protect the innocent, but none of this mattered to the ten desperate men who were only interested in saving themselves.

The first Advocate forced his way to the front of the queue. His bracelet unlocked the exit doors permanently allowing people to flow more freely to the outside world. Dozens started tumbling out into the unfiltered air. The crystal zone was set high in the mountains and the only direction they could go in was down, clambering over huge rocks and boulders. Some lost their footing and fell hundreds of feet to the ground below. Others carrying small children descended more slowly and carefully but were gripped by fear.

There were thousands still inside the domes waiting to escape when suddenly the projected blue sky and sunshine shut down. They all looked up to see the reality of the skies outside. Then the purified air stopped circulating and finally, the entire complex was plunged into darkness as the electricity was switched off. It all served to make the remaining population even more hysterical to the point where they were trampling over those who had fallen like cattle in a stampede.

Marcus went further into the complex of domes to search for Professor Hill knowing that at his age he would struggle to run to the exit, but he couldn't locate him. He found himself running in the opposite direction to the surging crowds and being constantly pushed out of the way. Then he spotted Finch. Never had he been so happy to see anyone in his life.

"I'm trying to make sure that no one is left behind," Finch shouted to him breathlessly.

Marcus shouted back. "Yes, I've got to make one more circuit of Eggshell just to be sure all the children have been removed."

Suddenly there was another crowd surge and they lost sight of each other. Marcus frantically headed back to Eggshell. It appeared to be empty but he had to be sure that all the toddlers were gone. It was a vast complex with large, segmented areas that were pressurised to accommodate the comfort of small ears. Now all the doors were open apart from one small room in the furthest corner. He imagined it was a utility space, but his gut told him to check it just in case. Guided only by fading daylight he made his way to the little room and forced opened the pressurised door, instantly it released the sound of a tiny infant no more than a week old, screaming its lungs out.

"Oh my. You poor little man. You're safe now, I've got you."

Marcus wrapped the tiny baby in a blanket.

"Food, you'll need food."

He looked around the room and found a satchel that had been left behind by one of the staff. He emptied the contents of the satchel then filled it with some nappies and bottles containing a white liquid. He then hooked it over his shoulder as he carried the baby close to his chest, protecting him from the turmoil of the relentless crowds. For a moment he thought about handing the infant to someone else, but something stopped him. He decided that the fate of this one tiny being was in his hands and that he would be responsible for his safety from that moment on. Marcus couldn't understand why the baby had been so isolated, in fact Marcus struggled to understand why there was a baby there at all. The Gen2 children were all a couple of years old now and there weren't supposed to be any new babies in progress yet.

The outside world came as a shock to the fleeing population as they made their way down the mountain. It was the first time they'd seen the real sky and breathed the real air, and many broke down in tears at the new experience. The ten Advocates had all made it out safely and instead of heading down the mountain they ran towards one of the craft that was docked to the side of the exit.

There were only six seats in the passenger cabin so the other four opened the cargo bay. There was enough room for twenty people inside it to sit on the floor, but the Advocates made no attempt to take any more passengers. Instead they closed the doors and set the automatic pilot to immediately take off and get them as far away as possible from the impending disaster.

Marcus realised that as much as his heart was telling him to get everyone to safety, his head was telling him that if he didn't get out of there now, it would be too late. He looked at the tiny baby in his arms and made the difficult decision to flee the complex. He only hoped that Finch would make it out in time too.

As he escaped through the exit with the baby now tucked safely inside his shirt he could see craft loaded with people departing the docking stations.

Then, just as he was about to start climbing down the mountain he heard a familiar voice. "Marcus, over here!"

He looked over and saw one final craft loaded with people.

"Come on Marcus, hurry!"

It was Finch. He ran over to him and jumped on board just as the doors closed and the ship took off.

"I don't know where we're headed, this thing is on autopilot, but at least we're out of there."

"Yes. But there are still so many people trying to get out Finch."

"I know, but we did our best, and unfortunately we can't save them all."

They sat down in the cargo hold with all the other people and Marcus took the baby out of his shirt, the baby had been silent up until that moment.

"I think he's hungry." Marcus took out one of the bottles from his jacket and fed the infant as Finch looked on in complete shock.

"You're just full of surprises aren't you?"

Marcus smiled. It was the first time he'd felt able to smile in a very long time.

"He's only about a week old, poor little guy."

"Well he's in the right hands, that's for sure. What are you going to do with him?"

"Oh he's not going anywhere without me from now on

Finch."

The craft was suddenly buffeted from a series of shock waves that came from the exploding domes of the crystal zone. Some of the people on board screamed and clung to each other.

"Do you know what happened? Marcus asked Finch. "How did things end up like this?"

"My guess is that the Leader had a failsafe programme installed in it so that if it was ever challenged or in danger, it would self-destruct and eliminate every trace of our existence. It killed Alex and John. Those poor men."

"I'm so sorry Finch. You've all been so brave, it's humbling."

They settled down for the journey ahead, hoping that in time they would see the ones they loved again.

"At least we've prevented the other drone strikes."

Marcus nodded as he watched the greedy infant guzzling down the liquid until he fell fast asleep, comforted by the warmth of Marcus's skin and the sound of his heartbeat.

After a few hours, the craft holding the ten remaining Advocates landed. They all breathed a sigh of relief and congratulated each other on surviving … then the doors opened.

An automated voice greeted the ten passengers. "*Welcome to the red zone.*" Then the craft powered down, never to restart.

CHAPTER 60

yellow

Marcus was lost in thought as the craft travelled to its new destination. The crystal zone was destroyed, and he couldn't help but wonder about the fate of its fleeing population. He thought about Professor Hill, Bibi, Cerine and Elise and hoped that they made it to safety. A great sadness swept over him when he thought about all the good the crystal zone could have done for the world in the right hands, and the selfishness of whoever created the Leader and programmed it to destroy everything that had been created. It was such a senseless waste.

"Where are we going to live?" One of the passengers sobbed.

"We're going to the yellow zone," Marcus answered, trying to sound reassuring.

"No! We can't go there, we'll all die!"

"Life is hard there for sure, but it is survivable," Finch said.

Marcus wondered how many of them were truly equipped to survive in their new destination. From what he could see they were nearly all Gen1s and had never had to provide for themselves or been exposed to a harsh climate. Everything they'd ever needed had been provided for them in a pristine world where life was easy.

One of the passengers placed his hand over his mouth. "What is that awful smell?"

Marcus realised that the baby had suddenly filled his nappy

and needed changing.

More of the passengers started complaining. "What a stench!"

"Alright. Alright. You were all babies once," Marcus growled, becoming impatient with his fellow passengers.

He immediately cleaned up the mess and changed the baby's nappy, wrapping the used one in a tight ball and placing it in his satchel to dispose of when the craft landed. He was counting the hours until they arrived in the yellow zone and he and Finch could find their way back to Feronia; back to Anja and Silvie. It had been nearly four months and he couldn't wait to see them all again, especially Anja. He looked at the baby in his arms and realised that he would also soon be meeting his own baby daughter for the first time.

"What are you going to call him Marcus?" asked Finch.

"I have no idea. I guess he needs a name though. I think I'll leave it up to Anja."

The noise in the cargo bay started to settle down as people began falling asleep, rocked by the gentle swaying of the craft. They were all exhausted and overwhelmed by what had happened to them, and their home. The only world they'd ever known was gone and their future was uncertain. Marcus remembered the first time he'd stepped outside in the yellow zone and what a shock it was, but he also remembered how quickly he and Finch had adjusted to a different way of life. He hoped it would be the same for all the evacuees.

Hours later the craft docked and the doors opened. An automated voice greeted the passengers. *"Welcome to the yellow zone."*.

The passengers stood up and peered out of the doorway at a strange new land. Nobody wanted to be the first to set foot outside. The cargo hold opened and the rest of the passengers surveyed the scene with a look of fear and uncertainty on their faces.

"It's so hot."

"And it smells bad."

"You'll soon get used to it," Finch said, as he shepherded

them out of the craft.

"I hate it here. I want to go home!"

"There is no home to go back to. This is your new home," said Marcus.

The passengers reluctantly began stepping out of the craft.

"Here, take these." Finch handed them breathing masks, bottles of water and bags containing pop up tents.

"Hey, how did all these things end up in here?" Marcus turned to Finch looking surprised.

"My crew fitted all the ships out with supplies last week just in case we needed to get out of here in a hurry," Finch said, winking at Marcus and feeling pretty pleased with himself.

All the ships docked at separate locations in the yellow zone and when Finch and Marcus finally stepped out they didn't recognise the port at all. It definitely wasn't the one they'd come into last time, so they had no idea which direction to head in or how far away they were from Feronia. The other issue was transport and the fact they had a week old baby with them. All the other passengers had headed off leaving Marcus and Finch alone with the craft. Finch had waited until they were some distance away before he opened the exterior side compartment which revealed just one hoverbike.

"Oh that's just great," Finch said sarcastically, as he rocked the infant in his arms to give Marcus a break. "I told them to install at least *two* bikes in every craft. Well you may as well try it, not that I hold out much hope."

Marcus tried to start the bike and nothing happened.

"Here." Finch handed the baby back to Marcus and put his hands on the bike. It started.

"I don't get it. Why did it work for you? I thought these only worked with a DNA skin match."

"It may be that all the bikes were matched to work with every Associate, but you know what? I don't really care right now."

They packed the satchel, water bottles and tent in the storage compartments of the bike. Marcus tucked the baby inside his shirt to protect him from the sun's ferocious rays before climbing on the back of the bike behind Finch, then they set off. All they could think of doing was to head north and hope that they'd pass something familiar. They had a long journey ahead and it would be much slower carrying two men, with frequent stops to feed and change the baby, but they didn't care just as long as they kept moving.

The only familiar site they saw were the rundown towns and bone dry countryside they travelled through. As the light began to fade on their momentous first day back in the yellow zone, they decided to set up camp in a field that was far enough off the road not to be seen by anyone passing by.

Marcus was devoted to caring for the baby who seemed to always be hungry and irritable. He had enough to feed him for another two days and could only hope that they would find their way back to Feronia before his food ran out. Finch camouflaged the hoverbike, determined that this one would not be stolen.

The air was still and oppressively hot, even as night fell. Marcus was concerned that the baby would overheat not having had time to acclimatise yet. He fanned the infant that lay next to him in the tent to try and keep him cool until he could no longer stay awake. Finch watched over Marcus and the baby for a few more hours until he too fell asleep.

The next day all were awake very early and Finch was keen to get going.

"I think we should head north-west today Marcus. When we were travelling last time, we could see that there was a large expanse of water in the distance behind Feronia, so we need to be high up on the other side of coastline from here."

Marcus nodded as he began packing things away in the hoverbike. He tucked the baby inside his shirt again and they headed off in the direction of the western coast. Neither of them had a clue where they were going, there were no maps to guide them, so it was purely down to instinct on Finch's part but Finch's instincts were good. They travelled another full day until they hit the western coast. Then Finch stopped.

"You see that crack in the road?"

"What about it?"

"I remember it. I remember it!"

"It looks like any other crack in the road Finch."

"No. I remember the first time I saw it. I thought it looked like an old man's face."

"If you say so."

Marcus was too consumed with a now crying baby to look at a crack in the road.

"We're going to have stop for a while, the baby needs feeding Finch."

"If you can both wait just a little bit longer ..."

Before Marcus could answer, Finch had taken off again. He was riding with a new sense of purpose, and fifteen minutes later Marcus could see why. There in the distance, high up on a hill was Feronia.

"We're nearly home!" Finch shouted.

Home. It felt strange to call it that, but it also felt right.

CHAPTER 61

yellow

The light was just beginning to fade as Finch, Marcus and the baby rode up the long winding drive towards the house. Both men felt as though their hearts were going to explode with happiness.

Winter looked out of the window and screamed.

"Well I'll be … oh my. Come quickly y'all."

Ling Ling, Silvie and Anja all made their way to the kitchen as fast as they could to see what was wrong.

"Look!"

They all peered out of the window looking at what Winter was pointing to. It felt like a miracle. Everyone, apart from Ling Ling, ran outside.

Finch jumped off the bike and ran towards Silvie. He scouped her up in his arms and swung her around and around as she squealed with delight.

"Ya back!" She kissed his cheek and hugged him tightly.

Anja ran over to Marcus, tears streaming down her face. "I can't believe you're really here."

She was just about to throw her arms around him when he put his hand up to stop her. Then he reached into his shirt and brought out the tiny infant.

"Oh my goodness. Who is this Marcus?" Winter said, walking over to Marcus and relieving him of the small bundle. She quickly examined the baby who had started crying. "He can't be more than a week old poor little mite."

Anja looked at Marcus then back to the baby.

"He needs feeding Winter," said Marcus, reaching into the satchel that was stowed at the side of the bike, pulling out a bottle and handing it to her. "Would you mind?"

"Now you come along with Aunty Winter you gorgeous lil' man." Winter happily took the baby into the house. Marcus's attention returned to Anja. "I'll explain later," he said, as he embraced her at last. "I've missed you so much."

"Promise me you'll never go away again," Anja whispered, as she clung to him. "Never."

"I give you my word. You're stuck with me now."

While the reunions were taking place outside, Ling Ling, always the perfect hostess, was busy in the kitchen preparing refreshments and keeping an eye on Astral. When Winter walked in with a baby in her arms, Ling Ling's face lit up.

"Another baby in the house, how wonderful!" She beamed as she pulled out a chair for Winter to sit on while she fed the hungry infant. "Now Astral will have someone to play with."

One by one they all came into the kitchen with Finch and Marcus, taking it in turns to hug Ling Ling.

"I swear all that has kept me going over the last few months was the thought of enjoying a cup of your delicious mint tea Ling Ling." Finch savoured the aroma of the steaming brew. "That and seeing you again Silvie."

"Where's Walter?" Marcus asked expectantly.

The mood in the kitchen changed from elation to sadness as Ling Ling told them that Walter had passed away and was now buried next to Harvey.

Marcus bowed his head. "Oh Ling Ling. I'm so very sorry."

Suddenly the cries of a baby in a cot in the corner of the kitchen broke the solemn moment. Anja walked over to the cot and scooped the baby up into her arms.

"Goodness me. I almost forgot! Marcus meet your daughter, Astral. Astral this is your father."

Marcus's eyes filled with tears. "Astral. What a lovely name. Oh Anja she's beautiful, she's perfect. Thank you."

"I couldn't have done it without the help of these amazing women."

"I'm almost afraid to ask, but what happened when y'all went back?" Winter asked quietly, as the baby in her arms was falling asleep.

Marcus and Finch took it in turns to tell the women about how they were incarcerated and then interrogated, the moment they arrived back in the crystal zone. They explained that they'd come up with a strategy that they had hoped would turn things around there, and just as they thought they were going to succeed, it all went horribly wrong and the crystal zone was destroyed.

The women listened, their eyes as wide as saucers, as they heard about how the Leader wasn't human after all, and that it had set off a series of explosions once it became exposed.

"So there is nothing for us to go back to. Good, I'm glad," Anja said.

Ling Ling crossed her fingers. "Does this mean there are no drones coming to kill us now?"

"We're safe from the drones now, Ling Ling," Finch said, reassuringly. "There is nothing for you to worry about."

"Well thank heavens for that. Now I can stop searching the sky in case they're coming for us. I have been doing it every day since you left."

A giant weight had been lifted from Ling Ling, and it was the first time in months that she felt she could relax and live in the moment once more.

"What his name?" Silvie asked, looking at the now sleeping baby in Winter's arms.

Marcus shrugged his shoulders. "We thought we should come up with one together."

They all looked at each other blankly for a few minutes before Anja whispered something to Marcus.

He smiled. "With your permission Ling Ling, we'd like to call him Walter."

Ling Ling burst into tears of happiness. "Oh yes, that would be wonderful. Walter would be so touched by this gesture."

In the days and weeks that passed, Walter grew stronger

and slept in a cot next to Astral. When one baby cried, the other would cry too. Fortunately, Anja had plenty of milk to feed both new-borns, which Marcus found amazing as he'd never witnessed a baby being breastfed before. Winter and Silvie enjoyed helping Anja with the babies, taking it in turns to have them in their rooms so that Anja could get a good night's sleep. These precious new lives gave everyone in the house something to feel joyful about, especially as they began to crawl and then to walk in the months that seemed to fly by.

Because the babies had been born so close together it was decided that they should celebrates their birthday's on the same day. So every year on their joint birthday, Ling Ling made special food and everyone else made presents to give them. It turned out that Silvie had a gift for sewing and she made them lovely clothes from leftover scraps of fabric she found lying around the house. Finch turned his hand to woodwork and made them wooden toys from the many dead tree trunks that littered the grounds of Feronia. Marcus and Anja handwrote stories for them which they loved reading to them at bedtime.

Astral was a playful and fun little girl who loved pretty colours, while Walter was the more serious of the two and seemed intent on making balls out of the soil, rather than playing with toys. Where Astral would use bright colours to create pictures, Walter grew obsessed with drawing circles and colouring them in using only black and dark brown.

When they were five years old, Marcus became concerned that Walter hadn't grown out of his rather strange behaviour. One day he discovered that Walter had pulled an old atlas off the bookshelf in the library. He was horrified to see that the view of Earth from space taken decades before, when it was affectionately called the blue marble, had been coloured in black. He sat down on the floor with him sensing that little Walter was unhappy and asked him why he coloured in the picture of the earth.

"Home."

"Home?"

"Yes. Home."

Marcus was taken aback. He knew in his heart that Walter

was special. Different. But he'd tried to suppress his gut instincts about the child over the years.

"Why is this home Walter?" Marcus asked, pointing to a now blackened planet earth.

The child stared into Marcus's eyes for a moment. "Dead," the little boy said, with tears starting to run down his rosy cheeks.

Marcus had his answer. An answer he didn't want to believe but couldn't ignore. He decided not to tell the others about their conversation. If he was right about the symbolism in Walter's art, he could see no point in sharing it. Life was hard enough.

"I understand Walter. You're a good boy."

He picked him up and cuddled him, while deep inside his heart was breaking with sadness. What had he saved the children for if there was no future?

CHAPTER 62

final observation

When I was born with full knowledge, I knew what had happened to everyone, and everything that had lived on Earth in the past. I also knew what my own fate would be, just as I knew the fate of all those around me. And I knew what lay ahead for our planet. The burden of carrying so much knowledge for all these years has been hard to bear.

I was brought up to be the son of Marcus and Anja, whom I adored, and I was privileged to have a sister called Astral. I remember Winter and Silvie, although my recollections of Ling Ling are less clear as she passed when I was just four years old.

When I buried my father Marcus, he was only 67. It seemed such a young age, but he was a PreGen, and given what he had gone through in his life, it was no surprise that his body could no longer cope with the harsh climate. He was an extraordinary man, kind and gentle, and he taught me so much about the history of our existence and the terrible mistakes that we made along the way. Naturally, I didn't let on that I already possessed all of this knowledge. Instead I enjoyed spending time with him and listening to all of his stories, and especially how he came to rescue me and bring me back here to become part of his family. When he died, I experienced the most intense pain and grief. Though what was even worse, was watching my mother's heart break, and that of the others who mourned him for so many years. It was just the beginning of a great sadness that came upon me.

One by one our little graveyard grew, and my extended family became smaller and smaller. When Winter passed away ten years after my father, and Silvie twelve years after that, I was struck by the fragility of life for PreGens. One day you can be laughing with someone, and the next crying over their loss. Even though I knew all that would befall us, it didn't make things any easier. If anything, it made things harder because I wouldn't, couldn't divulge my knowledge to anyone. Imagine being told you would die tomorrow. That would have been a monstrous thing to inflict on someone I cared about.

I was blessed to have my mother, Anja, with me for the best part of 125 years. She was such a beautiful and special woman, and I know that she loved me with her whole heart, just as she did her own naturally born child Astral. I miss her dearly. But equally I know that when she left us, she was ready to go. She had endured so many years without my father by her side and I know how awfully hard that was for her. Finch passed away two years later. He had been like a second father to us. As Gen1s, both Anja and Finch had lived the precise amount of years that science had programmed into their genetics.

And so now, 25 years on from losing my mother, I sit at the freshly dug grave of my beloved sister Astral who, as a hybrid, lived to be an astounding 150 years old.

I am now completely alone. I know that I am the last living creature on this dying Earth, and that having been created as the last great experiment of genetic engineering - a Gen3 - I have another 150 years of life left in me. I was programmed to live, and live I must, however hard the journey ahead is. I will remain here at Feronia as there is little point in relocating, and I have no means of transport anyway.

In my many years of life, I have learned how to cultivate enough food to keep me from starving. There is a library of books for me to read and reread, and I shall hope that my solitude doesn't make me lose my mind. One hundred and fifty years alone is the cross I have to bear for mankind's insatiable desire to prolong life. If the scientists who created me knew then, what

I have always known, would they have seen the futility of their obsession?

When I die, there will be no one to bury me. Nobody to say a kind word at my graveside. Not another living soul to mourn my passing. It will be the end of the chapter of our existence on, what must once have been, a truly special place to live. Books have shown me what life was like not that long ago, only a few hundred years ago in fact. I can't understand how, or why, the destruction of such a rich and diverse ecosystem was permitted to happen. It baffles me, just as creating a lifeform to live for 300 years makes no sense to me at all. Or perhaps it does. Perhaps I'm here as the final custodian of Earth, to guide it to its eternal resting place in a solar system full of all the other dead planets.

Perhaps we just didn't deserve to live at all.

Printed in Great Britain
by Amazon